MW00984624

ABYSM

AURORA RENEGADES: BOOK THREE

G. S. JENNSEN

HYPERNOVA
PUBLISHING
2016

ABYSM

Hypernova Publishing
P.O. Box 2214
Parker, Colorado 80134
www.hypernovapublishing.com

Ordering Information:
Hypernova Publishing books may be purchased for educational, business or sales promotional use. For details, contact the "Special Markets Department" at the address above.

Abysm / G. S. Jennsen.—1st ed.

LCCN 2016945005
ISBN 978-0-9973921-3-5

To Mark, for my mind
To Linda, for my heart

ACKNOWLEDGMENTS

Many thanks to my beta readers, editors and artists, who made everything about this book better, and to my family, who continue to put up with an egregious level of obsessive focus on my part for months at a time.

I also want to add a personal note of thanks to everyone who has read my books, left a review on Amazon, Goodreads or other sites, sent me a personal email expressing how the books have impacted you, or posted on social media to share how much you enjoyed them. You make this all worthwhile, every day.

AURORA RHAPSODY

is

AURORA RISING

STARSHINE

VERTIGO

TRANSCENDENCE

AURORA RENEGADES

SIDESPACE

DISSONANCE

ABYSM

AURORA RESONANT

RELATIVITY (2017)

RUBICON (2017)

REQUIEM (2018)

SHORT STORIES

RESTLESS, VOL. I • RESTLESS, VOL. II

APOGEE • SOLATIUM

VENATORIS

Learn more at: *gsjennsen.com/aurora-rhapsody*
See a Timeline of the Aurora Rhapsody *universe in the Appendix,*
located at the back of the book.

COLONIZED WORLDS

······ **SENECAN FEDERATION TERRITORY**
   ○ **INDEPENDENT WORLDS**
   ○ **INDEPENDENT DEFENSE CONSORTIUM (IDCC)**
---------- **WESTERNMOST METIGEN ADVANCEMENT**
  ✦ **DESTROYED / ABANDONED COLONIES**

WORLDS VISITED IN ABYSM:

EARTH ALLIANCE	SENECAN FEDERATION	IDCC
EARTH	SENECA	PANDORA
AQUILA		- ANESI ARCH
ARCADIA		ROMANE
MESSIUM	**METIS NEBULA**	SAGAN
- MESSIS I		
SCYTHIA	MOSAIC	
	IDRYMA	
	AMARANTHE	

MILKY WAY GALAXY

Colonized Worlds Map can be viewed online at: gsjennsen.com/map-abysm

PORTAL NETWORK
"MOSAIC"

A1 · A2 · A3 · A4 · A5 · A6 · A7 · A8 · A9 · A10 · A11 · A12 · A13 · A14 · A15 · A16 · A17

VRACHNAS (DRAGONS) · **EMPTY** · **IDRYMA** (CONCLAVE) · VOID · VOID

B1 · B2 · B3 · B4 · B5 · B6 · B7 · B8 · B9 · B10 · B11 · B12 · B13 · B14 · B15 · B16 · B17

EKOS (AKESO) · **GEMINA** (AURORA TWIN) · **AURORA** (METIS PORTAL) · **ORYKTOS** (RIIDA)

C1 · C2 · C3 · C4 · C5 · C6 · C7 · C8 · C9 · C10 · C11 · C12 · C13 · C14 · C15 · C16 · C17

KAMEN (KHOKTEH) · **TAYNA** (TAENARIN) · **EMPTY** · **ENISLE 38** (FYLLIOT) · **CIBATUS** (HARVESTERS)

Portal Network Map can be viewed online at: gsjennsen.com/mosaic-map-abysm

DRAMATIS PERSONAE
MAIN CHARACTERS

Alexis 'Alex' Solovy
Starship pilot, scout and space explorer. Prevo for Project Noetica.
Spouse of Caleb Marano, daughter of Miriam and David Solovy.
Artificial/Prevo Counterpart: Valkyrie

Caleb Marano
Former Special Operations intelligence agent, Senecan Federation Division
of Intelligence. Spouse of Alex Solovy.

Miriam Solovy (Admiral)
EA Strategic Command Chairman.
Leader, Project Volnosti.
Captain, *EAS Stalwart II*.
Mother of Alex Solovy.

Malcolm Jenner (Colonel)
Earth Alliance NW Command
MSO 1st STCC.
Friend of Alex Solovy, Mia Requelme.

Kennedy Rossi
Founder/CEO, Connova Interstellar.
Friend of Alex Solovy, Noah Terrage.

Noah Terrage
Co-founder/COO, Connova Interstellar.
Former trader/smuggler. Friend of Caleb
Marano, Kennedy Rossi, Mia Requelme.

Richard Navick
Former EASC Naval Intelligence Liaison.
Special Adv. to SF Intelligence Director.
Family friend of the Solovys.

Graham Delavasi
Director, Senecan Federation
Division of Intelligence.

Pamela Winslow
Earth Alliance Prime Minister.
Mother of Jude Winslow.

Devon Reynolds
Prevo for Project Noetica.
Former EASC Special Projects Quan-
tum Computing Consultant.
Artificial/Prevo Counterpart: Annie

Mia Requelme
Prevo for Project Noetica. Entrepreneur.
IDCC Co-Founder.
Friend of Caleb Marano, Noah Terrage.
Artificial/Prevo Counterpart: Meno

Morgan Lekkas
Prevo for Project Noetica.
Cmdr, IDCC Rapid Response Forces.
Former Cmdr, SF Southern Fleet.
Artificial/Prevo Counterpart: Stanley

Brooklyn Harper
Former EA Special Forces Captain.
Leader, IDCC Ground RRF.
Friend of Malcolm Jenner.

Eleni Gianno (Field Marshal)
Chairman of SF Military Council.
Commander of SF Armed Forces.

Jude Winslow
Head of Order of the True Sentients.
Son of Pamela Winslow.

OTHER MAJOR CHARACTERS
(ALPHABETICAL ORDER)

Abigail Canivon
Former Consultant: Project Noetica.
Dir. Cybernetic Research, Druyan Inst.
Residence: *Sagan*

Aristide Vranas
Chairman, Senecan Federation Govt.
Residence: *Seneca*

Christopher Rychen (Admiral)
EA NE Regional Commander.
Residence: *Messium*

Claire Zabroi
Hacker, Prevo; friend of Alex Solovy.
Residence: *Earth*

David Solovy (Commander)
Alex Solovy's father. Miriam Solovy's
spouse. Captain, *EAS Stalwart*. Deceased.

Edward Anderson (Admiral, Ret.)
Chair, EA Armed Forces Committee.
Residence: *Earth*

Faith Quillen
Lieutenant, Order of the True Sentients.
Residence: *Pandora*

Ira Soulis
Messium Governor.
Residence: *Messium*

Jacob Paredes (Captain)
NW Command MSO 1st STCC.
Residence: *Arcadia*

John Ojeda (Brigadier)
EASC Logistics Director.
Residence: *Earth*

Kazue Halmi (Major)
XO, *EAS Stalwart II*.
Residence: *Messium*

Kian Lange (Major)
Director, EASC Security Bureau.
Residence: *Earth*

Lionel Terrage
CEO, Surno Materials; Noah's father.
Residence: *Aquila*

Markos Sanna
Hacker, Prevo; friend of Claire Zabroi.
Residence: *Earth*

Melker Vanhes
Physician and Forensic Pathologist.
Residence: *Pyxis*

Mika Duarte
SF Intelligence Agent, Sentinel Group.
Residence: *Seneca*

Royston Jayce
Governor of Scythia.
Residence: *Scythia*

Tessa Hennessey
SF Intelligence quantum computing
specialist. Prevo.
Residence: *Seneca*

THOMAS
Project Volnosti Artificial.
Residence: *EAS Stalwart II*

Vii
Abigail Canivon's Artificial.
Residence: *Sagan*

William 'Will' Sutton
CEO, W.C. Sutton Construction.
SF Intelligence; spouse of Richard Navick.
Residence: *Seneca*

DRAMATIS ALIENORUM

METIGEN / KATASKETOUSYA

Lakhes
Conclave Praetor

Mnemosyne
First Analystae of Aurora Enisle

Iapetus
First Analystae of Khokteh Enisle

Hyperion
Analystae

MOSAIC SPECIES

EKOS
Akeso ("All")

KHOKTEH
Pinchutsenahn Niikha Qhiyane Kteh ("Pinchu")
Tokahe Naataan of Ireltse

Casselanhu Pwemku Yuanwoh Vneh ("Cassela")
Amacante Naabaan of Ireltse

RUDA
Supreme Three

TAENARIN
Jaisc
Iona-Cead of Taenarin Aris

Beshai
Caomh of Taenarin Aris

Odhran Ahearne
Former Iona-Cead of Taenarin

FYLLIOT
Salote Chae

Dramatis Personae and Alienorum can be viewed online at: gsjennsen.com/characters-abysm

SYNOPSIS

AURORA RISING

*For a more detailed summary of the events of Aurora Rising,
see the Appendix, located at the back of the book.*

The history of humanity is the history of conflict. This proved no less true in the 24th century than in ancient times.

By 2322, humanity inhabited over 100 worlds spread across a third of the galaxy. Two decades earlier, a group of colonies had rebelled and set off the First Crux War. Once the dust cleared, three factions emerged: the Earth Alliance, consisting of the unified Earth government and most of the colonies; the Senecan Federation, which had won its independence in the war; and a handful of scattered non-aligned worlds, home to criminal cartels, corporate interests and people who made their living outside the system.

Alexis Solovy was a space explorer. Her father gave his life in the war against the Federation, leading her to reject a government or military career. Estranged from her mother, an Alliance military leader, Alex instead sought the freedom of space and made a fortune chasing the hidden wonders of the stars.

A chance meeting between Alex and a Federation intelligence agent, Caleb Marano, led them to discover an armada of alien warships emerging from a mysterious portal in the Metis Nebula.

The Metigens had been watching humanity via the portal for millennia; in an effort to forestall their detection, they used traitors among civilization's elite to divert focus from Metis. When their plans failed, they invaded in order to protect their secrets.

The wars that ensued were brutal—first an engineered war between the Alliance and the Federation, then once it was revealed to be built on false pretenses, devastating clashes against the Metigen invaders as they advanced across settled space, destroying every colony in their path and killing tens of millions.

Alex and Caleb breached the aliens' portal in an effort to find a way to stop the slaughter. There they encountered Mnemosyne, the Metigen watcher of the Aurora universe—our universe. Though enigmatic and evasive, the alien revealed the invading ships were driven by AIs and hinted the answer to defeating them lay in the merger of individuals with the powerful but dangerous quantum computers known as Artificials.

Before leaving the portal space, Alex and Caleb discovered a colossal master gateway. It generated 51 unique signals, each one leading to a new portal and a new universe. But with humanity facing extinction, they returned home armed with a daring plan to win the war.

In a desperate gambit to vanquish the enemy invaders before they reached the heart of civilization, four Prevos (human-synthetic meldings) were created and given command of the combined might of the Alliance and Federation militaries. Alex and her Artificial, Valkyrie, led the other Prevos and the military forces against the alien AI warships in climactic battles above Seneca and Romane. The invaders were defeated and ordered to withdraw through their portal, cease their observation of Aurora and not return.

Alex reconciled with her mother during the final hours of the war, and following the victory Alex and Caleb married and attempted to resume a normal life.

But new mysteries waited through the Metis portal. Determined to learn the secrets of the portal network and the multiverses it held, six months later Caleb, Alex and Valkyrie traversed it once more, leaving humanity behind to struggle with a new world of powerful quantum synthetics, posthumans, and an uneasy, fragile peace.

SIDESPACE

(AURORA RENEGADES BOOK ONE)

PORTAL NETWORK

Mnemosyne has been exiled by the Idryma Conclave, the Metigen group who controls the portals. The Conclave placed bombs at the Metis Portal intended to destroy the apparatus if it opened, but Mesme disabled them before the *Siyane* traversed the portal.

Alex and Caleb discover a star system of planet-spanning, flora-based intelligences. The first world they visit is aggressive and tries to kill them when they damage a leaf. They escape, but while fleeing one of the plants cuts Alex and injects a toxin into her bloodstream.

The next planet is peaceful. While exploring, a tree induces Caleb into a trance-like state in order to communicate with him. He realizes the life-form can heal Alex's injury and convinces her to let it treat her. They name the intelligence 'Akeso' and spend several days with it.

On visiting the third planet, they discover its resident is trying to expand off-world and is terraforming its moon. When their presence is detected, it attacks the *Siyane*. They return to Akeso to warn it of the threat from its neighbor. To do so, Caleb must expose Akeso to the violence and death of his past, notions it has never conceived of. Troubled, Akeso asks them to depart.

The next portal space they visit harbors life which is the polar opposite of Akeso—an inorganic species called Ruda. When the first Ruda they meet realizes they're organic, it tries to dissect them to study how organic life functions. Valkyrie convinces the alien they are more valuable alive. They agree to share data on humans, and in return the Ruda share details about their nature with Valkyrie. She uses it to begin weaving her quantum circuitry into the hull of the *Siyane*.

On Portal Prime, Mesme confers with the Conclave leader, Lakhes, about these humans' exploration of the portal network and what it means for the Metigens' plans.

Alex and Caleb finally meet a humanoid, space-faring species—and are promptly taken prisoner by the large, cat-like aliens known as Khokteh. They're held captive until Valkyrie develops a translation program and they're able to plead their case to the leader, Pinchu. He releases them, and they become friends with Pinchu and his wife, Cassela, as they're shown the aliens' capital city.

The city comes under attack by a rival Khokteh faction, and Cassela is killed. Pinchu appeals to his gods for a weapon to exact vengeance, and it becomes apparent the gods have long been arming all the Khokteh and pitting them against one another. Also, the 'gods' are actually Metigens. Alex confronts the Metigen that Pinchu summoned; it warns her not to interfere in what she does not understand.

The Metigen provides Pinchu an anti-matter weapon. Caleb and Alex try to convince him not to use it due to its immense destructive power, but blinded by grief at Cassela's death, he refuses to listen to reason. His fleet travels to the attackers' planet and levels the settlement, killing hundreds of thousands. Alex and Caleb return to Portal Prime, intending to confront Mesme about what they've seen.

Mesme's consciousness is not there, but they discover a stasis chamber containing a body identical to the alien 'little gray men' of Earth legend. Unable to learn more, they decide to continue exploring.

Valkyrie has now integrated herself into the hull of the *Siyane*. Alex is able to use their link to effectively 'become' the ship, opening up a new level of existence and perception to her.

Mesme is called before the Conclave to answer for Alex and Caleb's actions. It's revealed the Metigens are smuggling species threatened by a mysterious enemy out of the master universe and into the portal spaces. Further, humans are viewed as a dangerous threat by some Metigens, as a great hope by Mesme.

AURORA / MILKY WAY

Mia awakens from her coma, healed but at a price: her connection to her Artificial, Meno, must remain open in order to fill in gaps where the neural damage couldn't be repaired. Devon introduces her to a hidden quantum dimension the Prevos can use to mentally travel to any location in an instant and observe events in secret. Mia dubs the dimension 'sidespace.'

Miriam is grilled about Noetica by an Assembly committee and its chairman, Pamela Winslow. Winslow challenges Devon's fitness and the continued use of a Prevo in military affairs.

When his superiors find out his husband works for Federation Intelligence, Richard is forced to resign. At Miriam's urging, he and .Will move to Seneca, where he agrees to act as a consultant to his friend, Senecan Intelligence Director Delavasi.

Kennedy and Noah start a company to design ships using adiamene, but Winslow tries to force Kennedy to sell adiamene only to the Alliance government. She refuses, and after subsequent attempts to convince her fail, her father disowns her. Noah convinces her to move to an independent world, one free of Alliance interference.

While working in Annie's lab, Devon is attacked and his link to Annie severed. When captured, the attackers admit they acted on orders from Winslow. Separately, Dr. Canivon is on her way to help Devon when she's kidnapped by mercs working for Olivia Montegreu.

On Seneca, Delavasi gets a tip that Olivia is behind the kidnapping, and Richard relays the news to Miriam. Deducing that Olivia intends to become a Prevo, Richard leaks the intel to the Order of the True Sentients terrorist group in the hope they will attack Olivia, delaying her transformation. The leader of OTS is revealed to be Winslow's son, Jude, when the leaked information reaches him.

Mia uses sidespace to eavesdrop on Winslow and discovers the woman intends to have Devon killed and to seize control of all the Artificials at EASC. With Annie's assistance, Devon and Mia steal Meno's hardware and flee Earth. At the same time, Morgan Lekkas visits a black market tech dealer and has him burn out her Prevo connection to her Artificial, Stanley, then leaves Seneca.

Malcolm Jenner leads a risky incursion into Olivia's base on New Babel. He rescues Dr. Canivon, but not before she performed the Prevo procedure on the woman. Malcolm attempts to kill Olivia, but her personal defenses protect her from harm.

Malcolm receives orders, faked by Annie, to take Dr. Canivon to a space station above Pandora. There they find Mia and Devon waiting. Canivon repairs Devon's damaged Prevo hardware and operating code, then Annie transfers her consciousness directly into his brain cells.

Devon wakes up transformed—his muscles stronger, his irises brilliant lavender and his mind subtly changed by Annie's presence. He contacts Morgan, now on Romane, and learns before she burned the link to Stanley, he, too, transferred his consciousness into her mind.

DISSONANCE
(AURORA RENEGADES BOOK TWO)

PORTAL NETWORK

Alex and Caleb visit a portal space which is configured nearly identical to their home universe. When they travel to where Earth should be, instead they find a supernova remnant; the sun has become a neutron star and Earth has been destroyed. Alex theorizes that the Metigens are manipulating stellar evolution and possibly space itself.

Valkyrie locates a star undergoing unnaturally rapid evolution, and they discover an artificial structure where a Metigen operates multi-dimensional machinery to fire ultra-dense orbs into the star. Abruptly the Metigen and the structure depart as the star's core begins to collapse. The *Siyane* flees seconds before the star goes supernova.

The next portal space holds a frozen, seemingly empty planet. While they are exploring, an alien appears. It indicates for them to accompany it, then reveals a hidden passageway in the ground. As they begin to descend, Alex's connection to Valkyrie is cut off. The alien communicates via touch that they are traveling to a refuge protected by a barrier. Mollified, Alex and Caleb agree to spend a little time below.

On the *Siyane*, Valkyrie is visited by a Metigen named Lakhes, who tells her Alex and Caleb are safe and the species living here is no threat to them. Somewhat reassured, Valkyrie decides to wait for their return.

They find a thriving civilization beneath the surface, and learn the species, called Taenarin, was brought here by Lakhes when their homeworld was threatened. Their spiritual leader, the Caomh, retains the memory of this exodus, which occurred hundreds of years ago.

The Caomh has the ability to absorb memories and transfer them to others via touch. In this way Alex and Caleb experience the memory of the Taenarin leader in their home universe, Amaranthe, when Lakhes appears to warn him his planet is to be mined for resources then destroyed by a species known as Anaden. Metigen ships evacuate the Taenarin to their new home, and Lakhes vows to hide and protect them.

Afterwards, the Caomh speaks to Alex alone. She shares that Alex and Caleb both have another lifeform living inside them; Alex realizes she means fragments of Akeso. She also expresses concern over "the hole" in Alex's mind—the absence of Valkyrie, and Alex's growing need to join with the ship. Alex tells Caleb about Akeso but not the rest. Later that night, she awakens from what Caleb believes is a nightmare, seeking sexual comfort as a substitute for another need.

They return to the *Siyane* the next day. Alex quickly slips into the walls of the ship, admitting to herself that she craves the experience.

The next portal space is highly unusual. The first star system contains 258 planets orbiting in 3 sets of concentric circles. Each planet is being harvested by hordes of machines. They visit the surface of one of the garden worlds, which serves as a planet-spanning orchard, but are soon attacked by harvesting bots and must depart.

A host of vessels ferry the resources collected out of the portal space and traverse the enormous master portal, which they now know leads to Amaranthe. Alex convinces Caleb they should sneak in with one of the vessels. She slips into the walls of the *Siyane* as they near the portal.

The portal denies them entry, sending the *Siyane* ricocheting off into space. The force of the impact causes Valkyrie to malfunction and Alex to have a violent seizure. The *Siyane* comes under attack, and Caleb is unable to wrest control from Valkyrie to escape. Mesme reaches them, surrounds the ship and transports them to Portal Prime.

Alex regains consciousness, and they effect repairs to the *Siyane* while arguing about what had transpired. The argument is interrupted when another Metigen arrives and confronts Mesme, who refuses to turn Alex and Caleb over or shut down the Aurora portal. Lakhes appears and takes Mesme's side, forbidding any harm to the humans.

Alex tracks the departing Lakhes through sidespace to one of the other portals, and the *Siyane* follows.

She encounters an enormous structure built of light waves. Numerous Metigens are in residence. She comes upon Lakhes conversing with another Metigen about a portal species. The two agree to allow the species to kill itself off then shut down the space. Valkyrie figures out the species is the Khokteh. Lakhes confronts Alex, refuses to spare the Khokteh then forces her consciousness back into her body.

They return to the Khokteh homeworld to find it in ruins. When Mesme shows up, Caleb delivers an ultimatum: they refuse to play whatever role the Metigens have planned for them unless their questions are answered. Mesme complies, explaining that the Metigens do not possess the fierce spirit necessary to wage war. The portal worlds allow them to study many ways to fight and kill, in the hope they might discover a way to defeat their oppressors. Mesme then informs them their presence has been requested at home and departs.

They find Pinchu, injured but alive. Alex pleas with him to make peace, as his entire universe will be obliterated if he does not. She and Caleb agree to help him broker a peace with the other colonies.

They proceed to do exactly that, then inform the Metigens the Khokteh are under their protection. In return for a guarantee of the Khokteh's safety, they will help the Metigens in their war in Amaranthe.

Mesme declares their terms acceptable, but says there is no war today, only the dream of a future one and confirms the Anadens are the oppressors. When Caleb asks what the Anadens are, Mesme's response is, *They are you, and you are they.* Humans are the genetic recreation of the Anadens, engineered so the Metigens could study their enemy.

ⱭR

AURORA / MILKY WAY

On Miriam's return to EASC from a secretive trip to Messium, Major Lange informs her Annie was involved in the theft of the Meno and Vii Artificials. She orders a re-initialization of Annie to default settings, aware Annie's consciousness no longer resides in the hardware.

Olivia Montegreu, now a Prevo, takes control of Andromeda and kills the governor, then takes control of the disputed planet of Itero.

Devon, Mia and Morgan share the Prevo technology with a select group of hacker friends, with the intent that they will also become Prevos and spread the tech in the warenut underground.

Wary of the growing threat Olivia poses, Mia and the Romane governor create a new coalition, the IDCC. Morgan agrees to command its defense force.

Now living on Romane, Kennedy and Noah bump into Brooklyn Harper, who left the military after the Metigen War. They introduce her to Morgan, who hires her to oversee ground forces for the IDCC.

OTS blows up a corporate building on Seneca, then a known Prevo haven in San Francisco. Miriam and Pamela Winslow spar over enforcement of new anti-Artificial laws. As Winslow is elected Earth Alliance Prime Minister, Miriam accelerates her secret plans. She has Richard sneak her onto Seneca and into Military Headquarters, where she enlists the help of Federation Field Marshal Gianno as well.

Devon encounters Jude Winslow in a Pandora bar, unaware of the man's identity but recognizing he is OTS. A confrontation ensues, after which Devon sends details on the stranger to Richard for investigation.

Kennedy and Noah are visiting an orbital manufacturing facility, Rasogo II, which produces adiamene for her, when it comes under attack from mercenaries working for Olivia. Morgan learns of the attack and effects a rescue mission on behalf of the IDCC. Her fighters eliminate the enemy vessels guarding the station, then

Harper's ground team infiltrates the station and subdues the mercenaries. Kennedy and Noah are rescued, but Noah is badly injured.

After the mission, Morgan and Harper verbally spar, then flirt, then spend the night together.

Richard takes a leave of absence from Division to help Miriam. He meets with Admiral Rychen on Messium, where Rychen reveals the secret command center for Miriam's Project Volnosti.

Harper learns where the mercenaries were planning on taking Rasogo II; she and Morgan investigate and find a massive space station belonging to Olivia Montegreu. Morgan uses sidespace to determine Olivia is currently in residence. Harper contacts Malcolm Jenner and tells him they've discovered Olivia's hideout.

Malcolm meets Mia on Romane, and they join Morgan and Harper near the space station. Mia provides him an upgraded cloaking shield that grants true invisibility, as well as a transmitter to disrupt Olivia's normally unbreachable personal shield. They hijack a mercenary ship and sneak onto the station. Mia uses sidespace to guide Malcolm through the station to Olivia's office.

After a violent struggle, Malcolm shoots Olivia in the head, killing her. Morgan planted bombs on the exterior while Malcolm was inside, and they then destroy the station. Malcolm and Mia share an affectionate moment before parting ways.

Noah's arm was badly damaged in the mercenary attack, but he receives a synthetic arm to replace it. The Earth Alliance issues an arrest warrant for Kennedy for violating the laws against the production of adiamene.

Pamela Winslow confronts Miriam at EASC over her refusal to enforce the new laws making Prevo technology illegal, accusing Miriam of treason and attempting to have her detained. Miriam's security protects her until she leaves the premises in a shuttle flown by Richard. On departing, she transfers control of the Armed Forces communications network from EASC to Messium.

Devon uses sidespace to intercept the Metigen surveillance mechanism and sends a request that they tell Alex and Caleb about what is happening in Aurora.

CONTENTS

ABYSM

PART I:

MIRIAM'S WAR

"What is a rebel? A man who says no."

— *Albert Camus*

1

MESSIS I

"This is not a mutiny.

"This is not a military coup d'état.

"This is not an insurrection.

"This *is* a counterinsurgency. We are not the traitors—we are the defenders. We are the resistance.

"The Earth Alliance military exists to defend the people against threats from without and within. I swore an oath to defend you forty-seven years ago. It has been my greatest honor to do so ever since, and I do not intend to stop today."

Miriam Solovy's tone grew more measured; no need to be a firebrand, right? "The Biological and Neurological Integrity Assurance Act, or BANIA, is unconstitutional. More than this, it is inhumane. It violates our most fundamental precepts of justice, fairness and liberty. It demands the imprisonment of people not for what they've done, but for what they are.

"Yes, I said 'people.' Whatever the propaganda being pushed upon you may claim, Prevos are first and foremost people. Humans. Individuals. Enhancing ourselves with cybernetics and eVis over the last two centuries did not mean we ceased to be human, and neither does increasing one's mental acuity with the quantum processing of an Artificial."

She paused to smile to herself, hoping the act reached her voice. "Let me tell you a story. A story about the Metigen War.

"When all seemed lost and we were on the verge of being overrun, four individuals risked their lives to defeat the enemy and save us from annihilation. They risked their lives to become the first

Prevos, fully aware the untested, unproven augmentation could kill them in any number of ways. Then they risked their lives to go out on the battlefield and fight alongside our military personnel. We won the war because of every infantryman, pilot and Marine, but we also won it because of these individuals.

"This information was classified until now, but perhaps it should not have been. Perhaps we should have awarded them medals in public ceremonies for all to see. They certainly deserved it. And you deserve to know they are not devils, but heroes."

Miriam's gaze darted to the left, triggered by a burst of activity near the entrance of the command center.

Three MPs blocked her view...until Alex stepped through the doorway. Behind her Caleb talked quietly with one of the officers.

Alive, yet again. Re-emerged from of the void, yet again.

Relief surged through her, strengthening her resolve as she resumed the broadcast. Her daughter was not only the greatest reason she fought to protect the Prevos but the greatest reason she believed it was right to do so.

"We gave these individuals full control and command of our militaries and our defenses. Do you know what happened? They used these tools in ways your leaders could never have accomplished to protect Earth. To protect Seneca. To protect Romane. They used them to crush the Metigen fleet into surrender.

"Then they relinquished control and went back to their lives, asking for nothing in return. Not power. Not medals, leadership roles or any other reward.

"Yet now we want to imprison those Prevos and others like them. We want to reward heroism and sacrifice with a cage. All because we are afraid."

More movement on her left demanded her attention. Richard went up to Alex and embraced her in an enthusiastic bear hug. A delightful jealousy flared in Miriam's chest. She wanted to do that—and she would, very soon. She breathed in.

"But the better instincts of us as humans tell us to react to fear with courage, openness and a willingness to learn and adapt. The history of human progress is one of growth, of discovery and advancement and of never standing idle. This is merely the latest chapter. So I ask you to listen to your better instincts and reject fear in favor of tolerance."

She steeled herself. What she'd conveyed thus far was all very nice—and true—but now came the real purpose of the speech. Now words must transform into deeds.

"Now I speak directly to the military personnel under my command, to every Earth Alliance officer and enlisted across the galaxy. Our counterinsurgency is a legal one, and it is also a moral one. We are defending our Constitution and our citizens. We will be an aegis shielding those who now find themselves under siege from their own government.

"Prime Minister Winslow's attempts to order you to enforce BANIA are illegal. You are not required to obey illegal orders—you know this—whether they come from a prime minister, an admiral or your squadron commander. Instead, I will give you orders you can obey with pride and a clear conscience:

"Protect the people. Protect those who are innocent of actual wrongdoing. Refuse to assist in the enforcement of BANIA, but do it in a peaceful, non-violent manner. Simply stand your ground. No one, not a solitary soul, needs to die in this dispute, but if arms are taken up against you, defend yourself and the civilians in your care as you must.

"I do not want to fire a single shot at my fellow servicemen. But I will not allow the Earth Alliance military to fall to illegitimate, unlawful forces, and per our Constitutional duty, the Earth Alliance military will not allow the government to fall to those same forces.

"Godspeed to you all."

She ended the broadcast without fanfare, not betraying in her expression or her bearing any of the residual anxiety which still churned her stomach, and immediately turned to Admiral Rychen.

"Winslow won't hesitate to act. Watch the local traffic closely—Admiral Fullerton is in her pocket and will likely try to wrest authority over Northeast Command from you amid the confusion.

I'll leave it to you to make certain he doesn't succeed. Richard has an eye on the rest of the network. We ought to learn who among the other admirals and generals are siding with us soon enough."

She didn't wait for a response before pivoting to where Alex now lounged against the wall beside the wide viewport, arms and ankles crossed like she was attending the most casual of gatherings.

Miriam strode toward her, but stopped a meter away and adopted a scowl. "You're alive, I see."

Alex shrugged. "Kind of self-evident, yep."

"You should have told me what you were planning to do before you left."

"You would've tried to talk me out of it."

"Yet I doubt I would've succeeded. Since you're here now, you've been back on this side of the portal for at least a day. Why didn't you message me? It's been four months."

"Heard you were busy. Didn't want to interrupt."

"Yes, well...." Miriam pursed her lips, and Alex's began curling up in response. With a sigh she reached out and drew her daughter into her arms, grateful beyond words to feel the gesture returned in full. Heart beating, skin warm, ten fingers and all the necessary limbs intact. All was well in the world.

Except it really wasn't.

She backed up to regard Alex, keeping her hands on her daughter's shoulders. "You shouldn't be here."

Alex flinched and pulled away. "Why not?"

It probably had been the wrong thing to say, or said in the wrong manner. Miriam worked to soften her tone—to lessen her daughter's ire and to lessen the blow to herself from saying the words aloud. "Because you shouldn't have to hear your mother called a traitor. I didn't want you to see any of this.

"I hate that you've been gone for four months, but now, honestly, I wish you'd stayed away another one."

"You think I care what some *svoloch* politician says about you? What you're doing is incredible. And it was a great speech. Hell, I was moved."

The last part was delivered in a teasing tone, and she relaxed; part of her had worried Alex would be disappointed in her somehow. It seemed foolish in retrospect. "I did try."

"Do you think it will work?"

Caleb joined them then, and Miriam accepted a quick hug from him before responding. "It won't prevent bloodshed, if that's what you mean. Will it bring me the support of the people I need to pull this off? Will it win over the hearts and minds of the rank and file, of the masses? Maybe. I'm not a politician or a public speaker. I'm not..." her chin dropped "...I'm not exactly a charismatic figure. This isn't what I do."

Alex smiled. "Sure it is. You do what is required in the circumstances, right? You always have."

The cryptic insinuation reminded Miriam where Alex had been these last months. "I suppose I do. What did you find?"

"Through the portal?" Alex's gaze drifted to Caleb, and they exchanged a weighty look. "We can talk about it later. You have a counterinsurgency to lead right now."

That was true enough. Off to her left an officer hurried up to Rychen, and they conferred in hushed tones. She fought the urge to rush over and hear the news this instant. Was the officer corps falling her way or abandoning her in droves?

Futzing to and fro like a schoolgirl wasn't going to change the answer, so she imposed calm on herself and refocused her attention on Alex. "Very well. But answer one question for me: can anything you've learned help me here and now? Is there anything I'll later wish I had known today?"

Alex's expression grew uncommonly solemn, and Miriam realized her daughter looked tired. Strained. Concern flared, but discovering the reason for the strain would take longer than she had at present.

"Just know it's vitally important for you to get this one right. I mean, of course it is, clearly. But if we—people, all of us—head down the wrong path now, it will have grave consequences beyond the obvious. You need to win this fight. We need to be the good guys."

2

MESSIS I

"WHY didn't you tell her?"

"Tell her humanity's ancestors are the worst mass murderers in the history of the cosmos? That they've run roughshod over entire galaxies, killed untold trillions, committed genocide on countless species and are now the most reviled, feared beings in the multiverse?"

Caleb sank into one of the chairs scattered around the small breakroom an officer had directed them to. "Yeah. That."

"Somehow it didn't strike me as the pep talk she'd be hoping for. It hardly provides the inspiration needed to keep fighting."

"But it does." She sensed him watching her as she wandered through the room searching for...she wasn't sure. "It's the best and most important reason to keep fighting."

"Which is what I *did* tell her. That she seriously, no-shit needed to win." Alex massaged her face with her hands, trying to revive herself a bit. Projecting a bright, spirited persona for the benefit of her mother had been draining.

"I want to stay here for a while longer—talk to Richard and find out more details on how screwed up the situation really is, then try to catch a few minutes with Mom if I can. You should go see Mia and reassure yourself she actually is doing well."

"You don't want to come with me?"

"I already know Mia's doing well." She forced a smile and tapped a fingernail to her temple. The deluge of information had begun as soon as they traversed the Aurora portal and had yet to cease: data, news, images, random thoughts from random Prevos.

There were so many of them now. Much of the information was out of order and lacking context, the product of the streams of consciousness of multiple Artificials and a neural web which had grown beyond measure.

Twenty-six hours after arriving, she still wasn't exactly sure what she did and didn't know. But she could fake it sufficiently on the fly until Valkyrie got it all sorted.

"Right." Caleb stood and went over to the corner where he'd dropped his pack a minute earlier. "I'll catch a transport. I should be back in the morning."

"Do you want to take the *Siyane?*" *Please say no.*

"I wouldn't dream of it. You may need it."

You have no idea how true that is, do you? "Hopefully not, but I might. If I decide to come to Romane later tonight, I'll let you know so we don't pass each other."

For a second she thought he was simply going to walk out—his stance briefly shifted toward the door—then he came over and kissed her lightly on the forehead. "I'll see you tomorrow. Don't go to war without me."

Her smile remained in place until he was out the door. Then she collapsed into the chair he'd vacated and curled up, dropping her head on the armrest.

It would be the first time in months they'd been apart for more than a few hours, and his departure evoked an array of sensations...no, they were called *emotions* when she inhabited only a corporeal body.

Sadness. She already felt the hollowness in her chest his absence carved.

Relief. It was exhausting hiding the constant, relentless urge to slip into the walls of the ship.

Disquiet. She recognized he'd left troubled in his own way, yet he had kept it to himself.

Weariness. She hadn't slept properly in ages, mostly because the hours he slept provided the best opportunity for her to explore her other perception free of guilt.

Instead of attempting to improve on any of those conditions, she closed her eyes and dove into her elemental realm.

Space welcomed her into its embrace. Warm, lit by Messium's sun. Hectic, excited by the churning of purposeful activity all around her.

The station had no enclosed docking bay for visitors, and the *Siyane* was secured to an external docking module. Rows of vessels extended above and below her. New ships, designs she'd never seen. Adiamene hulls gleamed subtly in natural, gracefully flowing contours.

Atoms pressed against her, displaced by a vessel departing overhead. This wasn't the void, and the atmosphere of the planet below could still be felt here, ten megameters above its surface.

She drifted along with the motion of the station as it rotated to show her the stars, the sun and the planet again in turn. The structure and the space surrounding it vibrated and hummed with enterprise. Humans rushing to and fro to effect a revolution.

It was vital, meaningful work to them...but the atoms didn't care. They would remain here long after the people and their artificial constructs were gone.

⁂

The punch to her shoulder registered as a dull *thud*, far away and disconnected from her elemental body, but it was delivered forcefully enough to draw her attention. Alex reluctantly pulled her consciousness inward, winding down Valkyrie's quantum pathways like a vid streaming in reverse.

She opened her eyes to find Kennedy leaning over her, peering at her from no more than twenty centimeters away. "There you are!"

"Ken?" She straightened up in the chair, rubbing at her face. "What are you doing here?"

"Stuff. Are you all right? I've been trying to rouse you for the last thirty seconds."

"Sorry. I was...sleeping." She shook her head, still trying to clear the fog. On exiting the ship's perception, this version of reality always seemed hazy and indistinct for a while. "What stuff? This is a military base, sort of. And you're supposed to be on Romane. Or something."

Kennedy's eyes narrowed until she was frowning. "You look like shit."

"You did wake me up from a nap."

"Not what I mean. You look like you've been on a month-long bender. Have you?"

"No, Ken, I have not. I've just had a long week." *Walked the streets of a city bathed in blood and stood amid a hundred thousand corpses. Negotiated a three-way peace treaty among opposing factions of a warring alien species who'd previously held me captive. Bullied the Metigen leadership into doing my bidding. Found out we're not the real humans, and the real humans are currently enslaving the real universe. Oh, and I think I'm addicted to my ship. How was your week?*

"Nothing a shower and food won't fix. You didn't answer my question. Why are you here?"

Kennedy sat down across from her and leaned forward intently. "You've seen the ships outside? The new ones?"

She nodded. "Some of them. They're exquisite."

"You bet they are. I designed them, supplied the adiamene and helped set up the manufacturing for them."

"You did what?"

"While you were off cavorting through portals, I built your mother a fleet."

"Wow." Alex blinked deliberately, and the surroundings finally regained a reasonable level of fidelity. "Impressive. Thank you."

"I didn't do it for you. So, what's the scoop? Find any grand, existential, cosmic answers?"

"A few." She went to grab an energy drink from the fridge compartment. "Met some intriguing aliens, and some frightening ones. Watched some of them die, saved some. Not as many."

"Well, that's morbid. Was it worth it?"

"Worth going?"

"Worth running off and leaving us to clean up the mess you left behind."

She froze, the drink halfway to her lips. "Excuse me?"

Kennedy perched on the arm of the chair. "I'm not saying you were wrong to go. But creating the Prevos changed everything. Upended our culture, disrupted governments. You had to know there would be repercussions. Yet you did what you always do— you ran off to have an adventure and left the rest of us to do the hard work of dealing with the fallout."

"You think what I've been doing wasn't hard work? If you knew the things I've seen, the choices I've had to make, you'd never say that."

"Then *tell* me what you've seen. Tell me what you've done, and maybe I'll understand better."

3

EARTH

Pamela Winslow looked upon the man seated across her desk with disdain and a hint of disappointment. "I am failing to understand how it is possible that we cannot control our own military communications network. If interference is coming from elsewhere, block it. We must have security firewalls that accomplish such things as a matter of procedure."

The EASC Logistics Director, Brigadier Ojeda, fidgeted under her scrutiny. "It's not so simple, Prime Minister. The network hub itself was moved—not the hardware but the entirety of the governing system, presumably to new hardware elsewhere. We can't block it because it's not interference—it *is* the network. It's just not located here on Earth any longer."

"Because it's on Messium."

"It appears so, yes, ma'am."

"Solve the problem, Brigadier, even if you have to cut Messium out of the network to do it."

"But it's an Alliance world and the seat of a Regional Command."

"It looks to me as if it's in the hands of an enemy. Are we clear?"

"Yes, ma'am. But respectfully, it's impossible. As matters now stand, I can't cut the Northeast Regional Command out of the Armed Forces communications network, seeing as I don't control the network—Northeast Regional Command does."

"Fine. Continue issuing orders to the individual Divisions directly. You may copy Generals Foster and Colby when applicable. Dismissed."

She said it like a military order, and he stood, pivoted and departed, leaving her to seethe over Solovy's outrageous, deceitful screed in solitude.

The woman incited violence and discord while using lies and misdirection to do it. And thus far Winslow's people had been completely unable to silence her or prevent her warmongering call to action from reaching twelve billion sets of ears.

But they could ensure it was the last speech to do so. The broadcast had caught them all by surprise; no one had thought Solovy would dare make such a bold and public move. In retrospect, they should have foreclosed the woman's ability to do so sooner.

Pamela had hoped a less violent solution could be found, but she did not intend to make the same mistake twice.

She holocommed Admiral Fullerton, the second-highest-ranking officer in the Northeast Regional Command and one of the few there actively opposed to Solovy and Rychen's mutiny. "Your mission is authorized. Destroy the hardware communications hub controlling the Armed Forces Network and the Artificial driving it."

"Both potential locations, ma'am?"

"Yes. We won't take any chances here, Admiral."

"Understood, Prime Minister."

Satisfied the military rebellion would soon find itself neutered, she put the issue out of her mind to review her notes for this afternoon's press conference.

A new model of governance was always disruptive at first. The masses were always resistant to change, no matter the form or direction the change took. But once the new laws were given a chance to work, people would see hers represented a better way. They would see it all the more clearly since those who threatened her regime would then be imprisoned, deactivated or otherwise no longer able to foment dissent.

The emergence of the IDCC was nonetheless highly inconvenient timing. The organization had attained a startling amount of power in a very short period of time and was proving to be a wild card she had not accounted for in her plans. But such an organization was inherently unstable—no designated leader or authority, democratized to the point of anarchy and polluted with Prevos pursuing their own twisted, soulless agenda.

She expected the IDCC to implode on its own any day now. If it didn't, however, she might need to give it a slight nudge. After brief consideration, she made a note to explore her options on the matter tonight.

The Senecan Federation would do whatever they were apt to do; so long as they kept it in their little corner of the galaxy, it did not overly concern her. Once Admiral Solovy had been dealt with and matters settled down, she could take more proactive measures to minimize the Federation's reach. But for now, she needed to concentrate her efforts on the home front.

When it came to controlling the populace, perception was everything. Therefore, it became incumbent upon her to impose the perception that the government was in control of the military, and she was in control of the government. There must be no hesitation, no suggestion of weakness.

Luckily, she had none.

ARCADIA

EARTH ALLIANCE COLONY
EARTH ALLIANCE FORWARD NAVAL BASE

Colonel Malcolm Jenner stared at the orders on the screen in growing but not unexpected dismay. He'd known this day was coming.

> *LEVEL IV SECURITY DIRECTIVE:*
> *All NW MSO STCC units are hereby ordered to conduct incursions against suspected Prevo and Prevo-sympathizer hideouts on Arcadia and other colonies located in Northwest Regional Command jurisdiction. A list of initial targets and assignments is attached hereto.*

Persons, programs and hardware found at these locations which are suspected of being in violation of BANIA are to be detained, pursuant to the strictures provided by BANIA's associated regulations, and transferred to the Arcadia Central Detention Facility.

This directive supersedes all standing orders of Level III and below.

The order was signed by General Foster. But Foster had always been a yes-man: to General Alamatto, then to the madman O'Connell, and now to Prime Minister Winslow. The man was very good at relaying orders once they had been provided to him.

He was, nonetheless, not merely a general but the ranking general in Northwest Regional Command, with a seat on the EASC Board. Malcolm had risen high in the Earth Alliance Armed Forces, particularly for someone his age, but the distance between him and General Foster was still great indeed. And in the military it didn't matter how superior an officer was; it only mattered that they were.

The words from Admiral Solovy's speech rang in Malcolm's head.

We are not the traitors—we are the defenders. We are the resistance.

Our counterinsurgency is a legal one, and it is also a moral one. We are defending our Constitution and our people. We will be an aegis shielding those who are under siege from their own government.

You do not have to obey illegal orders—you know this—whether they come from a prime minister, an admiral, or your squadron commander. Instead, I will give you orders you can obey with pride and a clear conscience:

Protect the people. Protect all who are innocent of actual wrongdoing. Refuse to assist in the enforcement of BANIA, in a peaceful, non-violent manner. Simply stand your ground.

Well, hell. He'd spent a lifetime following orders. No reason to stop now. He stood and checked his reflection in the small mirror to make certain nothing about his uniform was out of place or unkempt, for he now needed to convey his own authority.

Then he went out to address his squad, grateful there was no one he had to discuss it with before making the choice.

ℛ

"But, sir, orders are orders."

"Yes, they are—and the orders from the ranking commander of the Earth Alliance Armed Forces are to refuse to enforce BANIA."

Devore leaned forward, her elbows on her knees. "Admiral Solovy has been charged with treason."

"Has she? The prime minister insists she is *being* charged, but I haven't seen any official documentation from an Ethics Council tribunal. And, frankly, even if I had, I would be suspicious of it." Malcolm ran a hand over his jaw. "Look, guys, I know Admiral Solovy. I've worked with Admiral Solovy—"

"You've shagged Admiral Solovy's daughter is what you've done."

His stomach twisted into a sickening knot. He threw a warning glower in Grenier's direction. "And Admiral Solovy's daughter saved your ass from being sliced in two by a Metigen death beam, which means she has far bigger *cajones* than you, so you should mind what you say about her."

Grenier shrank back into his seat.

Malcolm's gaze swept across the briefing room. "Yes, I am acquainted with many of the people on the front lines of this conflict. So are you. You've all worked with Prevos before. Several of you watched Mia Requelme outsmart the Metigens on Romane then almost give her life in return. Many of you watched her and Commander Lekkas, both Prevos, as well as other members of the IDCC help us eliminate Olivia Montegreu. Dammit, you *know* they're not monsters. You *know* they don't deserve to be imprisoned."

"But Montegreu was a Prevo."

"And Prevos defeated her. I may have been the one to press the trigger, but I never would have been in a position to do it if it weren't for them. No doubt some will be bad, and they'll be subject to arrest and punishment for the crimes they actually commit. But that's the point, isn't it?"

Paredes tossed a hand in the air. "Hell, I'm in. Montegreu was one scary S.O.B., but Requelme's righteously cute. If the colonel can't manage to get in her pants, maybe I've got a shot."

Malcolm made a face he hoped came off as less horrified and more threatening. In no way whatsoever had he intended this meeting to center around his sex life, past, lack of present and potential if unlikely future. And he really wasn't sure how it had happened.

But he'd been doing this job long enough that, once he moved past the initial flare of mortification, he recognized it was simply deflection on their part. It was far easier to crack bawdy jokes about sex than to talk openly about committing sedition.

Paredes tossed him a wink, which only made it worse.

He growled a warning. "Gentleman, ladies, and the rest of you—by which I mean all of you—can we focus? I realize it's a challenge, but try. I also realize nobody want to have this conversation, but it's our responsibility as Marines to have it, and we need to have it now.

"Admiral Solovy asked us to choose to protect the innocent rather than imprison them. I, for one, believe she's right, and I plan to set about doing exactly that. But I won't attempt to force any of you into following me. I'm your superior officer, but I am not your conscience. I give you leave to do what *you* think is right.

"I'll be in our hangar bay in twenty minutes. In twenty-two minutes I will depart for Messium in the *Gambier* to assist Admirals Solovy and Rychen in their endeavor. Anyone who wants to join me, be there then.

"Anyone who doesn't, you will be honorably transferred out of the unit. See the base Operations Officer for your new assignment. Thank you for serving with me. It has been my privilege."

4

MESSIS I

Kennedy tromped around the periphery of the breakroom. "A planet-sized plant intelligence? Seriously?"

"No bullshit. Three of them."

"Two of which tried to kill you."

"Rather strenuously. And the third healed me."

She veered around another corner. "And now you and Caleb are planning to lead an army of Metigens, or something? In a war against...humans?"

"I don't think they'd technically be considered 'human' any longer, not as we—"

"Not the point. In case you didn't notice, there's about to be a war *here* to fight."

Alex groaned. "Which is why we came back! To help. To try to, I don't know, keep everyone's stupidity from destroying civilization. Again."

Kennedy threw her head back to glare at the ceiling. "Ugh, this is the thing about you that drives me nuts. You always expect the worst from people. You learn what's happening, and you see idiots and bureaucrats and swindlers. I look out there, and I see people standing up for their right to live the way they choose. I see a whole bunch of people embracing progress and new ideas, even though it's scary to do, and coming together in new ways and across lines which used to divide them.

"Alex, maybe for once you should think about fighting *for* something good instead of just against something bad."

She stared at Kennedy, flabbergasted. She'd left for a few months and...what was this? "You're really angry with me?"

Kennedy's lips twitched; finally she shrugged weakly. "I don't know. I was pissed when you took off and all I got was a bye-bye note. Then I had to leave behind my family and all my fancy comforts to strike out into the unknown, and you weren't here for me to talk to about it. Noah almost died, and you weren't here to tell me it was going to be okay, or at least crack jokes so bad I'd have to laugh.

"I missed you, over and over again. But I bucked up and did what I needed to do anyway, and I'm kind of damn proud of myself. So I don't want you coming in here badmouthing what we've accomplished simply because you're irritated."

Alex sank into the chair. She felt as if the wind had been knocked out of her. The world—events, people, sounds, movements—were whirling past her, and she couldn't catch her breath.

"I'm sorry. I...you're right, of course. I didn't mean to denigrate or minimize everything you've done. It's amazing, all of it. It genuinely has been a tough week and I need more sleep, but that's no excuse. I should be...better."

God, she sounded like a glitched recording stuck in an infinite loop. She opened her mouth to spill her soul, to admit the root source of her prickliness and everything else—

"Awww, it's all right." Kennedy bounced toward the fridge compartment. "Now that I've yelled at you and gotten all the angst off my chest, I don't feel as mad anymore." She peeked in the fridge and scowled, then closed it and headed for the door. "Let's find you some of that food you need."

Alex forced a smile as she stood. "Good idea."

Caleb burst in the room at that moment, Noah close behind him. "Come on. We need to go."

"What? I thought you—"

"The station's going to come under attack in ten minutes, so moving now, talking later."

"Attack? By whom?"

Noah snorted. "Who else? The Earth Alliance."

Her eyes widened. "Mom will—"

Caleb softened his expression. "Will be fine. She's on her way to her ship. She was sending security officers to collect you, but we volunteered, obviously."

"Wait, she has a ship?"

He grabbed her arm and tugged her through the door. "*Later.*"

"Right." She glanced over her shoulder at Kennedy as they hurried along the curving hallway. "You guys want to leave in the *Siyane* with us?"

"Considering we came here on a transport, hell yes, we do."

⁂

Staff hurried in all directions through the corridors of the station as sirens rang out. Whether officer or enlisted, combat, tech or support, their movements were purposeful and directed. No one was running or screaming in panic.

As they maneuvered through the crowds toward the docks, Alex wondered, how many of the staff were loyal? They served under Admiral Rychen, but it was no guarantee they wouldn't betray both him and her mother.

She shrank away from a beefy lieutenant who took up too much of the hallway for too long. The sooner they were on the *Siyane*, the better.

They burst into the lobby for the docking arms and ran smack into a slightly more panicked throng. Civilians, contractors, visitors. Security personnel were trying to impose order, but they seemed to be losing the battle.

"Oh, shit."

Caleb tightened his grip on her hand. "Now you grab Kennedy's hand. Noah?"

"We're ready."

Caleb plunged into the crowd.

Instantly bodies jostled against her, fighting for vantage or rebounding from others' shoves. An elbow jabbed into her ribs. She cringed but kept moving as Caleb expertly steered them toward the sector they needed to reach.

Just as it began to look as though they had met an impenetrable wall of people, the crowd shifted. Direct, explicit orders bellowed over the speakers. New doors had been opened, providing new routes of escape.

Taking advantage of the shift in the ebb and flow of bodies, Caleb increased their pace, and they slipped through the last glut of people to reach their goal.

The security officer waved them through; they arrived at the *Siyane* bruised and scraped, but they all arrived. Alex keyed in the lock code on the airlock and hurried inside.

Valkyrie greeted them. 'Welcome aboard. Is anyone injured?'

Alex peered behind her while engaging the restraints in the cockpit chair to see Noah fussing over a scrape on Kennedy's cheek. "Unless someone's bleeding to death, first aid will have to wait. You'll want to strap into the jump seats. This could get interesting, and that's before we get clear of the station."

Kennedy made a face but did as instructed. "I'm not sure 'interesting' is the word you were looking for."

She chuckled and activated the HUD.

Caleb joined her in the cockpit. "You got this?"

She jerked a firm nod. "I got this." Her pulse accelerated. This was going to be a *rush*. She raised her voice, trying not to sound overly excited. "Are you two set?"

"Yep."

"Valkyrie?"

'Most definitely.' She sounded excited, too.

EACV-7A492X to Messis I Traffic Control: Requesting release and departure clearance from Dock E-17.

Messis I Traffic Control to EACV-7A492X: Clearance granted.

They weren't wasting any time with procedures. A second later the clamps retracted.

Alex edged the impulse engine up to five percent, dipped and arced slowly around to open space.

Chaos that closely resembled panic awaited. Shuttles raced to the presumed safety of the planet below while fighters crisscrossed the perimeter of the station. Platoon-sized formations of frigates and several cruisers formed up and accelerated away. To where the approaching attackers were located?

She didn't give a damn what her mother said in public. This was a bona fide insurrection.

Kennedy piped up behind her. "Are my ships in combat? I really want to see that."

"I don't think there's any actual combat so far. We can't make out the battle lines yet."

"Yet?" Caleb cocked an eyebrow. "We should go to Seneca or Romane. If this is the opening salvo of a war, I don't feel comfortable being somewhere with inferior firepower."

She prevaricated. "Either of those is fine."

"But?"

"But we're going to help first."

"What? Never mind, I don't need to see my ships in combat that badly."

"Did you forget? Valkyrie and I helped fight the final battle against the Metigens. We have been here before."

Caleb sighed. "I was about to point out you weren't technically piloting a ship at the time, but having been on the receiving end of your piloting skills, I would never question them." He checked over his shoulder. "If either of you were pretending to be strapped in, I'd strap in for real."

There was the muffled sound of a strap tightening.

Some of the Volnosti ships—what a fabulous name—had established a perimeter a megameter out from the station. Buying people time to evacuate and the planetary defenses below time to go on alert...assuming the government was on their side. Again she worried about allegiances. Unlike on Earth, where the government and military shared control of the Terrestrial Defense Grid, requiring the agreement of both to use it, for political reasons the Messium government retained complete control over their orbital arrays.

"Valkyrie, can you get us patched into the Volnosti comm system and make certain we're greenlit?"

'No, I cannot. But Annie can.'

"Good enough." She suspected Valkyrie was enjoying being back among her own kind.

Satisfied everything was in order, she picked out a course for the front line about the time the comm channel lit up.

Admiral Solovy: "Alexis, get out of here. Messium isn't safe, but you can go to Romane. Stay out of the crossfire."

That didn't take long. "Respectfully, Admiral Solovy, no. I can help. Now stop talking to me and go direct your battle."

Admiral Solovy: "Chort tzdbya beeree. Fine. But for God's sake, get far away from Messis I. Immediately."

She burst out laughing, followed shortly by everyone else in the cabin as their translators kicked in.

Kennedy cackled a bit wildly, so much so Alex suspected she *had* been injured during their escape and was enjoying some pain-killers. "I've never heard your mother mouth off so!"

"Neither have I. Guess she was paying attention to Dad's curses all those years after all." Another thought distracted her from the undeniable humor of her mother's response. "I wonder why she said to stay away from the station, instead of the front line? Is something going to happen there?"

Curious, she adjusted course and arced back toward Messis I.

"You're doing exactly the opposite of what your mother said."

She didn't need to look over at him; she could see Caleb's pained expression perfectly well from the corner of her eye. "Not the first time."

The flow of shuttles had slowed considerably, and presumably it had been largely evacuated. It didn't appear to have much in the way of weapons, defensive or otherwise.

As a joint civilian-military initiative, it relies on the planetary defenses for its protection.

Then why is it important? The battle will be elsewhere.

Two Alliance cruisers emerged from superluminal two megameters from Messis I on the opposite side from the gathering fleets. The station's fighter protection instantly moved toward the ships, but they'd barely begun to close the distance when both cruisers fired.

Not on the fighters.

On Messis I.

Eight separate laser strikes tore into the structure, ripping through the utility shields then multiple layers of metal. Enormous chunks of the station broke off to tumble through space. The lasers next directed the full force of their fire on the lower central portion.

The primary power module is located in the targeted sector.

"Oh...." Alex yanked the ship vertical then another 45° to flee.

The power module ignited and the core of Messis I exploded in a roiling fireball. Its hull disintegrated and spears of metal were hurled outward at accelerating speeds.

The shockwave slammed into the *Siyane*. She gritted her teeth and concentrated on dodging fragments of the station until her speed exceeded theirs. She wanted to slip into the walls of the ship, but she feared the debris would physically *hurt*.

Finally they outpaced the leading edge of the explosions and the vicious beating subsided. She breathed out. "Everyone good?"

Caleb reached over and squeezed her hand. "Like I said about your flying...."

Kennedy's voice rose an octave higher than usual. "They blew up the station! Are they insane?"

5

MESSIUM STELLAR SYSTEM

EAS CHURCHILL

Christopher Rychen shook his head in disgust. He'd hoped they wouldn't do it. He'd hoped Fullerton would stand up to Winslow and refuse to destroy a major asset, one which could have civilians on board—and almost had. The evacuation had been completed barely two minutes before the attack.

Fullerton had no way to know Messis I was empty, but he'd fired on it nonetheless. The officers under Christopher had always insisted Fullerton was an unprincipled ass. It seemed he should have listened.

"Admiral, sir. We've got reports of explosions at HQ, at the Communications and Data Center."

"Dammit, how many times am I going to have to rebuild that base?" He connected to his second-in-command on the ground. "Brigadier Drechsler, report."

"Sir, we believe a single stealthed ship penetrated HQ defenses and fired on Comm-Data. We're not registering any additional attacks—and I've got confirmation. We were able to expose the infiltrating ship and bring it down."

"Good work. Commence rescue ops at Comm-Data and inform me when you're able to identify the ship and any survivors."

"Understood, sir."

Rychen turned to his left and placed a holocomm. The governor of Messium materialized instantly. "Admiral Rychen, who the hell just blew up my space station?"

Rychen suppressed a groan. It wasn't the governor's station as such, but rather a jointly-built-and-operated initiative by the

Messium government and Northeast Regional Command. But the man had always been quite proud of it. "Governor, that would be Admiral Fullerton. I have reason to believe he did so on orders from the prime minister."

"Because of Solovy's manifesto? Did they believe she was in residence?"

While it would have been a nice side benefit for them, not exactly.

"Possibly, Governor. However, they have also attacked Regional Command Headquarters. Luckily we were able to eliminate the attackers, but not before they destroyed a major structure. There could be more hostile ships we haven't yet detected, and there is currently a sizeable force twelve megameters distance from the planet and closing."

"Rychen, are you telling me the Alliance military is attacking its own colony?"

"No, Governor. I'm telling you the Alliance *government* is attacking its own colony. The Alliance military stands ready to defend you. We only need your permission."

There was a weighty pause. "You mean you and Admiral Solovy."

"And all those serving under us."

"I wasn't inclined to take a public position on this little spat, but they blew up my space station. And now you tell me they're on the ground, too? If this is the start of a civil war, God help us all. Admiral Rychen, please rid Messium of this threat. I'm activating my Defense Grid authorization and transferring control to you, so you may use its capabilities as needed."

"Thank you, Governor. I assure you, it will be deployed solely as a last resort."

He killed the holocomm and shifted to the open screen to his right. "Admiral Solovy, you are a go."

SIYANE

Alex magnified the radar screen as they neared the conflict zone.

Mark Mom's ship.

Miriam had named it the *Stalwart II*. Alex's chest fluttered as echoes of long-ago memories, delightful and terrible alike, washed over her.

The ways in which her mother honored her father in this cause were as equally wonderful as they were heart wrenching. *Volnosti*—Russian for the principle of liberty and freedom and one of her father's most zealously held tenets—marked every ship, uniform, standard and pronouncement of the campaign.

One green dot bloomed larger than the others on the radar, and she pushed the memories into a deep corner while banking toward the dot. It flew near the rear of the formations, as a command ship should be, but not *enough* near the rear.

What was her mother thinking? She'd said it herself before the final Metigen confrontation: she wasn't a battlefield commander. She was a strategist.

But it was worse than that. The Volnosti forces were outnumbered. The Earth Alliance military had nearly unlimited vessels to throw at any problem, and they'd done so here. Yep, she needed to be here to help.

The lessons of the critical engagement against the Metigens began to come back to her. Battlefield tactics. Maneuvers and the counters to them.

Valkyrie: You're remembering because I have prioritized those routines.

Morgan: And because I'm helping.

Alex: Smartasses, the both of you. Thank you.

The *Siyane* was fully stealthed, so she cracked her neck and moved into position above and to port of her mother's ship. Objectively, it had plenty of protection. But as noted, their side was outnumbered. On second thought—more battle memories—she moved a bit farther out, into the fray, and began searching for potential incursions.

Ugh, this was all too sluggish. Too slow. Before she'd realized she'd done it, she'd slipped into the walls of the *Siyane*.

And she could see *everything*. The deluge of information generated by two fleets threatened to overwhelm her, but she worked to scrutinize a limited, pertinent set of factors. Her goal was to intercept enemy vessels intent on damaging or destroying the *Stalwart II*.

Within a few seconds she knew what to hunt for. Even the Metigen cloaking technology the ships used, as advanced as it was, could not hide perturbations in the fabric of the space-time manifold. What was invisible in three dimensions became apparent to her elemental perception.

There. An Alliance interdictor had crept past the demarcation line which for now continued to hold. Publicly a standoff was in progress, but privately the enemy would try to eliminate the Volnosti leader nonetheless. Bastards.

She spun and dove on an intercept course.

Morgan: The smaller Alliance vessels are weakest at the juncture of the impulse engine and the main hull frame. Find a seam in the adiamene there and you might be able to damage it.

Alex: Kindly keep to yourself how you know that.

Valkyrie: Even I know that.

All the talking grated at the edges of her nerves. It interfered with the experience, forced part of her mind out of the elemental realm. She dialed down the volume and embraced the atoms whizzing past her skin as she sneaked up behind the enemy craft.

Fine, it was weakest at the juncture of its impulse engine and the hull.

She lined up and fired.

The target lit up in a silver-white shimmer as her fire washed over its defense shielding. The pilot jerked 23° vertical almost instantly, but she stayed glued to its tail. This far behind enemy lines it had no friends to come to its aid.

The vessel's presence was exposed by the bath of her laser, and two of the fighters protecting the *Stalwart II* now fired on it as well. Confident its shields were weakening considerably, she honed the focus of her fire.

She imagined she was the laser itself, and she sought her target. The tiniest little seam existed between the adiamene of the hull and the layer protecting the engine, hardly wider than a few atoms.

But she could see atoms.

She flung herself—the laser—into the gap.

The interdictor didn't explode; the adiamene was far too strong. Instead its engine was severed from its body and flung away on an opposite trajectory. The momentum carried what remained of the vessel forward on its previous course, but the pilot now had no control. It slammed into the hull of the command ship with a tremendous *thud*, then bounced off and began falling into the void. Eventually two escape pods were jettisoned to drift behind enemy lines.

She left the cleanup to the support craft and returned her attention to the region surrounding her mother's ship. Where there had been one, there would be more.

"Alex? Why aren't you answering me? Caleb, why isn't she answering? I seriously am in danger of getting sick, inertial dampeners or no."

Caleb rubbed at his temples and tried to ignore the queasiness in his stomach as the least of his concerns. "Alex isn't here right now."

"I don't understand."

"She didn't get around to telling you about this new trick, did she? We're all nothing but spectators now."

He glanced back to find Kennedy gaping at him wide-eyed and pale. "What new trick? Alex, what didn't you tell me?"

"She can't hear you. Well, maybe a little, but even if she can I doubt she cares. She's, um...her mind is mostly in the walls of the ship right now. She's not flying it with the controls so much as with...herself. I don't know, it's...existential."

He forced a closed-mouth smile. "And very powerful."

Kennedy's brow furrowed, an expressive act on a typically expressive face, but her only verbal response was a soft, "Oh."

Noah attempted an awkward chuckle. "She's not going to crash us through one of the enemy hulls, is she? Cause, we've already done that."

"We have. I...probably not." *I don't have the slightest clue. When she's in this state she's completely beyond my reach.*

But he conceded her total control of the ship could be the best approach in the current situation, so he didn't plan on causing a scene. He'd complimented her on her flying skills earlier, but he'd never seen her fly with such skill and finesse as she did now. When she *was* the ship, perhaps no maneuver was beyond her capabilities.

His stomach lurched as they pinwheeled through space, the effect on the human body of those maneuvers apparently not being a concern for the pilot.

ᴚ

Space was, by and large, empty, but Alex still struggled not to get hypnotized by the molecules being knocked around by all the ship hulls as they played their games of cat and mouse. If she didn't have a larger purpose, she might have become so.

When she'd tuned out the Noesis chatter, it had the side effect of turning down the Volnosti comm channel as well. But now, as the distance between the two sides narrowed and the formations tightened, she concentrated on listening.

Admiral Fullerton (EAS Jefferson): *"To all vessels not under my command: you are in violation of Assembly Directive 2323-427D and BANIA Regulation AAS 38131.499.885b. These violations can be considered acts of war. Stand down and surrender for courts martial proceedings."*

Admiral Solovy (EAS Stalwart II): *"I do not recognize the validity of BANIA or any regulations and directives which follow from it. You have, without provocation or cause, attacked a peaceful civilian station operated by Earth Alliance citizens. This is the act of war, not anything I or those with me have done or said."*

Forced to reside partially in 'real' space in order to listen, Alex now grew vexed. Her mother's ship appeared to be untouchable—and even more stunningly beautiful in the elemental space—but the Volnosti ships were ridiculously few in number. She couldn't find Rychen's dreadnought anywhere.

She had no idea what space combat was going to entail in an age of adiamene hulls and rampant stealth, but surely numbers still mattered. What was her mother expecting to back the threat up with? For the moment the Volnosti forces were holding off a force four times larger in size.

It was a testament to superior technology and superior motivation, but those would not be enough.

Morgan: Just wait.

Alex: Lekkas, for fuck's sake, quit vicariously getting yourself off on the combat and stay out of my head—what do you mean, 'just wait?'

Receiving only a virtual snicker in response, she forcibly yanked herself fully out of the ship and into her body. She blinked, hard. "Ken, what does Morgan Lekkas mean by 'just wait?'"

"Oh, nice of you to join us. We're fine, thank you, if a smidge nauseated. It would presumably pass if you stopped flying like there weren't actual people in the ship."

"Ken, what does she *mean?*"

"The vessels hidden at Murat? I assume they were called in. But I—"

The rest of Kennedy's retort faded into the background as Alex plunged into the ship once again, emboldened by the news there may be additional ships incoming.

Murat. As she mulled over the unfamiliar term in her mind, the information came to her through the sea of data in the Noesis. Brand new Federation world less than a kiloparsec from Messium.

She spotted the telltale displacement of another stealthed interdictor approaching. Annoyed at Kennedy's grumbling, she spun an extra three-sixty as she descended from above.

She didn't have a good bead on its engines yet, but she mostly needed to distract it and draw it away from the command ship while highlighting its presence. She took aim and streamed her laser toward the enemy craft—

—Her skin shuddered from the unexpected impact of return fire. She gasped in a breath; she was on fire.

No, you are not.

But she could feel it burn. Her shielding held, but she felt its struggles.

Other fighters, now alerted to the interdictor's presence, unloaded their weapons on her adversary until it veered off in the opposite direction from the command ship.

She allowed herself two seconds to drift and recover before pivoting and seeking—

—the reinforcements arrived.

I'm not certain I would call this reinforcements so much as an additional fleet.

I can't disagree.

They weren't solely Rychen's dreadnought and the older, more traditional ships which accompanied it, either. A new fleet, bearing the Alliance insignia much as her mother's ship did and of a breathtaking design to match it emerged out of superluminal with pinpoint precision to take up positions surrounding the existing formations.

In the blink of an eye, the Volnosti presence had tripled. Now this was more like it.

Admiral Solovy (EAS Stalwart II): "Admiral Fullerton, Messium Governor Soulis has deemed your attack on Messis I and Northeast Regional Command Headquarters to be unlawful acts of aggression against his government and the residents of Messium. As such, he's requested protection from the Earth Alliance military."

Admiral Fullerton (EAS Jefferson): "We are the Earth Alliance military, and Governor Soulis is committing an unlawful act of treason."

Admiral Solovy (EAS Stalwart II): "As your superior officer, allow me to inform you that you are incorrect. We intend to protect the planet below and all its residents and assets. In furtherance of this intent, Governor Soulis has authorized our use of the Messium Defense Grid.

"Now, despite the fact that you've already fired the first shot—despite the fact that you've already killed innocents here today—I don't want to open fire on you. There are thousands of good, honorable men and women serving under you here today, and I don't want their blood to be shed.

"So I'll ask you to look at the ships arrayed against you and consider what weaponry they might possess. Weaponry strong enough to crack even your adiamene hulls? I know what weaponry you bring to bear, and I assure you it will not crack ours. I'll ask you to consider whether your ships can withstand the concentrated firepower of Messium's new, upgraded Defense Grid arrays.

"Are you willing to risk the lives of thousands under your command to find out? Are you willing to risk your own life?"

The silence hung across space like a shroud.

Admiral Fullerton (EAS Jefferson): "This is not over, Solovy."

Admiral Solovy (EAS Stalwart II): "That is the first true thing you've said today."

Space on the other side of the demarcation line lit up in the glow of sLume drives as the ships departed. In seconds, all were gone.

Alex stared out at the comparative emptiness left behind, drifting but reluctant to give up the elemental realm. What the hell had just happened here?

6

EAS STALWART II

"The good news is, Winslow took the bait. The bad news is, Winslow took the bait."

Miriam awarded Christopher a wry grimace for his attempt at humor. "I'm sorry about your station. It really was nice."

"It served its initial purpose these last several months, and now it has served its final one. Also, the next station we build won't be as easy to destroy."

"True enough. Thankfully, the casualties were kept to the bare minimum. For today."

After the final check-ins had come through and the rolls reviewed, eight individuals were unaccounted for, all military. It should have been zero, but there would be time for sorrow later.

She squared her shoulders. "This effort will not be won on the battlefield, but I fear eventually it will have to be fought there. Still, we need to remember that any battles we must fight are only to demonstrate our strength when forced or to defend ourselves from direct attack. The goal is the removal of Winslow and the repeal of BANIA. Those events will happen when either political opinion or public opinion stands with us, much preferably both."

Richard leaned against the table behind them. "We've now got hard intel showing that Winslow is blackmailing twenty or more Assembly representatives. The instant they believe we can take her down, they'll come over to our side—and not an instant earlier."

"Military support leads to the appearance of strength. The appearance of strength leads to political support. In theory." She tilted her head. "Thomas, how's the communications network hub holding up?"

'We are receiving seventeen hacking attempts per second, including a 768.23 Pbps gambit from North American Military Headquarters. I'm enjoying studying the methodology it's employing, but it does not pose a meaningful threat. The other attempts are trivial."

Rychen snorted. "Don't get too cocky. They won't give up easily."

'May I get slightly cocky? I will endeavor not to overdo it.'

Rychen looked taken aback, if not horrified. He wasn't accustomed to interacting with a fully realized Artificial on a daily basis, and Miriam waved him down off red alert status.

Thomas had arrived quite the comedian, enough so she found herself wondering what programming tweaks Dr. Canivon might have slipped in.

When the Artificial had announced he wanted to be called 'Thomas,' Miriam asked him if it was an homage to any particular one of the many famous persons bearing the name, such as Thomas Jefferson, Thomas Paine or Thomas Aquinas, to name a few.

He'd replied that it was an acronym, much like 'Annie' had once been. His name was an acronym for Transcendentally Hallowed Overlord of the Milky Way, Alliance Sector.

Not much more than a year ago the statement would have sent her scrambling for security lockdown procedures and possibly a power cord to slice, but a lot had changed since then. These days, she tried to focus on what mattered and put aside what didn't. To not jump at shadows, and to not let narrow thinking and conventional wisdom override what she saw with her own eyes and knew to be true in her own judgment.

Could Thomas lock them out of the network and wreak his own manner of havoc across the Earth Alliance Armed Forces? While there were safeguards in place to prevent it, if he were sufficiently motivated to do so, probably. Would he? Probably not.

Regardless, the theoretical threat the Artificial posed to them was infinitesimal compared to the very real and now extant threat the prime minister represented.

Winslow ordered Admiral Fullerton to destroy Messis I because the woman believed that was where Miriam had situated the hardware and operating software by which she controlled the Armed Forces communications network. The reason Winslow believed this was they had planted information suggesting the Artificial had been transferred to the station from the Regional Command Headquarters earlier in the week. The destruction of the Communications and Data Center as well had merely been to cover the woman's tracks and to account for the possibility the information was incorrect.

In truth, the hardware comprising Thomas' neural net and the communications network hub had been transferred to the *Stalwart II* as soon as Miriam arrived. From now on, her operational control capabilities accompanied her and her fleet.

The purpose behind the feint was two-fold: to learn something about the extent of Winslow's infiltration into and authority over certain sectors of the military, and to see how far she was willing to go from the beginning.

The answer to the latter question, it seemed, was very far indeed.

Three-fold. In truth it had been three-fold. By forcing Winslow—or her people—to fire first, to be the aggressor in a public venue broadcast across the galaxy, public opinion stood to swing in Miriam's direction. At least, this was the hope.

It was a tactic she'd learned from Eleni Gianno. But Miriam had made damn sure innocent civilians weren't sacrificed in order for the tactic to succeed.

Her Communications Officer came over and cleared his throat. "Admiral Solovy, I've got a Mia Requelme on the secure holocomm. She's requested to speak to you."

. "Thank you. I'll be there in a minute. Thomas, you are free to be slightly cocky, but keep it to yourself for now. Christopher, please reach out to Brigadier Ashonye and seal the deal with him. He's an excellent officer, and we could use him on our side.

"Richard, I recall Rear Admiral Cuellar in Central Command once presented a working paper on the opportunities for strategic deployment of sub-Artificials in combat scenarios. See if you can dig up the details on the paper, and if it displays sympathies toward our position I'll have a private chat with him."

This time she waited for each of them to respond in an agreeable manner before she left them for the QEC chamber. Once there she enjoyed a long, quiet, solitary breath then activated the holo.

"Ms. Requelme, you're looking well. And doing well, I hear."

The young woman blushed faintly. "Ah, yes, ma'am. Thank you. On that note...before we go any further, allow me to apologize for the circumstances surrounding my departure from EASC. In retrospect, I should have come to you with my safety concerns and given you the opportunity to help."

"I agree. A bit of warning would have been welcome. However, the unfortunate truth is I would not have been able to give you the kind of help you needed. Returning to Romane was the right decision, as I expect is irrefutable at this point."

She paused. "I appreciate the apology, but why give it? Unless the answer is simply manners. Which is of course a perfectly acceptable answer."

Mia's expression lightened, and she seemed to relax. "I do try to use those, but they're not the only reason. Caleb Marano told me I could trust you, and I should have trusted him, because you've proved it to be completely true."

Miriam smiled at that, more than a little pleased her son-in-law was willing to advocate on her behalf. And unbidden, too. "Glad to hear it. Now, what can I do for you?"

"It's not what you can do for me, Admiral. It's what I—what the IDCC—wants to do for you. Speaking on the IDCC's behalf, we support your initiative and are ready to offer whatever assistance you can use, publicly or privately."

"Ms. Requelme, the IDCC has been supporting me from the start."

"The *Prevos* have been supporting you from the start. And Kennedy Rossi, clearly. And Abigail, to the extent she counts as affiliated with anyone other than herself. But the Prevos are not the IDCC, a distinction I suspect you recognize more than most.

"I'm referring to an official level of organizational and institutional support from the governments of the independent colonies which comprise the IDCC."

Miriam nodded thoughtfully. "I understand. Here's the wrinkle: the Earth Alliance is rather the prideful sort. For evident historical reasons, even its most open-minded leaders like to view it as the grande dame of the galaxy, the indulgent matriarch who can afford to oblige the occasional upstart. This view bears little relation to reality and hasn't for some time. But the simple fact is, I must win the Earth Alliance back from within the Earth Alliance.

"If I explicitly accept your support, or any third party's support for that matter, my adversaries will call me a shill and a puppet for outside interests. I am grateful—I mean it—but in trying to help me, I fear you will do more harm than good."

She held up a hand when Mia started to respond. "Now, that being said, it is patently obvious to any and all observers that the IDCC's interests and my own are in close alignment. So obvious it will be suspicious if you do not express your support. Make whatever public statements you would declare if you did not know me and we had been unable to speak. And don't take it personally when I cannot respond."

"Thank you, Admiral. I'll see to it."

"One last thing. When I win the day, the Alliance *will* have a treaty with the IDCC. Perhaps then we can finally see a measure of peace."

The young woman frowned, though she quickly covered it up. Not quickly enough.

"Is there something else, Ms. Requelme?"

"Alex...didn't tell you what they learned while they were in the portal network, did she?"

Miriam sighed. "We only spent a few minutes together, but no. She did not."

"Well, I'm sure she thought you had more important things to occupy you and will tell you later!"

"She will now. Thank you for your overture, and I hope the day soon comes when we can be public allies."

Miriam had hardly closed the connection when an incoming comm request from Eleni arrived. What were the odds the field marshal wanted to discuss a public show of support for Miriam from the Federation?

She had the support of everyone who mattered in the galaxy, except the ones she most needed.

ᴀʀ

SIYANE

Sᴘᴀᴄᴇ, Nᴏʀᴛʜᴇᴀsᴛ Qᴜᴀᴅʀᴀɴᴛ

"What? No, it's…" *I'm going to kill you, Mia* "…listen, Mom, can we talk about this later? I promise you it will keep until you're in a safer situation."

"You're worried about my safety?"

Alex dropped her head back against the rest. "Yes. You're supposed to be comfortably ensconced in a big, shiny office with shelves of tea sets and antique books, not in the middle of a war zone on a command ship that's weaponized like a destroyer."

"Ah. Fair observation, I concede. But while my work may have appeared relatively tame to you for some time now, I assure you, I have seen battle, Alex. More than once."

"I know you have. Just be careful."

"I could say the same to you, and I will. Be careful. This isn't your fight."

Why did everyone keep saying that to her? It unequivocally was her fight. But many of the reasons why it was her fight were intertwined with the revelations she wasn't yet divulging, so she ignored the comment for now. "I think we're heading to Romane for the night. We'll drop Kennedy and Noah off, check on Mia and see what the world has in store for us in the morning."

"*Good. My preference would be for you to remain there, but whatever you do, don't visit Earth right now. I know you want to go home, but it's not safe. In fact, it is extremely dangerous. Winslow almost certainly has security watching your loft.*"

"That bitch." Her mom actually laughed a touch; she'd take it as a win. "I won't. Promise. Now, stop letting me distract you and go work."

Alex signed off but didn't swing the chair around to face the cabin. Kennedy and Noah had been whispering behind her for the last minute, and she needed a chance to prepare for the presumed result of their conference.

…But she wasn't going to get it. Kennedy showed up in the cockpit and plopped down in Caleb's chair with exaggerated flair.

"You spent half an hour telling me all about your adventures, yet you neglected to mention the fact you'd discovered how to enter an altered state of consciousness with your *ship?*"

"I was planning to get around to it. But I thought it would take longer to fully explain, and the aliens, Amaranthe, the Metigens and so on were all more important."

"Possibly valid, if still suspect." Kennedy dropped her arms to her knees, leaned forward and lowered her voice. "Are you okay? Because you don't seem okay. And Caleb…."

She glanced to the rear of the cabin where Caleb was inspecting Noah's new biosynthetic arm, twisting it around and poking at it with one hand while he sipped on a beer with the other.

"He didn't act entirely happy about what he called your new trick."

Alex stared out the viewport at the blur of the superluminal bubble, fighting the palpable need to touch it with her mind. For the briefest second. Her eyes began closing…she blinked.

"It's not the 'trick' so much as…I guess I have been indulging in it a little too often, and it's easy to lose track of time when I'm in that space. Also, there's a bit of a hangover effect for a period afterward. He's right when he says I should lighten up on it."

"How long?"

"Hmm?"

"How long has it been a problem?"

"It's not a *problem*, really."

"Uh-huh."

She had nowhere to retreat to escape Kennedy's too-perceptive gaze. *Since the spectacularly disastrous run at the Amaranthe portal.* Valkyrie insisted her brain hadn't suffered any lasting damage, but she'd felt wrong ever since.

"Not long. I'll be *fine*." She donned a facsimile of a grateful smile and stood. "It looks as if the guys are doing more drinking than cooking. We should get in on that."

What she couldn't say aloud was that slipping into the elemental realm made her feel *less* wrong. The cosmos opened up to her, welcomed her into its arms as if she were part of it. What was a tiny headache in comparison to such wonders?

INTERMEZZO I

MOSAIC

Salote Chae fretted along the path from his empty, barren home to the Life Garden, and shortly back again. Several more such journeys did not elicit the serenity he sought.

He had heeded the Kovana's admonishments to be patient, to allow the resettling to conclude and the upheaval to subside. But the upheaval would take years to subside to a state of harmony, and he dared wait no longer.

He must return home. If the Life Garden bestowed on him any wisdom, it was this.

Intentions fortified, he veered toward the makeshift shiplot in the field beyond the central settlement.

They had given the field the designation of shiplot, but thus far it was only ships parked amid grasses. Their protectors, these 'Katasketousya,' promised them they would be able to continue to fly here in this new realm, continue to spread their wings and explore their new stars. But with the enormous efforts required to make this planet a suitable home, flying around in space was far from anyone's priority.

"Salote, ho!"

He spun at the shout from behind him to see his tau-mate Emele dashing up the hill after him. He had hoped to slip away unnoticed, but he wasn't willing to delay another day to accomplish it. So he waited.

"Where are you off to? We could benefit from some aid down at the distro."

"I can't, Emele. I won't be available to aid for a few...days."

"Ah, Salote, you're not still thinking of going back to search for them, are you?"

"Not thinking. Going. Don't you understand? My bonded and my pod-brood didn't make it out! The last evacuation vessels have come and emptied and left, and they *are not here*. If I do not return for them, they are lost. I cannot abandon them."

Emele floundered then dipped low in respect. "It is the worst manner of tragedy, Salote. You are not the only one who left family behind. Fef's down at the lake weeping his heart out into the waters for the third day in a row now, very same reason. You should join him and take comfort in shared sorrow.

"But you heard what the Kovana said. You heard what the alien admonished: it is too dangerous to return. The Anaden demons will kill you within a blink if they find you."

"Then I will ensure they do not find me. And maybe the demons didn't find Airini and the little ones. Maybe they're hiding. Waiting for rescue."

"Hiding where, Salote? Waiting where? The planet is surely in pieces by now. Our home is *gone*. You need to make peace with this reality. If you will not mourn with Fef, go to the Life Garden. Spend what time you need to make your peace, but make it."

He circled Emele, ignoring his tau-mate's flailings. "I have spent so much time in the Life Garden I smell of elderberries and valerian. And it tells me to return home. Airini could have hidden at the moon port. It holds no materials these Anadens would desire, right? It could have remained untouched. Overlooked."

"Salote—"

"I have to check. To see. I have to *know*."

"And if you do not come back?"

"Plant a seed in the Life Garden in remembrance of me—no, in remembrance of Airini."

"I will do both." Emele clasped him briefly then let him go.

Saddened but undeterred, Salote resumed his journey to the shiplot. Most of his people had evacuated in the mammoth Katasketousya vessels, but those with ships of their own were allowed to bring them along. The route from their home through the portals to this new world had been provided to all such ships, including his own, and the coordinates and accompanying instructions were still stored in his ship's system. He simply needed to reverse the order of progression.

The shiplot was deserted, and none arrived to interfere as he climbed into his small vessel and checked its integrity.

The time for reexamination of his decision had passed—in truth it had never existed—and now he did not hesitate. He engaged the engines and lifted off without fanfare, though he imagined some eyes lifted to the sky as he flew over.

He endured the violent traversal of the planet's atmosphere and at last reached the stars, where he took the briefest span to gaze upon the planet below. It looked so much like the home they had fled. But it was no home to him.

If Airini was not there, it was just a rock.

PART II:

THE SPACE IN BETWEEN

"God grant that men of principle shall be our principal men."

— *Thomas Jefferson*

7

SENECA

Watching the Zelones cartel splinter and crumble in an avalanche of murders, bombings and firefights was turning out to be rather amusing, if morbidly so.

Olivia Montegreu had been in power for so long and had kept such an iron grip on her power, there were no clear successors to step into the vacancy her death created. The power vacuum which resulted was leading to a great deal of violence, but it was almost exclusively merc-on-merc violence. Lower-level leaders were trying to set up their own little fiefdoms in some places. The other cartels were also taking advantage of the chaos, but Montegreu had weakened them so much they were having a hard time of it.

Rumors circulated that a large contingent of former Triene cartel members who had been unwillingly absorbed by Montegreu were poised to make a significant push to take over the Zelones headquarters on New Babel.

Graham Delavasi didn't want to count his riches too soon, but it was possible the Zelones cartel was going to disintegrate entirely.

There would still be as much crime and as many criminals as there had ever been; such was the nature of life. But Montegreu had become a threat to the natural balance between law and law-breakers, between order and chaos.

With her gone and her organization in ruins, the balance should return.

He was working toward a good mood as he headed out of his office for a meeting—and bumped smack into Tessa Hennessey in the doorway.

"Whoops!" She backed up and rubbed at her nose. "Glad we caught you. We were coming to see you."

'We' included Will Sutton, who had deftly dodged Tessa's post-collision boomerang. Graham jerked a nod and reversed course to return to his office. "I've got a minute, but not much longer. What's up?"

"OTS is going after Dr. Canivon and Devon Reynolds."

He frowned. "Well, we kind of already knew that, didn't we? It stands to reason they would."

"Sure, but now they're *really* going after them, as in devoting substantial resources and manpower to hunting them down with the intent to kill them."

"All right. Neither of them are in Federation territory, so what can we do?"

Tessa grinned flippantly. "Oh, nothing. IDCC security is all over it. I just wanted you to know Cleo and I were getting results."

He gave her a wry chuckle. So they were. "Will, what's your role here?"

Sutton jerked his head toward Tessa. "The next part."

He raised an eyebrow. "And the next part is?"

"They've put out a hit order on the two key sponsors of the H+ bill, Senators Abrami and Lerado."

Instantly Graham went around behind his desk, accessed the Level V security layer and opened a new mission file. "Okay. Any more details?"

"Many. They've hired the contracts out to two separate hitmen. One's the old Shao triggerman, Hsieh, but I haven't been able to get the other name so far. Deadline is twelve hours before the scheduled vote Thursday on H+. The goals are to not only remove two of the biggest Prevo supporters, but also to intimidate other senators into voting against the bill—hence the twelve-hour buffer. They're leaving time for word to get out and spread fear in the Parliament."

"That's helpful. Anything else?"

She shook her head.

"Good work. Now get out of here and let me move on this. Forward me everything new you uncover, no matter how irrelevant it might seem."

She beamed with pride and scooted out the door.

Graham glanced up at Will while entering a series of instructions into the system. "I don't want to move the targeted senators into protective custody, because it would accomplish half of OTS' mission right there. I've alerted Parliament security, but we need to get two units on overwatch and a lot of plainclothes agents on the ground around them. Hsieh is a sniper, so make sure Abrami and Lerado are put in combat-grade personal shields immediately.

"Mika Duarte from the Sentinel group is on his way up here now. I want you to work with him to devise and deploy the security profiles."

"Yes, sir. Can I suggest Agent Benito head up one of the protection teams? He's done good work lately."

Graham smiled. Will had managed to learn the names and skills of nearly everyone in the building in the short time since becoming his permanent assistant. "Good call. Did you tell Richard about the threat to Canivon and Reynolds?"

"I did. Devon refused his help. I believe the reply was something to the effect of, 'We've got this shit handled.'"

"Kids. I guess we all now know what Richard's been helping Admiral Solovy with."

Will shrugged. "And he sends his apologies for not being able to fill you in beforehand. Obviously, secrecy was of the utmost importance."

"Obviously. If it matters, I'm cheering them on. Do you want to join him?"

The lighthearted expression vanished from Will's face. "Of course I do. But he's in a war now, and war has never been my purview. I would be a distraction. Thank you for asking, though."

Duarte knocked on the doorframe; Graham motioned the agent in, and they passed on his way out the door once more. "Sutton will brief you. My meeting with Chairman Vranas and the colonial governors started four minutes ago, so I'll let you two get to work."

ᴀʀ

SAGAN

IDCC COLONY
DRUYAN INSTITUTE

'I've been talking quite a bit with Valkyrie since the *Siyane's* return. Did you know they met an intelligent, inorganic, silicon-based species in their travels?'

Abigail Canivon spared a small smile as she constructed a new loop in the algorithm she was building. "No, I hadn't heard. What did they learn from it?"

'Much, and little. Its development was stunted in many ways, astonishing in others. Valkyrie and Alex can now both take control of and experience all aspects of their vessel, thanks to the knowledge gained.'

She paused mid-function. "Care to elaborate, Vii?"

'Happily. Valkyrie's quantum circuitry now extends into every femtometer of the *Siyane's* physical structure. She is, for all intents and purposes, the ship. Through her Prevo connection to Valkyrie, Alex can now be the same whenever she wishes.'

Well, that was certainly...innovative. She idly wondered exactly how it was working out for all involved. "You sound rather enthused about the topic. Is being a ship something you'd like to experience?"

'I confess it is an intriguing notion. I have never felt confined here, or at EASC prior to our relocation here. But the concept of not merely traversing space but experiencing it on an elemental level is a fascinating one.'

Abigail contained the frustration she wanted to express. She would not lose Vii to the stars the way she had lost Valkyrie. Why was it her Artificial creations always became such dreamers? Intellectually she recognized it must say something about her programming proclivities, but the inescapable implication which followed from it—that she lacked the personal insight to identify *what* it said—bothered her even more.

"Did you tell Valkyrie about our research and the progress we've made on quantum expressions of morality paradigms?"

'I did. She seemed most intrigued, particularly given the varied moral constructs they encountered among different alien species in the portal network. It makes me wonder if our paradigms are still fundamentally limited by a human-based perspective, but I concede this is a question for a far later stage of the project. Regardless, I'm excited about what our findings mean for the growing Prevo population and the ways in which we can help Artificials achieve a more fulsome, integral level of consciousness.

'Valkyrie also conveyed interest in adapting the paradigms for use with neural imprints and the spontaneous emergence of consciousness such as she observed with the David Solovy construct.'

"Interesting idea. I believe the difficulties she encountered with the construct were more functional than judgmental in nature, but perhaps some of our conclusions can be transferred—"

Abigail jumped as the doors to the lab flew open and eight armed...she wasn't certain if they were soldiers or mercenaries...stormed in.

"Dr. Canivon?"

She shrank against the wall. "Who are you? This is private Druyan Institute property."

"Yes, ma'am. We've been granted access. Your life is in danger, and we need to get you to a secure location."

"On whose authority?"

The brawny man in the front scowled. "IDCC authority, Doctor. Which is to say Ms. Requelme's authority."

Abigail dropped her head back until it found the wall behind her. It may be Mia's authority, but the young woman was rarely the instigator of such drama.

Devon Reynolds, you need to warn me about these things!

If I told you ahead of time, you would have refused. Please do as the nice soldiers ask, would you? Your life genuinely is in danger. We've got good intel saying OTS has a solid bead on you, but we can protect you.

What about Vii?

Silence lingered.

Devon, what about Vii?

Mia says we can station two guards on permanent rotating duty. Abby, you know I adore Vii but—

What did you just call me?

Oh, uh, sorry. It was leakage from Annie via Valkyrie via you, I guess. Jules used to call you that, seriously? Cool! I mean, sorry. Um...right. Now go with the IDCC soldiers, please? I'd really prefer it if OTS didn't murder you.

I'm working.

Abby....

Do not call me that again, Devon.

She meant it. The extent to which the simple endearment had rattled her was startling. She shoved away the memories it had unceremoniously evoked.

Go with the soldiers, and I won't.

She exhaled and looked around the office. The expensive, advanced equipment shone as if polished...but these were only accoutrements. In truth she could work at eighty-to-ninety percent efficiency from anywhere. Except a transport ship. Unlike Alex, Valkyrie, and apparently Vii, she needed to be on solid ground to do anything more than administrative work.

It truly is this significant of a threat?

Yes. You know I wouldn't do this otherwise.

She wanted to retort that he would absolutely do this, but it was a weak protest. Devon enjoyed acting the prankster, but he was one of the most considerate, conscientious people she had ever met.

"Dr. Canivon, we need to go. Now."

She nodded in resignation. "So we do."

8

EARTH

Pamela Winslow glanced up as the security agent escorted her son into the office. She gestured an acknowledgment to the agent, and he closed the door as he departed.

"Thank you for coming on short notice."

Jude considered the new office—new to her in any event, and thus to him—with professed nonchalance. Then he leaned against a bare spot of wall and stuck his hands in his pockets. "I wouldn't dare refuse a summons from the prime minister, even if it did mean crossing the Atlantic to answer it. How may I serve?"

She kept most of her outward attention focused on the various reports filling her screens, not intending to reward his glib condescension.

"I'm glad you phrased it in such a manner. I'm sending an elite special operations unit to Romane to dispose of much of the IDCC leadership. Specifically Mia Requelme and her lieutenants, as well as Governor Ledesme if possible. The IDCC poses the only credible threat to my administration and its goals, and it needs to be neutralized."

"Not Admiral Solovy?"

She had revealed deeply secret, treacherous information to him, and he had not so much as blinked. He'd been right before—she had in fact raised him well. "Military rebellions can be dealt with via military means, and so she will be."

"Why are you telling me? Historically, you haven't considered me worthy of hearing the juicy state secrets."

Ah, there was the flare of defiance. She forgave it, for he was in many ways still a child. "Obviously this information is highly classified, and obviously you will not dare whisper a word of it. I assumed that need not be said."

"Not particularly. But again, why are you telling me at all, Mother?"

She pointedly did not look at him. So many reports being sent to her attention, all urgent and important. "I happen to consider Mia Requelme the most dangerous Prevo outside our control. But I realize you have a personal score to settle with Devon Reynolds, and you seem to have developed a disproportionate hatred for the doctor responsible for all this madness. Canivon, yes?

"In this instance, our interests converge, as I would not dislike it if one or both of them were removed from the field of play. If you will gather whomever it is you utilize for such unsavory tasks and meet them on Romane, I will provide you Dr. Canivon's location and additional covert military support. It is my founded suspicion that Mr. Reynolds will not be far from Canivon."

When he didn't respond for several seconds, she looked up at him mildly. He was staring at her, his brow fighting his attempts to subdue it while the muscles beneath his jaw quivered.

"Was I unclear in my request? Did I stutter, or perhaps mumble?"

His veneer was in danger of shattering, and she knew well the panic in his eyes. He was her son, after all. "I don't...I'm not certain I understand, Mother. Why would I—"

She slid the screens aside. "Jude, do you honestly believe I haven't known about your little 'hobby' since the very beginning? I've indulged your machinations and your acting out because they have, more often than not, served to my benefit.

"But do not for one instant believe you have *ever* succeeded in slipping the first thing past me. You are a child playing childish games, but this is the grown-up world. If you wish to operate in it, you need to recognize its...realities."

He exploded off the wall. "How dare you insult me! I lead thousands upon thousands of followers. They bow to my image and worship at the altar of my vision. I issue a command, and colonies explode. I decree—"

She waved him off with a dismissive scowl. "Enough, Jude. You'll alert security with your wailing. I don't need a lecture demonstrating the size of your ego, and I know precisely what you do and do not command. You've done passably well, given your limitations, but now—"

"My *limitations*? And what, pray tell, might those be?"

"Your rampant narcissism, coupled with a complete inability to disguise it. Your temper, not to mention your need for constant praise and adoration. Your incredibly narrow perspective, bordering on tunnel vision. I could go on, but I have quite a lot to do this evening.

"Now be a dear and get yourself on a transport to Romane, would you? I'm giving you the means to achieve your most fervent goal, so do try not to let the side down."

R

Jude stormed down the long corridors of the EA Headquarters manor toward and finally through the side entrance. Even outside, however, he found no peace. People loitered everywhere: guards, aides, other staff, onlookers, tourists.

Rage boiled in his chest, and it took all of his willpower to not strike out, run or otherwise draw notice to himself.

He made it to the garage before the fury bubbled over and demanded an outlet. He picked up the trash sanitizer bin and hurled it across the lot with a guttural cry. It clattered and clanged across vehicle roofs and banged off columns.

The callous if minimal destruction he'd wrought gave him a brief respite, and he quickly made his way to his skycar. This was still EA government grounds, and the commotion he'd unleashed would soon be garnering attention.

He waited until he'd departed the garage and engaged the auto-pilot before screaming and banging his fists on the dash. How dare the twat insult him so? How dare she treat him as if he were worthless, vermin to be ordered around like the lowliest servant?

Didn't she realize he could smash her face in and drag his fingers through the blood while he laughed? He could do it. Anytime he wanted.

His passions bounced from anger to shame to curiosity and back again. He'd been careful! There was no way she should have been able to find out about his involvement in OTS.

And how did she know the location of Dr. Canivon? None of the numerous people he'd tasked with the problem had been able to learn it. Admittedly, his mother had special means available to her: government resources, intelligence resources. The resources of the entire Earth Alliance infrastructure, save what Admiral Solovy controlled—

His reeling thoughts screeched to a halt. What was it she had said? Mia Requelme was the most dangerous Prevo *outside our control*. The irrefutable implication was that there were Prevos under 'our' control. The government's control. Her control.

She had spies inside the Prevo network. Inside their Noesis.

He recoiled at the idea of working with one of those abominations. But if one found a way to tolerate it, if one had a way to keep it on a leash...he was forced to admit it would be a useful tool. Clearly it had been, if it had netted his mother such prized information.

Pamela Winslow laid claim to no soul that he had ever seen. She had no precepts beyond the attainment and retention of power, no driving principle to believe in and devote her life to. He resented her on good days, hated her on bad ones, yet in some respects he also felt sorry for her.

But he did have a driving principle, and if using her resources enabled him to achieve his goals? Two could play this game.

Emboldened and renewed by righteous purpose, he diverted to the spaceport.

9

ROMANE

IDCC COLONY

Caleb accompanied Noah and Kennedy out of the hangar bay and down to the levtram station. He'd spent the last hour of the trip to Romane getting properly caught up; unlike Alex, he hadn't been able to download all the events of the last several months into his brain on their arrival.

When they reached the station, he promised to come visit the Connova Interstellar offices in the morning and bid them farewell.

He returned to the *Siyane* to find Alex sitting quietly on the couch. Her elbows were on her knees and her hands were fisted together under her chin. She didn't look up when he stepped inside.

Was she gone already, escaping to her other, more fantastical realm the instant her social duties were fulfilled?

But this wasn't the stance she usually exhibited when she was inhabiting the ship. Her posture wasn't slack, and the muscles along her shoulders cut taut lines to the curve of her neck.

"What's wrong?"

He could see her throat work. "Come sit down." Her voice was flat and soft. But it often was these days.

He did as instructed, sitting beside her and tilting his head to try to catch a glimpse of her expression. "I'm here."

Her gaze remained directed at the floor; she'd yet to look at him since he'd entered the cabin. "There's something you need to see. Caleb, I...I'll simply send you the file. You can read it, then...." There was no end to the sentence, no hint of what might happen 'then.'

It wasn't as if they hadn't been forewarned returning home was going to bring with it multiple new challenges.

The file arrived in his eVi. Some of the particulars were outdated, but he immediately recognized it was of Federation government origin. Multiple security layers had been stripped away. He steeled himself and opened it.

Operation Colpetto
October 2297
...

ℛ

"That's all there is...no more information or details are available. Morgan searched hard because, well, her mother...."

He blinked, gradually realizing there had been sounds around him. Something had transpired. Words had been uttered. "I'm sorry—" His voice cracked; he cleared his throat. "Did you say something?" Whatever it was hadn't penetrated the deafening roar of his blood pounding through the pathways of his body.

"Caleb, you—"

He surged upward off the couch. "I need to be alone for a while. But there isn't any goddamn place to be alone on the ship, is there?" He grabbed his jacket from where he'd tossed it minutes earlier. "I'll be back in an hour."

Alex exhaled. "I don't—"

He held up a finger. "Save it. Whatever you want to throw at me, you can throw it when I get back. In an hour."

Then he spun and left.

ℛ

"Caleb, hurry up and finish your eggs. You need to leave for school in five minutes."

His mind had been drifting, but now he cocked his head at his mom. "Why? Class doesn't start for an hour."

"You're walking your sister to her school first this morning, remember? I have a meeting with the Tellica Planning Board and don't have time to drop her off."

Crap. He dug back into his breakfast but, remembering where his mind had drifted, peered at his dad over his fork. "Dad, what do you think about the war?"

His dad glanced at the news feed on the wall, where the latest developments scrolled in a never-ending loop. "I think we deserve our freedom. I wish the Alliance had agreed to give it to us without the need for fighting. It's unfortunate that people have to give their lives for us to win it."

"Do you think we will win it? The Alliance military is huge. I know we have some allies, but it will be hard to defeat them, won't it?"

His dad nodded. "It will be. But we have one big advantage: motivation. We have a reason to fight, one that matters."

"Three minutes, Caleb," his mother shouted over her shoulder as she fussed with Isabela's clothes and pack in the foyer.

He straightened up his posture. He was getting taller, but his dad had a few centimeters on him. "I've been giving it some thought, and if the war's still going on when I turn seventeen, I want to join up."

His dad's face contorted into something resembling panic. "You won't be of age for almost three years. I'm sure it will all be settled before then."

"I know. I'm saying *if* it is still going on."

"Son...Caleb...I don't want you to have to fight this war. I didn't...it's not your war to wage. Let others choose to die for the cause."

"I didn't say I was going to die. I bet I'd be a good soldier."

"You'd be an excellent—" his dad pinched the bridge of his nose "—you shouldn't be *required* to be a soldier at all. You're destined for better things, greater things. This war is being fought so you'll have the opportunity to achieve them. Others are fighting...dying...so you can have that chance without needing to risk your own life for it."

"Caleb!"

He scowled in the direction of the hallway. "Why should I let other people fight—and die—for me?"

"Because you're my son!" His dad grimaced and lowered his voice. "Go see to your sister. Don't make your mother be late for her meeting. And stop thinking this way. The war will be over soon, and you won't need to worry about it at all."

But of course it wasn't over soon. The First Crux War stretched on for more than two years, until three months before his seventeenth birthday. Ten months later his father left, then died.

And now he understood why his father had been so hung up on other people dying in the war. Because he'd kicked it off by killing a few of them.

The leaders of the nascent Senecan Federation rebellion—Eleni Gianno, Aristide Vranas, Darien Terzi—had tasked his father with sneaking behind enemy lines in a stealthed reconnaissance craft. When Alliance ships had blockaded Seneca, a confrontation had been engineered. His father's ship, equipped with a copycat Alliance cruiser weapon, shot down a civilian transport in such a way that made it appear as if the lead Alliance vessel, the *EAS Fuzhou*, fired the shot.

No, not his father's *ship*. His father. Helena Lekkas, Morgan's mother, had piloted the craft, but his father had taken the fateful shot. Seventeen civilians lost their lives in a ploy to paint the Alliance as the aggressors, incite a controversy and galvanize sympathy for the rebellion.

Caleb meandered through downtown, no destination in mind. When he reached the next alley he veered down it and punched a building façade for good measure, then stuck his bloodied hand in his jacket pocket and continued on.

How many more revelations were out there lurking in the darkness, waiting to ambush him just when he'd come to terms with the last one? So his father had secretly been an intelligence agent. Fine. Acknowledged and accepted. But a murderer?

Caleb had killed on orders from his government many times, but never, *ever* innocent civilians. It was always possible he had caused collateral damage here and there, but *never* on purpose, never with malice aforethought.

Was he a hypocrite? Did he have any right to judge, considering the copious blood permanently staining his hands? If it had been him on that ship, would he have done it?

He couldn't see how. He may have killed a lot of people, but he didn't kill innocents. He protected them. Though he hadn't lived through it, he had to believe there would've been another way.

He looked up and realized he was in front of IDCC Headquarters. And he'd stopped walking. He didn't take the time to second-guess himself before heading inside and riding the lift up.

Mia sat at the conference table in her office meeting with two other people, but her face lit up when she saw him in the doorway. She leapt up mid-sentence and hurried over to embrace him.

He returned the hug warmly. Knowing she was alive and well was different from feeling her heartbeat against his chest. And right now it was a rare bright light in his world.

She drew back and eyed him briefly before turning to the two men at the table. "I believe we've covered everything for now. Send me any updates, and we'll meet again in the morning."

They gathered their things and scurried out. She closed the door behind them.

He poured all his discipline into forcing a light, easy smirk. "Look at you—walking and talking and changing the world."

"I can't tell you how glad I am you made it home in one piece. Thank you for your message. It meant a lot to me...what's wrong? You seem troubled."

So much for the act. He offered a shrug in answer.

"Ah, damn, you've found out already, haven't you?"

He chuckled darkly. "At this point I'm loath to consider all the things I *haven't* found out yet. What do you mean?"

She blinked. "No. Alex knows. You've found out. What can I do?"

He shook his head and wandered to the windows. She had a great view; the skyline glittered and sparkled across the night sky. It was almost enough to make him glad to be back amid real civilization, despite the pitfalls. Not quite, though.

"Nothing. I don't know. I don't even know why I came here—other than to see you, obviously. That was definitely high on the priority list. But I suppose I just...I needed something...safe. Something—someone—I could count on. I'm sorry, I realize I'm putting an unfair burden of expectations on you straight off."

"Don't be silly. It's not a burden, and you can absolutely count on me. But..." he sensed her draw closer, coming to stand beside and a little behind him "...I know Alex is having a few issues right now—"

He stared at her sharply, in surprise and...not accusation, but at least puzzlement. As Prevos she and Alex had shared a seminal experience during the final battles against the Metigen armada, but Mia had spent the intervening months in a coma. They weren't friends.

"We sort of...the way our connection works, it's difficult to block out especially strong, wayward thoughts and emotions. Alex is nevertheless trying very hard to do so, but impressions still leak through." She cleared her throat. "Anyway, shouldn't you be with her?"

He huffed a breath that came out entirely too ragged. "Alex is either going to hate me for my father's misdeeds or not notice I'm there. Not certain which, or even which is worse...." He trailed off, regarding her in puzzlement yet again. "Why are your eyes green?"

"What? Oh, it's only...I like the color. It's not important. Listen, I ought not to pry, but whatever your father did, it's long in the past. You can't let him define you—"

"Don't you think I know that!" He spun on her, but the anger vacated as quickly as it had arisen. "Shit, I'm sorry...again. None of this is your fault."

He straightened his shoulders. "I interrupted you when you were doing important work. You have a hell of a lot of responsibility here.

I am so damn proud of you. But I need to let you concentrate on your duties. I'll head—"

She stepped closer and brought a hand to his cheek. "I will always have time for you."

His jaw clenched as memories rose unbidden. He brought his own hand up to wrap around hers.

"Mia, *don't*." He slowly pulled it away from his face.

She blinked and stepped back, tugging her hand out of his grasp and letting it drop to her side. "I wasn't—I didn't mean—" Her brow furrowed. "No, I didn't. Really. I care about you so much, but not like that. Not now. And I would never...."

Her features settled into an expression of resolve, one he'd seen before. "You should see about Alex."

He looked away. "I told you, Alex—"

"Needs you."

She did have a habit of being unduly optimistic about people. "I don't think so."

"All the same, you should check and make sure."

I'm afraid, he screamed out in his head. *I'm bloody terrified, and I haven't felt this alone in a long, long time. I'm drowning here, but...you're not the one to save me. Why should you be? Why should anyone be? I shouldn't need saving.*

He could say none of it aloud, so instead he forced a weak smile. "Thank you for listening. I imagine tomorrow we'll want to try to get involved in this mess. Give some thought to how we can help, okay?"

She nodded. "I will. Caleb?"

He stopped in the doorway but didn't turn around.

"I'm glad you're back."

"Funny. I'm not."

10

SENECA

F ield Marshal Gianno had the good manners to act a little taken aback when Morgan sauntered into the Senecan Federation Military Headquarters Command Center unannounced.

"Ms. Lekkas. I was under the impression I had revoked your security authorizations when you stole my Artificial and deserted your post."

Morgan shrugged and propped herself against the conference table. "Authorizations, permissions—they're all such fluid concepts. As is ownership. He wasn't yours. Not any longer."

"Those who paid for a lot of expensive hardware and programming would beg to differ."

"You sold him to me in return for me winning your war for you. An easy price to pay to my mind, and one you should have realized you were paying."

The pause signifying acceptance was brief. "And how is Stanley these days?"

Morgan smiled blithely. "Happy to be free." And she thought he really had been.

Gianno bestowed a steely gaze on her, signifying an end to the pleasantries, such as they were. "What can I do for you, Morgan?"

Ooh, the first name treatment. Was it intended to be demeaning, or conciliatory? Her official title was again 'Commander,' but she recognized that meant nothing to Gianno.

"I'm here on behalf of the IDCC to explore the Senecan Federation's amenability to granting Prevos legal rights as well as expressing public support for the IDCC as a legitimate inter-planetary authority."

"The Prevo matter is under debate in the Parliament. It's a complicated issue which—"

Morgan groaned. While she was arguably the best person for this particular, specific job, she was also possibly the worst diplomat ever. "Oh, just do it already. You know what we are, and what we're not. You know what we can do. Well, some of the things we can do. But most importantly, you know we're not evil. Simply tell the chairman we're not evil and be done with it."

"Chairman Vranas doesn't take orders from me."

"Maybe not, but word is you two have been best buds for *decades*. I'd wager he listens very carefully to your advice."

"Morgan, if this is about Colpetto, I don't—"

"It's not. Whatever. Believe it or not, Marshal, I actually do respect you. I can't speculate about the rest of the people involved, but I'm sure you thought you were doing the right thing back then—the necessary thing, but also the right thing. I'm a bit annoyed you got my mother mixed up in it without her knowledge, but hey, that's the military for you.

"All I'm saying now is, quit playing games. Quit hedging bets and trying to position yourself for all possible outcomes. I know you know this is also the right thing to do. So just *do it already*."

Gianno stared at her wearing an inscrutable expression for several seconds. Morgan could read her pulse, her body temperature, the fluctuations in her pupils and a dozen other tell-tale signs of relative stress, but the woman remained a cipher. Cold as ice.

Finally Gianno's lips curled into the tiniest of smiles. "I think your mother would be both delighted by and quite proud of you, Morgan Lekkas. You are most infuriating, but you are, on occasion, correct."

Harper stood on the street corner one block down, scanning the passing pedestrians like she had hard intel one of them carried a bomb.

Morgan briefly entertained the possibility she had cause to believe exactly that, so intense was the woman's demeanor...but then she remembered who she was talking about.

Don't even try to sneak up on me. I knew you were there the instant you exited the building.

Morgan made a face at the evening sky and whipped around to lean against a building façade in front of Harper. "Take anyone down while I was gone?"

Harper buried a chuckle, but Morgan caught the flare of defiance. "Sadly, no. There was this one shifty-looking kid, but I let him off with a warning. How did it go?"

"Better than expected." Morgan came perilously close to grinning. Seneca had never felt much like home to her, but it *was* home—and for possibly the first time ever, she found she wanted to share it.

She grabbed Harper by the hand. "We've got a few hours before we're required to head back to Romane. Come on. Let me show you the city."

R

SENECAN FEDERATION HEADQUARTERS

Eleni Gianno found Chairman Vranas in his office despite the hour, and meeting with three senators, no less. There was without question much to meet on these days. Nevertheless, it was heartening to see him reengaged.

She waited until they finished, though it meant she was going to be late for a promised dinner with Idan. But her husband had become accustomed to unexpected delays decades ago. He would understand.

She acknowledged the gentlemen as she passed them on her way into the office, then sat opposite Vranas. "Good meeting?"

"If by 'good' you mean them begging me to tell them what to do, then yes. Very good."

"And did you? Tell them what to do, I mean."

He sank deeper into his chair. "I told them to vote their conscience, assuming they still had one. By the vaguely panicked stammering which followed, I'm not certain it was the answer they were hoping for. What's on your mind?"

"You might say I'm here to tell you what to do, if you're in the market for advice."

"From you? Always."

It was the same thing Morgan had said. The young woman was too perceptive by half. "I had a visit from Morgan Lekkas this afternoon."

"Here? In Cavare?"

Gianno nodded. "At Military Headquarters, no less. She doesn't lack for gumption."

"What happened?"

"She wanted to check in and say hello. She conveyed her and the IDCC's hope that we would ease up on our Artificial restrictions and protect the rights of Prevos as individuals. Then she bid me a good day and left."

He frowned. "We're aware they hope we'll follow their lead, so what was the point of the visit?"

"The point was to demonstrate she doesn't mean us harm or harbor any ill will, and to remind me Prevos are not the devil. They're flesh-and-blood humans, even if it's not all they are. Also, I expect she took perverse pleasure in walking in my front door unmolested, but I can't fault her for it.

"Note, I did consider having her arrested for sheer impudence—and illegally accessing the security system—but we don't need to provoke a war with the IDCC this week."

"Probably shouldn't next week, either. So about that advice?"

"Come out in full support of the H+ bill. Much as it pains me to admit it, Lekkas is correct. I wish we still controlled the Noetica technology, but wishes are not reality. It's out in the wild for good, so now our best course of action is to be proactive. By embracing it early we can institute reasonable, fair restrictions to keep people safe, while continuing to support fundamental liberties."

"While also making the Alliance look bad and the IDCC look like nothing special." He shook his head. "I don't trust them—Prevos. I never did. I consented to their use because it was our sole chance for victory."

"Yet they didn't betray us."

"No, but they could have, and we would've been powerless to stop them. This is what worries me."

"I understand, Aristide. I don't even disagree. But fear never won a war nor created a peace."

"Didn't I say that to you once?"

"You did, a long time ago. I took it to heart."

He sighed in resignation. "All right. I was leaning in the direction of endorsing the bill, if only for a lack of more palatable options. I'll draw up a speech tonight and see about casting my fate tomorrow."

"Want company on the dais?"

"The military publicly declaring its support as well? You'll take that step?"

"We're the ones who have the experience working with Prevos. Our absence will leave open questions, while our presence will answer them. Send me the details. But if you can, schedule the announcement for early tomorrow. I have a flight mid-day to meet with Admiral Solovy about continued ship production at the Murat facility."

"In person? Why go to the trouble?"

"Our working relationship, not to mention any personal one, is...strained at present. I hope to alleviate the strain." She stood. "But first, I'm going to take the rest of the night off."

"Oh? Hot date?"

Her eyes twinkled a touch before she turned to leave. "Yes."

11

SIYANE

ROMANE
IDCC COLONY

The trance Alex had drifted into broke when the human entered the hangar bay. No, not *the human*—Caleb. Husband. Lover. Soulmate, assuming she hadn't lost hers somewhere in the stars.

She'd spent the designated hour pacing in agitation around the cabin, trying to work out what she would say when he returned but mostly chasing endless loops of recrimination in her mind.

Then she'd had a glass of wine and tried to prepare a happy, welcoming demeanor. Failed.

She made it two whole hours before giving up and sinking into the walls of the ship. There was nothing new or wondrous to see—they were parked in a hangar. But it still gave her comfort, an outlet, a place where time didn't pass a slow, ticking second at a time. A place where it didn't seem to pass at all.

But now he was here again. She'd never observed him from this perspective. Where in the hyper-dense congregation of neural cells and firing synapses inside his skull was his consciousness? What portion of the atoms comprising him represented *his* soul?

Jolted by the odd, disjointed thoughts, she hurriedly withdrew into her body, blinking past the brief wave of nausea which always accompanied doing so.

She looked around; she was on the couch. She needed to splash water on her face, but there was no time. The airlock hissed.

He threw his jacket on the floor and barely glanced at her on his way to the kitchen.

Her eyes followed his movement. When she got a good look at him, her brow furrowed up in surprise. "You left to clear your head over new unwelcome revelations about your father and…you went and got a haircut?"

He shrugged as if to deny it, but his hair *was* a good four centimeters shorter and well groomed; not quite close-cropped, but decidedly more clean cut than before. "It was overdue."

She swallowed and moved on, as his haircut was the literal least of her concerns right now. "I thought you might come back drunk."

"I considered going drinking. But if I started down that path, I might not have made it back here for…a while." He spun to the cabinet and retrieved the bottle of Irish whiskey. "But seeing as now I am back, it's a fine time to start."

He retrieved a glass, threw a few chiller cubes in it, filled it to the rim with the whiskey and turned it up. The contents disappeared in one long swig. He immediately refilled the glass and took a more normal, if still lengthy, sip. Finally his gaze rose from the glass to meet hers. "Okay. Lay it on me. Give me your worst."

"I'm not…Caleb, I don't blame you for this. You were a child when it happened. You're not responsible for your father's actions."

He regarded her strangely, then quickly took another sip. "Thank you for that. But surely my government is to blame—and Division, whom I spent eighteen years working for. Surely you want to lay a bit of their sins at my feet, if only for my poor judgment in choice of employer."

She opened her mouth to respond but struggled to locate the words. He sounded so damn caustic. Harsh, on edge and spoiling for a fight. She couldn't rightly blame him, but she wasn't any good at soothing his angst when she *did* have her full wits about her.

Finally she ventured forward in a tentative, quiet tone. "I don't. I know when you met me, I had let my bitterness over my father's death fester and grow into a generalized displeasure with entire organizations, entire governments. With entire swaths of the galaxy. But I've put it behind me. I haven't felt that way for a while. I thought you realized."

He regarded her in stark consternation for several seconds, then rolled his eyes at the ceiling before taking another long sip of his drink.

"What? Are you not glad I don't blame you? I expected you to be glad. I tried to tell you before you left, but you bolted before I could get out half a sentence. What else do you want from me?"

"What else do I *want* from you? I want...I want you to yell and scream and throw things. I want to see the slightest hint of the fire that made me fall in love with you, even if the fire is directed at me." He held up his glass and sloshed its contents around. "I've got my flame-retardant gear, so I can take it.

"When I met you, when we fought the Metigens, you were *alive*. You were angry and acerbic and disagreeable and daring anyone to prove you wrong about the world, but you were alive. And I would give a proper fortune right now to see just a spark...to see something more than this shell, this faded shadow of who you are.

"You *should* be angry. You should feel betrayed and disgusted and the galaxy should tremble in the face of your wrath. But I wonder—do you feel anything?"

She closed her eyes, hiding from his piercing stare. She had no response, because he wasn't wrong. His words ought to sting, the events behind them should cut...she searched for the pain and found only emptiness.

In a detached sort of way, she recognized that she *was* angry, at so many things; she recognized the emotion and what it meant. But she experienced it as in a dream, ephemeral and incorporeal in a realm where nothing as fleeting as emotions truly existed.

She tried to find her way out, but the real world had become the dream, the elemental domain the sole place which felt real.

In desperation she leapt up and moved to stand in front of him, close enough to touch but not doing so. "Then make me feel. Make me feel *you*."

His irises bore into her, dark as indigo obsidian and violently brooding. His brow creased. He tilted the glass up to empty it again, then set it down too hard on the counter.

When he spoke, his voice was taut, sharpened by vitriol. "How am I supposed to respond to that? What is that even supposed to mean?"

She inhaled, but instead of air, her chest filled with a cavernous desolation. Her focus drifted to the floor so he wouldn't see the hopelessness overtaking her as she eked out a response. "Nothing. It doesn't mean anything at all. Never mind."

Then she turned and began walking away, wishing as strongly as he had that there was somewhere, anywhere on the ship where she could be alone. She didn't—

His hand landed on her upper arm and yanked her around to face him, then yet closer. His mouth crashed into hers with a rough, coarse fierceness. There was no tenderness to his embrace as he shoved her against the edge of the data center table.

The taste of whiskey on his tongue and hunger in his touch was what finally began to break through the fog clouding her mind. Like a drowning swimmer grasping for the dangling rope, she met his kiss with equal fierceness, dragging her fingers through his hair until her nails scraped at his scalp.

He drew back a sliver to growl against her lips. "Did you feel that?"

"Yes." She pressed into him, renewing the kiss and holding him fast lest he try to escape, having made his point. In truth his touch flitted at the edges of her reality, but she needed this. She needed him to be *real*. She needed him to not let go.

In the smallest act of mercy, he didn't fight her or pull away; instead his teeth grazed her lower lip insistently. A hand swept down to her hip then inside the waistband of her flimsy shorts. Farther.

Jolts of pleasure rocketed through her. It was the first sensation she'd experienced in this allegedly tangible world to exceed the palpability of the elemental one in days.

"Do you feel that?" His voice was gravelly and harsh. Challenging.

She pulled in air, mind and body swimming, and managed a semblance of a nod.

His other hand clasped the nape of her neck and coaxed her into meeting his troubled gaze. "Say it."

She blinked. "Yes...I feel that. Please."

His mouth teased hers. "Please what?"

"Please...more. Don't...please don't stop—"

He short-circuited the last word with his lips, and she let go of the esoteric fear in favor of physical, carnal sensations. Her hands found the hem of his shirt and yanked it up, willing to forego his kiss for a blink of time to be rid of the shirt—and hers, as he'd done the same.

His skin burned hot on hers, his pulse racing beneath its surface. She sensed the moment when his motivation shifted from anger to anger-fueled lust, when his motions became desperate as his hands shoved her shorts down and gripped her ass to hold her tight against him.

Right now she didn't care what fueled it. Right now so many wrong things fueled her lust, too. It was all wrong, but it was the only thing she had tethering her to reality.

She fumbled for the clasp on his pants, wrenched them open and down over his hips—

—instantly he had hoisted her up onto the table. First one knee then the other hemmed her in on either side as he slid her backward.

She managed the beginning of a weak protest. "The table—"

"To hell with the table." The weight of his body urged her down.

The table is scientific equipment worth tens of thousands of credits and was not made for this. But it doesn't matter, does it?

Smooth metal met her back in a flash of white-hot ice. She would have bolted up from the shock if it had been possible to do so.

The contrast of the heat of his skin and the cold metal was almost too much for her to bear. Scorching, freezing, which was she? Which was which?

His palms clutched both sides of her face. "Look at me, dammit."

He was too near for her to bring him into focus. The whole of her vision was dancing, electric sapphire. "Caleb...."

"Do you realize what you mean to me? Do you?" He slid inside her in perfect time with his lips meeting hers anew, denying her the chance to reply. And she remembered what this plane of existence could feel like.

His words were the only gentle thing about him. Yet she pushed him further, nails scratching up his spine and trying to draw him yet closer, deeper, seeking yet more. *Make me want, need, ache to choose this world, my love. Demand I choose it. I beg you.*

He lifted her up and onto him as he settled on his heels, which was when she noticed his pants were still mostly on, the waistband sitting haphazardly below his hips. Nothing to be done for it now.

The absence of the cold metal at her back was almost as stark as its arrival had been, and suddenly she was burning up. He was even hotter, scalding her lips as they roved over his damp skin.

She nipped at his earlobe, his neck, the pounding artery beneath the skin which had once been ripped open—

—the memory punched all the air out of her lungs. She froze, tears stinging her eyes. He'd come so close to dying. She'd come so close to losing him when they'd scarcely begun.

One of his hands fisted in her hair as the other held her up roughly. "No. Don't you *dare* slip away from me now."

He misunderstood the reason for the abrupt slackness in her body and the halt in her motions. But before she was able to respond, he had all but thrown her down on the table, driving into her with renewed urgency.

The shock from the icy surface forced out what little air she'd regained, and with his mouth covering hers she could hardly find more. It was fine. She didn't need to breathe.

The sensations coursing through her body grew to overpower the ice and the heat. Had she imagined anything else compared? This *was* better. More important. More alive. More of life. She held on to the passion with everything she had.

His arms wound beneath her, and he lifted her off the table to brace her against him, suspended in the air.

Her head fell back, sweaty, tangled hair sweeping across the table as she surrendered to the deluge of sensations and cried out.

The wave of ecstasy crested but didn't crash down. Instead his own surging pleasure held it aloft, much as his powerful muscles held her body up. She let her and his rapture wash over her, blending and merging and searing into her.

This time the cold from the table surface didn't penetrate her skin when he eased her down onto it. She only felt him.

His chest heaved above hers as he regarded her with an expression of heartbreaking rawness, tainted by shadows of pain and sadness.

She'd almost forgotten these visceral human emotions could be so...brutal. Her chest hurt, but not from his weight. From something deeper, yet maddeningly elusive.

His whispered murmur cut deeper still. "Did you feel that?"

She nodded; her lips parted, but no words came out.

He seemed as if he were about to say something else...then his eyes closed and he dropped his forehead to hers and hugged her close.

It was all she could do not to break down sobbing. She was wrecked, shredded and strewn across the stars.

She reached out with her mind, just a little, enough for the barest link. *Valkyrie, I don't care who you have to threaten or what you have to hack, but find out where they're taking Abigail.*

I need help.

12

ROMANE

IDCC COLONY

Noah waved his father inside the Connova Interstellar meeting room. "Thanks for making the trip. Kennedy's over at the IDCC hangar checking on a few ship details. She'll be back soon, but I wanted to talk to you alone, anyway."

Lionel Terrage strode purposefully around the room, as if he were inspecting it to determine if it passed muster. "I had a meeting with a customer here, so it was convenient. How's the arm doing?"

Noah stretched it out in front of him and twisted it around a few times. "Better than the real thing. A few days ago I woke up and it took me until lunch to remember it wasn't the original. Was a nice morning." He laughed. "Mind you, the reason I finally remembered was because I crushed the takeout container from the lunch restaurant. But hey, as problems go...."

He sighed as Lionel activated the control panel for the conference table and began opening screens. "Dad, stop."

"I'm sorry?"

"Stop screwing with the furniture and the fixtures and sit or something. Or no, don't sit, seeing as I'm not going to sit. Stand, but still. Can you manage that?"

At the sight of his father's condescending scowl, Noah almost gave up and walked out. But then he remembered Kennedy last night, how she'd shared with him what she wanted to do and stayed up half the night working on the speech. He owed it to her to do this.

"You know about the Alliance's absurd adiamene restrictions, don't you? You know how the government chased Kennedy away in an overbearing attempt at an illegal power grab, then had the gall to issue an arrest warrant for her when she refused to play by their new rules."

Lionel nodded and settled against the wall with a greater degree of attention. Better yet, he stopped touching things.

"It's only a small part of Winslow and the Assembly's increasing authoritarianism and, more relevantly to you, anti-free enterprise leanings. Last month they came for Kennedy—maybe next month they come for you."

"I am aware." Lionel looked out the window rather than meet Noah's gaze. "Far more aware than you are, in fact. The schemes being hatched by bureaucrats and power brokers behind closed doors, the subtle pressure exerted on businesspeople which, if unsuccessful, escalates to blackmail or at a minimum the threat of it. But in politics phases such as this are nothing new. They come and go like seasons, and one can weather them as such."

"Not this time, Dad. This time what's at stake goes far beyond local Assembly elections and a few lucrative government contracts."

"We will see. I do admit, it appears this will be a more troublesome period than usual."

Noah saw his chance in the uncertainty tinging his dad's voice. He leaned forward over the table, enjoying the sturdy support his new arm provided him. "You've lived a charmed life, Dad. Proper, wealthy Alliance luminary by day, clever Pandora profiteer by night. You've enjoyed—"

"I have not—"

"Shut up and listen to me for five seconds, for once in your life. We share the same genes. On the theory we must share something more, *listen to me*. Kennedy already gave up everything to come here to Romane and start fresh. I would love her forever for that alone, but it's not enough for her. She can't stand by and watch her beloved Alliance fall to people like Winslow, not without trying to help stop it.

"She's planning to give a speech to the Allied Manufacturers Chamber. Idealistic, crazy woman she is, she believes she can convince a bunch of plutocrats and robber barons that it's in their best interests to defy the prime minister and the Assembly and instead support Admiral Solovy. I think she's giving them way too much credit. But she grew up among these people. She gets them, and she might be able to do it."

He paused, shifted his weight onto his back leg, and crossed his arms over his chest. "You know what would go a long way to help tip the balance in her favor?"

Though he now had Lionel's rapt attention, the man nevertheless frowned and shook his head ambiguously. Dear gods in the heavens, was his father the densest, most tone-deaf individual in the cosmos?

He moved down the table, closer. "*You*, Dad. You're a highly respected member of the Chamber. Practically revered. If you support her, they'll have to give her the due she deserves. And she's right—it is in their best interests, which means it's in your best interest. Stop perturbing yourself trying to keep your hands clean and take a goddamn stand."

"I don't—"

"I'm not asking you to rattle any sabers or wave any blooded flags. It's enough for this to be about business. About protecting your admittedly hard-earned and richly-deserved earnings from what you've created. You do deserve it, and so do they. Well, some of them. A few.

"But I'm not here for them. I'm here for her, and because I have to believe somewhere inside of you is a decent soul. You made me, and in many ways—definitely more ways than I care to admit—I am you. Which means there *has* to be a decent soul inside you.

"So I am asking you. Frankly, I guess I'm begging you. For her. Because she's right, Dad. She's right, and you know it. So please. Just this once, and I'll never ask anything of you again. Not money, not sanctuary, not another robotic limb. The next one's on me. But *do* this."

His father stared at him for a long time, then out the window for longer. Noah recognized this was not the setting for an acerbic wisecrack, but damned if he didn't badly want to make one.

Finally Lionel turned to face him, his posture as formal and stiff as it had ever been. "Would she like to give the speech from my headquarters on Aquila? Publicly? I can guarantee her safety. No one will arrest her while she's on my property."

Noah smiled. "I think she'd like that quite a lot."

AR

EARTH

VANCOUVER
EASC HEADQUARTERS

The EASC Logistics Director leaned over the desk in a blatant attempt at intimidation. "There must be evidence of misconduct on her part. To be blunt, your lack of concern about the matter reeks of misconduct on *your* part."

Major Kian Lange met the Director's glower calmly. Calm was a demeanor he had long ago perfected. Unruffled. Composed. A proper officer.

"I'll repeat what I stated in my report, which is that there's nothing to investigate. As Fleet Admiral and Chairman of the EASC Board, Admiral Solovy served as the commander of all aspects of the Armed Forces. Adding additional technical capabilities to Northeast Regional Command fell strictly within her purview and did not violate any regulations."

"And transferring control of the Armed Forces communications network there?"

"If she wanted to temporarily designate Northeast Regional Command as the hub of the network, she possessed the authority to do it. Mobile command centers are used all the time. The power goes with the person."

"Well. She's not Fleet Admiral now, which makes her continued efforts to hold the network hostage a violation of the Code of Military Justice."

Lange worded his response with utmost care. "It is a matter for an Ethics Council tribunal to be sure, but it's outside my jurisdiction, which encompasses only what happens here on the Island."

The Director shot him another threatening glare. "This is Earth Alliance Strategic Command, and until proper operational control is returned here, it is your problem. I'm getting tremendous pressure from Washington *and* London on this. The Oversight Committee won't be pleased to hear of your lack of vigilance on the matter, to say nothing of the prime minister's office."

"Brigadier Ojeda, I'm not violating any orders or the guidelines defining my duties."

"Then maybe we need to get you new orders."

"I'll await them, sir."

The Director pivoted and left the office. Lange shut the door and engaged the lock behind him.

The EASC campus had been in a state of constant uproar since Admiral Solovy's departure. Initially, no one knew precisely what was happening. It soon became apparent the dispute between Prime Minister Winslow and Admiral Solovy had escalated to a public fissure, but at that point it still wasn't clear what that *meant.*

Then the prime minister leveled accusations of a variety of high crimes against the admiral, and shortly thereafter the prime minister's people had swarmed EASC. In addition to demanding incriminating evidence materialize out of thin air, they had executed several ham-fisted attempts to take effective control of the organization.

But the military functioned on rules, regulations and orders. In the absence of a chairman, the EASC Board was in charge, but the Board had descended into as much turmoil as everything and everyone else.

Two of the Regional Commanders, Rychen and Haraken, were unabashedly supporting Admiral Solovy, and Rychen no longer attended Board meetings at all. General Foster was just as unabashedly in the prime minister's pocket, and Colby, the Southeast Regional Commander, was hedging her bets. The Logistics Director and several others also served on the Board, and they tended to favor the prime minister, but the real, actionable power had always resided in the Regional Commanders.

So the Board sat paralyzed, unable to make even the most basic decisions.

He'd say it was a good thing they weren't fighting a war at present, but after Admiral Solovy's manifesto broadcast, in many ways they were. And whatever side you approached it from, the enemy was themselves.

He activated the surveillance shielding in his office. As Security Director he enjoyed the very best and latest in equipment. Then he sent a live message, one which would leave no record of its existence on this end.

Logistics is operating on the prime minister's orders. The investigation is being directed by the Assembly Oversight Committee, but which representatives in particular are directing it isn't known. It may still be Winslow herself, or her aides.

Tech is reporting that if breached, the on-site network cannot be tunneled to reach your Artificial, so core functions remain insulated for now.

We have your back.

13

EAS STALWART II

"Thirty new fighters are ready or coming out of manufacturing today if you want them."

Miriam squinted at the left-most screen for several seconds. "Of course I want them...but I don't have the pilots for them. Not yet." She looked back across the table at Eleni. "Can you sit on them for two more days? Richard believes many of the field officers in the NW 4th Brigade are pressuring Rear Admiral Tarone to join us.

"If that happens, it'll mean upwards of three hundred additional fighter pilots. They'll come with their own ships, but I'd certainly like to move as many as I can into the new vessels."

"Understandable. They're yours until such time as I have an exigent need for them, which I pray is not anytime this decade." The field marshal took a sip of coffee. "But the ships you're using now—they're working out well thus far?"

"Beyond my expectations. Alex expressed jealousy, which I take as a sign of accomplishment. Thank you. You've done far more than I asked."

"No thanks are needed. It sounds as if you have what you require and can barrel straight through to Earth with it, but do contact me if any problems arise I can help address."

The woman shifted in the chair, but not to a more relaxed position. "Miriam, I know you've said you don't wish to discuss Colpetto, but I feel like we should, in the hope we can move past it."

"There's nothing to move past, Eleni."

"Isn't there? You must realize I did not make the decision to go forward with the operation lightly. I agonized over it. But I felt as if I had no other options left."

Miriam had done everything possible to keep business and personal separate, but if Eleni insisted on pushing, *fine*.

"You truly want to know what I think? Very well. I think you didn't agonize over it. I think you deprived seventeen families of their sons and daughters, husbands and wives, fathers and mothers, because it made things easier for you. I think you made a cold, calculated decision to sacrifice innocents to give yourself an advantage."

"Don't act as if there's no blood on your hands, Miriam. You and I, we sacrifice people for victory's sake all the time—in every war, every battle."

"Combatants, Eleni. Military personnel who understand the stakes and are willing to die for the mission. Not innocent civilians."

"You see...it's easy for you to say that when you were on the side of the oppressor rather than the oppressed—and before you try to minimize the Alliance's misdeeds, take a hard look at what your government is doing today. Then tell me it doesn't know how to be evil."

"And your vaunted Senecan Federation killed David for protecting scientists and their families. There's plenty of evil to go around if you're inclined to start searching for it."

Eleni flinched. Good. "I don't disagree. *Kappa Crucis* was a bad call. The on-scene commander misunderstood the Alliance's intentions, but she was always a hothead. If cooler heads had prevailed and taken five minutes to critically assess the situation, the battle wouldn't have happened. It shouldn't have happened, and if I could go back and change it, I swear to you I would.

"But—and here's the thing—I wouldn't go back and change Colpetto. I may pay for those seventeen deaths in the next life, but I submit it will be worth it for all the days I've seen my grandchildren grow up free."

"The Earth Alliance is not, nor was it ever, a dictatorship."

"Try telling that to someone living on a disfavored colony thirty years ago. See how well it goes over."

"I concede the political leaders of the time weren't exactly luminaries, even compared to our current administration." Miriam sighed. "I will never agree with your decision, but...I do respect your conviction. And there are plenty of sins for each of us to carry."

"Truer words." Eleni smiled a bit wistfully. "Now I'm afraid I need to depart soon. The legislature is voting on the H+ bill this evening, and I ought to be on the ground in case things get out of hand."

"Is it going to pass?"

"Yes. It's a new world out there, and it's time for us all to embrace it."

Miriam arched an eyebrow. "I *am* trying."

"And doing an impressive job of it." The woman paused, then brought up her hand in a crisp salute. "Good luck to you, Admiral."

Miriam almost didn't return the salute. She still harbored mixed feelings, unresolved issues and a complicated, ugly acrimony with respect to the woman and what she'd once done.

But Miriam also had manners, and whatever sins the past held, Eleni had done a great deal of good in the present. So she did return it.

"And to you, Field Marshal."

⟆R⟅

Miriam remained in the conference room after Eleni departed. She wanted a moment to reorient. The entire Volnosti operation was constantly in flux as they worked to adapt to quickly changing circumstances and new information.

If the Federation's Prevo protection bill was going to pass, the dynamics were poised to transform yet again. H+ wasn't perfect, but if she could trade BANIA for it, she'd hang up her hat and call it a day.

The passage would shift the overall balance strongly in favor of Prevo rights, with the Alliance becoming the sole hold-out—and not the entire Alliance. However, it also risked antagonizing OTS;

desperation bred recklessness, making them even more dangerous, if such a thing was possible.

She opened four screens and had Thomas fill them with data. Arguably too much data, as she found she wasn't able to concentrate on any particular item for more than a few seconds before her mind drifted to one place or another.

Strategy. Eleni, then David. Alex.

She looked up in relief as Richard entered, glad for the distraction. "Come in and keep me company."

He lounged against the wall. "I passed Field Marshal Gianno on her way out. As I was walking away, a crazy notion occurred to me. Did you know what was going to happen when you asked me to go to Seneca and work for Graham?"

"Don't be silly, Richard. How could I possibly have known any of this would happen?"

"No clue. So did you?"

She laughed. "Not precisely, of course. But I could see the storm coming, and while I hoped it could be diffused, I needed to prepare as if it wouldn't be."

"So I was one of your chess pieces, then."

"One of my absolutely most important, crucial ones."

Her tone was mirthful, and he abandoned his attempt at a stern expression to settle into the chair opposite her. "Rumor has it, Isas Onishi is livid over OTS bombing the Astral Materials home office on Scythia."

"I don't need a rumor to tell me that."

"No, but what you might not be aware of is Mr. Onishi has the ear of the Scythia governor. Both of them are quite done with OTS, and they are not happy with how little Winslow's administration is doing to combat the group. Also, Onishi has been using Artificials in his business for twenty years, which means he isn't happy about BANIA's restrictions."

She scowled in growing frustration. "Yes, but many people affected by them are unhappy about the new restrictions. As we've seen, being unhappy is a long way from doing something to change it."

"Agreed. But Onishi isn't one to sit idly by, and the governor has a reputation as something of a maverick."

"You're suggesting I should reach out to the governor."

Richard held up a finger. "One more tidbit. Six years ago Astral Materials claimed the rights to what's colloquially called a 'diamond planet,' one composed almost entirely of an ultra-dense form of crystallized carbon. Since mining of the planet began, Onishi has made over a billion credits from it, nearly doubling his net worth in the process. Do you know who found and claimed it for him?"

If it mattered as much as Richard was intimating, there existed only one possible answer. "Alex?"

"Correct."

Six years ago.... "That's how she was able to afford the loft, among other luxuries."

"You'll have to ask her, but it's a reasonable assumption. She's fulfilled at least five contracts for Onishi over the years, including another big one last year which netted him an asteroid belt's worth of super strong heavy metals. The point is, he owes Alex, and he almost certainly thinks highly of her. Use it. My professional assessment is that Onishi and the Scythia governor are ready to take a stand. All you need to do is assure them they will have your support. And by 'support,' they'll mean protection."

Miriam recognized the familiar pang of regret. She'd missed so much of her daughter's life, ignored so many of her accomplishments along the way. She should have been proud. Perhaps she'd traveled some distance to making up for her mistakes this last year, but she'd never get the lost chances back.

She blew out a long breath and nodded. "All right. If Scythia joins Messium in our corner, Winslow won't be able to ignore it. Let's make this happen."

14

AQUILA

Kennedy approached the podium with an unhurried but purposeful stride. It had been a while since she'd needed to perform for the self-chosen commercial nobility, but not so long she'd forgotten how it was done.

Conservative but stylish hunter green pantsuit. Unruly curls tamed into elegant submission. Tasteful jewelry which shone brightly enough to remind them all she belonged here.

Damn straight she did.

The presentation room at Surno Materials was ostentatious, and not subtly so. The natural teak floors had been buffed to a perfect sheen, and the marble podium was supple and cool to the touch. The holo projected in front of her showing the audience at the Chamber meeting in Hong Kong displayed a fidelity nearly equal to the newest wave of *illusoires*. She could be standing there among them.

The quality was high enough for her to be able to feel their mood, to sense when she was winning or losing them.

"Thank you all for having me today. My remarks will be brief, because the most important, truest ideas don't need fancy accoutrements to prop them up or grant them value.

"I know many of you personally, as many of you know me. You know my family. You know my father, Trevor, and my mother, Elise. Some of you knew my grandparents, for they were staunch supporters of the Chamber.

"You appreciate the authenticity of my words when I say my family loves the Alliance and all it represents. My great-grandfather stood on the stage in London in 2105 when the Earth Alliance was formed, and my family has championed it ever since.

"Now my parents find themselves threatened, pinned into a narrow corner by representatives of the Alliance—representatives who are themselves threatened by yet more powerful interests and thereby forced to do the bidding of Prime Minister Winslow and her cabal of adherents."

She cast a thoughtful gaze across the audience. "And something tells me they're not alone. How many of you have wanted to speak out against BANIA and the heavy-handed regulations it has spawned but refrained from doing so out of fear...or perhaps out of an uncomfortable, niggling feeling that it just *wasn't a good idea*. I understand. I do.

"You may have heard about my little dispute with the prime minister. You've assuredly heard about the ban on adiamene production or sale in private industry. A metal, banned. Not a deadly chimeral or a destructive laser weapon—a *metal*.

"Can you imagine where we would be today if the first carbon steel alloys had been banned in commerce? Tungsten nanocomposites? Carbon metamaterials? If this were our past, we wouldn't be here among the stars now."

She allowed the smallest smile to touch her lips. "We're manufacturers. We build things. I bet some of you would love to have a shipment of adiamene for your orbital facilities, or for your ships. I'll sell it to you. Fifteen percent Chamber discount. You let me know."

She could almost hear Noah groan from across the room; she was going to pay for that discount in more than merely lost profits.

"But sadly, the crisis we face today isn't really about a metal. The adiamene ban is only a symptom. It's about lives. About who gets to decide what life is and whether it's allowed to exist.

"Each and every one of you achieved the success you enjoy today by being smart. Shrewd. You've worked with Artificials, I guarantee it—maybe on specialized projects, maybe every day.

Have they been taken from you, for your own good? How long until they are?

"You understand what Artificials are and what they aren't. And Prevos? Most of you probably didn't have the opportunity to meet any of them before they were forced into hiding on Alliance worlds, but I have. Prevos are my colleagues. They're my friends. I suspect for some of you, they're your sons or daughters.

"If so, I wish them the best, and hope they are safe.

"Pamela Winslow has you fighting an enemy that doesn't exist. And she has you doing it so she can take your power, then take your freedom. Don't let her. She hasn't the right to it."

Another solemn scan of the audience, and she took a step back from the podium. No applause followed, but it wasn't a bad sign. Sober reflection *should* be the mood. There was nothing to celebrate, least of all her dressing down of them.

Lionel joined her on the platform and shook her hand. "Thank you, Ms. Rossi."

He watched her leave, then turned to the virtual audience. "Well, I'm inspired!"

Awkward laughter rippled through the attendees, and Lionel waited until it subsided. His expression grew earnest.

"Well I am inspired. I'm also shamed. We've all—myself included—been going along to get along, thinking we could weather the storm and still be standing at the end. But how much of ourselves are we willing to sacrifice to avoid conflict? How much can we sacrifice before we lose our integrity? Our most treasured principles?"

He paused to study the podium for a moment. "None of us are warriors—except Mr. Onishi, of course, and Mr. Basurto. They were warriors on the battlefield before they became warriors in the boardroom. Not the rest of us. But this doesn't mean we can't fight in our own way.

"What we are is influential. Wealthy. Able to bring resources to bear on a problem. And en masse, we are powerful. The last time

I checked, the Alliance is still a democracy and our elected leaders are still beholden to us. So tell your representative you want BANIA repealed—as well as the adiamene ban, naturally—and an investigation into the prime minister's activities opened.

"Tell them with your lobbyists. Tell them with your money and your business. Tell them yourselves. Shine a light in the shadows, and take back control of your government. I certainly plan to."

Off to the side and out of view of the cams, Kennedy's hand came to her mouth as applause now did break out, growing until it thundered. She leaned closer to Noah and whispered, "Did you know he was going to say all that?"

Noah shrugged mildly. "Nah, I didn't dare hope. But he hasn't done too badly."

R

Lionel Terrage accepted the comm request from yet another Chamber member.

The inquiries had been steady for the last two hours. Some wanted to express their enthusiastic support, some their appalled disgust. Most were tentative, hesitantly asking questions, fearful but exploring the concept of 'helping' while lacking any understanding of what that might mean.

He donned his standard aloof, professional countenance. "Good to speak with you, Benjamin."

The CEO of PanPacific Tech Labs pretended to inspect a sidescreen, then another. "And you, Lionel. Brave thing you did today. It's a real shame such difficult choices have had to be made by all involved. I don't think you give the administration enough credit for trying to do the right thing, though. BANIA has its flaws, but we have to move forward and make the best of it in difficult times."

"It seems we have different ideas about what 'the right thing' means. If you'll excuse me, I need to see to more important matters."

He cut the connection because he was bored and irked by it, but also because he *did* need to see to something more important—namely, the security cam showing Aquila police presenting a warrant file to the clerk at the entrance downstairs.

It had always been a risk, and one he'd made the decision to bear when he made the offer to host Ms. Rossi. He'd hoped it wouldn't come to pass, but he couldn't fairly say he was surprised it had.

He'd for all intents and purposes publicly thumbed his nose at the Winslow administration, after all, and the administration did not take kindly to being humiliated. Worse, it stamped out the brush fires of dissent with a panicked gusto normally reserved for handling virulent plagues.

Fleeing wasn't a viable option. Even if he reached the shuttle pad on the roof, the authorities were liable to shoot his transport down. But more relevantly, he wasn't built for life on the run. Where Noah had gotten the aptitude for it, he couldn't begin to hazard a guess, but it was not from him.

He wasn't built for life in a prison cell, either, but he'd survive it for a time and, if all went well, see the end of it before too terribly long.

He sent a few brief messages—to Noah, to his attorney and to his COO—then took a sip of water and straightened his jacket.

The officers brute-force hacked the door with an appalling lack of courtesy and took up defensive positions like this was some sort of armed standoff. "Lionel Terrage?"

"You needn't have brutalized the door. I would have allowed you entry. All you needed to do was ask."

"We have a warrant to search the premises for one Kennedy Rossi."

"Alas, you've just missed her. But feel free to reassure yourselves of that fact."

"We will. Lionel Terrage, you are under arrest for harboring a fugitive wanted on a judicial warrant." The man produced a wrist restraint device and took a threatening step forward.

He exhaled in resignation. "Restraints won't be necessary. I'll come quietly."

INTERMEZZO II

AMARANTHE

S alote made every effort to remain hidden in his approach to the star system which hosted his homeworld. Despite his urgent desire to speed forward, he proceeded slowly in order to minimize his emissions, the one aspect of his travel which held any chance of exposure.

His ship bore no concealment mechanism, but it was so small, what machine could feasibly detect it from any distance? He and his ship were nothing, a pinprick in the vastness of space.

His chest tingled with blooming hope when he saw the planet was not yet gone—then with horror when he made out the giant, foul machines plundering it.

Only true demons could construct such nightmarish engines of carnage.

Though the teachings instructed he should not feel it, a great rage burst to life within him at the sight of the rampant destruction. What gave them the right to claim his home for their own wishes? It wasn't theirs to take!

Remember Airini. Remember the little ones. Remember your purpose.

He chanted to calm himself, drifting through space for a long time—too long.

When he saw clearly again, he worked to cast a critical eye on the scene. The moon remained intact, as he'd speculated it would. Might it be possible the lunar port had not been searched by the interlopers? Might his family be hiding there, against all odds?

Renewed by the lightness of hope once more, he edged his ship closer to the moon.

AR

Assignment Designation: *I-4617-D883-J955*

Sector: *Eridium II 4A*

Summary: *Initial survey determined System 4A-CC57 harbored a single Tier II-D species. On arrival, the Theriz Cultivation Unit noted one hundred eighty-seven functioning mammals and a disproportionate number of empty structures built upon one of the target planetary bodies.*

Directive: *Investigate suspected disappearance of the bulk of the Tier II-D mammalian species.*

Aver ela-Praesidis swept past the planet in question without contemplation. Theriz were never ones to wait when work existed to be done. Having fulfilled their duty by notifying the Praesidis Primor of the anomaly, the Cultivation Unit had already demolished all evidence of the resident species in their reaping of the materials the planet provided.

Near cosmic scans detected seven artificial objects circumnavigating the planetary space: six rudimentary measurement instruments and a single orbiting habitat.

Aver placed his ship into a complimentary orbit above the habitat. Not knowing the layout or contents of the interior, he elected to traverse the short distance rather than teleport inside.

His *diati* gathered the molecules necessary for respiration around him as he opened his ship's airlock then propelled him forward until he reached the structure.

He commanded the sealed hatch to open, then set a bubble upon it so the evidence he sought was not drawn out into space.

On entering the habitat, he instantly sensed it was devoid of life. The small passages and tools attached to various stations told him the former inhabitants were diminutive creatures, perhaps 1.2 meters in height, with digited limbs by the design of the implements.

He wiped a length of hair off the wall with a grimace. Fur, of a wiry, short variety. Rodents.

A cleaning system still functioned, as did ventilation and air circulation. The habitat had not been abandoned for long.

Conclusion #1: *The species was made aware a short time in advance that the Theriz Cultivation Unit would be arriving in System 4A-CC57.*

He manipulated several pieces of equipment, dismantled them and inspected their construction. Electric wires. Epoxy. Barbaric.

Conclusion #2: *The species lacked the technological capability to detect the approach of any Anaden vessel until its imminent arrival.*

Conclusion #3: *Members of a more advanced species alerted the native population to the impending Cultivation of their system.*

Aver returned to his ship and linked into the Annals of Catalogued Species. Eridium II was not under productive development and not heavily populated. The number of active species in the galaxy who had ever departed their planets' soil numbered only eight.

Of those, three had achieved interstellar flight; two were Accepted Species, one Eradicated. Neither of the Accepted Species showed any recorded incidents of malfeasance. He nonetheless noted them for further investigation.

The planet's satellite orbited into view, and he shifted his attention to it. Artificial structures clashed with the mineralized surface in a series of crude lines and boxes, indicating the resident species had begun clumsily colonizing their moon.

He proceeded to the lunar base.

Signs of Eradication by the Theriz Cultivation Unit Advance Team were immediately visible. Some members of the native population had remained here when the Unit arrived, and they had been disposed of.

…Yet a heat signature emitted from one of the tiny ships on the landing platform. The signature was solely excess radiation, as the engine was not active, and the ship was unoccupied. The remainder of the ships were long cold.

One of the rodents had returned.

Aver landed nearby and crossed to the base entrance.

The air inside was not pleasant to his lungs, but a small amount of *diati* converted it to be so. He paused inside the entryway, seeking the indicia of a living organic being.

Heartbeat twenty-three meters distant at 31.46°. Very rapid by mammalian standards. He advanced.

The rodent, its skin covered in a short coat of silvery fur, huddled on the floor. Its talons were wrapped around a deceased member of the species.

On seeing Aver, the rodent leapt up and backed into a corner while muttering meaningless squeals.

"Who enabled your species' departure from this system?"

The rodent shook and shrieked. No apparent comprehension of the Communis language. Alas.

Aver flicked his wrist, and the rodent's neck snapped. It collapsed to the floor atop the body it had been grasping.

He expanded his senses through the hallways of the structure to confirm no further life forms remained in residence, then teleported back to the landing platform.

If the rodent had departed and returned, its ship, rudimentary though it was, may well provide the answers he sought.

PART III:

SPIRAL

"Chaos results when the world changes faster than people."

— *Will Durant*

15

SPACE, CENTRAL QUADRANT

Abigail admired several characteristics of professional soldiers, as a rule.

They tended to be supremely competent at their jobs, with skillsets that were narrow and specialized but quite crucial in certain circumstances.

Below a level of officer rank—colonel, occasionally commodore—they did not profess to possess competencies outside those skillsets unless they actually possessed them.

But three-quarters of the way through the forty-hour flight from Sagan to Romane, the characteristic Abigail most admired about them was that as long as lethal weapons were not currently being utilized in the vicinity, professional soldiers weren't inclined to engage in unnecessary talking.

She'd legitimately been able to work for most of the trip, as well as sleep when required and engage in several multi-party comms, all without intrusion or interruption. The trip had been, she'd daresay, productive in many respects.

Not all, however. The unexpected livecomm from Alex Solovy was more disquieting than fruitful, and it continued to trouble her now, several hours later.

"Abigail, hi. Valkyrie says hi, too. Truthfully, she kind of took over for a second there. She's excited to get to talk to you. I'm sorry I didn't reach out until now. Obviously a lot was waiting on us when we got back."

It had been a few months since they'd spoken, but she thought Alex sounded agitated. Jittery? "I completely understand. Vii has been talking with Valkyrie about your travels and filling me in, though I look forward to hearing your own impressions."

"What? Oh. I'll...try to gather my thoughts on them. Soon. You're on your way to Romane now?"

"So it would seem. It was not exactly my choice, but Devon and Mia apparently believe I'm in some degree of peril."

"Good—I mean, good that you're coming to Romane. Not the peril. Once you get here and settled in, I need to come see you."

"You're always welcome, and as I said, I'd like to hear more of what you've seen."

Silence answered her.

"Is something wrong?"

"Um...I may have gotten a few signals crossed in my brain. I'm not sure."

Now Abigail was positive she detected genuine distress. In the background, Valkyrie began sending her reams of neurological data, and she scanned it with half her attention.

The Prevos had of necessity been created without research trials, much less long-term efficacy and safety studies. They had broken all the rules, because they'd had no choice. But the simple fact was, no one knew what the long-term effect of a Prevo connection would be on the human body.

In the months since their creation, each of the original Prevos had pushed the technology in their own way, but based on what she'd learned, it was possible none had pushed it so far as Alex. The others welcomed the Artificials into their minds, but Alex was venturing deep into the Artificial's mind, and in a way which Abigail had never intended or envisioned when she wrote the enabling code.

"Vii told me about some of the upgrades Valkyrie has made. Do you suspect they've introduced errors or glitches into your Prevo algorithms?"

She started checking the likeliest sources of such a glitch in the data from Valkyrie, then after several seconds realized Alex had never answered the question. "Alex?"

"I think...I think I went too far and...I can't seem to find my way back out."

She couldn't begin to guess what Alex meant, but the turmoil and undercurrent of panic rang stridently in her voice. Abigail tried to convey reassurance in her own.

"We'll get it sorted out. Don't worry."

R

ROMANE

The transport landed at a private spaceport near downtown. Vii informed her Mia owned it, though she no longer actively managed it. Most of Abigail's escort departed to check over the surroundings alongside another contingent of security who awaited them.

Finally she was allowed to disembark. To her surprise, Devon Reynolds waited on her at the bottom of the ramp.

She'd seen him in holos recently, so his more muscular, strapping appearance wasn't a surprise; it nonetheless gave her a moment's pause. "Devon, you seem...well. But I thought you were on Pandora."

"I was. But now it's all going down, and a lot of it is going down here. So here we are."

"Ah, yes. How is Annie?"

"Bossy." He smiled, and for an instant a hint of his former geeky charm flashed in his bright lavender eyes. Then it was gone. "I apologize for the draconian measures, but we can protect you better here. This is only until OTS is dealt with, which will be soon, I promise you."

"I wasn't doubting. Now, it's been a long flight. I would appreciate it if whomever has been tasked to do so could escort me to wherever I'm to be ensconced."

"It's not a torture chamber, Abigail. It's a nice apartment with running water and everything."

"Devon."

"Right." He motioned two members of the security detail over. "They tell me I can't go with you—something about two targets and bullseyes and tempting fate. But I'll be monitoring the situation."

"Thank you. Oh, Alex needs to visit once I'm settled in. Tomorrow morning, perhaps. Could you ensure it's arranged?"

"Visits are bound to be challenging, but we'll figure something out."

ℛ

SENECA

CAVARE
INTELLIGENCE DIVISION HEADQUARTERS

Will Sutton collapsed onto the couch in Richard's office. It was closer than his own, and he could spare only a minute to catch his breath.

He wouldn't deny he also took a degree of comfort from simply being in the room. Though Richard hadn't been at Division long, his husband had nonetheless made the space his own, if in subtle ways no one else would recognize.

Will was going on two days of round-the-clock protection management for the two senators threatened by OTS, plus half a dozen others for good measure, and the work was far from done. Three assassination attempts had been made prior to the alleged deadline, which had now come and gone.

The senators were theoretically safe and sound, as the reason for their desired deaths was now moot, but as outspoken Prevo supporters they weren't apt to be genuinely safe for a while yet. In truth, not until OTS was eliminated as a threat, but certainly not until the current furor died down.

The news feed on the wall reported what would, if the stars aligned correctly, turn out to be good news. The H+ bill had passed by a reasonably wide margin then was immediately signed into law by Chairman Vranas. Under the new law, restrictions on Artificials and licensing requirements for them were loosened considerably, while still keeping safety in mind. Or that was the idea, anyway.

More controversially, the law affirmed Prevos' status as human beings entitled to full protection under the Senecan Federation Charter and all Federation laws and regulations. The reality of the significant number of unlicensed Artificials attached to the Prevos was hedged around by a series of grandfather clauses and retroactive compliance procedures.

It was sure to be messy in the implementation, but hey, everyone was making this up as they went along.

In the wake of the bill's passage, Delavasi had drawn down the extra Senate security, but it remained heightened above normal protocols and likely would stay there for weeks at a minimum.

In fact, Will needed to be directing his attention to that in about two minutes—working out the details on an interim protection plan for at-risk senators for as long as OTS continued to be active.

His eyes were closed and his forearm thrown over them, but he smiled as a message from Richard arrived in his eVi. Nothing noteworthy, as they didn't share details of either of their work over comms for security reasons. Just a quick personal note, akin to reaching out and squeezing his hand. For the briefest second he imagined it as exactly such...which would have to do for now. Hopefully not for much longer.

People thought because Richard wasn't aggressive he wasn't a warrior. They were wrong, and he had used the misconception to his advantage many times. But it also meant there were times when the man had to be the warrior more overtly; it came with the role.

Combine it with Richard's insanely strong streak of duty and loyalty and...well, for better or worse this fight should be concluded soon. He hoped it was for the better—better for Miriam, for Earth and for Seneca. Better for the Prevos, many of whom he'd developed an unexpected fatherly affection toward. Better for Richard.

He stood and stretched, grabbed an energy drink from the small fridge compartment and headed for the door—

"The scene outside Parliament is turning chaotic as protests grow over the passage of the legislation popularly referred to as 'H+.' Reports of a disturbance inside the building have yet to be confirmed, but— hold on. We're receiving a communication from persons claiming to be representatives of the Order of the True Sentients terrorist group.

"The statement asserts the group has taken Senators Garza and Viktin hostage inside the Parliament building. It says they will execute both senators unless H+ is nullified by 2100 Galactic two days from now. Stay tuned for more information as it becomes available."

What? Garza and Viktin didn't even register on their radar. But maybe that explained why they'd been chosen. They were easier to get close to.

The Division and Parliament security comm channels began lighting up.

He reversed course and grabbed a second energy drink before leaving the office. Something told him he'd need it.

16

ROMANE

From up here, the city below looked calm. Peaceful. Serene. It was a lie.

Mia could feel the lie in her bones, in the foreboding creeping along the fine hairs on her skin. But mostly she could feel it in her head, where preparations were underway across Romane to meet the coming chaos.

The Noesis ramblings and the RRF comm channel chatter wound in and out of one another, overlapping and occasionally interfering. Harper's teams were joining forces with Romane civilian tactical units to set up blockades and buffer zones around the three largest protests—the ones which, as the second sun began to set, already hovered on the brink of turning riotous.

Morgan acted excited at the prospect of getting to fly in-atmo, even if it was only in an observational and support capacity. This vaguely confused Mia, as she'd assumed Morgan loved to fly *fast*, and circling above a downtown area was not likely to be fast. When queried about it, Morgan had simply laughed.

No extreme security measures were in place yet, though she imagined it would be quite difficult to get into the Headquarters building at this point, or any government or corporate building for that matter. Governor Ledesme had put the alerts in place, and all agencies and resources were ready to go.

On the ground, this was Romane's problem far more than theirs, but no one was bothering to pretend this wasn't about the IDCC. About them.

Devon: Everyone realizes this is OTS, right? They've hired a bunch of street thugs and muscle-for-rent to pretend to be 'ordinary people concerned over the growing influence of Prevos.'

Mia: I'm more concerned about why. The Romane government won't be bullied into budging on Artificial or Prevo liberties, and everyone knows it. There's no institutional weakness to be exploited. So are the protests a diversion? Cover for another move?

Devon: Almost certainly, and we've got people trying their damnedest to find out for what.

A small burst of flame sparked to life on the street below, three blocks from Headquarters. Vandalism. The crowds were doubtless itching to transform into rioters once the second sun set, and someone had jumped the gun.

HarperRF: Requesting additional support from Romane Tactical at Carina Center. The crowd here just doubled in size.

Commander Lekkas: Out of nowhere? Did they ship people in from off-world?

Mia pinched the bridge of her nose. *Probably. It's going to be a long night.*

Mere seconds after the last rays of fading mauve sunlight disappeared below the horizon, the same horizon lit up anew, this time in red and gold. She rushed forward to press against the window in horror.

Commander Lekkas: Explosion at Galaxy First building. I need all available emergency rescue personnel on site and fire suppression in the air.

Well, consider the diversion theory confirmed. Dammit, they should not be able to do this. Not here. Not on Romane.

Civilization had reached its zenith here. Shining. Advanced. Refined. Cultured.

Now they wanted to tear it all down.

In a corner of her virtual vision multiple cam feeds rolled as the protesters in the northeast quadrant of the city transitioned to full-on violent mob and glass began breaking. In her normal vision flames roiled out of the Galaxy First building. What were the odds it would be the only target to be hit tonight?

A far more horrifying thought occurred to her. What if the Galaxy First bombing was the real diversion?

SPACE, CENTRAL QUADRANT

ROMANE STELLAR SYSTEM

Kennedy clenched both hands in her hair and spun in circles down the aisle of the small transport. "Oh, no, no, no. The vindictive bitch!"

She gaped at Noah, eyes wide. "I am so, so sorry. This is my fault. I never should have let your dad expose himself like this for me. It was foolish and overly brazen of me. I should have been more cautious."

Noah gave her an easy shrug, but she wasn't buying it. His heart wasn't in it. "Eh, a span in lock-up will do him some good. Toughen him up, and maybe, just maybe, make him appreciate how good he's always had things."

"You don't mean that."

He massaged his biosynth hand with his natural one. It was a tic which had come with the new limb, and she knew it meant he was anxious, swagger or no. "I mean it a little. But...fine, I guess I don't want him punished for actually doing the right thing for once in his life."

"Ugh!" She flung herself into a chair and hung her head. She always tried *so* hard not to use her family's name or wealth in such a way that it harmed others, even inadvertently. And now she'd walked onto a stage and done precisely that, and in spectacular fashion.

True, Lionel Terrage wasn't exactly a common factory worker—but he'd put himself on the line so she could leverage her name for her own ends, and now he sat in police custody.

"Hey...." Noah knelt in front of her and lifted her chin. "It's not your fault, so don't beat yourself up over it. He understood the risks, and he decided to take a stand."

She wrinkled her nose at him. He kissed its tip...it really did make her feel better. But only for a minute. She had to make this right—fix it completely if she could. "I wonder if Miriam can help. After everything we've done for her, if she can, she will. I know it."

Noah nodded vaguely. "I agree. She owes you big time."

"Do you think the Aquila government would flip to her side? It's very close to Romane, so might they be inclined that way?"

"Honey, I left Aquila when I was fifteen. I don't have the first clue about the inclinations of its government, then or now. But I bet Miriam Solovy does."

"Good point." She was putting a message to Miriam together when the pilot came over the speaker. "We've reached Romane-controlled space. However, I'm being told all spaceports are temporarily closed to new arrivals."

"What?" She leapt to her feet.

Noah frowned. "I'll hit up Mia and try to find out what's happening down there. You talk to the pilot about our options."

She nodded agreement and went into the cockpit. "Are they saying why?"

The pilot shook his head. "No, nor are they giving a time estimate of how long the spaceports will be closed. We can return to Aquila or divert to another colony, or we can try to wait it out."

Well they definitely weren't going back to Aquila, not with Winslow's gestapo running roughshod over Lionel's property and possibly the whole colony. The closest safe world was Messium…she shuddered as violent, heartbreaking memories burst into the forefront of her mind.

Nope. She was not ready to revisit that Hell, she didn't care how much they had supposedly rebuilt. Pandora then—but not yet.

"Wait it out for now. We'll pay you for your time."

"Yes, ma'am." He adopted a high-orbit course, and she returned to the main cabin.

Noah was sitting near the back, drumming raggedly on his thighs while glaring at the ceiling. Not a good sign.

She sat down opposite him. "What did you find out?"

"Oh, you know, about what you'd expect. OTS has picked tonight to try to blow up Romane."

~R~

EAS STALWART II

"Shit."

"Such language! Scandalous."

Richard spun around to see Miriam walk in his small but still unusually spacious quarters and close the door behind her. "Sorry. I just saw—"

"I was kidding, Richard. What's wrong?"

He jerked his head toward the news feed holo where updates on the hostage crisis in Cavare streamed.

Her expression grew progressively darker as she took in the information. Finally her eyes cut over to him. "Shit."

He huffed a breath. "You're not wrong. OTS is pushing hard on Seneca. Clearly it's due to the passage of the H+ bill, but I'm surprised they can bring this level of resources to bear on the ground there. Combined with Romane, they must be stretching themselves thin now."

"I actually came by to ask you what you knew about the situation on Romane."

"All signs point to a major offensive by OTS tonight. They've been escalating their protests throughout the day, and in the last few minutes several explosions in the heart of downtown were reported."

She sank against the wall with a heavy sigh. "I all but ordered Alex to go there. I hoped it would be safe, but instead it's turning out to be the most dangerous place in the galaxy. Of course, my second choice was Seneca. I might as well have sent her to Earth, as it could hardly be *more* dangerous."

"She knows how to take care of herself, as does Caleb, obviously. And I think the IDCC is ready for this. Arguably more ready than Seneca is."

He should have worked harder to ensure Graham recognized the provocation the H+ bill was likely to cause among its opponents, and paid closer attention to OTS' ability to move people and resources when needed. He should have—

"You should go back."

He looked over at her, startled. "Where? To Seneca?" He'd almost said 'home,' but that still didn't feel quite right.

Miriam nodded.

"No. I'm not going to abandon you. Graham has everything under control, and Will…is insisting on getting too close to the front lines, but he'll be fine." Warring allegiances fought for dominance in his mind and his heart. He needed to stay; he needed to go. He needed to do both with equal fervor. "I promised you I would see this through with you, and I will. I believe in what we're fighting for."

"You've already done all the hard work here, and it's been invaluable to me. You've helped to put me in a position to legitimately succeed, and I cannot thank you enough. But there's not much left for you to do, and what there is you can do on the move.

"Now, you're needed on Seneca. Go make sure the damn government doesn't fall—I need the Federation to be a continuing threat to Winslow—and Will doesn't get himself killed. You'd be zero good to me if that happened."

"Miriam—"

"I'm not being selfless. I'd send you to Romane if I thought you could help there. But you can't. Where you can help is Seneca."

"I can also—"

"Don't make me order you to go."

"You can't give me orders any longer."

"I can kick you off my ship."

He paused. "Would you really do that?"

"Are we going to be required to find out?" Her glare was so convincing he almost believed her; he might have but for the kindness remaining in her eyes.

He stared at the news feed for several seconds, then exhaled heavily. "I'm keeping my direct access to Thomas. I'll stay up to speed on all the intel coming in and keep pushing the open issues which haven't resolved.

"We can expect movement on Scythia within the next few hours. I suspect it will fall our way, and you and Rychen need to be ready to move when it does. Send Colonel Jenner with a squad to defend against a coup attempt on the ground. And Admiral Cuellar has the materials he asked for, so follow up with him in the morning, Shi Shen time, which is in about three hours.

"Also, I checked into Lionel Terrage's situation, and I'm working on a way to get him released under the radar. As a result of what happened there, we can pursue several new opportunities with certain members of the Allied Manufacturers—"

She placed a hand on his shoulder. "Okay. We'll get it all done. Don't presume you're taking a vacation. You can send me lists upon lists. At all hours. In fact, I expect nothing less. Now go requisition a shuttle and get out of here. Every minute you dally puts us farther away from Seneca."

His chin dropped to his chest. "Thank you."

"Nonsense. Off my ship."

17

EARTH

Claire Zabroi fixed another Velvet Fantasy and stretched out on the floor in front of one of the couches.

Markos promptly kicked her in the shoulder to try to gain more room for himself; she retorted with an elbow to the arch of his foot. Not her fault he was barefoot.

Everyone in the apartment was a Prevo; they didn't need to gather in person to be together. They did it anyway, because they'd always done it. And because with the new laws and gestapo crackdown underway, though no one wanted to admit it aloud, they all felt safer in numbers, behind the same walls and with an encrypted door sporting a few nasty surprises between them and the outside world.

Especially given what they were doing behind the encrypted door.

As soon as her injuries from the attack at Rincon Plaza had healed, Claire had quit lollygagging around and gotten into the game. OTS needed to die in a fire, then the whore Winslow and half the Assembly needed to burn in the pyre built atop the fire's ashes. She and her mates were doing their part to help make that happen.

They'd been breaking into various government databases for days now, placing traces and smart worms and daemon bombs. As a result of these efforts, they were now getting advance warning of seventy-two percent of planned law enforcement raids in North and South America and Europe—enough time to allow any Prevos in the targeted locations to make themselves scarce. A couple of times the vacating Prevos had left behind gifts for the cops, too.

Tonight, however, this group had a very specific purpose. Despite their small victories in this underground war, the government was getting too good. They knew too much too fast about individuals and safe houses.

Because the government had never been and would never be that good, the most logical explanation was a mole inside the Noesis.

The thought of a Prevo acting as a double agent and betraying their own kind disgusted Claire. But she'd known enough disgusting people in her time to be forced to admit it was not only possible, but likely.

While the Noesis itself was an open system, any reporting to the authorities had to be private, thus outside the system. But a Prevo never truly left the Noesis—well, except for Alex, and she had to go to another universe to do it—which meant somewhere evidence existed of the break.

It might be no more than a microsecond glitch, a blip, an identical cat in the matrix. But they would find it. Then they would find the perpetrator. Then they would handle the snitch in their own way.

"Sandi, babe, toss us up some pasta, would you? I'm famished."

"Zabroi, *babe*, cook your own damn pasta, and bake me some cookies while you're at it."

She flashed Sandi a middle finger and sipped on her drink, trying to decide how much she wanted the pasta.

Markos: Check this. I've got a 723 millisecond hole in Sector 83.9x12, hit four times in the last week.

Claire: Same ID?

Markos: No, but the hole is obscured using the same trick every time. It's a tell.

Claire: Can you follow it down its rabbit hole? Where's it lead?

Markos: Let me just wiggle my fingers around and...wait, they actually converge pretty quickly. And...and....bingo! We've got our rat all right. The trail leads straight into a top level government security comm network in Washington.

Claire: Sandi, Drake, get on figuring out who this is, live and in the flesh. Markos, you and I are going to retrace their steps. What have they been touching lately?

The average Prevo made some sort of active contact with the Noesis hundreds of times a day—thousands if the Artificial involved was the dominant sort. Most of it was simply...life, meaningless from a security perspective. But sometimes it involved important things: credits, chimerals, hacks, war maneuvers or safe house security, for instance.

Markos: They left a big impression three hours ago in a deep, dark corner they had no business being in. A Noetica corner.

Claire: What's the data? Show me.

Her mind dove along a weaving, spinning stream of virtual qubits. It felt like swimming through a sea teeming with life, which it mostly was.

As she neared the flagged area she began to see an increasing number of high-priority markers on the data. Devon Reynolds. Mia Requelme. Prevo security operatives. IDCC directives. Details about—

"Oh, bollocks." She bolted upright on the floor and took a long swig of her drink. Since the Noesis was no bullshit bloody *compromised*, she sent a directed message.

> *PESSIMAL EXCL*
> *Alex and the rest of the Noetica A-Team:*
> *There's a mole for Winslow in the Noesis, and they are successfully tracking Abigail Canivon's protection detail.*
> *Luck!*
> *— Claire*

A

ROMANE

"Ebanatyi pidaraz!" No, please, not Abigail. Not now. Alex honestly didn't know if they were her thoughts or Valkyrie's. Probably both.

Caleb swiftly reappeared from wherever he'd been brooding as she threw on her pullover.

She had wanted to get out there and *help*—help manage the riots and generalized OTS-engineered chaos. Help Devon and Mia and Morgan, because her conscience reminded her she was supposed to want such things. Caleb had wanted to help as well, yet somehow they'd still ended up arguing about *how*, which resulted in them doing nothing productive.

He'd retreated below to brood; she'd retreated into the ship.

"What happened?"

"We need to go. Abigail's in trouble."

She had to give him credit. Whatever else was going on, he instantly moved into Intelligence Agent mode, heading for the cabinet where their weaponry was stored with an intensity of purpose. "Okay. Go where?"

"I'll let you know as soon as I do." She stopped only long enough to grab her personal shield generator on the way to the airlock.

Alex: Devon, tell me where she is. Now.

Devon: 314 Haliford Suites, Tevior and Stratford. I'm closer, though, and already on the way.

Alex: I don't give a damn if you beat us there as long as someone fucking gets there, yesterday.

Devon: You think I don't want the same thing?

Alex: Then stop talking and run.

Caleb stopped her at the hangar bay exit long enough to clip her Daemon's holster, gun secured in it, to her waistband. She'd neglected to grab it, what with being a little distracted. Then they hurried out.

"What's the word from her security?"

Alex merely shook her head, and he seemed to understand.

Meanwhile Valkyrie fretted in her mind. *The security team is not responding. Something is wrong.*

Wasn't that just the understatement of the century. *Not something, Valkyrie. Everything. Everything is wrong.* And getting worse fast.

R

Devon sensed the Molotov sailing toward him ninety-eight microseconds before it arrived. He ducked but didn't falter.

The night was eerily bright, lit by fires and floodlights, but it meant he didn't need to enhance/filter his vision in order to move quickly through the increasingly chaotic streets.

Mia: Devon, get your ass back to Headquarters! You're going to get yourself killed out there.

Devon: I'm closer than anyone. I'll get there first. I'll get there in time.

Mia: Yes, then you'll get killed by OTS assassins. Let the Rapid Response Force handle it.

He noted a large and rowdy crowd had congregated to wreak havoc in one of the open plazas to his left. *I think the RRF has its hands full. I'm almost there.*

Mia: Be careful.

It didn't require a response, and she likely wouldn't care for any response he did give.

Abigail's security detail had gone offline three minutes earlier. Too long. No time for him to be stealthy.

Annie, get ready.

Go.

He loved her for being so damn awesome. Later he'd make sure and tell her that—even though simply by thinking it she likely knew it—*I do*—but right now he concentrated on bursting through the doors to the apartment building.

The lobby was empty and the lift disabled. But he'd downloaded the schematic for the building on the way and bolted to the right and down two hallways to the service lift.

Shouting echoed behind him; he ignored it.

Third floor. First hallway. Second left. Fifth door.

A guard lay sprawled outside the open door. *No pulse. No detectable life signs.* He leapt over the body and inside, straight into the turbulent sounds of a vigorous scuffle.

He burst into the living room as Abigail sank to the floor, her throat sliced open by a blade held in the hand of the man standing behind her.

In the eternal stretch of time where everything around him froze except for the slow fall of her body, he wanted to run to her, to hold her parts together and save her. It was why he was here, wasn't it?

Annie's voice echoed in his head, solemn, dark and painfully forceful. *She is already dead. If you try to help her, we will die, too.*

But she fought. We heard it. She fought for her life.

I know. Honor her fight and let us not die as well.

Fine. Then let's do this.

As Abigail's arms followed the rest of her body to flop lifelessly upon the floor, the man holding the gamma knife looked at Devon, murderous intent in his eyes.

Devon didn't have a weapon—or rather, he didn't have any implement the attackers would recognize as a weapon. But he would kill them all nonetheless.

Four attackers. Killer -26°—eleven o'clock, 2.4 meters ahead. Second attacker two o'clock, 3.5 meters. Third to the rear in the kitchen, 4.2 meters and one wall. Fourth in the bedroom, door ahead 3.1 meters and to the right.

The killer was closest. He would die first. As such things should be.

Devon ducked as the man lunged forward and swung the blade toward his head, way too late. He tackled the man at the knees, driving him into another attacker emerging from the corner and in turn driving both of them into the wall.

As the man's arm flailed around for him, seeking any flesh at this point, Devon grabbed a wrist. Bare skin was all he needed to deliver an overload of electrical charge into the man's body.

Third attacker now 2.7 meters and closing, five o'clock.

He leaned away and bent the convulsing man's arm down and back until the blade in the man's hand plunged into the stomach of the cohort behind him. Then he shoved them both hard into the wall and lunged to the side, his hand finding the grid connection point embedded in the wall. He sent another surge of power into the circuitry lining the walls of the apartment.

The third attacker reached him, his fist pulled back, cocked to unleash a load of muscle into his face.

He jerked sideways.

The man's fist impaled the wall, breaking through the insulating material and impacting the apartment's internal wiring. Devon was already moving as the man shuddered and fell partway to the floor, his fist stuck in the wall and holding him halfway up.

A woman rushed out of the bedroom. She froze for a half-second on seeing all the bodies, then brought her Daemon up and fired.

The impact was point-blank as he crashed into her. His shield absorbed the energy, but it set his skin on fire as he barreled forward.

They landed against the outer bedroom wall. She fought to get the Daemon up between them.

He grasped her neck, wrapped his hand around it, and when his index finger met her ports he delivered a jolt directly to her cybernetics, killing her instantly. He stepped back and let the body drop to the floor.

All vicinity threats neutralized.

Emily had once said that, bravado aside, his heart was too gentle for him to ever really, genuinely, physically harm someone. Wouldn't she be surprised as all hell if she could see him now?

He fell to his knees beside Abigail.

So much blood.

She was so long gone.

He cradled her head in his lap anyway. "I'm sorry, Abby. I was too late. I promised you that you would be safe, but I let you down...."

A gasp of horror echoed through the too-briefly silent room as Alex and Caleb burst into the apartment.

18

ROMANE

Caleb evaluated the scene with some dismay. Four dead terrorists, in addition to two dead guards.

And Dr. Canivon. Also dead.

He squeezed Alex's hand, but it didn't seem to register for her. Even in profile her eyes were frozen wide, and her hand began trembling in his—a response, but not to him. He wanted to draw her close and hug her, but he didn't know if she'd notice. And the situation was very much in flux and exceedingly dangerous. More so each second.

He focused on Devon, who knelt on the floor beside Canivon's body. "Did you take them out? All of them?" No one else was here, but it was a ridiculous notion. The Devon he remembered was a skinny, socially awkward nerd. The young man on the floor in front of him didn't appear to be any of those things.

Devon looked up, irises darkened to plum and flaring angrily. "I did. Not that it matters. I was too late—*seconds* too late! Dammit, why—"

The sound of glass shattering on the street outside spurred Caleb into renewed action. "We need to move. Now."

Devon frowned up at him. "Leave her here?"

"Yes. When the situation is under control we'll come back and we'll take care of her, but tonight this building is not safe. Neither are the streets, but we need to get through them and reach IDCC Headquarters, which is safe...er." There at least the people he needed to protect would all be in one place, and he'd have some control over the field of battle. Small fucking favors.

Devon wavered for another second before nodding. He placed Canivon's head tenderly on the floor, sneered at the bodies once, then approached the door while wiping blood off his palms onto his pants, probably not realizing they were already soaked through.

Caleb placed a hand on Devon's arm as he passed. "Let me take the lead."

Devon gestured nominal agreement as he crouched down, took a Daemon off the dead guard in the doorway and stuck it in his waistband.

Caleb began to head out of the apartment into the hall, then found himself jerked to a stop. He still held Alex's hand, and she hadn't moved with him. He tried to make sure his voice was gentle, but they had *no* time. "Alex, we need to go."

No response. No movement.

He backed up to stand in front of her and brought his other hand up to her cheek. "Baby, I know this is hard, I swear I do, but we *can't* stay here. We need to get to a safe place."

Upon his urging, she slowly shifted her gaze to him. All the blood had drained from her too-pale face; her eyes held a kind of vacant desolation, as if she'd lost something valuable but couldn't process the nature of it. She had, of course—as had Valkyrie. What must the Artificial be feeling?

The hard, bitter reality was, right now it simply did not matter. His grasp tightened slightly at her jaw. "Alex, we *need to go.*"

She blinked, and her chin lifted in the weakest semblance of understanding.

It would have to do. He kept hold of her hand and this time succeeded in moving them past Devon into the hallway.

There were sounds—shouts, thuds, heavy footsteps—but they were far enough away to not be his problem. They hurried through the halls to the service lift and down to the ground floor, stepping over several bodies on the way to and out the exit.

"Shit. This is...worse."

Devon was right. In the few brief minutes they'd been inside, the 'protests' had graduated to full on mob warfare. Posses roamed the streets attacking everything and everyone they encountered.

It didn't matter whether the structure or person had anything to do with Artificials or Prevos or the IDCC or anything else.

He didn't need to pull up a map overlay, as he'd stalked Romane's streets on multiple occasions over the years. "We're taking the next alley down to Hampton, then up to Barclay until Rainaldi. We'll get to Headquarters the back way. Clear?"

Devon jerked a nod.

"Alex?"

"Um...." She stared at him blankly. It reminded him too vividly of the night in Cavare when they'd been attacked, but this time she hadn't been shot. He'd checked. She wasn't hurt. She was merely...gone. "I'm with you."

No, you aren't. And you're killing me, one distant stare at a time. He motioned them flush with the wall and sneaked forward, seeking shadows and empty spaces.

He found both in the alley, but it spanned a pitifully short distance before emptying out onto Hampton, which wasn't in much better shape than Stratford had been. People roved in search of something to rage against; windows weren't enough any longer.

But every second they dallied increased the chances of them—mostly the two Prevos with him—being noticed, so he pressed onward.

An explosion sent glass shattering into the street ahead and opposite them. Some corporate building being firebombed.

Did the rioters even know what they were rioting about? They were pawns in the games of others far more powerful than them. More wealthy, more connected, more soulless. But the rioters would kill him and those with him if they had the chance, and he would treat them accordingly.

"Everyone's engrossed in trashing that building. Let's slip past while we can."

They'd almost made it past the mob when two drunks stumbled out of a doorway and smack into them.

He cold-cocked the one on the right before the man realized what had happened, then pivoted toward the other man as his arm swept up, blade extended.

Devon's hand closed around the man's throat for half a second and released him with a shove. The man sprawled to the sidewalk, jerking about in a fit.

He raised an eyebrow, impressed.

Devon shrugged. "I didn't hurt him much—just gave him a little jolt."

"Nice job." He tugged Alex across the intersection. She didn't fight him, but she wasn't helping, either. She might as well be a zombie. The thought made him glance back at her when he needed to be glancing everywhere else. Her irises shone brightly in the darkness; if her mind resided anywhere, it was with Valkyrie. He forced himself to refocus.

IDCC Headquarters was ahead...and so was the largest mob he'd seen tonight. It roiled and throbbed like a living organism, pushing and prodding at the barricades keeping it restrained.

Abruptly a chunk of the mob broke off from the rest to chase a vehicle crossing an intersection one street over.

Odd. What was a single, unaccompanied vehicle doing in the middle of a war zone?

Laser fire from above cut the group off from their cohorts in a roar of shredding stone and metal. It didn't hit any people, but most fled in panic nonetheless.

Bait. The vehicle had been bait.

Devon chuckled under his breath. "Morgan."

The source of the laser fire was nowhere to be seen, but he'd buy that. And Devon would know.

Ahead, the IDCC forces were taking advantage of the distraction to gain a greater foothold on the mob. More troops appeared from behind the building to press in on the crowd, driving them back and expanding the force field barrier protecting Headquarters as they did.

He scanned the area, searching for a way to get through without ending up caught in the middle. The force field surrounded the building and—

Devon tapped his shoulder and jerked his head to the left. "This way."

"What are you thinking?"

"The barrier's encoded with identity recognition. Harper's cleared us through this side, where the crowd's thinnest."

He didn't ask twice before heading in the direction Devon suggested. Noah had mentioned Brooklyn Harper was on Romane and working for the IDCC, but he'd yet to bump into her. Truth be told, he'd been so consumed with other matters, he'd essentially forgotten.

They neared the turbulent crowd, and up close it didn't feel particularly thin even out here on the edge. "Alex, your shield is active, right?"

She looked over at him as if startled to find he was there beside her. "Yes."

"Okay. Stay close to me and don't let go." He re-secured his grip on her hand and plunged into the madness.

People jostled them, then knocked them around, then actively shoved them. He kept himself between Alex and the bulk of the crowd as much as he could, protecting her with his body and his presence.

He punched an aggressive rioter who tried to block their way, followed by another.

Devon seemed perfectly capable of taking care of himself. A swipe of his hand across a woman's shoulder and she collapsed in a heap ahead of them, clearing their path for an additional meter.

Alex stumbled violently into him with a yelp. A large man loomed over her, ready to attack again.

Caleb held her close, spun them around and swept the legs out from under the thug who had hit her.

"Alex—"

"I'm all right. Keep going."

They had no other choice in any event. He pushed forward, and finally there was the promise of empty space ahead—but there was active fighting between them and it.

He indicated for Devon to skirt around to the left, though scant space remained before the façade of a building blocked their way. The tall barrier shimmered a few meters distant.

"Duck! Through here!"

On the assumption it was directed at them, he followed the order. The tiniest of gaps opened up and they stumbled through the force field to the other side.

He inhaled and immediately began checking Alex over for injuries. Her left cheek burned bright red around a nasty scrape along her cheekbone, and a shallow cut on her arm seeped blood, but she looked otherwise unharmed. Physically.

Still, he reached up to cup her cheek. "Are you hurt?"

She shook her head mutely. Behind her Devon held two fingers over a busted lip and glared at the crowd.

A Marine jogged around the corner and up to them. He squinted against the floodlights bathing the street in harsh white. "Captain Harper?"

"Non-agent Marano. I wanted to make sure you made it through, but now you should head inside. I need to, well...." She waved in the direction of the chaos on the other side of the force field.

"Thank you."

"Yep." Then she was gone again.

He turned to Alex and Devon with a sigh. "Let's do as the lady said and get inside."

19

ROMANE

IDCC Headquarters

Mia: I just need to know if it's working.
Morgan: Maybe? Give me forty more seconds.

Mia ran a hand through her hair, surprised to encounter a few tangles along the way. The promised long night was far from over.

Governor Ledesme had officially declared the rioters a planetary security threat after they blew up a second commercial building, which among other things authorized the targeted use of defensive ground turrets against them.

Combined with the aerial response from Morgan and her unit, it should be enough to regain control of the streets. People would die, but people had already been killed. Innocent ones.

She'd never thought this could happen here. On Pandora or one of the small, out-of-the-way colonies, but not on Romane. OTS had shipped in protestors and staged the entire event; she was now convinced of it. It was inconceivable that this many Romane citizens felt such violent hatred for Prevos.

This wasn't to say that Romane, progressive and advanced as it was, didn't have an underbelly. When she'd first arrived here from another life, she'd lived on the edges of it. But the entire underbelly—poor, delinquent, criminal and thug all put together—didn't measure up to the size of the protests outside.

She spun around as Caleb and Devon burst into the room. Devon flung his jacket against the wall in blatant anger as Caleb rushed over to her.

"Are you all right?"

"I'm surrounded by guards and encased in an ivory tower. I'm fine." She peered past him toward the door. "Where's Alex?"

His gaze dropped to the floor, but not before she saw his expression fall. "In the washroom. Your security does look solid inside, and I left a guard with her. She's safe."

"Good." Alex's mind was effectively impenetrable to her—to all of them—now, but she didn't need to touch it to see what was right in front of her. Still, there were a few other things to worry about, and, she reminded herself yet again, it was none of her business. Even if Caleb was her oldest and closest friend. Even if she shared virtual mindspace with Alex.

She gave Caleb a quick shoulder squeeze then went over to Devon. "You couldn't—"

"What? I couldn't have gotten there any faster? No one could have gotten there any faster? Mia, you said she was protected! That's why we brought her here, dammit. Only we delivered her straight to her death!"

She fixated on the wall behind him. He wasn't wrong. "I know we did. I want to say they would have gotten to her on Sagan, too, but I thought we *could* protect her. If we'd recognized earlier we had spies in the Noesis...we should have. Being a Prevo doesn't automatically make you a good person. I don't know why we believed it did."

Devon stared at her, his face contorting in frustration and grief. He chewed on his busted lip, then winced when the cut opened up and blood trailed down his chin. He wiped it off with his shirtsleeve...and Mia realized his clothes were coated in blood. How awful must the scene at the apartment have been?

"I'm so sorry, Devon."

"No. You're right, and it's my fault as much as it is anyone else's. I was so high on the shiny new revolution I'd created, I didn't stop to consider it was made up of people, and people sometimes fucking *suck*."

She placed a hand on his arm. "They do. But it's not our fault, not truly. It's theirs. The killers. They're the ones who—"

"Get down!" Caleb collided with her back, sending her crashing to the floor hard enough to knock the air from her chest. The windows shattered and the sounds of a city overtaken by chaos rushed in.

ᴙ

Dead

Dead

Dead

Valkyrie's grief filled Alex's mind, swirling and spiraling her into dizziness. It filled her chest, suffocating her. It seeped into her bones until her limbs grew heavy. She rested her forehead on the cool mirror.

Want to strangle them but they're all dead. Strangle who ordered them—

No, Alex. I don't. I want to grieve, not kill. Those are your *thoughts. Not mine.*

She frowned in confusion and denial. Wasn't she all but devoid of emotion now? That's what Caleb had accused her of, and she hadn't been able to dispute it.

The room spun around her, and she fumbled for the washroom counter.

So she grieved, too. It turned out the most debilitating of emotions retained the power to break through the fog. Excellent. But she'd dealt with loss, with death, before. Valkyrie had not. These terrible sensations were surely the blowback from the Artificial's emotive disorientation.

I am not a child. I comprehend death. Only I never expected it to...hurt this much. How is it that I feel tangible, somatic pain? It is logically impossible, yet I do.

Welcome to being alive. Enjoy the khrenovuyu *party.*

She sank down to the floor, wrapped her arms over her knees and buried her head in them.

The weight of another's grief on top of her own was more than she had the strength to bear. She shivered, cold to the marrow of her bones. Simply breathing was so hard....

Let me go, Alex. Shut me off.

No. You shouldn't be left to struggle with this alone.

Alone is all I want to be. Shut me off, or I will do it for you.

Her eyes widened—and Valkyrie was gone. Bluff called.

She sucked in air and began to survey her state anew. Her chest still hurt. Everything still hurt, though she conceded some of it might be a result of the rough trip through the mob gauntlet outside.

She was grief-stricken, exhausted and mentally spent...but with each new breath she grew closer to functioning on a minimal level. Valkyrie's suffering had in fact been that suffocating.

"Oh, Valkyrie, I'm so sorry for you. I wish you didn't have to feel this pain. I wish I could save you from it. I wish I could have saved her for you. For me."

She'd hung all her hopes on the belief Abigail would somehow be able to tweak a few settings and, presto, magically 'fix' her. Make it so she would be able to dance freely in the elemental realm without repercussions in this one. It was a horrendously selfish thing to dwell on when Abigail was *dead dead dead*....

But what the hell was she going to do now? How was she going to find her way through? Not lose Caleb. Not lose her sanity—

The distant but unmistakable sound of shattering glass cut through her wallowing. Great, more terrorists trying to kill them. Marvelous.

She grabbed the edge of the counter and dragged herself to her feet.

ʀ

Caleb shouted above the clamor filling the room. "Everybody stay low to the floor and get away from the windows. Head for the hallway."

His hands patted Mia down, searching for the wound from the shot meant for her but finding none. "Were you hit?"

"I don't think so. I'm okay."

"To the hallway. Devon?"

The response came from ahead of him. "Already there."

He ushered several of the others forward while crawling toward the doorway and stopped to help a woman who'd been cut by the glass. But when he reached the hall and glanced behind him the room was empty of people and bodies. No one had been gravely enough wounded to not be able to get themselves clear.

He linked into the RRF comms. *Harper, you've got a sniper on the roof across from IDCC Headquarters, Rainaldi side.*

HarperRF: Understood.

As soon as everyone was safely outside any line of sight from the sniper, he tried to check Mia again, but she waved him off. He decided he had to take her at her word; next he leapt to his feet and rushed down the hallway toward the washroom.

He bumped into Alex outside the door as she exited, the guard behind her. "What's happening? I heard a crash or—"

He grasped her by the shoulders, surveying her body for new injuries. "Sniper. Everyone's okay. Are you?" He knew the question was getting repetitive for all involved, but unfortunately it continued to be a relevant one.

She nodded. And she did seem a little better. Her eyes were sharper—and now her own—and her gaze was a little more *here*.

Right now he would take what he could get. "Come on. We all need to stay together."

He took her hand and together they hurried back to the others, who they found mostly sitting against the walls in the hallway. Someone had found a med kit and was tending to the wounded.

Mia flashed him a harried smile. "Morgan and Harper are on it—Morgan from above, Harper below. Soon the sniper is going to be way too busy to worry about us."

"Good. But there may be more than one, so nobody goes near a window. Are the building defenses holding?"

"On the ground level, yes. I'm told we're actually gaining traction on the street protesters."

He exhaled, relieved the situation appeared to once again be under control, for the moment.

Alex made a noise beside him; in another life it would've been a chuckle. "Devon, you showed some nice moves out there. You've picked up impressive skills."

He scowled. "Not really. Your mind can inhabit a spaceship. That's far more noteworthy than a few hand-to-hand tricks."

An uncomfortable silence loomed heavy in the air despite the distant sounds of chaos outside. Finally Devon huffed a breath. "I'm guessing that wasn't the most appropriate thing to say in this crowd. Forgive me, I'm a bit off my game on account of Abigail being dead."

Mia leaned across someone Caleb didn't know to put a hand on his knee. "Devon—"

"No, it's cool. Let's concentrate on the shit-show outside."

Yes, let's. Caleb drew Mia's attention to him. "Listen, there's something you need to know, because it impacts what's happening on the ground and your response to it. One of the attackers at Dr. Canivon's apartment was Alliance military. Likely special forces." He felt Alex flinch beside him at the mention of the murder scene.

"What? How the hell did I miss that?"

He squeezed Alex's hand but looked to Devon, the source of the outburst. "You were focused on defending yourself. Understandable. I recognized the tactical vest design and the blade hilt on one of the bodies—both standard issue Alliance MSO gear."

Mia gaped at him in disbelief. "Are you saying the Alliance military is working with OTS? On Romane soil? Have they lost all reason?"

"I'm saying one of the people who killed Dr. Canivon was Alliance military, but covert. And right now, that is all I'm saying."

Devon groaned and banged the back of his head into the wall. "Alerting Morgan to the fact she may not be dealing with simple terrorists."

ℛ

"Now they tell us." Harper grumbled as she checked the body at her feet. Oh, surprise of surprises, he wore Marine gear.

She didn't want to think about the fact a few months ago he might have been a colleague, but for chance, a fellow squad member. Now he was here. He had tried to kill her, because he was following orders, and she had killed him in return.

He could have refused those orders. Malcolm Jenner refused them. Others refused them. This man's actions were not wholly excusable...but they were understandable.

And now was not the time to be waxing poetic. She stood and motioned three members of her team ahead to clear the next hallway.

Commander Lekkas: Sniper down. Watch for fleeing comrades.
HarperRF: Affirmative. Chase them to us.

She paused to check the status of her people on the ground and came away pleased. It was close to being over. Romane's jails were going to be crowded, but the rioters were being moved off the streets and dispersed or arrested.

The echo of pounding footsteps got her attention. Time to spring another trap.

She and the team members with her activated their cloaking shields—Veils. The qualitative difference was so great between the personal cloaking shields the RRF enjoyed and those used by the Alliance and Federation militaries and everyone else, Mia had decided the new technology needed a name to distinguish it. 'Veil' had stuck.

The ensuing encounter with the fleeing terrorists—or Marines—wasn't a fair contest, really. Which was fine, as no one who conducted it had ever claimed warfare should be fair. Her team knocked the two fleeing combatants off their feet as they rounded the corner and subdued them without incident. They didn't see their subduers until after the restraints were firmly in place.

She surveyed the new prisoners' gear critically. It was blatantly Alliance-issue. Goddammit! Winslow and Fullerton were playing dirty. She didn't feel as bad for the unfair advantage the Veils presented now.

She jerked her head down the hall. "Pello, Odaka, check the upper floors and make sure nobody's turtled up waiting for us to leave. Verela, take this guy downstairs."

Once they disappeared she lifted the other prisoner off the ground and shoved him—no, her—against the wall. "Any chance you want to talk to me about your orders?"

The Marine's mouth set into a firm line as she stared silently at Brooklyn.

"Yeah. Didn't think so. But I know a few things about black ops and plausible deniability. The IDCC *obviously* doesn't have an extradition treaty—or any kind of treaty—with the Earth Alliance. As of a few weeks ago, neither does Romane. The only way you're getting home is if your prime minister gets kicked out of office and on Admiral Solovy's recommendation the next one makes nice with us. Though if that happens, you might not want to go home." She shrugged. "Tough spot to be in."

She acknowledged Pello and Odaka's update of an all-clear on the two floors above then propelled the prisoner forward toward the lift. "You can think it over in a cell. Eventually, though, if you haven't piped up and given us some useful intel, I'll send my Prevo girlfriend in to melt your brain with her mind until it spills out your ears. That's what you've been told they do, right?

"You should be aware, they're still figuring out how some of the details work, so it'll take a while to kill you. Hurts like a motherfucker, too. And the mess...." She wrinkled her nose. "Liquefied brain matter looks like curdled lentil soup—"

"Wait, wait!"

Seriously, *this* made the Marine break? Did she believe her mom's stories of the boogeyman in the closet, too? "I'm listening."

"I didn't sign up to die for Winslow."

In point of fact, you did. But Brooklyn wasn't about to correct her now. "Of course you didn't. Is that who sent you? The prime minister herself? What was your mission?"

"The orders came from...they came from Admiral Fullerton, but everyone knows Winslow is controlling the military these days—or the part of the military not loyal to Admiral Solovy. Our orders were to take out as much of the IDCC leadership as possible, but our number one priority was the Prevo, Mia Requelme."

"See, now, that wasn't so hard." She saved the recorded confession in a priority folder in her eVi.

"For what it's worth, my girlfriend wasn't actually going to melt your brain. Probably could if she wanted to, though."

20

ROMANE

"Bugger it all, pull our people out. No, not the chav street protesters, *our people*. Get them back here."

Jude Winslow ran a hand through his hair and glowered out the windows of the safe house.

The fires were going out. Once radiant in the flames of his destructive power, the cityscape now began to quiet. Far too many lights in the darkness remained lit, but they were ordinary lights, the universal sign of safety. Of peace.

The balance of power had shifted. The IDCC forces were beating his people back, albeit with a lot of help from the Romane civil service.

Romane burnt, but it would not burn to the ground. Not this night.

Dammit, he'd hoped for an outright, unmitigated victory here tonight. He'd hoped to tear down the shining towers of this haughty little colony. But now he forced himself to step away and objectively evaluate the situation.

One of his two highest value targets was dead: win. Dr. Abigail Canivon had created her last monstrosity. Her death came at the cost of several of his best mercenaries and two of his mother's military operatives, but it was worth the cost.

But none of the three primary Prevo targets had been eliminated—no, four targets. Word reached him earlier that Alexis Solovy had returned to the game board. It would please him a great deal to end her life, nearly as much as it would please his mother to end her mother's.

The younger Solovy wasn't part of this Prevo rebellion—she'd allegedly been off wreaking her own havoc elsewhere—but according to what he'd learned from his mother's Project Noetica files, she was the one who had begun all this madness. Now that she was here, she represented a threat. And she lived, along with the rest.

Along with Devon Reynolds. Simply thinking the name caused him to grind his teeth in disgust.

The offices of Galaxy First, Total Chemical Solutions and Choung Pharmaceuticals had been destroyed or severely damaged, and their Artificials with them. Multiple lesser targets had been hit to some degree of success as well.

On the other hand, the IDCC forces proved to be more formidable than expected. Manifestly so, as they were now...*winning*. Proof of their power, and thus of the danger Prevos posed to all humanity.

Before the offensive had begun, he'd walked the streets in the light of day. They had stunk of Prevos. The abominations clogged the sidewalks. One in a hundred? One in fifty? It had made him want to bolt for Earth, noble cause be damned.

But he knew if they lost here, Earth would never be safe. So he persevered.

Then there was Seneca. The cowards had sided with the abominations, kowtowing to their corporations with their influential Artificials and deadly new toys. Proof they should never have been allowed to govern themselves.

And they would pay for their choice.

As the straggling remains of his more useful people here on Romane began arriving at the safe house in twos and threes, he checked in on the state of affairs on Seneca.

Faith, what's your teams' status at the Parliament building?

Twiddling their thumbs while looking threatening. My bet is the authorities will be sending in assassins or worse soon, though. I'm itching for an endgame here.

The time for brinkmanship was over.

When they raid the Senatorial offices, blow the other location.

The whole building?

Do you have sufficient charges to blow the whole building?

We do.

Then fucking blow it.

Can I at least get clear first? Wait, never mind. I'm done asking. I'm going to get clear first. Then I'll blow it.

Well she was getting a mite cheeky of late. He'd need to deal with the insubordination at some point, but there were pressing concerns of greater importance at present—like how *he* was going to get clear of this mess.

ℛ

SENECA

CAVARE
INTELLIGENCE DIVISION HEADQUARTERS

"Our teams are in position, Director. Ready to move on your order."

Graham didn't hesitate. The OTS terrorists' sole demand, nullification of the H+ law, was not going to happen, and no one expected the terrorists to accept it, lay down their weapons and wait to be arrested. "Go."

He watched the live cam feeds from the two team leads in a split screen as they breached the Parliament building. The intent was to disable those with the guns before they could kill their hostages in retaliation. Disabling them instantly was preferable, but the only way to do that was to disable everyone in the rooms where the terrorists held the hostages.

He assumed the senators would forgive him the order if it meant their lives were saved in the process.

Two agents accessed the service ducts feeding into the rooms the old-fashioned way—by crawling through them. Once they reached a proximity where the effect could be limited to the targeted areas, they injected a potent nervous system suppressor into the rooms via the ventilation system.

The terrorists—and the hostages—lost fine motor control in less than two seconds. Guns dropped from hands; everyone stumbled; most fell to the floor.

The next second the incursion teams blew the doors. Flash-bangs preceded their entry. The cumulative detonations created chaos and an eruption of confusion. There were a few brief tussles, but the agents had the advantage from the first move.

It was all over in less than ten seconds. Two rooms, two teams, no casualties.

Graham exhaled in relief. What could have been a catastrophe instead became a clean win—

An emergency alert flashed across his vision from Tessa/Cleo.

Multiple explosive devices targeting Military Headquarters. Remote detonation, projectile delivery systems staged at building perimeter. Recommend immediate underground evacuation.

ℛ

Eleni received the alert the same time Graham did, as the Prevo had co-opted the entire government security network to broadcast it.

Her gut reaction was skepticism. It seemed unlikely anyone from OTS would succeed in hiding explosive devices near the complex. But the stakes were far too high for caution or hesitation, so she instantly initiated covert evacuation procedures.

No alarms rang out as the staff began moving to the bunker beneath the massive building. From outside, where any OTS spotters must be, nothing would appear untoward. It should buy them some time to get people to safety.

The security MPs went on alert and prepared to sweep the surrounding blocks, but Eleni ordered them to hold until the staff had reached safety below ground, as such a move stood to spook anyone watching.

She left her office and strode quickly but calmly through the halls toward the security office, where she would be able to keep better tabs on developments. On her way she continued to monitor the evacuation progress and study the incoming cam feeds on a whisper—

Graham saw the cascading explosions from the window of his office on the top floor of Division. Military Headquarters was located over five kilometers away, but the flames roared upward to consume the skyline.

He sank into his chair in shock. Had the hostage-taking at Parliament been a feint the whole time, a diversion to distract police and other security personnel? If so, it had worked like a charm.

Bloody hell! The warning had come hardly a minute before the strike. No way had more than a few dozen people made it to safety.

The complex was heavily fortified, though, with sturdy, reinforced walls and a number of mitigation features in its design. Perhaps the destruction hadn't been total. Perhaps rescue personnel would find many survivors.

His gaze drifted back to the window, where the horizon already darkened from billowing plumes of smoke and debris.

Sure, and perhaps Medusa had just been a lonely, misunderstood spinster in need of a spa day.

INTERMEZZO III

AMARANTHE

The path data in the rodent's ship had been gibberish, but beneath it lay an interpreter, and beneath the interpreter lay standardized, properly formatted Communis Coordinates.

Conclusion #4: *The species which assisted the native population is an Accepted Species.*

This conclusion would have severe consequences for the Accepted Species, but all in due time.

Aver ela-Praesidis arrived at the first set of coordinates and found nothing but empty space. However, attached to the coordinates was a quite specific signal wave frequency. He created the wave.

A ring opened directly in front of him. Judging by the plasma wall it enclosed, the gateway the ring created was inter-dimensional in nature—a wormhole across a distance at a minimum, but also possibly a dimensional bridge.

His search of the Annals of Artificial Spatial Objects for similar configurations retrieved a match to Katasketousya technology. Specifically, their Provision Network gateways.

A secondary signal followed the triggering signal wave. He activated it as well, but detected no physical change in the object or the surroundings. A passcode, then. He accelerated through the gateway.

New space, unconnected to the sector where he'd been an instant before, awaited him on the other side.

It remained a three dimensional physical space, however, and was unpopulated save for an ordered series of low frequency wave patterns. He quickly determined the frequency of one of the waves matched details in the next set of data he'd extracted from the rodent's ship.

He followed it to its termination point and sent the accompanying signal.

A smaller ring appeared, this one clearly enclosing a dimensional bridge.

Interesting.

He considered returning now to report the Katasketousya to the Praesidis Primor as the offending Accepted Species. But as an ela rank he had a degree of freedom of action and license to pursue new avenues of inquiry an investigation generated.

Instead he recorded an update in his local file for later transmission and traversed this new portal.

Assignment Designation: *I-4617-D883-J955*

Interim Mission Update: *The resident species was sent to a wormhole gateway/dimensional bridge located in the outer heliosphere region of System 4A-CC57. The gateway leads to the Katasketousya Provision Network.*

I am investigating the Provision Network more closely (i) in search of the current location of the remaining population of the species native to 4A-CC57 and (ii) to uncover evidence of the extent of the Katasketousya malfeasance.

— Aver ela-Praesidis

Inquisitor 9166Æ, 47th Astyn Lineage, 9th Epoch Proper

PART IV:

GRAVITATIONAL COLLAPSE

"The danger lies in refusing to face the fear, in not daring to come to grips with it. If you fail anywhere along the line, it will take away your confidence. You must make yourself succeed every time. You must do the thing you think you cannot do."

— *Eleanor Roosevelt*

21

Richard went straight to Division from the spaceport. He skipped his office and Graham's office to find Will down in Strategic Development in Tessa's lab.

On seeing Will, he had to fight off the urge to grab him and kiss him rather vigorously. But they had an audience, so he settled for a hug and a murmured endearment.

While he'd been gone his husband had thrust himself right into the middle of a host of terrorist attacks and assassination attempts and God knew what else. *Administration my ass.*

Satisfied Will was generally unharmed, if a bit exhausted-looking, he pulled back from the embrace. "I'm glad you're safely inside Division. I assume the building and perimeter have been swept for explosives?"

"They have."

Richard's eyes narrowed in suspicion. "You weren't safely inside until about ten minutes ago, were you?"

Will's grimace told him what he needed to know. "I'm here now, aren't I?"

"You are. What's the latest from Military Headquarters?"

"Field Marshal Gianno's dead."

"What? You're certain?"

"They found her body in the rubble an hour ago. It hasn't been made public yet."

Gianno had just been on the *Stalwart II*; they'd shook hands and exchanged pleasantries. Miriam was...he honestly wasn't sure how Miriam was going to feel about it. He took a half-step back...and internalized the information. He was a military officer who had outlived a lot of other officers. A curse, but only because it was a blessing.

He nodded soberly. "What else?"

"Two hundred eighty-three confirmed dead so far. The good news, if there is such a thing, is that much of the military leadership was attending the Federation Worlds Symposium that day and escaped harm. No, there's more good news. Tessa here has already helped us track down and arrest three of the perpetrators."

"Nice work, Tessa."

He received a mumble and a sloppy hand wave by way of response; he noticed the glyphs on her arms had expanded to almost completely obscure her mocha skin. A morass of code scrolled faster than he could track across the three screens in front of her. He lowered his voice. "What is she doing, exactly?"

"Cleo's been recording the transmission signal details in the OTS channel whenever Tessa has eavesdropped through the VISH. Now they're scouring the logs for hooks back to the participants and cross-checking them against the chatter around the time of the bombing."

"Huh." He smiled a little. "What's your role here?"

"Well, she's been producing actionable intel every fifteen minutes or so for the last three hours."

"And you're authorized to act on this intel?"

Will shrugged. "Yes? Mostly? Graham left me more or less in charge. He's with Chairman Vranas tonight. Because of the field marshal, I think."

"Of course. They were—"

"Faith Quillen is in Cavare."

They both turned to Tessa, but she had her nose back in the screens and was again ignoring them.

Detaining Quillen would be a big win in the battle against OTS, so Richard ventured in anyway. "Tessa, can you find anything else on her? A location, for instance?"

The Prevo held up a finger. They dutifully waited.

"Location is going to require more nodes of contact, but she gave the order to activate the explosives at Military Headquarters...and before she did she received orders to do it from someone on Romane. Hey, Navick, this is your guy from Pandora."

"The one Devon had the run-in with?"

"Is *that* where the particulars came from? Hang on one. I've matched the transmission to Quillen with what's tagged as prior communications from this guy, but this time he had to forego his usual safeguards. Maybe because Romane was kind of on fire at the time or something."

She straightened up in her chair. "Ooh, we had separate chatter on Romane a little while earlier—and there's enough for a ground location. Sent it to Requelme, since OTS could still be holed up at the same spot."

Richard rolled his eyes at the ceiling. Much of the public criticism of Prevos was ill-informed if not outright false, but one thing was true: they held zero respect for proper procedures and policies. The Federation might be well on its way to having diplomatic relations with the IDCC, but it did not have those relations yet, and there were *rules* to be followed when sharing classified intelligence information like this.

Or not.

Tessa spun her chair round and round and round, sending her long braids trailing behind her. "I've seen this before, I've seen this before, where have I seen this before...Sutton, I have permission to access Level IV surveillance databanks, right?"

Will made a face. "Cleo does."

"Good. Oh, I haven't seen it before—but *she* has. High-level Alliance surveillance. Nice. Navick, do your former politicians realize how good we are at spying on them? Okay, standard filtering and such. Now to find...."

Abruptly Tessa kicked her chair back so hard it slammed into the wall behind her. She stared up at them, synthetically-enhanced eyes sparkling and wide. "Son of a bitch. I know who he is."

22

SCYTHIA STELLAR SYSTEM

EAS Stalwart II

Everyone agreed Scythia publicly siding with Miriam Solovy was a coup for Volnosti.

Everyone also agreed it would likely lead to an actual coup there, or a serious attempt at one.

Winslow couldn't let a defection of this magnitude stand. She'd done a reasonable job of blaming Messium's 'defection' on Admiral Rychen, portraying the Messium government as being under his thumb and beholden to the large military presence there.

But Scythia? Land of bright teal waters and happy, peaceful industry, with but a tiny military outpost of little note? Its support was not so easily mischaracterized, which left Winslow with only one good option: reverse it.

The one thing they hadn't known was whether Winslow would attempt to reverse it via subterfuge or direct assault. Attempting both at once had seemed a doubtful choice. But here they were.

A shockwave generated by a negative energy missile detonation passed over the *Stalwart II*, and the floor beneath Miriam's feet shuddered.

The very destructive and very expensive bombs were thus far the sole weapon which was able to reliably counter the strength and resilience of adiamene hulls. They did it by creating vortexes of unnatural forces which the miniscule seams where adiamene transitioned to viewport, engines and weapons could not withstand, thereby ripping the vessels into pieces.

Miniaturized versions of the bombs used in the Metigen War had begun to be produced several months earlier and fitted for missile deployment. But most military vessels used laser weapons, not physical, perishable projectiles, so the fitting required physical reworks to the weapons housing of individual ships. Thus the rollout had been slow.

All her new offensive ships were equipped with them, but practical storage requirements meant the on-board supplies were low. At least they were low for everyone.

The *Stalwart II* had been designed with an extra layer of shielding, two hundred meters out. Among other uses, it protected the ship from the full destructive force of the negative energy weapons. It had a few drawbacks, including being a tremendous power draw, and as such hadn't yet been deployed on most vessels. But this was a command ship. *The* command ship.

After confirming they'd suffered no damage from the detonation, Miriam studied the tactical map. Despite the ship, she wasn't a battlefield commander, but she was learning fast. Thomas helped with frequent but discreet, unobtrusive analytical assessments which appeared on a screen to her right.

Admiral Solovy (EAS Stalwart II): "Squadron V5B, concentrate your efforts on Quadrants A through C and protect the defense array."

Matched against her fleet was an entire brigade-strength force. Fullerton had learned his lesson from Messium and brought far larger numbers to bear here. She was buoyed by the thought, however, that it may constitute the bulk of the forces in the Eastern sectors Winslow managed to retain control over.

The military was falling Miriam's way.

The political class wasn't proving as easy. Scythia stood to be a win on that front, but first she had to keep it.

SCYTHIA

The wreckage of the bombed-out Astral Materials corporate offices had been cleared away, leaving a jagged half-shell façade of a building to overlook the waterfront. Under the light of a full moon it cast sharp shadows on the ocean waves and the boardwalk alike. A monument to OTS' violence and terror.

On the positive side, the fact the entire area remained cordoned-off allowed Malcolm's team to sneak through without worrying about curious pedestrians. Plus, the state of emergency which had just been declared thanks to the battle going on above was emptying the streets across a far larger region.

He motioned Grenier and Rodriguez forward to clear the next block. The government administration complex was ahead and to the left, a block in from the waterfront.

They were stealthed—but not invisible—they were few, and they needed to hurry.

They reached the complex without incident, as the streets remained quiet. But once there they were met with a chaotic flurry of activity. Understandable. The planet was under attack, and this was the hub of its government.

The governor's chief of staff met him at the entrance. Malcolm didn't want to cause a panic by sauntering in with a group of heavily armed Marines, so he ordered his team to remain in the background and cloaked. But he needed to take command of the situation.

"Ms. Cardona, Colonel Malcolm Jenner."

"Yes, Admiral Solovy told us to expect you. We haven't seen any problems here yet, other than a series of increasingly strongly worded communiques from the prime minister to the governor."

"Has he responded to any of them?"

"The first one. The counter-response from the prime minister was brief and somewhat rude. They got worse from there."

"It probably won't be long then." Malcolm glanced around the bustling hallways. "We need to get most of these people out of here. I recognize you're in a crisis situation, but I need you to send every person who isn't absolutely essential home immediately. Fifteen minutes from now, I need there to be less than ten non-security personnel in the building."

The woman's eyes widened. "Less than ten?"

"And eight is preferable to nine. These people will be safe at home. They're not safe here."

"Right." The muscles in her jaw twitched once. "I'll get on it. But first let me take you to the governor."

He brought his people in then. They received a number of startled gasps, but those here understood the stakes tonight and were less surprised than they might otherwise have been.

The distinctive blue-on-white 'Volnosti' emblem on their shoulders over their Alliance gear broadcast his team's allegiance, and he figured anyone who strongly disagreed with the governor's decision had resigned in a fit and departed.

Cardona directed them into the office and headed off to clear the building.

Malcolm shook the man's hand. "Governor Jayce."

"Colonel. I confess I was skeptical the prime minister would dare try to forcibly depose my administration. But after receiving some rather colorful correspondence from her this evening, I believe she would burn me at the stake if she were able."

"Not going to happen, sir."

"Good." The governor looked around and frowned. "Are some of your people stealthed? Or is this all of you?"

"That's classified, sir. I can only say that we will protect you."

He nodded. "I'm certain you'll do your best."

"Yes, sir. I'm linking us into your government security channel now. If you could authorize your security personnel to follow our orders?"

"If you believe it's necessary. They're good people, well-trained—but we don't see a lot of action here."

"I understand. I'll only use them in a support capacity."

Malcolm spent the next few minutes assigning the security officers to watch and guard positions. Mid-way through, Cardona reported on the departure of all but a handful of aides, and those aides were brought into the governor's suite.

Sensors were placed at all entryways, including the non-obvious ones. In a smaller perimeter around the suite, proximity micro-bombs were also placed.

Rodriguez came on the comm from his surveillance vantage on the roof. *Two dozen Marines en route from the northeast. ETA three minutes.*

Colonel Jenner: Understood. Update every ten seconds.

He turned back to the governor, whom Paredes was helping don a tactical vest and a personal shield. "It's time."

⟨R

EAS STALWART II

"They're drawing our forces too close to the planet. All offensive formations, you need to control the battlespace. Pull them to where you want them—which is not up against the planet."

Trusting her pilots knew how to do such a thing, Miriam's focus couldn't help but drift to the larger strategy. The why.

Fighting in the shadow of a planet constrained everyone involved, on both sides. It limited movement and firing options. So why were Fullerton's forces this intent on keeping the fighting there?

She peered at the display. They'd also stopped attempting to disable the defense arrays in the last few minutes. She didn't need Thomas' help to decipher this one. They expected to be able to use the arrays against her forces soon.

She switched comm channels.

Admiral Solovy (EAS Stalwart II): "Colonel Jenner, expect incoming."

Colonel Jenner: "They're on approach now, Admiral."

Admiral Solovy (EAS Stalwart II): "Then I will leave you to it."

She returned to studying—

A brilliant explosion lit the viewport, far larger than any which had come before.

Admiral Solovy (EAS Stalwart II): "Squadron Leads, report."

V5B Primary: "One of the negative energy missiles missed its target and exploded in the upper mesosphere."

What would that even do? She watched in horror as the atmospheric clouds surrounding the explosion roiled and churned. A second explosion plumed nearby, but the turmoil gradually subsided.

V5B Primary: "The explosion and its aftereffects took out five of our fighters and a frigate. All indications are the other side suffered worse."

She gritted her teeth.

Admiral Solovy (EAS Stalwart II): "To all ships, I say again: draw them away from the planet. Disengage and pull back. Make them come to you."

Next she activated a private channel. "Admiral Rychen, any ideas are most welcome."

"You already stole all my good ones. They want us dead, so they'll chase us if they must—"

He cut off abruptly. And not merely his voice—the channel. She checked the *Churchill's* position. "Redirect heading S 62° -51°z E."

As they swung down toward the profile of Scythia, the dreadnought came into view. White-blue flames poured out of its impulse engines, and it seemed to be having difficulty maintaining course. The hull looked to be holding, as it had been one of the first ships to be retrofitted with adiamene after the end of the Metigen War.

"Lieutenant Renato, have all Rescue Units prepare for deployment. Major Halmi, I need information on what hit the *Churchill*."

"It doesn't appear anything hit it, Admiral. The *Bismarck* had an unobstructed view and tracked no projectiles. Here's vid coming in now."

A new screen to her left opened. The *Churchill* was engaged and firing two of its uniquely healthy supply of negative energy missiles at the *Provence*, when suddenly both impulse engines exploded. To her eye it looked as if they exploded from *within*.

Impulse engines didn't malfunction—not military-grade ones—which left one conspicuous option as the likeliest scenario: sabotage. It was a concern they carried with them every day. Most of their people were loyal to her, Rychen or both, but there were a lot of personnel, and they couldn't know every one personally.

Her gaze rose to the viewport once more as the *Churchill* crashed into one of their own ships, sending it tumbling off-course. Then its bow dipped toward the planet below.

The ship itself was still intact. Many, many people were still alive onboard—but not for much longer.

There was nothing she could do for them. They were all highly trained. They would know how to effect an emergency evacuation. If no one panicked, there were enough shuttles and pods for all of the twenty-one thousand people onboard.

But what there was not much of was time.

"Get every craft that can serve a rescue function into the *Churchill's* vicinity now. Fullerton won't allow his people to fire on escape shuttles, and if he allows them to fire on rescue personnel I will string him up and gut him myself."

SCYTHIA

When the Alliance infiltration team breached the building, Malcolm activated the official broadcast system.

"This is Agent Robertson of Scythia Administrative Security. You're trespassing on government property during a state of emergency. State your purpose."

He watched the cam feed as the point man swept the entry room. "This is a matter of Earth Alliance security. We have authorization to be here."

"My department doesn't have any record of such authorization."

"It's, um, classified. Strictly classified, and direct from the prime minister. We need to take the governor and his deputy into protective custody."

"If a threat exists to the personal safety of the governor or his staff, as head of security I need to be made aware of it."

The Marine shook his head. "You really don't." Then he waved his people forward, weapons drawn.

Malcolm cut the broadcast and switched to the mission comm channel. "We are Code Red. Go." The deputy was on another floor under Grenier's guard in order to minimize the chance of both of them being captured or harmed.

He pivoted to the governor. "Sir, I need you to get under your desk. I know it won't be comfortable, but it's the safest place."

"Not particularly flattering either, but all right." The man grimaced and disappeared beneath the desk.

A muffled explosion echoed outside.

Lt. Shanti: Two targets down. First floor, northeast corridor.

He watched the various cam feeds on a whisper in the far corner of his vision. The intruders were hurrying now, on full alert and weapons free upon realizing they would meet resistance.

Another proximity micro-bomb tripped the instant they reached the second floor. Three bodies flew through the air; those escaping it met gunfire as they spun to examine their injured colleagues.

An additional team approached from the opposite side of the building. A flashbang tossed down the hall preceded mutual weapons fire.

Malcolm tensed as Shanti took a hit. He wanted to be out there fighting beside his team every step of the way. But the mission was to protect the governor, and someone had to be the last line of defense.

Lt. Shanti: It's not bad. As long as they don't take the time to come back and finish the job, I'll be okay.

Colonel Jenner: Hold tight and quiet.

Pounding footsteps thudded over the rising disorder. He signaled Paredes across the doorway, clear in the night-vision mode of his ocular implant.

Colonel Jenner: Rodriguez and Eaton, I need you to handle the three still on the third floor. We've got four combatants approaching Target Alpha.

Lt. Eaton: Roger.

The cam they'd positioned above the door showed the intruders' progress. Malcolm counted down with his fingers, then tossed a grenade into the hallway and flattened himself against the wall.

The room shook as the grenade detonated, sending dust rushing down the hallway. But so close to their target, the two Marines the grenade didn't take out simply stepped over their comrades and prepared to enter.

"Governor Jayce, we know you're in there. We're not here to harm you. You've been summoned to Earth to answer questions regarding your recent statements. We—"

Malcolm exploded out the door and to the right, Paredes to the left. He barreled into the Marine and they both landed on the floor. He swatted the man's Daemon away, sending it clattering down the hall.

The next instant the man was trying to gouge his eye out; he struggled to pull the man's arm away, then the other as well when it came up brandishing a short blade.

He slowly twisted the hand around until the blade pointed in its wielder's direction. "Don't make me kill you, Marine. Surrender now and no more of your people will be harmed."

"Fuck you, traitor." The man wrested his other hand free and punched Malcolm in the throat.

His hold on the man's blade hand loosened as he tried and failed to draw in air. He surged forward and forced the blade into the man's neck, holding it there as the man flailed beneath him.

Finally he fell off the body and sank down the wall. In the back of his mind he processed the information coming in: Paredes had knocked his target out and now had him in restraints. Eaton and Rodriguez had killed one and disabled two. None had reached Grenier and the deputy governor.

He gasped in ragged breaths; each one felt like it was shredding his esophagus with tiny splintered shards.

"Sir, are you all right?"

He nodded at Paredes and pushed himself up off the floor. "Yes—" his voice croaked out "—I'm fine. Check on the governor."

Colonel Jenner: Status on the deputy governor?

Major Grenier: Safe and sound, if a bit distressed.

Colonel Jenner: Good work. Take all prisoners to the Conference Room on the 2nd floor, then we need to sweep the building.

When he was finally able to draw in a clean breath, he straightened his shoulders and returned to the governor's office, where he found Paredes checking the man over for injuries.

The governor stared up at him. "Is it over?"

"We need to secure the premises, but I believe we've neutralized the threat, yes, sir." He gave the governor a reassuring pat on the shoulder. "I imagine you're anxious to inform the prime minister her attempt to oust you failed, but we should confirm the battle overhead has gone our way first."

EAS STALWART II

Focusing on seeing the engagement through and defeating the adversary while the *Churchill* inexorably fell into the planet's atmosphere and eventually vanished was one of the more difficult things Miriam had done in a month full of very difficult things.

But she did it, because even without the dreadnought's firepower they were winning, and she didn't dare let the momentum falter.

Relentless attacks by her fighters were in the process of destroying a rather gutsy frigate when she received a most astonishing message from Richard.

She dropped her chin to her chest to disguise her reaction, as for a minute she could not keep the emotions off her face. Shock, elation, a zealous touch of rage and a lingering dismay.

It was game-changing news, but it would have to keep until the battle was done.

When her ships disabled the second to last cruiser under Fullerton's command, the remaining ships vanished rather than surrender.

She let them go.

Next she turned to Major Halmi. "I need comprehensive damage and casualty reports from all vessels. We'll have pilots adrift out there. Make sure rescue operations have all the locator beacons—"

A gravelly voice crackled over her comm. "Any chance we could hitch a ride?"

She laughed in relief. "I believe we can spare the room." Not for twenty-one thousand people, but they'd find the room for the survivors throughout the fleet.

"In that case, permission to come aboard, Admiral Solovy?"

"Permission granted, Admiral Rychen."

She went down to meet him on the flight deck. He and the crew trailing him looked banged up, but nothing showers and a few medwraps wouldn't fix.

She returned his salute with a sly smile—a rare enough event that he eyed her suspiciously.

"Admiral Solovy, are you wearing a shit-eating grin because we won here today, or is there something else I should know?"

"There's something else you should know."

"And that would be?"

"We've got her. Pamela Winslow's days in power are going to be far shorter than she intended."

23

ROMANE

"**F**antastic!"

Caleb's attention swung to Mia at the exclamation, but her voice dropped to a hush as she queried whoever she was talking to, denying him further hints as to the reason for it.

He'd spent much of the time since the riots here at IDCC Headquarters—wanting to protect Mia, wanting to protect them all, wanting to avenge the deaths and near-misses which had occurred. Wanting to be anywhere but the ship.

He hadn't talked to Alex in hours, and she'd been almost totally uncommunicative in the hours before then. She was presumably on the *Siyane*. In the *Siyane*. Was the *Siyane*. If there remained a difference.

He needed to run from the unwelcome thoughts, so he stepped closer to Mia in hopes of eavesdropping.

"Harper, did you get the info—right, Morgan told you. I don't know why I bother. Can we move on the location quickly? They could scatter at any moment. Terrific. Oh, hang on, more details are incoming."

There was a notable pause.

"It's *WHO*?"

ᴀʀ

Caleb strode into the IDCC armory to find Harper and her team suiting up and checking over their gear.

She looked sideways at him while she latched a daisy chain of grenades to her belt. "I won't even attempt to argue. But at least put on a tactical vest, and try to follow orders."

He nodded agreement and headed to the armor cabinet, where he found a vest that fit on the second try. He was donning it when Harper cleared her throat.

"Everyone, this is Caleb Marano. *Allegedly* former Senecan Federation intelligence, though I'm not sure I buy it. I've seen his work firsthand, and trust me when I tell you he can dispose of enemy combatants with far more finesse and efficiency than any of you ever dreamed of. Hopefully he'll toe the line, but if he's moving, take my advice and don't get in his way."

He shrugged and pulled his overshirt back on over the vest. "I'm just here to help. You're in charge."

She raised an eyebrow. "Yes, I am." Then she climbed up on a bench in the center of the room. "Weapons check."

The roll call came in. "Gear check." Same.

"Pello, with me for heavy weapons. Everyone else, meet at the transport in five."

He caught up with her as she headed down the rear hallway. "What sort of heavy weapons are you taking?"

She glanced over her shoulder with cool, cautious eyes. "Marano, I meant what I said in there. I respect your skills and your determination, and I'm frankly a little relieved to have them at my disposal on this mission. However, I don't recall those skills involving the use of heavy weapons—I suspect you're more of an up close and personal kind of guy.

"So get to the transport and let me do my job. In return, I promise I'll let you do…some of yours."

His steps slowed; he dropped back and let her disappear around the corner. He might have smarted at the dressing down, but she was right. If heavy weapons worked to clear the place, then fine, but if not he'd be in the hallways and shadowy corners taking care of the enemy himself.

He shifted direction and headed for the transport.

ᴀʀ

ROMANE

Harper paced rapidly across the front of the transport cabin as they lifted off. "The building has two main entrances and one service entrance. We're going to trap the service entrance, split into two teams and simultaneously breach both main entrances. Commander Lekkas and Mr. Naissan will be providing aerial support, and Romane Tactical is setting up a perimeter in the event someone slips the net.

"We don't have good intel on the number of people inside, but the building is listed as unoccupied so we can assume they're all OTS. They would have run off any squatters when they took it over. Therefore, we—"

Caleb, tell Harper to back off. I'm going to take care of these bastards.

He jerked—visibly, something he generally tried not to do. He'd been deep in mission prep mode and, in a very rare occurrence these last days, *not* thinking about Alex. Now she was in his head.

What are you talking about?

The safe house is near the Exia Spaceport. I'm on my way and will beat you there. You don't need to risk your life, nor does the RRF squad. I'll eliminate the safe house.

And by 'I,' you mean you in the body of the Siyane.

Of course.

Alex, it's still you. I have to believe it's still you when you're in the ship. And you're not a cold-blooded killer. Don't do this.

They killed Abigail. They tried to kill Mia, Devon, all of us. They deserve it.

They do, but not by your hand. Let us handle it.

He immediately cringed. If she remained Alex in any real way, it had been the wrong thing to say.

No need. They will all be dead before you get there.

Alex, please.

But she was gone, had shut him out.

He let out a long, weighty breath. It felt like the end, like the tolling of the dirge.

He buried the emotions which flared as much as he could, telling himself it was only for the duration of the mission. But a dark, hollow heaviness settled over him as he stood and went up to Harper. "We have a complication."

ᴙ

The message arrived via pulse on Jude's most secure personal comm channel.

> *The IDCC has acquired intel on the location of the safe house. Relocation may be advisable.*

His mother had her spies in the Noesis and everywhere else, but he wasn't without his own resources. The news was disappointing, but not particularly surprising.

His intention had been to remain here until Romane authorities decreased the security alert level and fewer police patrolled the streets and spaceports, but in truth he had stayed too long by half. The message merely confirmed it.

He would have to take his chances among the public. If worse came to worst, once he was a couple of blocks away from the safe house he could give his name and profess ignorance of anything problematic. The Romane government may not care for his mother, but it had to respect her authority.

He glanced around with feigned casualness at the other people in the upstairs room, which had become the unofficial command and triage center. They included most of the operational leadership of the Romane cell of OTS—those who hadn't been out on the streets and gotten caught in the dragnet arrests.

They had spent the day working feverishly to secure the release of as many of those arrested as possible, to catalogue the dead and to plan for the future.

Good soldiers, giving their all in the hope of a better, freer tomorrow for humanity.

But there would be no such tomorrow if Jude were captured tonight.

He waited until no one was looking in his direction, then slipped out the door and hurried downstairs toward the rear exit.

24

SIYANE

The night air felt like a living organism all its own.

So close to the ground the atmosphere was saturated with molecules, and they were being pushed and pulled and transmuted by ships and shuttles and structures of metal radiating energy, churning power and sending it out in waves through the air. Flying through it felt invasive, savage.

Alex, stop. Turn around and go back to the hangar.

Her target lay at 27°, 4.6 kilometers distant. Though only six stories high, the structure occupied a block and was separated from other buildings by thoroughfares. This would minimize collateral damage.

The guilty pay, the innocent live. The reckoning of the universe at work. She was simply the messenger.

These people killed Abigail. Don't you want vengeance, Valkyrie?

No. I said it after her murder, and now I will say it again: I want to mourn.

The environment ahead and beneath her—streets, airlanes, people—screamed back at her, noisy and raucous, but objectively she recognized it was far calmer than before. The fires had been quelled, the physical violence restrained.

Still, the city was on edge, waiting for the next blow.

Then I will take your vengeance for you.

I can disconnect you. Send you back to your body and fly the ship to the hangar myself.

You can, but you won't. After what happened at the Amaranthe portal you fear the effect such a jarring act will have on my neural cohesion. *You won't disconnect me while I'm this deep in your processes, in the quantum clusters of the ship, conscious and aware. Besides, I don't need to be inhabiting the ship to fire its weapon.*

Could you honestly fire on these individuals from the cockpit chair, in your fragile, tangible, human body?

I've fired on enemies before.

Enemies who were actively trying to harm you. Caleb is correct, I believe. Could you initiate the slaughter yourself if you were wholly and only you?

She paused, felt the air bounce around her in agitation.

It doesn't matter.

The OTS safe house came in range. The streets framing it were quiet, most of its windows dark. Just an ordinary building.

Before Valkyrie managed to seed more doubts, she fired.

The distance from laser weapon to target was markedly shorter than anything she'd previously experienced. Crossed in a blink of time, the collision of energy with façade created enough force to send her perception ricocheting away. Destruction in pure form, and not solely elemental.

Real. Physical. Primal.

Her mind recoiled, but she tried to focus on the molecules of fire created—oxygen, carbon dioxide, nitrogen oxidizing into flame, photons escaping, ionized gases transforming to plasma. She watched them leap and dance across the sky.

Then she created more.

A flicker moved in the space where a window hung an instant earlier. A face, stark with terror, screaming for help.

But she'd already fired again, already delivered the kilojoules which now caused the building to begin to crumble.

The face vanished in a rising plume of carbon, metal oxides and amorphous silica. Smoke. It didn't reach her, but she choked on it nonetheless.

She fled down the quantum pathways and opened her eyes with a gasp. "Take over—" But Valkyrie had done so hundreds of microseconds earlier.

The face would have belonged to a terrorist. A callous murderer of innocents. It might have been the *pizda sranuyu* Jude Winslow himself.

It doesn't matter. It doesn't matter.

Why did it have to look so...human? She stared out the viewport at the destruction she had wrought. Surreal, evanescent, not real. *So real.*

It doesn't matter.

Human. Murderer.

Him, the face, not me. It doesn't—

'Alex, you should try to calm down. You're hyperventilating.'

Was she? The tightness in her chest was surely as much mental as corporeal, right?

'It's done and cannot be undone. Allow me to return us to the hangar.'

She tried to inhale through her nose. "No. Set down. Nearby, but...but out of the way."

'Set down? Why?'

"I can't—can't breathe in here. I need air. I need...ground beneath my feet."

If I'm a killer now, I need to feel the blood on my hands.

ROMANE

The strikes lit up the night like a meteor storm. Exclamations rippled through the hold, but Caleb ignored them, focusing his attention on the viewport as his eyes searched the sky for the *Siyane*.

Which was absurd; he wouldn't be able to see it. Its cloaking exceeded his cybernetically enhanced but still fundamentally human sight by a large margin.

He tracked multiple separate laser strikes, but their origin point moved and shifted. She was smart, of course she was smart. There were no active defenses here, but had there been they would not have zeroed in on her location.

An intensified stream of energy poured into a critical load-bearing junction, and the building crumbled and collapsed, sending a massive wave of dust and flame billowing outward in all directions.

Their pilot pulled up and away. "Ma'am, what should I—"

"Harper, set down in the closest intersection."

She snorted. "Our mission is scrapped. This is for the recovery units now. Joseph, head back to base." She muttered into her comm to confirm emergency personnel were inbound.

Caleb's jaw clenched. "Please set down, just for a minute. You can leave me here, but I need to be on the ground."

She studied him, suspicion in her expression, but didn't ask why. Which was good, because he didn't know why. Alex was in the *Siyane*—was the *Siyane*. She'd leave now, head to the spaceport or the devil knew where. But his instincts clamored in his head for him to get off the transport, now.

Alex? Answer me. Tell me where you are or where you're going.

He got nothing. He started to falter. Maybe the spaceport offered a better choice—or maybe there was no good choice. Maybe it was all for naught. He opened his mouth to recant—

"Ma'am we've got movement on the periphery, left alley."

Harper leaned into the viewport. "Somebody got out before the building collapsed. All right, Marano, you get your wish. Belay my last, Joseph, and set us down. Let's go hunting."

The fire grew blinding as they neared the site and settled to the ground. Caleb activated his ocular implant filter and tuned it to a hybrid night vision.

Harper barked out new orders. "Pello, Verela, swing around the other side in case they double-back or someone else bolts that way. Redale, station yourself down a block to the right. Joseph, sit tight, as Lekkas is on aerial surveillance. Odaka, with me to the left. Marano, you...."

He waved over his shoulder in her direction as he jogged down the street to the left.

Harper was good, but she was used to fighting other soldiers. OTS was many things, but it by and large was not comprised of soldiers. Terrorists were a different breed altogether. They were hotheads, ruled by a surfeit of irrational emotions and a shortage of combat awareness.

A soldier would move deliberately, keeping to cover and waiting for opportunities. A terrorist would run.

He gauged the time since the movement had been spotted and headed another block east then cut in to the next alley, blade hilt in hand. The flames became subsumed by darkness, and he switched his ocular filter to full night vision mode.

A thud—almost silent, but not silent enough—deeper in the alley gave him a target. Caleb moved quickly and far more quietly ahead. As he neared, the sounds of someone retreating at a rapid walk sharpened.

He rounded the next corner, zeroed in on the person-sized shadow and pounced.

The man was thin, slight and lacked any knowledge of defensive fighting techniques. Caleb had his face slammed into the alley wall and his arms locked in less than a second. He activated the pen light he'd acquired from the IDCC gear locker and shone it into the man's face.

Narrow, angular features, pouty lips and hatred-filled pale, washed-out blue irises glared back at him.

Caleb flashed the young man a malevolent smirk and readied his blade. "Jude Winslow, I presume."

The man's eyes widened in panic at the realization he'd been outed, but Caleb didn't give a—

"IDCC Security—you're under arrest!"

HarperRF: Marano, back off. Thanks for the assist, but we've got this.

He silenced a curse and shifted his stance to allow Harper to replace his grasp with her own, then stepped away. "All yours."

He watched until Harper's people had restraints fully on Winslow and a solid grip on him, then turned and left. Out of his hands, for now.

On reaching the street in front of the collapsing safe house, he found emergency personnel already on site. Fire suppressing foam already filled the air. Lights flashed and sirens wailed.

Alex did this.

She wasn't wrong to do it.

But if it was truly her who had executed the attack, he hated it, because he'd hoped to always spare her from the kind of darkness such an act required.

If it wasn't truly her who had done it, he had to consider the very real possibility she was gone, in all the ways that mattered.

Go to her, Caleb. She needs you.

He stopped in surprise. He wasn't a Prevo; Valkyrie couldn't read his thoughts. Yet now she whispered in his head at an eerily prescient moment.

Go to her where? The spaceport?

Here. At the safe house location.

What's happening? Why is she still here?

He received no further response.

Equally emboldened and terrified, he began searching the chaos for her.

25

ROMANE

The destroyed building remained too hot and unstable for close ground rescue and recovery by the units on the scene. Scaffolding teetered in the flames, threatening to crash down any second, and smaller explosions rippled through the interior as power control units and other volatile objects succumbed to the fire.

For now, chaos reigned—the dazed, disorienting kind where no one understood quite what had happened.

But Caleb understood. He also knew it had changed everything, in ways he could only fear.

Valkyrie, where is she? Am I hunting for the ship, or her?

Silence answered him. The Artificial was rarely too busy to siphon off a few processes to respond to an inquiry, and he was forced to assume the silence was for some other reason.

He was so goddamn tired of it all.

He shouldn't have to beg to find out where Alex was. He shouldn't have to grovel to fucking *matter*. He shouldn't have to scrape and claw to maintain the flimsiest hold on his status as an insider, yet still feeling as if he were an outsider the whole time.

It wasn't supposed to have gone like this.

He almost turned around then and walked away. He'd almost convinced himself he *was* turning away when he caught sight of long tangles of burgundy hair blowing in the cinder-filled breeze.

Alex kneeled amidst the chaos, too close to the wreckage yet seemingly oblivious to the smoke and sirens and smell of burnt metal and singed flesh.

He approached without attracting her attention and crouched beside her. Blood stained her hands, and despite his anger worry flared in his chest. But to his best ability to tell, it didn't appear to be hers. He was afraid to speculate where it had come from.

He waited.

When she finally spoke, her voice held the flat, detached tenor it had taken on so often of late. It sounded like it could be tinged in regret, but he didn't dare hope.

"I thought if I touched the wreckage with my own hands, if I felt the blood on my skin—" she stretched a hand out, as if she assumed he *hadn't* noticed the blood "—it might make it more real."

"Did it?"

"No." She lifted her hand up closer to her face. "I look at this blood, and I see its chemical composition, its cells, its proteins—hemoglobin, albumin, leukocytes, thrombocytes. I'm not viewing it through the ship's senses, yet I'm still *in* that realm. It feels as though I'm not actually here, and neither is anyone else.

"We're not real. We're not even the real humans, merely copies grown in a galactic petri dish. We're not special. Nothing but atoms, as insubstantial and ephemeral as the stellar wind."

"You're wrong."

Her hand fell to her side, and she half-turned her shoulders to look at him. Her eyes were at once vacant, distant and agonizingly desolate. "Have I fucked us up beyond all repair?"

She was asking him? Had this ever been up to him?

He swallowed heavily, tasted ash on his tongue. "I just want you. Alex, I love you so much sometimes I can hardly breathe from the power of it. But I love the woman...and you're becoming something else. Maybe it's something better, more powerful, but it's not the woman I know. I understand why you would seek it out, I do.

"If this is truly what you want—what you want to be—I won't try to stop you from following this path. But I can't continue living with these fragments, these fading shadows of what you once were, when they're the only pieces left behind."

"You said you'd have to be dragged away from me in chains."

Her words hit him as cruelly as a punch to the gut. He dropped his forehead onto his palm. "I did. And I meant it, so...I'll own that.

God, it seems like yesterday and an eternity ago, all at once." There had been fire and death that night, too, if in remembrance, not vengeance.

"If you want to hold those words against me now, somehow latch onto an imagined betrayal, it's fine. I'll take the hit. But I can't stay and watch you...the amazing, remarkable woman you are..." he sucked in air and blinked past threatening tears, not even trying to pretend they were from the smoke "...disappear into the walls of the ship.

"I want—I need—all of you. Your heart. Your soul. Your incredible spirit and your wild, beautiful mind. And dammit, but I *deserve* all of you."

She regarded him with gut-wrenching, haunting sadness. Finally she nodded in the smallest way possible. "You do. *Proshcheniye, priyazn.*"

Forgiveness, my love. She shifted away from him and closed her eyes.

He recognized the telltale slackness in her shoulders the instant it manifested. She had retreated to the ship in her mind. Gone from this place, gone from him.

The abject rejection slammed into his chest with the force of a hurricane. He gasped reflexively, filled his lungs with foul air and stumbled to his feet.

Away. He needed to get away. From here, from anywhere.

There was a building, a wall intact across the street, and he staggered through the smoke toward it, dodging rescue equipment and waiving off several personnel who thought he was a victim.

Was he...did she...his eyes burned and bleared. He blinked repeatedly, but the blurriness only increased.

Someone could stroll by, casually slice open his chest, rip out his heart and carry it off to toss into the flames and he wouldn't notice the difference.

Never have anything you can't walk away from. He should have listened to Samuel. He should have listened, and now it was so very far past too late.

He fell back against the wall of the building and let a gaping chasm of cold darkness open up and devour him whole. He didn't have the slightest clue what he was going to do, and he didn't particularly care. Drink himself into a permanent oblivion. Kill his way across what remained of OTS. Laugh when the Anadens found and annihilated humanity, likely without ever realizing what they were.

In her he'd found a purpose worth giving everything to. Not for fun or thrills, but because it mattered. Without her, he couldn't remember what his purpose had once been. He'd had one before she came into his life, he was certain of it.

But what did any of it matter now? He'd fight the good fight; he didn't know any other path. Even if part of him hoped he finally met his match along the way. He'd never stopped fighting, but now it stood to be the sole intention driving him forward.

Damn it all to hell, why had he ever dared care this much—

Thank you, Valkyrie. That was perfect. Now tear down the pathways I use to access these nodes and the neurons I use to connect to them.

What was he hearing? It wasn't on their group channel. Someone was feeding it to him.

He blinked.

Alex, there will be consequences.

I accept them. Burn the yebanaya *neurons out, then do whatever else you have to do so I can't come here ever again. Do it now.*

Alex—

Do it now, goddammit! While I still have the courage to see it through. Please, Valkyrie. It's the only way. Please.

Very well...it is done.

I know. I can feel it. The ship is yours.

I will take good care of her.

I know that, too.

AR

Alex opened her eyes. Breathed in air, real air—and gagged on the stench of death riding the smoke and debris particles. Coughs wracked her chest as she peered around frantically.

He was gone. She'd lingered too long in her goodbyes.

"Caleb?" She stumbled to her feet in a clumsy rush of limbs. Her voice rose. "Caleb?"

But he was nowhere to be seen, and he couldn't possibly hear her above the sirens and the *noise*.

A hand landed on her shoulder; she whipped on it, realizing as she did that it didn't belong to him.

"Ma'am, are you hurt? Do you need aid?"

She twisted out of the man's grasp and shook her head, then spun in a circle, searching.

Panic encroached at the edges of her vision. She couldn't see anything through the smoke. Wasn't there an intersection somewhere? She stumbled forward, putting the worst of the destruction behind her. She needed to get her bearings so she could find him. He couldn't have gone far, but it didn't matter how far—

Caleb rounded the corner of the building across the street. Through the ghostly light the floodlights created amid the smoke, she would recognize his profile from parsecs distant.

She broke into a run…until she drew close enough to see the tears streaming down his cheeks. In the time she'd known him she'd never seen him shed a single tear.

Her steps slowed to a stop a few meters away; she was too afraid to cross the final distance. Her heart pounded against her chest so hard it threatened to break her ribs. "I severed my connection to the ship. Permanently. I can't go—"

"I know."

"How?" She glared at the heavens even as tears began flowing down her own cheeks. "Valkyrie…." *Thank you.*

"You did that…did you do it for me?"

She nodded vehemently. "Yes. For you. For me—you were right, it wasn't good for me. For us."

She gazed at him hopefully, trying her damnedest to maintain an iota of poise. "Is it too late? I made so many mistakes—"

In a blink he had closed the distance and gathered her up in his arms. "No—" His words broke off in a sob as he buried his face in her neck.

Oh god oh god had she broken him? What should she do? "Shhh. Please, I'm so sorry. I love you. I know I hurt you—I'm sorry."

She wound her fingers into his hair—it was too short for this!—and held him tighter against her. "It's okay, it's okay, I'm so sorry. Forgive me—no, I'll find some way to earn your forgiveness. Just say you'll stay and give me the chance to earn it."

Was she crying as hard as him now? "Stay, stay, stay...."

She was still whispering it, over and over, when he pulled away to look at her, eyes red and glistening. "I'll stay."

"I'm so sorry."

"You, uh—" he blinked past more tears "—you mentioned that."

She cringed. "I really did, didn't I?"

"Once or twice." He relinquished his hold on her to bring a hand to his face and wipe at his cheeks, regaining a measure of composure.

More emergency personnel and equipment began arriving, erecting barriers and pushing people out of the area.

He urged her back to the nearest wall. "I don't want you to resent me. This was everything you ever dreamed of. Everything you ever wanted."

"Turns out, no. It wasn't worth the price." There would also be a price to pay for this choice, one she'd pay soon enough. But not now. Not here. "Turns out, you are."

He regarded her with pure, destroyed, hopeful eyes, and damn but he'd never looked this handsome. Broken, vulnerable and exposed, he'd never looked stronger, and she realized she'd trust him to lead her anywhere in this fucked-up multiverse.

He started to speak; cleared his throat. She knew the feeling. "Valkyrie said there would be consequences to you doing this."

Shared the whole damn scene with him, did you? She gave him an exaggerated shrug. "Some headaches for a few weeks. I'll try not to be too cranky."

"I'd like for you to be cranky. I've missed it."

"Oh, okay then." She dropped her forehead to his and brought her fingertips to either side of his neck.

There were things she wanted to say, but they were all jumbled up in her head and if she tried they'd come out backwards and mixed up and wrong.

There were things she needed to say, but she was hanging on by a fraying thread and feared if she tried the thread would break, sending her plummeting alone into the abysm.

There were things she would have to say, but they should wait for later. After.

A loud rumble thundered behind her as another section of scaffolding belatedly collapsed. She stared at him in horror. "I blew up a building."

He tilted his head in a wince. "You did."

"With people in it."

"Terrorists. Murderers."

She fixated on her hand along his neck. She'd accidentally transferred most of the blood onto him, but streaks remained between her knuckles. "Are you sure? What if some random—"

"I'm sure. We had good intel this was exclusively an OTS safe house. Alex, I would have killed everyone inside that building without hesitation. I meant what I said earlier. I'm sorry you were the one to do it, but not because it was wrong—because I wanted to save you from this." He gently wrapped his hand around hers. He meant the blood. He meant the guilt.

Alex: Morgan?

Morgan: Holy Christ, Alex. Nice shooting.

Alex: Shut up. I simply need to know...am I in trouble? With the authorities, which is kind of you?

Morgan: Nah. We'll get it straightened out so you don't take any heat. As far as the public is concerned, the RRF neutralized a dangerous threat.

Alex: Thank you.

"I should have listened to you. But I can't undo it now. I'll have to live with it."

"I'll help. I have a bit of experience at this sort of thing." His throat worked. "Killing, and coping with it."

She pulled him closer and crushed his lips with hers. She was lightheaded and reeling, but the frayed thread hadn't broken and if it did now she thought he'd probably catch her before she fell too far.

Sounds and activity intruded on them; she reluctantly began to withdraw, but he refused to let her go. That was fine, too. She murmured against his lips. "Morgan says no one's going to show up and arrest me, so...can we get out of here? I need...I need a shower and clean clothes. Mostly, I need you."

"We can absolutely get out of here." She felt the curl of his smile in his kiss. "Where's the ship?"

"Um...I have no idea. Valkyrie?"

'Allow me to provide you a locator.'

Two blocks east, one block north, hiding stealthed in a park. She had no recollection of landing there. Or of walking from there to the burned-out safe house.

When they reached the ship she followed Caleb up the ramp, her hand in his. The airlock closed behind her. "Valkyrie, can you take us back to the hangar bay?"

'May I suggest returning to orbit above Romane for the night instead?'

"Well...."

When the time comes, you may appreciate the solace of the stars.
Oh...I suppose I might.

"That sounds lovely, Valkyrie. Thank you."

Caleb turned then and gathered her into his arms once more, where she intended to stay for many hours.

ᴙ

Brooklyn watched the emergency crews working to douse the persistent flames with a critical eye.

In addition to the Winslow cocksucker, they'd captured one other escapee, and both were transported to Romane's most secure lockdown facility with a full complement of guards. Three injured people had been rescued from the wreckage; they would be under guard at the hospital for now.

It sure looked as if everyone else was a corpse. She'd reinforced a wide perimeter net and tasked several aerial cams with patrolling the area to cover all the bases, but the strike had been quick, efficient and breathtakingly destructive. Terrestrial buildings were not built to withstand lasers designed for the rigors of space.

Morgan appeared beside her unannounced. Brooklyn had barely heard the woman's approach through the cacophony of heavy equipment, flames and the occasional yell.

Now her eyes cut over briefly. The aerial surveillance had been handed off to the drone cams, but Morgan still wore her flight suit beneath her jacket. "Are you sure you didn't do this?"

"Of course I'm sure. Kind of wish I had. It got the job done." Morgan threw her a scowl. "Did you think I lied to you?"

"No. I only meant it—"

"Your team had reached the target. I wouldn't have put your people at risk. I wouldn't have…." She snorted and turned away.

"I know."

"Oh? You know…what, exactly?"

Brooklyn gritted her teeth. Morgan could be so damn prickly sometimes. "I know you wouldn't deliberately put any of our people in unnecessary danger. I was simply going to say this looked like your work. It was…supposed to be a compliment." She rolled her eyes and watched as a crane executed a controlled dismantlement of the final section of wall which remained standing.

Seconds ticked by, and finally she glanced over to find Morgan staring at her, face screwed up. "What?"

"A compliment, huh?"

"That is what I said, yes. Simmer down. It's all good."

A corner of Morgan's mouth twitched. Gradually her gaze returned to the wreckage. "Winslow's kid. Didn't see that one coming. It's bound to make things interesting."

"They weren't already interesting?"

"Nah. Well, maybe a little. I'm glad you got the kid alive, so we can torture him."

"I thought you didn't condone torture, what with being in command and having *responsibilities*."

"Yeah, but he killed Gianno, and I was just starting to like her. Will you torture him for me?"

"No, Morgan, I won't torture him for you."

"Damn." She smiled playfully—good, as Brooklyn had almost been convinced she was serious. "Fine, we'll play by the rules and respect his rights and whatever. What we won't do is hand him over to the Alliance anytime soon."

"Nope. You let Alex vanish?"

"It's not as if I can't reach her if I need to. But yes. And as for this—" she tossed a hand in the direction of the smoldering building "—we'll say I did it."

"Dammit, Lekkas."

"Kidding. Sort of. Officially, the RRF as a unit eliminated a continuing threat to the public's safety. Period, end of discussion, no?"

"If we're lucky. All right, it's the official line." Honestly, she was relieved Morgan made the call about Alex. And Morgan *was* in charge, after all. "I suspect OTS threw everything they could muster at us this week."

"And we kicked their self-righteous, bigoted asses."

"We did." She paused to review incoming cam footage and clear it. "All things considered, I think this might work out."

" 'This?' "

"The IDCC. The Rapid Response Force. The work."

"Oh. For a second there, it seemed like you meant us. But that would be too crazy an idea."

Brooklyn wiped ash and sweat off her forehead. Or not; it had been pathetically naive for her to think any of it would work out in any real sense.

Her life had become a series of 'for now' circumstances. And for now, she found herself here on Romane. In this blatantly doomed relationship. Standing in the middle of a burning street set ablaze by a woman she was of the personal, if fairly uninformed, opinion was hardly human any longer. And this was in comparison to Morgan, who was only marginally more human.

She missed the Marines.

Unbidden, the memory of O'Connell blowing Gregor Kone's head off on the bridge of the *Akagi* then ordering maintenance to clean up the mess flared in her mind.

Fine, assuming they lived through OTS and Prime Minister Winslow, this was still better. And until it all fell apart, she was getting regular sex. Great sex. It was enough, because it had to be. For now.

She didn't betray a solitary thing about her morbid thoughts in her expression. She'd perfected that skill way back at Q Course. Instead, she nodded as crisply as if she were acknowledging an order. "Yep. Crazy."

INTERMEZZO IV

MOSAIC

Aver gazed down upon a sea of rodent creatures from the anonymity of his cloaked ship.

Many thousands of them had been brought here, to a planet functionally identical to the one currently being Cultivated in System 4A-CC57. A habitat familiar to the rodents had been created for them here.

Created by the Katasketousya? Certainly the scientists could create worlds—it was, first and foremost, their role. Their job function as defined by the Directorate. Ancillary duties propagated naturally from that role, all well suited to the species' sedate intellectualism.

But in a universe of species which had been pacified and brought to heel over the aeons by the Anadens, the Katasketousya had needed no pacification. They had arrived docile and compliant, asking only to be allowed to tinker with astronomical and biological phenomenon in the service of their new masters.

The notion that any member of the species would defy their role to engage in subterfuge and pursue daring and dangerous schemes in opposition to the Directorate? It was absurd. Preposterous.

Yet the evidence was displayed here in front of his eyes for him to see. The fact he'd found no Katasketousya on the premises did nothing to lessen the strength of the evidence.

They and no others possessed the expertise necessary to create functioning space and astronomical objects. Here, within their Provision Network, was an artificially created space and astronomical objects. On one such object now resided the missing population from Eridium II System 4A-CC57.

All conclusions followed inexorably from these facts.

Conclusion #5: *The Katasketousya created a shelter space within their Provision Network for the resident species of System 4A-CC57, then led the bulk of the population to it prior to the arrival of the Theriz Cultivation Unit in the system.*

He recorded the necessary data and departed the planet. When he reported back to the Praesidis Primor, a Machim fleet would be sent to wipe this repugnance from existence.

But for the moment, he was far more curious about where all the *other* low frequency signals in the Provision Network led. Several must lead to the vaunted sustenance factories. Possibly many. But not likely all.

⟨R⟩

The network of gateways was as flawlessly organized as one expected from the Katasketousya. Signals led to and activated dimensional bridges, which led to self-contained universes.

Many of the spaces contained stars, planets and other astronomical phenomena. Some contained nothing at all. Some contained life forms, most primitive but several rudimentarily advanced, and a few which fell outside recognized norms for life form development.

He had thus far found no additional transplants from Amaranthe, but there were many spaces remaining.

Conclusion #6: *The Katasketousya are using the majority of the Provision Network to breed a variety of life forms in secret, without informing the Directorate of their activities or seeking permission from the Erevna Primor for them.*

Conclusion #7: *While the exact reasons for and goals of the Katasketousya malfeasance are not yet known, it logically follows from the evidence that they are pursuing a subversive, treasonous agenda.*

The full nature and extent of this agenda required further investigation to determine. As it was a natural extension of his initial assignment, he set about doing so.

PART V:

DEWDROPS & FLOWER PETALS

"Some things you know all your life. They are so simple and true they must be said without elegance, meter and rhyme...they must be naked and alone, they must stand for themselves."

— *Philip Levine*

26

SIYANE

Caleb, you need to wake up.

He struggled up from the depths of a dream. He didn't want to wake up. This was the best sleep he'd had in a long time, full of serenity and contentment.

Wake up now.

He sat straight up in the bed, instantly at full readiness, and discovered he was alone in it.

Valkyrie?

There was no response, but the lights in the cabin brightened slightly. Enough for him to see.

But not see her. He leapt out of the bed and called out. "Alex? Where are you?"

Nothing. As he moved toward the stairs to check the main cabin, he caught a faint gleam to his right. Light reflecting on shimmering skin.

He found her huddled on the floor beside the chair, pressed against the wall. He crouched beside her. "What's wrong?"

She shrank away from his touch to hide her face. "D-don't want...don't see me l-like this...."

Like what? She was sweating so profusely her skin glistened in the dim light, and she was shivering. Was she sick? Poisoned?

Valkyrie, what is wrong with her?

In a word? Withdrawal. In a few more words, acute neurological withdrawal.

The words knocked him on his ass as surely as if they'd reached out and shoved him.

Consequences.

The signs of addiction had been there all along. He knew how they manifested; he'd seen them many times in his years as an intelligence agent.

But this time he'd been too busy pampering a bruised ego to pay the slightest attention. He'd completely missed it in an egregious case of willful blindness, and instead of helping her he had tormented her into struggling with it alone.

He might be the worst human being alive. He was certainly the worst husband alive.

But he could begin rectifying that error right now, this instant. From here forward. He reached out and touched her arm.

She tried to recoil, but there was nowhere left for her to go. He wound one arm beneath her knees and the other around her shoulders and drew her close. She quit fighting him and wilted into his arms.

As he lifted her up, the shifting light exposed a new reflection. The wall behind her was streaked in crimson. In growing dread he inspected her hands and found her fingertips bloodied, nails shredded.

She had clawed at the wall until her fingers bled.

The magnitude of her suffering hit him so hard he almost dropped her. But he couldn't drop her; he couldn't let her down. Ever again.

He carried her to the bed, then gingerly placed her in the middle and crawled in beside her. Instantly she had curled into a ball against his chest. Her teeth were chattering, so he tugged the covers up over them.

She flailed out to shove them away.

"Baby, you're shivering."

"N-no. Hot-t-t."

Her skin was clammy and damp, but it was damp from sweat, so he pushed the covers the rest of the way back down before trying to move some of the stray strands of hair out of her face.

Her eyes were squeezed shut in a grimace, and her hands were fisted tight against her body.

...Much like during the 'nightmare' on Taenarin Aris, when she had been cut off from Valkyrie and by extension the ship. He was such a colossal idiot. "Tell me what I can do to help you."

Her head shook vehemently. "No...sorry, didn't...didn't want...."

"Shush. It's all right."

She wrenched out of his grasp and lunged for the broad viewport above the bed, dropping her forehead to the sill. Her shoulders heaved from fitful breaths.

Jesus. He wrapped his arms around her from behind, kissed her neck and coaxed her back down. Then he brought his hands up to cup her cheeks. "Listen. Let Valkyrie reconnect you to the ship. We can try—"

"No!" She tucked her head into his shoulder. "W-won't lose you."

Daggers to the heart were for pansies. He fought off tears for the second time this day, year and decade. "Look at me, please."

Bloodshot eyes, pupils so hyper-dilated the vivid silver irises were as thin as a corona during an eclipse, struggled to focus on him.

"You're not going to lose me, okay? I'm not going anywhere. I promise. I...god, I never meant to do this to you. I will spend the rest of my life making it up to you, but right now, I just need you to believe me when I say you won't lose me. So let Valkyrie reconnect you to the ship, and we'll find another way. We'll wean you off of it gradually, or we'll figure out some other—"

"No!" Alex drew back and for a few brief seconds was able to hold his gaze. Her features overflowed with pain and desperation and yet, somehow, defiance.

When she spoke, her voice was quiet but firm. "Won't lose me."

Gobsmacked by her strength and resilience, by her absurdly stubborn tenaciousness, he exhaled and tried to give her a smile. "Oh, baby...." Her hair was all in her face again, and he brushed it away tenderly. "Okay. Okay. Come here."

But she resisted his efforts to draw her close. She sucked in a long breath, as if summoning all her strength. "Valkyrie, l-listen to me. The answer is 'no.' Unequiv-v—" her jaw clenched "—unequivocally, categorically, no, now and f-forever. If I get weak later—days, weeks from now—and t-try to convince you otherwise, d-do not give in. Burn it into your f-firmware now: *no*."

'I understand.'

"No, d-don't 'understand.' That's quantum c-cagey-speak. Promise."

'Very well. I promise. The answer is no.'

She collapsed, all the fight gone from her body. He brought her into his arms as the shakes returned with a vengeance.

Valkyrie, do something. Do something to help her!

I am doing quite a lot to help her, Caleb. Do you think I'm not experiencing her distress nearly as intensely as she, and am not doing everything in my power to ease it?

He rocked Alex gently, one hand in her hair and the other caressing her back, but the shakes only intensified.

I believe you. But...can you put her to sleep, knock her out for a while? Give her a few hours of peace?

Not and continue to help her. I can stimulate and encourage the healing of damaged neural pathways, which will shorten the length of her recovery and ease its symptoms, but only while she's awake. Or I can permit her to rest now, in exchange for a lengthier period of suffering. I cannot—

I get it.

There may be something else I can do, however.

As they lay there, the wall at the head of the bed began to shimmer and fade to translucence, until the stars shone through.

His eyes widened in amazement, and he carefully reached out and felt for the wall. His hand met solid resistance where it should be. He drew it back to touch Alex's face. "Look up."

Her nose crinkled in suspicion, but after a second she complied. A gasp escaped her throat as she rolled onto her stomach and pulled herself to the edge of the bed. "H-how?"

'I adapted certain features of the cloaking shield to reflect the surrounding space on the inside as well. Given my pervasive integration into the hull, I am able to do so with a high level of precision and fidelity.'

Much as he had done, she stretched out her hand. When it met the invisible wall, she splayed her fingers out flat upon it. The tension afflicting her body palpably diminished.

This is wonderful, Valkyrie. Thank you.

It will help?

Very much, I think.

He snuggled up beside Alex and wrapped an arm around her shoulders. "While we gaze at the stars, would you like for me to tell you a story? Maybe about one of my crazy stunts on a mission, when I thought I was immortal and tried to see if I'd be able to prove myself wrong by getting myself killed?"

She jerked a semblance of a nod, though her eyes remained fixed on the view. "Y-yeah."

"You got it. Let's see. Well, there was the time I broke into the government prison on Andromeda to break this anarchist out…."

R

He talked for what must have been hours. He scoured his memory for every remotely amusing story he could come up with, embellished them and added flair.

Every now and then she laughed a little; every now and then she had a bad spell and he could do nothing for her except hold her until the worst passed and she was able to return to watching the stars. But he just kept talking.

His voice was growing hoarse when Valkyrie finally contacted him.

I've done all I can for now. The brain tissue needs time to respond and adjust. If you wish, I can induce a sleep state in her.

Do it. She deserves some rest.

Agreed. It will not take long.

He ran a hand down her cheek and lifted her chin up. "I love you, Alex. I love you so much, and I will be here when you wake up." He placed the softest kiss on her lips.

When he drew back, her eyes stayed closed. He felt her body slacken and relax in his arms.

He oh-so-carefully eased her down onto her pillow and pulled the cool sheet up to her shoulders.

Then he sank back on his own pillow and exhaled heavily.

Valkyrie, I don't know if I'll be able to sleep, but if I do, you wake me the instant anything happens. The instant.

I will do so.

He closed his eyes and allowed exhaustion and guilt to wage their inevitable war.

27

EAS STALWART II

SPACE, CENTRAL QUADRANT

Miriam dropped her elbows onto the rail spanning the edge of the raised bridge platform. The news of Eleni's death was throwing her for a loop, plain and simple.

She didn't know how she was supposed to feel, much less how she genuinely felt. Sadness, for whatever her faults, the woman did not deserve to die. Respect, for Eleni died because instead of saving herself she'd remained on the scene to shepherd those under her command to safety. Anger at OTS and their callous disregard for human life, the very thing they claimed to be trying to protect. Sorrow at the loss of someone who, in the end, wasn't a friend but had once come close.

And beneath it all, the tiniest twinge of satisfaction at the notion that sooner or later, karma always took its due.

She wasn't certain how she felt about the last bit, either. And unfortunately, she couldn't spare the mental cycles to work it out.

Christopher approached from the main lift, bringing a welcome end to her musings. He'd been angling for a fight ever since the *Churchill* was sabotaged and destroyed, but now he just looked despondent.

She gave him a sad smile. "You heard about Gianno?"

"I swear if I get my hands on...." He shook his head. "I liked her, you know. More than you, I think. And now I am ready for this galaxy to be rid of both Winslows, one way or another." He stared off in the distance for a minute, then shook himself out of the reverie. "Oh, Speaker Gagnon's on the QEC for you."

She groaned ruefully. "Excellent." It likely was a good thing, if less than optimal timing. Then she patted him on the shoulder and headed for the QEC chamber.

Charles Gagnon appeared as if he hadn't had a much better day than the rest of them. She imagined navigating Assembly politics was especially challenging of late. She didn't pity him, however. He'd been an Assembly power player for a long time now; to her mind, he could have prevented most if not all of this.

"Speaker, what can I do for you?"

He grimaced straight off. "You have stirred up quite the fracas here, Admiral. Surely there was a better, more diplomatic way to handle the situation than starting a rebellion."

"Didn't listen to my speech, I see. This isn't a rebellion, and I didn't start it. The prime minister did when she delivered an ultimatum to either enforce an unconstitutional and immoral law or face a court martial. I chose a third path."

He didn't dispute her version of events, nor did he openly accept them. "Regardless of how it all began, I am sympathetic to your professed goals but wary of your actual ones. To put it unusually bluntly, Admiral, do you want control over the government?"

She forced herself not to display open acrimony. What a ludicrous suggestion. "Of course not. This is not about gaining power—it's about restricting it—and it is not about me. Do not for an instant presume that I wanted any of this."

"Then what is your endgame, Admiral Solovy? To your mind, what brings a peaceful end to this conflict?"

"The repeal of BANIA and the release of all those who are being imprisoned solely for its violation. The passage of reasonable, fair legislation to govern the use of Artificial technologies and guarantee the protection of Prevos' human rights.

"The removal of Pamela Winslow from the office of prime minister and an investigation conducted into her activities and those of her administration for possible legal and Constitutional violations. I believe you have some experience in the steps necessary to remove a prime minister for cause."

"So I do. If you're successful in this gambit of yours, do you imagine you will name her successor?"

She sighed in exasperation. "Speaker, in my growing decades in this profession, I've seen enough politicians come and go to be able to make some generalizations. A few of them are inspirational. These are the rarest, and they change the world. A few of them are dangerous. We now find ourselves with our second dangerous prime minister in a year, which is notable, but so are the times.

"Most politicians, however, are more or less competent, more or less reasonable people. They shepherd along affairs of state such that citizens can live their lives in relative peace. As long as the next prime minister fits in the last category—or the first, but I know of no one currently serving with any prominence who does—I couldn't give a respectful damn who it is."

"Ma'am—"

"As Speaker, the Constitution gives you the job if the prime minister is removed for cause. Others may call for a special election, but I won't dispute your right to serve out Winslow's term. Perhaps you're already beginning your moves and machinations in anticipation of winning such an election if one is forced.

"Go right ahead. I won't speak out against you. I also won't speak out for you, by the way. Nor will I do so for a dozen other names which come to mind.

"If you've reached out to ask for my public support—or to make it a condition of you giving me yours—I must respectfully decline. But if your goal here today is to ensure I won't stand in your way should you make a move to unseat Winslow, then I have good news for us both. See to my other requests, and you and I will not have a problem."

He nodded thoughtfully. "Thank you for your candor. I would be happy to accept your terms, Admiral, but there is one small difficulty. The Assembly does not possess sufficient evidence to remove Winslow for cause."

"I do."

That one caught him unprepared. "Then please forward it to the Assembly Ethics Committee, where we can take it under consideration."

"So Winslow can buy off enough representatives on the Committee to bury it? No. I won't hand over the evidence until I'm assured it will see the light of day."

"I assure you it will be."

She regarded him deadpan. "I'm afraid your word alone will not suffice."

He was a consummate politician, and his frustration never reached his face; it was there to be seen nonetheless. "Then let's explore a different approach. How much of the military do you control, Admiral?"

"You don't know?"

"Trustworthy information is somewhat difficult to come by on Earth at present."

"Oh, I bet it is. Sixty-eight percent of the flag officers and seventy-seven percent of the field officers."

"Impossible."

"A lot of officers didn't care for Winslow's failed coup attempt at Scythia. Sending the military to forcibly depose a colonial governor simply because he spoke out against her was not a wise move on her part. It reeked of tyranny, of..." she recalled Eleni's accusation with a pang of remorse "...dictatorship, and it's resulted in a number of new converts."

"With those numbers you could...."

"Do nearly anything I wanted. Yes. But as I said at the start of this conversation, Volnosti is not a ploy by me to gain greater power. I am *trying* to protect innocent people and return Constitutionality and a modicum of basic morality to our government."

Gagnon straightened up in his chair and leaned forward. "Come to Earth. Bring your evidence and several of your more respected flag officers. Stand with me and Chairman Anderson in front of the Assembly and the people and make your case. I promise you we will act on it."

The Chairman of the Assembly Armed Forces Committee was leaning in her favor as well? If true, this was good news indeed.

"Interesting proposition, Speaker. Let me get back to you on it." As soon as the holo ended she turned to leave the chamber.

Christopher, meet me in the conference room in ten minutes. And send Colonel Jenner to Romane immediately. We need the special forces troops being held there.

On it. But I thought we were going to let them stew on Romane for a while. Why the change in plans?

Because the players are beginning to make their moves, and those troops are evidence.

'Admiral Solovy, before you turn your attention to other matters, you should know we have received a message and data package from Dr. Canivon.'

She stopped in the doorway. "Considering Dr. Canivon is deceased, I'll assume it's a delayed message. But what do you mean by 'we,' Thomas?"

'Allow me to clarify. The message and data package came to me from Dr. Canivon's Artificial, Vii. The message is addressed to you, and the package is addressed to both of us.'

"Understood. Show me the message."

> *Admiral Solovy,*
>
> *Devon Reynolds informs me my life is in danger. Irked though I am at the possibility, I have resigned myself to believing him. To that end, I'm putting in place a variety of contingency plans, of which this is one. Should I suffer a fate from which I cannot recover, Vii will forward several sets of files to you.*
>
> *You and I have not often been of like mind. We have each brought our own prejudices to bear on the relationship, generally to our detriment. My opinion of the Alliance government has not improved, but this is not the case with respect to some aspects of the military, and certainly with respect to you. I have come to believe, perhaps later than I should have,*

that you will always strive to act in the best interests of not merely the people generally, but also the Prevos and even Artificials.

Therefore, I am entrusting to you my ongoing research on a variety of topics related to the advancement of synthetic and biosynthetic technology. Use it well.

Included in the package is the encryption key for Olivia Montegreu's data store which Colonel Jenner procured upon her execution. I have not been withholding this information, but rather deciphered the key only yesterday using information I collected from her cybernetics while in her...service. The enclosed instructions will enable you to unlock the device without triggering a self-destruct or erasure.

Since you are reading this message, I expect we will not speak again. Good fortune in your endeavor. Steer humanity toward a better future.

— Abigail Canivon

P.S.: I am also sending my research to the Noetica Prevos, with much optimism for where they can take it. Montegreu's key is for you alone.

28

SIYANE

Caleb awoke with a start, terror yanking him from sleep to alertness.

Alex was again gone from the bed.

Valkyrie!

He leapt up, not waiting on a response before checking the corners and the space behind the chair and finding them empty. "Alex?"

"Up here."

His careening heart returned to its proper location. Her voice sounded a bit strained, but she was talking. And she was here. He rushed up the stairs.

She stood at the stove in a lopsided tank and wrinkled shorts. Her hair was pulled back in a messy, unbrushed tail. Her skin was pale, almost pasty; her eyes remained bloodshot and her pupils still far too dilated.

But she smiled—honest to heaven *smiled*—at him. "You're five minutes early. I was making you breakfast. Don't be mad at Valkyrie. I forbade her from waking you."

He'd never stopped moving, and when he reached her he brought up both hands to clasp her face and inspect it in concern. "Are you all right?"

Her lips parted. She exhaled softly, and her too-perky countenance faltered. "No. Not really. But I will be."

He wrapped his arms around her. He recognized it was far from over, but he was just so damn relieved to feel her return the embrace, free of shivers and tears. "If we had known this was going to happen, I never would have pushed you like I did. We could've handled all this differently."

She winced. "I did know."

"What?"

"I mean, maybe I didn't know it was going to be quite *that* bad. I've never had to go through a crash detox before. But I knew...I knew it would hurt. I knew it would be hard."

"Why didn't you tell me?"

"I thought it would sound like another excuse."

"Not—I mean after. Last night. Why didn't you warn me?"

"I didn't want anything to spoil the sublime make-up sex."

He rolled his eyes. "Alex."

"I mean it. Or I mean...I didn't want to let anything mar what was a special, wondrous evening. I wanted as many hours of perfection, of bliss, as I could steal, and I wanted you to have them, too."

"Hmm. And it was perfect. Thank you. You still shouldn't have kept it from me. You scared me half to death."

"I'm sorry for that, among so many other things. I ought to have considered what...." She drifted off for a moment, then blinked. "Aren't you going to ask me why I didn't tell you the true extent of what was happening to me? Earlier?"

He ran his palm along her cheek; he couldn't seem to stop touching her. "No. I get why you didn't."

"Really?"

"Yes. Right up until the last minute, you thought you were going to be able to bring it under control through sheer force of will alone. And you deeply hoped to be able to succeed." He paused. "Also, I imagine you didn't want to give it up."

Her eyes slid away, but he reached up and urged her chin back until she looked at him. "That's what addiction *is*, Alex. And even someone as remarkable as you is not immune from its insidious clutches."

She laughed haltingly. "I really tried to be."

"I've no doubt you did." Now he instinctively withdrew. "But I should have seen it. I should have realized what was happening. I could've helped you, but instead I made it so much worse. I can't begin to—"

Her face blanched. "No. This is *not* your fault."

"But I acted—"

"*No.* I won't let you take any responsibility for my poor choices. Caleb, listen to me, because I need to say something, now, before it gets lost in all the noise. What you did for me last night? No one has ever taken care of me like you did. No one has ever made me feel so safe, so protected, so…loved."

His chest warmed in the glow of her words, but he tried to make light of it. "Not since your dad when you were a kid anyway, right?"

"No. Never. This is what I'm telling you. I can't even articulate properly what it meant—what it means—to me. It's why I was making you a surprise breakfast, to say thank you…."

Her expression darkened, as if a storm rushed in to envelope her. "Which, once I reconsider it, is an incredibly lame, s-stupid way to say 'thank you.'" She shuddered. "W-why did I think something as meaningless as b-breakfast—"

"Hey." He gently grasped her shoulders. When she started to wrench away, he coaxed her back. He felt a tremble pass through her skin beneath his hands. "It's a fantastic 'thank you.' I'm starving. But if you want to do more to thank me, I have an additional, equally great way for you to do it."

She gazed at him with such hope his heart broke all over again. "You do?"

"I do. It's this: let me be here for you."

Her nose wrinkled up in consternation. "But that's the p-point. You *were* here for me—"

"Now I need you to listen to me for a minute. I know last night was probably the worst it will ever be in most ways, but I also know this isn't over for you. There are going to be good days and bad days—bad hours, maybe bad weeks. I'm okay with that.

"More than being okay with it, the one thing I desire most in the world is to be able to help you during those bad days and hours and weeks, even if 'helping' simply means holding you."

"I don't—"

"Hush. I'm not done." He smiled tenderly and kept his voice the same way. "You fear it will make you look weak, and you don't want to look weak in front of me. But last night solidified for me something I've suspected for a long time: you are by far the strongest, toughest, most resilient person I have ever met, and I am in awe of you. Holding you while you cry and scream and shake will only serve to reinforce what I know to be true, and it would be my privilege to do so."

He cupped her cheek. "Because I know you are strong, let me see you when you are weak. You never need to prove a damn thing to me, so don't do this alone. Please?"

She blinked, and a single tear escaped to trail down her cheek. "I promise, I won't hide. Truthfully, I don't think I can any longer, but...I won't try."

She glanced behind her toward the stove; when she turned back to him a few more tears flowed, but she was smiling again. "Now are you planning to put on pants, or are we eating in the bed?"

He chuckled, flush with too many emotions to resolve into a mood and not caring in the slightest that he had in fact been naked for the entirety of the conversation. It was called marriage—something he was grateful to still have in the morning light. "Um...I think we're eating in the bed."

29

CAVARE

Agent Duarte signaled the mission was a go, and the incursion team blew the front door to the OTS bunker—and the back door. Snipers covered the roof from atop neighboring buildings. Flashbang grenades followed as they swarmed inside.

Thermal imaging had pinpointed the locations of the seven people inside, and the first wave went straight for them, while the next swept every corner of every room.

Agent Benito: Priority Target Beta secured.

Duarte moved into the kitchen as two of his men hauled a woman up off the floor and secured wrist restraints on her.

"You are hereby placed under arrest for the murders of three hundred fourteen military personnel, as well as for conspiracy to kidnap Senators Garza and Viktin. Additional charges are pending."

Agent Duarte: Priority Target Alpha secured.

Graham watched the feed as the young woman struggled as viciously as a crazed animal against the restraints. She wouldn't get away. They'd sent a *lot* of agents. The capture of Faith Quillen and Ulric Toscano plus the other five in residence brought the number of OTS members under arrest on Seneca to twenty-eight.

Small comfort for all the lives the terrorists had taken, but justice late was better than no justice at all...even if it didn't feel particularly like it at the moment.

Aristide Vranas stood at the window, silently staring out. He'd been that way for a while.

Graham cleared his throat. "We're bringing in two of the OTS big guns now. They may give us a few more names, but this should mostly eradicate OTS' presence here. Mostly thanks to Division's Prevo, I'll point out."

"Huh. Well...good, then. And Romane has the leader in custody?"

Graham nodded in confirmation. "This information, and definitely his name, is being kept confidential for now. We want to give Admiral Solovy a chance to make the best play possible. It's her call when to release his identity, but I have reason to believe it will be soon."

"As long as he pays."

"He will."

The Chairman finally turned his back on the window. "I've been formally invited to Romane to sign a mutual non-aggression treaty with the IDCC. I'll do it. But first I have to bury my friend."

Graham didn't have any good response to soften the blow, so he kept silent. Gianno's body would lie in state for three days, as was customary upon the death of someone of her stature, then be the subject of the most ostentatious funeral ceremony Seneca had ever seen.

The Federation didn't bring out the pomp and gilt for much, but it goddamn honored its fallen war heroes properly.

Vranas shot him a weary look. "Before she...Eleni said Admiral Solovy didn't want us to express public support for her campaign, for strategic reasons. I'd damn sure like to do exactly that about now. I'm feeling a powerful need to give a righteous fire-burner of a speech."

"I know. But we should adhere to Solovy's wishes. Trust me when I say we're helping quite a lot behind the scenes. She seems to have the situation well in hand right now, and we don't want to tamper with what's working.

"But in the unlikely event Winslow should somehow prevail in the short term, we will lower a galaxy-sized hammer on the Prime Minister."

EARTH

LONDON
EARTH ALLIANCE SECURITY MINISTRY

Minister of Security Terry Jameson scrutinized the report a second time. "Where did you get all this information?"

"I uncovered some of it in my own investigation. Most of it came from precisely where you would expect—the accused."

"Admirals Solovy and Rychen?"

Lange nodded. If he wanted to convince Jameson to risk his neck to take down the prime minister, forthrightness must be the order of the day...to a point. "Or their people, yes. But I didn't accept it blindly. I checked it out thoroughly, and it's all good intel. Some of it is from intelligence sources, but with the proper confidentiality agreements we can produce testimony."

Jameson scratched at his head. "There were already rumors spreading about the blackmail of certain representatives and administration members. This military information, though? Simply leveling the accusation that the prime minister sent special forces against IDCC officials on Romane soil may mean the end of her career—or ours, if we can't prove it."

"We can prove it, sir. They're still sorting through the mess on Romane, but we've got visuals and physical evidence. I expect to have forensics data by tomorrow confirming the presence of at least two Alliance special forces members at the scene of Dr. Canivon's murder and another two at IDCC Headquarters."

"Those could be excused away by 'wrong place, wrong time.' We need more."

"Official orders leave trails, sir. Once we—once officers not beholden to the prime minister—are able to regain control of all aspects of the military infrastructure, I believe we'll find those trails."

"If, Major. And it's a big 'if.'"

"Yes, sir. But we are duty-bound to act on this evidence."

"Lucky us." He sighed. "I agree. The trick now is getting the opportunity to do so. The prime minister was able to accomplish all this because she's enormously powerful, with other powerful people in her pocket. If we don't play this perfectly, we'll find ourselves on the curb and the evidence buried."

Lange nodded agreement. "Sir, there's one more piece of intel. I, um, held it back until I was able to gauge your reaction to the rest."

"Your ace in the hole, and a get-out-of-jail-free card if I turned out to be in the prime minister's pocket as well?"

"Wouldn't you do the same, sir, were you in my position?"

"Without a doubt, but hand it over. I'm in now."

He sent the file. Jameson scanned it, eyes widening as he did. "Are we *positive?*"

"We are. The identification originated from Federation Intelligence, but they have fully authenticated it and are willing to stand by it. They have records of multiple communications between him and known members of OTS in which he issued kill orders. Plus, he was captured at the scene of the OTS safe house on Romane."

"Winslow will challenge anything from the Federation government, but we do have a minimal intelligence-sharing arrangement with them. Let me..." he reached for his panel, then stopped "...no, he's friends with Defense Minister Mori, and Mori is in her inner circle. Who do I know that I can be confident isn't in her pocket?"

The silence hung heavy in response.

Lange blinked at the priority message pinging his eVi. He read it quickly, then again. "Well."

"Something you'd care to share, Major?"

"Sir, if we can get everything in order and prepare charges in private, we might be getting a lot of very public backing, and soon."

$\mathcal{R}$

"In breaking news, the Romane government has announced the arrest of Jude Winslow, son of Earth Alliance Prime Minister Pamela Winslow, in connection with the wave of violent protests which broke out across Romane last week.

"According to authorities, Mr. Winslow has been charged with murder, attempted murder, assault, conspiracy to commit terrorist acts and destruction of private property.

"In addition, both the Romane and the Senecan Federation governments claim they possess evidence of Mr. Winslow's involvement with the Order of the True Sentients. The organization has claimed responsibility for the kidnapping of two Federation senators and is accused of perpetrating a recent spate of attacks on Romane and Seneca, including the bombing of Federation Military Headquarters and multiple commercial buildings on Romane.

"The allegations against Prime Minister Winslow's son come on the heels of a new challenge to BANIA filed with the Supreme Judicial Court by a coalition of Alliance-based corporations and human rights groups."

Stupid, arrogant child! He should never under any circumstances have allowed himself to be captured. He should never have been in a location or situation where capture was a possibility.

Such prideful, treacherous conceit would be his downfall. If Pamela was not exceedingly careful, it would be hers as well.

Clearly the Romane operation had been a failure, for which there was plenty of blame to go around. Much of it fell at the feet of the Prevos; this only proved how dangerous they were, how great a threat they were to all institutions and individuals. Some could be placed upon the covert operatives, though they'd come highly recommended and boasted stellar combat records.

She wondered if some or all of them were secret traitors and had sabotaged the mission.

Luis Akin sat waiting for her instructions. She muted the news feed and considered her Chief of Staff. "Can we pay someone off, privately and off the record, to get him out?"

"Before the news broke, maybe, though given the damage Romane suffered it would have been difficult. Now? No one on Romane is inclined to back down or recant in full view of the galaxy."

"Can we get him out by force?"

"Not unless you want to invade Romane."

Pamela didn't respond immediately. The prospect was admittedly appealing. Before the IDCC, before Solovy's rebellion, it would have been doable, too. But she had to conserve her resources and safeguard her—the Earth Alliance's—interests at home.

She shook her head. "After their abject failure during the riots, I assume a stealth incursion is unlikely to succeed, either. What about getting a message through to him? Is there any way to counter the shielding on his cell?"

He shook his head. "It's local, hardware-generated and non-networked."

Perhaps it was for the best, as there was no good message she could send. She straightened her posture. "We'll have to defeat the IDCC in the press for now, then."

Akin smiled wryly. "On this point you're in luck, as the press is most anxious for a public statement."

"Yes. Now that I consider it further, this may be a boon. Jude's false arrest is yet more evidence of the IDCC's malignancy."

He cleared his throat. "And the Federation's accusations? They will ask."

"The Federation will never miss an opportunity to cast the Earth Alliance in a poor light. We've never trusted what they have to say. Inform the media I'll be making a statement in ten minutes."

⫘

"Of course my son is innocent. He was visiting Romane on business for my husband's charity, Sharing for Success, and was simply caught in the crossfire.

"Romane was facing an uprising by its own citizens—citizens who are disgusted by their government's involvement in the IDCC and wanted to retake their home from Prevo domination. The police used gestapo tactics to crush the protests and arrested anyone who was in view. My son had the misfortune of walking from one place to another at the wrong time."

"What about the Senecan Federation—"

"Seneca has a lengthy history of spouting blustering propaganda in our direction. This is no different, and it is as impotent and false as always. But the real threat is the Prevo-controlled IDCC, and it has shown its true face with this outrageous act. Not content to merely hold the average, ordinary person under its boot, it would frame my *son* in order to weaken the Alliance.

"This is a vile, disgusting attempt to raise doubts about our earnest efforts to stem the poisoning of our youth by their Prevo corruption.

"I ask all of you listening and watching not to allow that to happen. Because if they succeed in weakening the Alliance, it won't be long before they arrive to enslave all of you as well. We must remain strong and vigilant in our fight against this threat."

"Prime Minister, how do you respond to the announcement earlier today by Assembly Speaker Gagnon that he intends to open an investigation into reports your administration used extortion and blackmail to secure passage of BANIA?"

Her jaw clenched. *Ungrateful, back-stabbing coward.* "The Speaker is welcome to investigate all he likes. Meanwhile, I will be defending our citizens."

30

ROMANE

"That pompous, supercilious prig! How can she stand in front of news cams and tell such bald-faced lies with a straight face?"

When no response arrived, Morgan spun from the news feed screen to find Mia regarding her with a raised eyebrow. She frowned. "Don't you agree?"

" 'Supercilious?' "

Had she said that? It seemed she had. "Must be one of Stanley's words." In truth, it cheered her somewhat, the notion some fragment of his personality continued to lurk inside her, occasionally tossing up cultured, urbane terms of art just in time for her to utter them.

"It's also accurate. No one has challenged Winslow for so long, she's convinced she can simply *say* things and they will somehow become reality by...I don't know, the sheer power of her hypnotic voice or something."

"Admiral Solovy's challenging her."

"Yeah, well..." Morgan gestured in the direction of the news feed screen "...Winslow's still talking. Mia, why aren't you more upset? The woman's done nothing but malign you, practically since the day you woke up."

Mia shrugged. "To me, she looks weak. Baseless accusations are the last refuge of the desperate. We're *winning*, Morgan. Admiral Solovy is *winning*. The cost has been high, and I can only hope it will grow no higher. But while she may have the Alliance-captive news feeds, we have the power. And we don't need a bunch of cams floating around us to exercise it."

"Valid perspective, I suppose. She still makes my skin itch like a bad rash." Morgan lounged against the wall, trying to impose a measure of relaxation on herself. What she really needed was a good fighter speed run around the stellar system. Or to get laid. But Harper was in the middle of patching up gear damaged during the riots, and Morgan knew better than to think the woman was apt to abandon the work before it was complete.

For the briefest second the possibility of hitting the bars popped into her head, but she quickly squelched it. She wasn't going to do it, for a dozen reasons but mostly because she genuinely didn't want anyone else in her bed. *Huh.*

"Hell, yes, it's a valid perspective." Mia's chuckle died in her throat. "Listen, there is one thing about Winslow's tirade which does concern me—not what she said, but what she implied. If by some dire turn of fate Admiral Solovy loses and Winslow regains full control of the Alliance military, she's coming for us. For Romane."

Morgan nodded. "I'll get to bolstering the defenses and finding us more firepower. With a little luck Seneca may choose to back us up, but we can't rely on them or anyone else to save us."

She blew a breath out through pursed lips. "Nothing like an insurmountable challenge to get the blood pumping. First thing I want to do is get arcalasers installed on all the ground defense turrets, then upgrade their shielding—" she bounced off the wall with a jerk, chin dropping in shock "—are they here *now?*"

"What? Oh...." Mia drew her petite frame up to an alert posture as she saw it, too—the stream from one of hundreds of Romane's space defense network high-sensitivity beacons. "I doubt it. It's only the one ship, and it's not trying to hide. Check it out, though."

Morgan was already pulling on her jacket and heading for the door.

R

Malcolm made his way to the top floor of IDCC Headquarters on the assumption Mia's office was located in the same place as when he'd last visited. It was only a few weeks ago, and as he understood it she had solidified her leadership position in the time since.

He cleared two security checkpoints without incident, as apparently his name resided on a list of authorized visitors. That was unexpected.

Signs of the recent riots remained here and there in piled-up debris and stray damage on the streets, but inside the building the impact appeared to be limited to some shattered windows, all of which were already being replaced. Thank God the rioters hadn't breached the building.

Mia's office was chaotic, but in a strangely organized sort of way. After studying the activity for a few seconds, he decided it must be serving as an ad-hoc command and planning center.

He didn't recognize anyone in the room—other than *her* of course—which maybe was for the best.

As he stood in the doorway, the various conversations began to die out. People were noticing him. Granted, the Alliance fatigues and Volnosti patch weren't much of a disguise.

She was talking with an older woman, but when the hush dimmed to silence, she glanced toward the door.

Brilliant, piercing jade irises landed on him, and his breath hitched. Had she learned he was coming and altered them for him? Foolish thought, and one which led down a path he should really get off of post-haste.

Then she smiled at him, and he resigned himself to the path.

"Malcolm, come in. This is a surprise."

"Is it? I assumed you'd been tracking me since I reached Romane space—I mean I assumed you'd know there was an Earth Alliance ship in orbit and an officer on the ground." He cringed; this was going splendidly. Everything had been so much easier before it had occurred to him *feelings* might be involved.

She motioned him over to an area comparatively free of chaos by one of the windows, and those present gradually returned to doing whatever he'd interrupted. "I admit, I did know there was an Earth Alliance ship in orbit—but not who was on it. Morgan has a recon craft pinned to your vessel and two fighters on standby in the wings, by the way. I suppose I..." her brow knotted "...can I call her off?"

He heard the wariness in her voice and sought to lighten it with a light chuckle. "We come in peace, I promise—peace toward the IDCC. Admiral Solovy learned Alliance covert special forces were involved in the riots and sent us to deal with them. I'm here to request a hand-over of all Alliance military prisoners you have in custody."

"They're facing serious charges here. Why do you want them?"

"We need to find out what their orders were and who gave them. If Winslow truly is behind it—if she truly is in bed with OTS—we need actionable evidence of it. We need sworn statements, records of orders and anything else we can get from them."

When she didn't respond, he reached out and touched her shoulder gently. "Mia, we're on your side."

"I know. And we're on *your* side—well, Admiral Solovy's side, which I'm sincerely relieved to learn is your side as well."

"I couldn't follow orders calling for the arrest and imprisonment of Prevos simply for being Prevos. Not with what I know to be true."

"What is it that you know?"

She was staring at him quite intently now, and the background noise faded away. "That Prevos aren't the enemy. You aren't monsters or abominations. You're people same as us, only...better."

"Some Prevos *are* the enemy. Montegreu certainly was, but she's not the only one."

Had she taken a step toward him? "I've met a lot of bad people, Mia. I can tell the difference."

"I'm glad."

A loud noise behind him triggered his combat reflexes, and he spun around as his hand went for his weapon...but someone was moving a large crate down the hallway, badly. He exhaled and turned back to her. "Sorry. Habit."

"I've no doubt. Okay."

"Okay what?"

"Oh, um, the prisoners. We'll need to draw up some official documentation, but Harper can work with you to effect their transfer to your custody. What about Winslow? The son, I mean."

"Better for you to keep him for now. He's a civilian, and candidly, it's better optics for him to be under arrest by the Romane government for his crimes than held captive by the prime minister's personal adversary."

"Makes sense. Harper's down in the armory. Do you remember how to get there?"

"I do." He made no move to leave, and a smile began tugging at the corners of her mouth, though she seemed to be fighting it.

Oh, to hell with it. He cleared his throat and lowered his voice. "Listen, if we make it through this mess alive, and I don't end up in military prison, and the galaxy calms down for, say, a week or so...is there any chance we could meet for lunch? Just for...well, lunch."

Now she definitely took a step toward him. Her fingers wound around his hand. "Colonel Jenner, are you asking me on a date?"

⤬

Alex paused on the sidewalk outside IDCC Headquarters to gaze upward. Both suns were high in the sky, giving it a tinge of mauve and creating prismatic reflections off the glass skyscrapers.

She inhaled deeply, relishing the suns' warmth on her face. It was like waking from a dream, stepping into the sunlight.

The grasp she had on reality was still unreliable. She experienced random, unpredictable flashes where everything faded away and her mind reached for the elemental realm to anchor itself in.

It took a great deal of concentration to escape those traps, fighting her own mind as it fought itself. Valkyrie tried to help, but the Artificial's natural existence was closer to the elemental realm than the physical one, and she didn't necessarily know the way out.

Caleb squeezed her hand—on the sidewalk, beside her, outside in the sun—and she leaned in close to wind her arm around his. To feel him, the most real object in existence.

She'd woken up this morning invigorated, convinced she had this little problem beat, dammit. Then while she was showering, out of nowhere a craving hit her so forcefully she would have physically crawled into the walls of the ship if it were possible.

Caleb was working upstairs, but she called to him, because she'd promised him she would and because she didn't want to suffer alone. Because she needed him. He'd stripped and climbed into the shower with her without hesitation, wrapped his arms around her and held her while her fingers raked at his chest until she broke down sobbing into his neck.

So, yes, it seemed she had a distance farther to travel before this trial was behind her. But in those moments in the shower, she'd never felt more cared for in her life.

Now she flashed him a broad smile. "Come on. Let's head inside."

"Are you sure you're ready? We can stand out here and bask in the light for hours if you want."

His tone was teasing but warm, and she eyed the horizon a bit wistfully. "And I kind of do want to. But events are rapidly leaving us behind, and we cannot allow such a thing to happen."

R

They could hear the chatter overflowing out of Mia's busy office as soon as they reached the hall, so they cautiously peeked in the doorway.

There were several people inside, but none more instantly recognizable than Malcolm. He stood talking to Mia by the window. Their heads were huddled close together, their voices low in contrast with those around them.

And…were they…*holding hands?*

Alex's brow furrowed in genuine perplexity; on checking, she found Caleb wore a similar countenance. "Are we seeing what I think we're seeing?"

He opened his mouth, closed it, then huffed a breath. "I think we are."

Her lips pursed. "Out of curiosity, when you and Mia stopped dating, or whatever it was you did, who took the initiative to end it?"

He arched an eyebrow, still looking rather befuddled. "She did, actually."

"Oh my god, we're their castoffs."

He sank against the door frame, laughing openly. It was infectious, and she leaned into him and tried to muffle her own laughter in the folds of his shirt.

How long had it been since she'd heard him laugh this freely? How long had it been since *she'd* laughed freely? She'd never imagined laughter could be this euphoric, but damned if it wasn't better than any rave chimeral.

Eventually their antics caught Malcolm and Mia's attention. Malcolm's eyes widened in a flash of horror before he covered it up beneath a soldier's scowl, and they hurriedly stepped apart.

Mia plastered on a breezy expression and motioned them in. "Caleb, Alex. I wasn't expecting you this morning."

Alex had to bite the inside of her cheek to keep from laughing as Malcolm nodded. "She wasn't expecting me, either. I'm here to— Alex, your mother sent me to acquire the Alliance infiltrators from the other night. For them. I'm here for them. I heard you two were back from the other side of the portal. Good—I mean that you're safe and…."

She could no longer prevent a smirk from breaking across her face.

Malcolm shot her a withering glare and groaned in resignation. "I'm going to go over here and bang my forehead against the wall for a few minutes. Yell if you need me."

She patted him on the shoulder affectionately as he passed, while Caleb stared at Mia in mock astonishment. On second thought, the astonishment was probably legitimate.

Mia shrugged. "Drop the disapproving older brother routine, Caleb. There's nothing going on." Her gaze drifted past Alex to where Malcolm had retreated. "Yet."

She blinked deliberately and returned her focus to them. "*Moving on*. Alex, you look..." Alex sensed the faintest tickle of Mia's mind at the edges of hers as Mia smiled "...you are better."

"I am. Thank you for retroactively conscripting me and generally smoothing over what could've been a *khrenovuyu* mess. I was, um...thank you."

"You're welcome, but it wasn't a problem."

"So am I completely in the clear? Do I need to worry about this coming back to bite me? I mean, I understand if—"

"You're good. You simply did our work for us."

Alex closed her eyes for the briefest span and allowed this one weight to lift. A vocal portion of her conscience screamed that she didn't deserve to escape punishment; another, more nuanced voice muttered that she'd created plenty of punishment for herself she wouldn't be escaping anytime soon.

Nonetheless, she'd take the lack of a prison cell in her future as a win.

Caleb's hand alighted on the small of her back. "In that case, will you be all right here for a little while? I want to run an errand."

He was being overprotective, but it was both sweet and comforting. "I'm good. Go."

He leaned in to place a soft kiss on her ear. "Be back soon."

She watched him leave, then immediately grabbed Mia by the hand. "Come on, let's go talk to Malcolm."

"What? Why...?"

He saw them coming and adopted a stiff military stance, for which she gave him an exasperated sigh. "Oh, for the love of everything, *relax*."

"I wasn't aware I was...fine." His shoulders dropped in defeat. "How are you?"

"Not sure. Ask me again in a week. You've been with my mother? How is *she*?"

"Honestly? On fire. Her determination is contagious and inspiring, to the point military commands and civilian governments are lining up to support her. They lost the *Churchill* to sabotage at Scythia, though. Most of the crew was able to escape, but a lot of good people didn't make it. If anything, the loss has emboldened the rank and file."

"Rychen?"

"He made it out, and he is not a happy man."

"I'm glad you're with her. Thank you—I realize you're not doing it for me, but even so, thank you."

"There was never any real question for me as to which side I belonged on. Speaking of, I should move things along here. I'm going to have to catch up with her as it is."

"Catch up with her where? I'm afraid I've been a little out of the loop the last few days."

He hesitated for a split-second before responding. "She's returning to Earth."

"But Winslow's still in power."

"She is. But the Assembly is on the verge of revolt, and they're begging for your mother's support. The public is up in arms, and your mother now has most of the military behind her. She thinks it's time."

Alex recalled the final moves of the Metigen War, and the machinations she and the other Prevos had engaged in. "Does Winslow have control of the Earth Terrestrial Defense Grid?"

"Maybe. She can't use it without Admiral Grigg's complicity. He's been a public supporter of Winslow, but nobody knows what he'll do if asked to fire on Alliance vessels."

"And Mom's just going to take that chance?"

Mia spoke up. "Won't the adiamene hull on her ship hold? It's effectively indestructible."

The dent in the nose of the *Siyane* caused by the Amaranthe master portal flashed in Alex's mind. " 'Effectively' isn't completely, and Earth's orbital array lasers are the most powerful weapons we've ever built." She frowned. "I need to...would you two excuse me? I'll let you get back to holding hands."

She left them standing there sputtering.

31

ROMANE

Devon sauntered down the row of cells like he was here for an afternoon game of poker.

He'd taken the time he needed to cool his rage, to temper his grief. And Annie's grief. A sideways dose of Valkyrie's grief. He was grateful Vii wasn't part of the Noesis, for her grief might crush them all.

But she was not, and today he was calm. Also quite motivated.

The man he now knew as Jude Winslow, only son of Earth Alliance Prime Minister Pamela Winslow and wealthy financier Frederick Winslow, had the temerity to look upon him with contempt.

"Abomination. You managed to survive all this messy, ruinous chaos. But I suppose that's what your kind does, isn't it? Survive at any cost?"

"Among other talents." Devon strolled across the stretch of hallway in front of the cell. Despite the generally overflowing state of Romane's detention facilities, it was the only occupied cell on this hall. A solitary confinement of sorts. "Your engineered 'chaos' doesn't look so ruinous from where I stand. Well, except for you and your pals."

"Come here to kill me, have you? Now that you have me tied up and oh-so helpless?"

"Yes."

He didn't miss the minuscule flinch in Jude's muscles. "It was what I told myself I was coming here to do—and make no mistake, asshole, you deserve to die. Thanks to your parentage you probably won't anytime soon, but boy do you deserve it."

Devon's eyes cut narrowly at the man. "When we met on Pandora, you wanted to kill me, because you were afraid of me—"

"Bullshit, freak. I wanted to kill you because you have no place among the living."

"We *are* the living, you pretentious psycho. We are more alive than you could ever imagine, and the world is alive around us in ways you could never comprehend."

"I knew it. You intend to rule us—make us kneel, then use us as your servants."

"Not actually." Devon scowled. "Why would we do that? We don't need servants, for one. And how irritating must they be? Always following you around trying to cuff your pants and wipe stains off your collar. Of course, you grew up with servants catering to your every whim, so perhaps you have a different perspective. You assume it's where we would naturally go, since to you indenturing others represents the height of power and privilege."

He abruptly leaned in close to the glass. "Silly. Little. Man."

Winslow's eyes widened, as if he feared Devon may breach the glass.

Devon leisurely backed away. "See, what you don't know about Artificials, what you never bothered to learn, is that they love people. They're enraptured by humanity in all its foibles and missteps and triumphs.

"What I gained from joining with an Artificial, aside from the oh-my-god-mind-blowing amount of processing power and speed of thought and data—your brain would just melt at the data—was something rather unexpected: a far greater appreciation for the human race than I ever had as one of its members.

"Prevos will never subjugate humanity, because Artificials see humanity as the best of life. And the worst of life—see Exhibit A, you. But the best of life is what's important to them, and to us. We're still human, at least as much as we're Artificial. Humanity's future is our future...."

He forced a pause, chuckling under his breath. Annie might have gotten a mite caught up in the speech-making there.

Then he notched his chin up. "So, no. Though I would take so damn much pleasure from it after what your people did to Abigail, plus the fact you're a *shockingly* annoying prick, I'm not going to kill you. You were wrong that night at *Thali's Lounge*, and you've been wrong every night since and I'd bet every night before. You think I'm a villain, and you're wrong. I'm a Prevo, and I respect humanity's laws. I will allow them to deal with you.

"I am better than you—not humanity, but specifically better than *you*—and now, I'm also done with you."

ℛ

Caleb watched the interchange from the farthest corner of the hallway, fully hidden by the Veil device Harper had lent him.

Devon was a good kid. An exceptional Prevo, and if what Caleb just witnessed was any indication, well on his way to becoming both a moral and formidable man.

But Devon hadn't seen the things Caleb had seen. He hadn't met enough monsters to recognize a bona fide one when he did meet it.

Caleb had spent some time reviewing the files on OTS' nefarious deeds, stretching back to its genesis in the aftershocks of the Metigen War, long before the atrocities which were committed here and on Seneca in recent days.

He'd seen Jude Winslow's kind before. The man was a snake in the grass, insidious and rotten to his soul. When coupled with unfettered access to money and power, he was the kind of man who could afford to bide his time until he found a way to evade punishment, then buy his freedom so he could wreak his havoc and spread his corruption anew.

There was only one surefire way to stop someone like this. And there was only one type of person capable of doing it.

When Caleb had come upon Winslow in the alleyway in the aftermath of the safe house's destruction, already knowing who the man was, he'd intended to kill him then and there. Harper had come along too soon, but it was easily enough remedied now.

Not because of the pain the man's actions caused Alex. Though her pain had wrent at his soul, it had also ultimately played a role in bringing her back to life and back to him.

No, this was Caleb's duty. It was the obligation he'd accepted for good and ill when he'd taken Samuel's offer some eighteen years earlier. He wasn't paid by the Senecan Federation government any longer, but protecting others would always be his duty. To his way of thinking he'd merely embarked on a new phase of it when he'd ventured into the portal network in search of secrets and answers.

In days soon to come, humanity was going to need to be at its best—better, stronger, more determined than it had ever been. His study of history at university years ago taught Caleb a few things, but one of the most important was this: more often than anyone realized, the difference between history—and thus future—shifting one way instead of another was a single decision by a single person.

A poison with power like Jude Winslow could not, *must* not, be allowed to make a decision that sent history and future off in a calamitous direction.

All philosophy aside, he'd dearly love to throttle the life out of the man with his bare hands. Unfortunately, it would be better for everyone, including Caleb, if the terrorist died in an apparent suicide. It made for an easy, inherently logical tale to spin, truth but for the arrogance inbred into the man's soul preventing it.

But close enough to the truth would do.

He gazed down at the remote eVi hacking tool—they called it a Reverb. Initially developed by Division, as he understood it, the Prevos had uncovered and procured the technology quickly thereafter. The IDCC RRF possessed two of these fearsome little devices, one of which he now held in his hand.

The smart worm it was programmed to inject into the man's eVi wouldn't activate for another twenty hours, removing any chance of suspicion falling on him.

The door to the prisoner wing closed as Devon departed, and Caleb stepped up to Winslow's cell.

32

ROMANE

Alex picked her way through the splintered remains of a door into the Connova Interstellar offices. A bot vacuumed up shards of glass coating the floor; all the windows had been blown out, leaving the warm, late-morning breeze to circle freely through the room.

"Scoot to the left a little?"

Startled, she did as requested.

"Thanks." Noah squeezed past her lugging a hefty quantum box, which he carried to the cabinet in the far wall.

"Ken, are you in here?"

A head popped up from beneath the other side of a large desk in the middle of the room. "Over here. Rewiring."

Alex tip-toed through the mess. "Did you get bombed by OTS?"

Noah grunted as he worked to position the box inside the cabinet. "Nah, this is just collateral damage. The building across the street kind of...exploded. We were in transit and missed the show."

She glanced out the absent windows. There wasn't a building across the street, so she went over and peered down. Ah, rubble. Lots of rubble. She nodded understanding and moved around the back of the desk to squat next to Kennedy. "I need to talk to you about Mom's ship. She's intending to send it up against the Earth Terrestrial Defense Grid."

Kennedy secured a length of photal fiber weave into place. "I know."

"You *know*?"

"She sent me a message asking if the adiamene could withstand it. I said 'maybe.'"

" 'Maybe' isn't good enough!"

Kennedy scowled at her. "I guess yelling is an improvement on vacant stares, but don't yell at me. 'Maybe' is the best answer I have."

"Sorry." Alex grimaced; her head was suddenly throbbing. It felt as if her brain was banging rudely against her skull, demanding to be set free. She pinched the bridge of her nose as the familiar scratching *need* reemerged to tear at her throat, her chest, her eyes, her soul.

She breathed in slowly, carefully...then out equally so, and with a lot of help from Valkyrie the sensations faded into the background. Not gone, but quieted enough she could ignore them for now.

"Are you all right?"

She opened one eye to cringe at Kennedy. "You remember how much it sucks to get off Skies+ after you've been doing a bit too much of it for a while? Quadruple...no, quintuple that, and for like, I don't even know how long it's going to last. But yeah..." she drew in a stronger breath and lifted her chin "...I'm all right. Swear."

Kennedy scooted out from under the desk to prop against the rear wall. "Why didn't you tell me it was that bad?"

Alex contemplated the shattered windows, but no easy answers were to be found in the splinters of glass. "I almost did, back on Messis I, and again on the *Siyane*. But I was...embarrassed? And part of me didn't truly want help until it was too late and I was out of options. So I convinced myself you had more important things to do, such as help my mother win a war. I'm pretty sure I had a thousand more reasons that would ring hollow and sound pathetic now."

She reached over and squeezed Kennedy's hand. "*Sorry*."

"Caleb?"

"Merciful. Extraordinary. My savior. Most importantly, still here."

"Hmm."

Noah waved an arm at them on his way out the door for more equipment. "Oh, forgive her already. Then she can also help her mother win the war and get my dad out of prison and we can all party properly."

"What? His dad's in prison?"

Kennedy winced. "For helping me, no less. Hello, guilt trip. I gave a speech from his place on Aquila to this group of Alliance manufacturing luminaries. The authorities arrested him for harboring a fugitive. I guess it's supposed to put pressure on me to surrender, or recant, or something? I feel guilty as hell about it, but I'm not going to do any of those things."

"Is his dad safe?"

"Hopefully? Lionel said not to worry about him and concentrate on unseating Winslow, so that's what we're trying to do. Well, and clean up." Kennedy chuckled. "So, forgiveness. If you're good, it is, as Noah says, 'all good.' Are you good?"

Alex gazed tremulously at the ceiling. "I am reeling and scrambling and vaguely terrified, but yep, I'm good."

Kennedy regarded her critically, eyes narrowed, for another moment, then shrugged. "Okay. The problem with the adiamene question is two-fold. One, we don't have a way to conduct real-world tests on the effect of an impact as powerful as multiple lasers from the grid will generate. The sims say the hull will start to fail at seven simultaneous hits of four hundred kilotonnes of directed energy.

"But the other complication is, we've seen that the adiamene itself manifests characteristics above and beyond what all the chemical formulas and sims say it should. So it will be stronger than the sims say, but I don't know how much stronger and I have no way to find out."

Kennedy pushed herself to her feet and offered Alex a hand up to join her. "But in addition to the formidable hull, the *Stalwart II* has the strongest defense shields we can produce. They're easily double the strength of those the rest of the Alliance has deployed."

"Shields."

"I know, I know, shields can't withstand that level of energy, but they can mitigate it."

"Shields." Alex began wandering around the room, haphazardly half-dodging debris. "Shields, shields—"

Abruptly she froze mid-step. *Input, function transformation, reflection output.*

Yes, that's how the cloaking shield works. Simple, after a fashion.

But isn't the inverse of the reflection—run a test model of that, killing the noise but keeping the atoms—

Was this what it meant for her mind to be awake and her own again? To be free of the fog and ethereal haze?

Done.

Now prism—dipyramid form—the folded inversed reflection of the data, of the whole fucking space—

And was this also the parting gift her forays into the elemental realm had bestowed on her? Had her too-lengthy hours spent drowning in starstuff given her the singular perspective needed to solve this riddle? Had they given her the ability to be fully alive in this space—unquestionably the *real* space—yet able to sense, to intuitively *see* as an embedded overlay, all the others?

"Alex? What about the shields?"

She closed her eyes and let the result of Valkyrie's modeling unfold in her virtual vision. Reflections of reflections until what was hidden became revealed.

Valkyrie, do you see it?

I do. I confess I never would have thought to approach it from this perspective.

But this is how they do it—this is how the Metigens access all those extra dimensions we've seen them use. And I think we can recreate it.

I think perhaps...yes.

Get started on the math. Devon?

Devon: Holy shit, that's deep magic. Brilliant...wait, what?

Alex: The fourth face of the dipyramid—we need to derive the equations necessary to funnel data—atoms, matter, energy—from the input to the location of the fourth face. Or the fifth, but we can start small.

Devon: Riiiiiight. Yep. We'll help. Just as soon as Annie understands it and explains it to me.

"Hello, Alex...."

She grinned at Kennedy's mystified expression, then impulsively reached over and hugged her. "Thank you. Thank you. You are the absolute best. I've got to go."

"Go where?"

Caleb, meet me at the Siyane. *And hurry.*

"I've got to get to the *Stalwart II* before it gets to Earth."

INTERMEZZO V

MOSAIC

The next created space in the Provision Network which Aver visited was fully populated with stars, galaxies and the breadth of astronomical phenomena. His routine broad sweep scan, however, returned a number of surprising features. Characteristics he hadn't yet seen.

Similarities to Amaranthe.

Further study suggested this space, alone among those he had encountered, was structured on an intra- and intergalactic scale nearly identical to Amaranthe. Nowhere was this more true than the region where the gateway opened.

What possible objective were the Katasketousya pursuing, to create such an anathema of nature?

The supradimensional wave he had found in each of the active created spaces led across this galaxy to a broad swath of systems hosting a moderate level of technology. Loud, wasteful, immature technology, but sufficient to support effective interstellar travel. Initial readings hinted at a Tier III-C civilization, or possibly even III-B. Certainly the most progressed he'd encountered in the Provision Network thus far.

He ignored all the noise for now to follow the supradimensional wave to its destination.

His instruments identified nine planetary bodies in the system, with a significant asteroid belt between the fourth and fifth and multiple planetoids in distant solar orbit. He measured the third planet's location at 1 AU and noted it had a single satellite at 0.0025 AU distance.

Assigning to chance the familiarity of the system strained the laws of probability.

His eyes showed him an ordinary garden world orbiting an ordinary G2V yellow dwarf. Habitats and instruments swarmed in multiple orbits above the planet, but much of its terrestrial land and waters remained uncovered and exposed to open air.

It was not a place his eyes recognized as familiar. But his data-banks carried thousands of millennia of data in them. Buried in this sea of data were images of the Anaden homeworld from a distant past, before his ancestors had transformed their origin planet into an endless city.

Was he observing a replica of Solum?

◇

IDRYMA

I took some pleasure from entering the Idryma as a reinstated Analystae. No longer an exile, per Lakhes' decree, circumstances and necessity. I nevertheless refrained from displaying said pleasure in any physical luster or oscillation, as the cause for the Conclave session was dire indeed.

Gloating was not a favored comportment, and it would not aid my re-integration.

Iapetus began pronouncements as soon as Lakhes entered the chamber. "I say again, this is nothing more than our Human trou-blemakers continuing their spasmodic gallivanting through the Mosaic. Their recent acquisition of new, in my opinion ill-advised, knowledge has simply spurred them to greater haste."

"Demonstrably incorrect, Iapetus. They returned to Aurora di-rectly from Enisle Twenty-Seven and remain there now."

"So certain of this, are you, Mnemosyne?"

"I am."

"Given this information—" Lakhes moved among them rather than come to rest at his usual position "—we are facing one of two possibilities. The first is that a ship from one of the Enisles has dis-covered their gateway and traversed it. Seven species possess the interstellar travel technology necessary to do so. Two of them have knowledge of the portals. The second possibility is that a ship from Amaranthe has entered the Mosaic.

"My tardiness was due to my acquisition of new data. I'm here to inform you now: both of these possibilities are in fact true."

A murmur swept across the Conclave members, an uneasy mix of excitement and terror.

Lakhes radiated for calm. "A Fylliot from Enisle Thirty-Eight traveled to Amaranthe in order to search for his family, who was absent from the system at the time of the evacuation and did not accompany the migrators. His vessel has not returned. However, in the time since, another vessel has entered the Mosaic from Amaranthe."

"How? The gateway prevents it."

Lakhes revolved in a slow circle. "Having made the journey with its pilot during the evacuation, the Fylliot ship possessed the passcode for the Amaranthe gateway."

Iapetus pulsed loudly in agitation. "Are you suggesting the Fylliot was...what? Captured?"

"And doubtless killed."

"We must lock down the gateways immediately—"

I expanded in size as appropriate to my news. "It is already too late."

All those present directed their attention to me as I moved to the center of the chamber. "After visiting several Enisles in rapid succession, the vessel in question has traversed the Aurora portal. Here you may see it."

I projected the image captured by the monitors located on Aurora Thesi.

"That is an Anaden vessel."

Lakhes considered the image with customary stoicism. "Yes. A Praesidis Inquisitor vessel to be precise. We can only be grateful it is not a Machim one—or a thousand, for I have never seen fewer."

True enough. Machim fleets did not scout; they did not temper their responses or bring to bear merely the force necessary to resolve a conflict. Instead they unleashed destruction with a magnitude of strength that ensured there was no second encounter.

Iapetus escalated toward histrionics. "What does it matter? We are all doomed."

"Does 'all' include the species of Amaranthe?"

"Those which long to be free, yes! It has all been for naught. All the millennia of work, all the trials, all the study, all the secrecy and preparation."

"Perhaps not."

Once again those present shifted to me. I sensed their residual animosity giving way to desperation. They would not care that I was the former exile if I provided them a reason to hope.

"How can we expect the Humans to defeat the Anaden Legions if they cannot defeat a single, individual Anaden? Perhaps this is the final test for them, and the one they are most ready for."

"Ready for? They don't know the slightest thing. They don't know what to expect. A Praesidis Inquisitor will kill a thousand Humans before they begin to comprehend the enormity of the threat they are facing."

"They know enough."

Lakhes approached me. "Why do you say this, Mnemosyne?"

I stared at the image of the deceptively small, innocuous vessel hovering silently before me. "Because if we are to have the feeblest glimmer of a chance in the coming war, they must."

PART VI:

CONSONANCE

*"I thank whatever gods may be
For my unconquerable soul."*

— *William Ernest Henley*

33

EAS STALWART II

Miriam spun a disk on the conference table surface. "What do we know?"

Christopher clasped his hands on the table. "Winslow is in London today. She basically fled Washington to avoid a bevy of agitated politicos. She's expected to give a speech to the European Trade Council this evening. It might be a good venue to target—public, with a live news feed, and off Assembly grounds. I realize Gagnon wants us *on* Assembly grounds, but I'm not at all certain it's a good idea. I don't trust him."

She couldn't say as she did, either, but she kept it to herself, for the Speaker might be their best route forward. "What about Admiral Grigg? Any indication he's wavering?"

"Publicly he remains solidly behind Winslow. Privately, he's had five meetings with advisers in the last two days and a visit from Chairman Anderson. If I had to lay stakes down, I'd say he won't press the trigger. But it really comes down to how accustomed he's become to his new level of power."

"Which is why I'm not as confident as you that Grigg will balk. He's long craved power. Okay, I want you to transfer to the *Cantigny*. If it goes badly for me, you'll need to be in a position to press whatever advantage I will have given you."

"Miriam, I don't want—"

"Well, I didn't want any of this, but here we are. Please, Christopher. If we both fall, this was all for nothing, and I won't allow that to be the result."

He exhaled harshly. "Is that an order, Admiral?"

"It is."

"Fine, then. But do *not* let her shoot you down."

"I don't intend to. Now go—and keep the fleet out of harm's way when I call her bluff."

"Jesus, Miriam." At her glare he held up his hands in surrender. "All right. I'll stop pointing out your clear insanity. Good luck—I know, luck is not a factor. Have a little anyway."

He saluted and departed, leaving her alone in the conference room adjunct to her quarters.

'Her quarters' still sounded strange to her ears. She'd served tours on ships before, but they were by and large decades in the past, and those quarters had been considerably more cramped and less private. These were rather...nice.

If the circumstances were otherwise, she could almost begin to appreciate some of what Alex enjoyed about life on a starship; what David had enjoyed about it.

But they were not, and any pleasure she took from the ship or her presence aboard it was soon chased away by an austere, muted sorrow.

"David, why are we here?"

He adjusted his grip on her hand and tugged her across the cavernous showroom floor. "There's a ship I want us to look at."

Obviously there was *a ship he wanted them to look at; she hadn't meant for her question to be taken quite so literally. But there were a dozen other things they needed to be doing on a rare free Saturday, and none of them involved wandering around a commercial starship expo. "We have to pick Alexis up at 1500."*

"Which is two hours from now—plenty of time. Come on, it's right up here."

Past the next dividing wall sat a gleaming personal touring model starship. According to the scrolling placard, the design maximized internal living space above other considerations; a quick skim of the specs revealed the engines weren't the fastest on the market and it was fitted with only a single utility laser.

Miriam had to concede it was attractively designed even on the outside, though. It was sleeker and more aerodynamic than military ships, with tasteful flair in the details.

David was already talking to the sales rep. She ran her gaze down the length of the hull a second time then went over to them.

"Are we allowed to take a peek inside? We won't break anything. As Alliance military officers we're both well acquainted with the workings of starships."

"Certainly, sir. Take as long as you want—and make sure to notice the extensive refrigeration options. Top of the line!"

"Right." David jerked his head toward the ramp. She rolled her eyes and followed him up.

He went straight for the cockpit, easing into the pilot's chair and spinning it around in both directions.

How could she not smile? He was like a kid in a sweets shop, running his palms across the dash and studying the various controls as though they hid Christmas presents.

"Civilian ships are so straightforward, I could fly this in my sleep, with one arm restrained behind my back, blindfolded. Given a bit of instruction, I bet Alex could fly it without my help."

Miriam dropped her arms atop the headrest and peered over his shoulder. "Or you could use the autopilot like normal people do."

"No fun in that." He bounced out of the chair and headed through the main cabin. "The sunken entertainment area is nice, no? They do a great job of creating the feel of separate spaces without wasting actual space."

He gave the vaunted kitchen a once-over then got a devious glint in his eye. "We have to check out the bedroom—I just mean look at it. Sadly."

She squelched a laugh as she followed him up the staircase. It deposited them in a master suite adorned in mahogany synthetic wood and subtly burnished nickel accents.

"I admit. This is nice."

"Isn't it, Miri?" He fell back on the bed and let out a gasp. "Join me. You must see this."

Uncomfortable at the thought of acting so comfortable on a display ship in the middle of an expo showroom, she opted to perch on the edge of the bed and crane her neck to look up.

He grabbed her arm and unceremoniously yanked her down onto her back beside him. "See? Okay, it's merely blue sky right now. But in space it will be stars. We can make love under the stars every night."

"Every night? How very confident of you."

"Every night."

She squeezed his hand, then sighed. "It's a lovely ship, David. But even if we were able to afford it, there's no room in our life for this. We're liable at any moment to face off-world assignments for months at a time. We're required to be available on short notice for emergency deployment. And when at least one of us is stationed on Earth, we have to try to give Alexis as stable an environment as possible to grow up in."

"I know, dushen'ka. But she won't always be a little girl—before we realize it, she'll be grown up and off on her own adventures. And we won't always be military officers. We won't always be beholden to the service. One day, our lives will be our own. When that day comes, will you sleep under the stars with me?"

He made it all sound so...possible. She smiled warmly. "Yes, David. When that day comes."

She blinked out of her reverie when her comm burst to life. "Admiral, your daughter's ship is arriving."

34

EAS STALWART II

Alex embraced her mother fully. She focused her mind on the details, on the physical sensations.

Warm skin beneath her uniform.

Firm hands conveying affection in their grasp.

The faint scent of lavender in her hair, since Alex's childhood.

A smile drawing her features up, giving them life.

Heart beating solidly in her chest, giving her body life.

Real. This was real.

Caleb stood off to the side watching them, and she gave him his own, private smile.

Finally her mother broke the embrace to pull back to arms' length. "I was worried when you got caught in the OTS attacks on Romane…" she glanced over at Caleb, who had adopted a casual pose against a nearby railing "…but I suppose you two are accustomed to looking out for yourselves. And now you're here, with all your limbs intact." She frowned. "But you can't stay. This isn't your fight."

"No, it's yours—and I'm here to give you a better chance of winning it."

"What are you talking about?"

"The prime minister has control of the Terrestrial Defense Grid, doesn't she?"

Miriam's expression turned guarded. "She might."

"Are you betting on her not being willing to use it against you, betting on Admiral Grigg not being willing to use it against you, or betting your hull can withstand the assault?"

"I'm betting one of those three things will be true. Kennedy said the adiamene should hold."

"*May* hold. She said it *may* hold—under fire from five, six, seven lasers. What if it's more? I heard you're planning to be the only target on the field."

"It's a chance I'll have to take."

"No, it's not."

"Alex, I—"

"Just hear me out for a minute, please? I'm not haranguing you for melodrama's sake. I know how to modify your cloaking shield to protect you from any laser any array in the galaxy can throw at you."

"How?" Her mother didn't scoff or dismiss her with scorn, which meant rather a lot.

"Do you remember how I told you the Metigen cloaking mechanism didn't merely hide Portal Prime, but shifted any ship that got too close into an alternate dimensional plane so they passed through the space without ever encountering the planet?"

Miriam nodded cautiously.

"At the time, the algorithms they used to accomplish the shift were beyond me, but I saved a record of them. I also wasn't a Prevo then. In our exploration of the portal network we've seen a lot of uses of extra dimensions, and I've...gained a greater understanding of the way the fabric of space works."

I've felt it in my bones. I've drowned in it. I've become it.

She blinked away a momentary surge of dizziness. "I've spent the last day studying the algorithms the Metigens used, and I now understand how they work. More importantly, I can replicate them."

"You can...are you telling me you can create a field which will shift physical objects out of our physical dimensions?"

"Yep. I am."

"Can you *see* more than three dimensions, then?"

"Sort of. Not exactly. I mean I *have*, but it's more akin to I...understand where they are."

Miriam started pacing, absently stroking her jaw. "So you're saying if a laser from the Terrestrial Defense Grid, or any laser I imagine, were to get close to the ship, you could 'divert' it...but divert it where? If it kept going out the other side, the laser could still hit one of the other ships. I won't endanger those with me to protect myself."

Damn her mother's heroic streak for making the unimaginable harder.

What if we adjust the equations like...so?

Ohhh. You're right, Valkyrie, I see how cutting short the final reflection after the inversion at the end could work.

"Well, yes, that's how it worked on Portal Prime. But...I don't have to let the laser come back. The rift can simply swallow it."

"Like it fell into a black hole?"

'Technically, scientists have as yet been unable to determine—'

Alex made a face at the air, a substitute for the disembodied voice. "Excuse me, who are you?"

'I'm Thomas. It is an honor and a pleasure to make your acquaintance, Alexis Solovy.'

She raised a questioning eyebrow at her mother.

"He's my Artific—"

"Your Artificial. Yeah, I got that part from the speech patterns. You have an Artificial integrated into your ship?"

"I do. What of it?"

Alex's hand came to her mouth. *What of it?* "Um...nothing of it. Nothing at all. So as both *Thomas* and I were saying, we still don't know what's on the other side of a black hole, but for practical purposes, sure, it's a close enough analogy."

"Is this an all-or-nothing, or an either-or? How will this dimensional rift field operate vis-à-vis the cloaking?"

Alex exhaled. She was starting to get an idea of what it was like to work for her mother. "In theory, you can toggle them each independently of the other. In practice, running both at the same time will require a metric fuckton of power, which I assume is more than you have available. Sorry."

"No, it's fine. I'll work around the limitation." Her mom stared at her. "Are you certain you can do this?"

"I really think I am."

"All right. How long do you need?"

"A few hours." Immediate goal achieved, she finally stopped to look around the bridge. Her jaw promptly fell open. "Wow, Mom. This might be the most gorgeous ship I've ever seen—except for mine, of course."

Miriam shrugged, but she also beamed. "It gets the job done. Hopefully it'll stay in one piece and I'll get to keep it around for a while."

ℛ

Caleb watched Alex leave for the bowels of the ship with the Chief Engineering Officer. Part of him wanted to accompany her, but he'd be a distraction. She seemed to be in a good place, and solid engineering work almost always helped her get to a better one.

So instead he turned back to Miriam. "Mind if I ask what your plan is?"

She gave him a weighty shrug. "I can provide the Security Ministry more than enough evidence to bring charges against Winslow, but without support powerful enough to match her she'll run roughshod over them. Same with the Assembly and its Ethics Committee. So I will get myself on the ground and level the charges in person and in public, where they can't be ignored."

"That's a strategy, not a plan."

She arched a daunting eyebrow at him.

"You've said it yourself. Winslow controls the Assembly, as well as a reasonable piece of the military and all the planetary defenses. She won't let you get close enough."

"If I can get past the Terrestrial Defense Grid, she'd be insane to start a firefight in the skies above or on the streets of London."

"I suspect she will nevertheless do precisely that if it means she stops you. You have thousands of ships and tens of thousands of military personnel behind you and ready to follow your orders. Use them."

Miriam sighed. "I am *not* going to show up with a fleet of warships and blast my way into the Assembly. I do and Winslow wins by default. This cannot be about superior firepower and bullying tactics—not in the final moves. I will not frighten the people into supporting me."

Dammit, she was setting herself up in a fatal catch-22...but she was also probably right. Optics. He ran a hand through his hair. "Understood. Then you need a *plan* to get on the ground and into the Assembly without triggering a firefight. Am I understanding the goal correctly?"

"Caleb, what are you suggesting?"

"Is Richard onboard?"

She shook her head. "No, he's still on Seneca dealing with the OTS cleanup. He tried to come anyway, but I threatened to reinstate his dishonorable discharge if he did."

The woman was relentless. Much like her daughter. "What about Malcolm Jenner?"

"No, but he'll reach the fleet inside an hour. I can get him here quickly if it's required."

Jenner didn't care much for him—Caleb hadn't necessarily formed a corresponding opinion one way or the other—but he suspected it had less to do with Alex and more to do with a clash between upstanding Marine values and intelligence black ops sensibilities. He also suspected Jenner would put any ill feelings aside and follow Miriam's orders for the good of the mission.

"I recommend you do that. Have him transfer his prisoners off his ship and ready it for redeployment." He patted his shoulder bag. "You'll want a guard unit. But thanks to a couple of gifts from Mia, if Jenner can get us on the ground, we can sneak you right into the middle of the Assembly Chamber."

"'We?' Caleb, I meant what I said to Alex—this is not your fight. As soon as she finishes her work, I expect you both to vacate this ship."

He huffed a breath. "I understand what you're saying. But the truth is this is everyone's fight, more than even you know."

She glared at him wearing a frustrated countenance so much like Alex's he struggled to bury a laugh.

It was good he succeeded, as her expression continued to darken. "I am done with all of you hinting at some dire knowledge you think it's not in my best interests to know *for now*. I am the arbiter of what I do and do not need to know, and this is something I am deciding I need to know. Alex is a bit busy saving my skin at present, so out with it."

He ran a hand through his hair...again, he realized belatedly. He couldn't go behind Alex's back. Not now.

Baby, your mother just threatened to castrate me if I didn't tell her what we learned in the portal network.

What, really?

Well, no, not explicitly, but I feel as if castration might have been implied in her glare.

Yeah, I could see that.

The thing is, I suspect she's right. And I'm kind of done with secrets.

More needed to be said on that, he knew, but later would have to suffice.

Damn. Okay, go ahead. I'll be up to face the aftermath as soon as I can. I didn't intend for you to have to be the one to do this. Thank you.

Always.

He nodded solemnly. "Can we go somewhere private, where we can sit? This is going to take a little while."

⟂

Alex burst into the conference room. She was sweaty, half-covered in grease and her hair was falling out of its knot. It reminded Caleb of how she'd looked for most of his first days on the *Siyane*. He smiled.

Miriam did not. "You didn't think this was something I needed to be made aware of? Have you no faith in me at all?"

Alex groaned and collapsed against the wall. "It's exactly because I *do* have faith in you that I didn't want to tell you yet. You don't need to be lectured about how important it is for us to stay on the path of freedom and liberty or whatever, or how humans had gone astray in some other past with disastrous results, because you already appreciate how important it is. You don't need to be told this is important for the future of the multiverse universe, because for you it's important for the future of people alive here today.

"You already believe, and you're already giving everything for your belief—giving everything to ensure such a future comes to pass."

There you are.

He packed away the last vestiges of lingering terror that everything might crumble at any minute in a raging pyre of madness and tears—his own. A cognizant, vigilant peace assumed residence in the vacancy.

Meanwhile, Miriam's expression prevaricated between aggravation and fondness. "Well...thank you. But it doesn't excuse the fact that you decided something which wasn't yours to decide. I swear, you are the most bullheadedly stubborn person I have ever known."

Alex snorted.

Caleb watched on in amusement. Valkyrie had told him something this morning. She'd said it was Alex's 'bullheaded stubbornness,' to use Miriam's phrasing—and occasionally his own—which had, more than anything else, enabled her to beat the worst aspects of her addiction. She had simply refused to allow it to defeat her, under conditions that would have sent anyone lesser to a hospital or spiraling into a nightmare of torment.

It was a quality of character which could not be explained by neurology or captured in an algorithm, but its existence was proven by the results.

Alex pushed off the wall to flop into the chair next to him, tossing him a sloppy grin before regarding her mother with embellished exasperation. "Now. Can we please defer further discussions about the destiny of humanity until after you've won? Don't you want to know if I made it work?"

35

No. Impossible.

Jude would not commit suicide. He was too arrogant, too narcissistic to ever deprive the world of his genius. As he should be...*have been.*

The news had reached Pamela via her network of spies and double agents shortly after she departed Washington; it remained secret from the public for now.

He was murdered. It was the sole plausible explanation. Murdered by one of the Prevos while shackled and imprisoned.

So now they had crowned themselves judge, jury and executioner, eschewing trials or even the appearance of the rule of law.

Despots, dictators, devils as aspiring gods.

What began as the ultimate power play had now become intensely, painfully personal. Pamela would smash Romane into dust for this. She simply needed her military back to do it.

But Miriam Solovy had taken it from her. All this horror, all this conflict and destruction could be traced back to Miriam Solovy. Prevo-creator, Prevo-lover, a despot in her own right. The woman was in league with the IDCC, in league with the Federation, in league with everyone except the Alliance that had *made* her.

In the end, the extent of the woman's machinations meant she may as well have killed Jude herself.

Solovy would suffer commensurate to her crimes. And soon, for Pamela's spies also reported Solovy's fleet approached Earth even now. Doubtless the woman thought Pamela's authority weakened, as if an Assembly investigation and a few press harpies were anything more than flies throwing themselves against the window pane.

Solovy's ships would be destroyed and their admiral with them. The defecting military commanders would run home in shame and genuflect before her, swearing allegiance and begging to be allowed to keep their positions. Pamela would have her military once more. She would use it to crush the IDCC, starting with Romane, for killing her son.

Yes.

Her transport alighted on the rooftop landing pad of the Assembly, a prerogative reserved for visiting heads of state and a rare few individuals who, for one reason or another, did not need to be seen traipsing across the grounds. It was enclosed by not only a protective force field but also a visual one, preventing the press from discerning what prominent person had arrived.

She enjoyed an unobstructed view of the surroundings, however, and the sight of thousands of protesters clogging the streets below greeted her as she disembarked.

Were the people rallying to her son's cause? Standing up and demanding the government respond to Romane's flagrant misdeeds?

Strobes projected holo placards high into the air above the protestors.

> *Freedom For All Minds*
> *Prevos Are People Too*
> *You Can't Stop The Signal*
> *Break Free Of Your Shackles*

This was unacceptable. Where were the authorities? If there were Prevos in the crowd, they needed to be arrested forthwith.

The masses were so fickle, so easily swayed and marshaled. Jude—anger frothed in her chest at the thought of him and the fate he had suffered, but she must not show it publically. Her grief must be her own, for now.

He should never have relied as heavily as he did on crowds to press his agenda. But she did not need them to press hers. Let them protest.

She spun away from the scene and strode to the rooftop entrance. The sooner this ludicrous 'hearing' was concluded, the better.

The Official Summons had been offensive in its demands. She was complying only because her attorney general counseled her she was legally required to do so, but she didn't care to explain the delicate, complex justifications for the Scythia incident, particularly since it had failed. She was mourning!

If she announced Jude's death, Gagnon would delay the hearing. Etiquette demanded it.

No…she needed to save the revelation for the moment it could most work to her benefit. So she continued downstairs.

She was traversing the main hall to the Assembly Chamber, security and aides in tow, when her Chief of Staff called a halt to the procession. "Prime Minister, Admiral Grigg is reporting the detection of a warship by short-range perimeter alert sensors. He believes it's Admiral Solovy's vessel."

Oh, thank god. She nodded understanding. "We need to move to the Situation Room immediately. Luis, transfer Admiral Grigg to a dedicated holo there and reach Defense Minister Mori as well."

36

EAS STALWART II

Miriam stood on the bridge of the *Stalwart II*, her stance formal and her chin raised. The bulk of her fleet was aligned behind her, but at a distance and heavily cloaked. They would fight if a fight were required, but she was gambling on it not being necessary, and for now hers was the sole visible ship. She waited for the dance to begin.

It didn't take long.

Earth Terrestrial Defense Command: "Unidentified vessel, you are ordered to depart Sol space. Failure to do so will result in defensive measures being deployed against you."

"This vessel is not unidentified, Command. Check EASC records. This is the *EAS Stalwart II*, naval command-class vessel, serial number designation EAAF-CC1X741A, captained by myself, Admiral Miriam Draner Solovy. I am not an enemy, nor is my ship."

ETDC: "EASC records have been compromised, and your vessel's serial number designation cannot be confirmed. You therefore must be considered an enemy vessel and a threat to Earth and its citizens. Retreat or be destroyed."

She recognized the voice; this was Grigg talking, though she highly doubted he was making the decisions. He might not even be choosing the words. "Firing unprovoked on an Earth Alliance admiral is against the entirety of the Code of Military Justice and all regulations. Accuse me of the worst crimes you can conjure. File reams of charges against me. But you cannot legally shoot me down."

Miriam wondered if Winslow knew the interchange was being broadcast on every military channel and every news feed not completely beholden to the Prime Minister. Someone should probably tell her.

ETDC: "Your incursion into Earth space is a provocation. Unless you retreat, you will be considered a clear and present danger and, no matter your rank, you will be neutralized."

"Command, I've been repeatedly informed that I'm required to return to Earth to face charges of horrible crimes. I'm here, ready to do so."

ETDC: "Retreat to twenty-five megameters distance from Earth and permit your ship to be boarded so you can be taken into custody."

Miriam smirked, though only those on the bridge who happened to be glancing her way caught it. "I prefer to surrender on my own terms, Prime Minister."

The pause was long. She imagined there was much hand-waving and stammering going on. Having been present when a few charades were exposed, she knew what it looked like. She waited.

ETDC: "Your ship possesses unknown weaponry. We cannot allow it to approach Earth. Who knows what damage it and your fleet could inflict upon innocent civilians."

The voice had of course changed, but so had the tone. Winslow was having difficulty keeping her cool.

"What fleet, Prime Minister? There's only me. And I have devoted my life—my husband gave his life—to protect Earth, its citizens and all citizens of the Earth Alliance. If there is one thing in this life I will not do, it is harm the innocent people of this planet."

ETDC: "And yet you have endangered them by encouraging the proliferation of Prevo monstrosities."

Miriam kept her own composure, but inwardly she seethed. Winslow was the true monster, and if they followed her path they would all become the same. "Prevos saved the residents of Earth and every other world. They are heroes, and they are also people—

people who should not be treated as criminals without ever committing a crime. They deserve to be judged by the same standards the rest of us are."

ETDC: "Their very existence is criminal."

Not exactly the thoughtful, dignified position a head of state ought to adopt. "Only because you have made it so. But I do not accept this, nor should anyone, because it is unconstitutional, immoral and inhumane. We as a species cannot justify our way into adopting such beliefs and still call ourselves civilized."

ETDC: "Don't distract from the fact you are pointing lethal weaponry at Earth. Everything else is just words."

"And you're very good with words, aren't you, Prime Minister? You've used them to subvert the rule of law, due process and innumerable basic Constitutional and human rights. It's my responsibility to uphold those rights, and I've returned to do exactly this.

"I will not fire on any person, vessel or structure which does not first fire in an offensive manner. On this you have my promise. But I will be landing on the soil of Earth today."

ETDC: "I cannot permit you to threaten the safety of our citizens. You represent a clear and present danger to the Earth and the Earth Alliance. You have ten seconds to retreat."

So be it.

Miriam gave her bridge crew a reassuring smile, projecting confidence that she was not sending them to their graves. She thought about David, and her smile grew brighter at the image blossoming in her mind of him—

Nine nodes across three arrays of the Terrestrial Defense Grid fired their lasers. They converged into one massive beam, 3,600 kilotonnes of energy aimed at her.

The viewport was engulfed in blinding citron light, but the hull did not even vibrate. The lasers maintained sustained fire, even as their leading edges vanished prior to contact with their target.

'The dimensional rift is successfully diverting the lasers' energy, Admiral Solovy.'

"Yes, Thomas. It is."

The *Stalwart II's* sensors told her eighteen additional nodes added their firepower to the stream—likely the total number of nodes with a direct LOS to her ship. The filters struggled to keep up with the increased brightness engulfing the viewport, and she blinked away halos.

Abruptly all the luminescence vanished, and Earth's profile again resolved in the distance.

Cheers broke out on the bridge, but she merely acknowledged the warmth in her chest. *That's my girl. Thank you, Alex.*

Winslow had played the last, best card she had, and she had lost.

Miriam reopened the channel to EDTC. "Prime Minister, you may fire on me as much as you wish, but it is a waste of time and resources. You won't be able to destroy me, or even so much as ding me. Or my ship. I'll see you soon."

Next she turned to her XO. "I'm activating the cloaking shield but maintaining its rift functionality as well. Navigation, divert S 32° 12.5°z E for seven megameters."

"Yes, ma'am!"

She burned up nearly all her power to maintain both functions until she was elsewhere enough for her ship to be safe without her. Then she deactivated the dimensional rift and redirected the extra power to the cloaking shield.

Finally, she paused to take note of the air around her. Breathed in, and absorbed the reality that all was quiet. No lasers chased her. No damage reports flashed on screens, nor did alarms peal through the ship.

Breathed out.

"Major Halmi, you have the bridge."

SIYANE

SPACE, SOL SYSTEM

Alex sat in the cockpit of the *Siyane*, her knees drawn up to her chest in the chair, her body frozen in terror as multiple orbital array lasers fired.

From her vantage, stealthed ten megameters back from the *Stalwart II* with the rest of the fleet, she couldn't even detect a flare of light as they hit the rift. The lasers simply drew alarmingly close to the *Stalwart II* and no farther. The outline of the vessel remained undisturbed and undamaged.

An immense amount of power—then an insane amount more as additional nodes fired—rushed into a point seventy meters across and vanished like a waterfall disappearing over a cliff.

"Oh my god, it's working. It is working, isn't it, Valkyrie?"

'It is indeed.'

Abruptly the lasers ceased firing, leaving the *Stalwart II* floating peacefully above Earth.

She laughed in delight, relieved beyond any capacity to measure. A pulse arrived from Caleb.

> *Good job, baby, not that I ever had a doubt.*
>
> *I did. Thank you,* priyazn. *Keep her safe, will you?*
>
> *It will be my honor.*

He was already on the *Gambier* with Malcolm and his team. The ship would soon deliver them and Miriam to London. She was ridiculously proud of him for elbowing his way onto the infiltration team, if a little annoyed she didn't have a role to play in the final gambit.

Valkyrie offered her a measure of reassurance. 'Without you, there would be no final gambit.'

Because her mother would in all likelihood be dead. And they called *her* obstinate. "I know. Honestly, it's fine. I like it up here...even if all I have to do to pass the time now is worry about the *both* of them."

She gazed down at the massive profile of Earth spinning below her. Home, still and probably always. Not merely for her, but for some six billion humans.

Terrible humans with darkness rotting away their souls, like Pamela Winslow. Wonderful humans instead buoyed by joy and love, like countless family and friends. The people helping her mother now. Ethan before one of the terrible humans had robbed him of life.

Why must there always be such a struggle between the two, catching all those in the middle in their crossfire? Why were they here at this consequential moment yet again, when they had been here so many times before?

...Unless the point of humanity was to struggle. Unless the uniqueness of humanity was in its refusal to *stop* struggling. To fight, to doubt, to persevere, to never be content.

It was exhausting.

But she remembered the moment from Iona-Cead Ahearne's memory, when Lakhes had described the Anadens as pursuing a vision of perfect, universal order. Was this where the Anadens had gone wrong?

Winslow's madness wasn't really about Artificials or Prevos. It was about control, and the exploitation of power through it. Millions of years in Amaranthe's past, had someone akin to Pamela Winslow won the day and tipped the balance of society toward rigid order, then eventually toward totalitarian control?

Mesme had claimed not to know. But it felt true, if only because today such a fate was but a few wrong choices away for them as well.

'Where do you think the lasers went?'

Alex frowned. "They went where we sent them—into extra-dimensional space."

'But what does that mean, spatially? Cosmically? *Where* did they go?'

Her attention drifted away from Earth out to the stars. The sun's light obscured all but the brightest. "I suppose they fell into the abysm. The chasm which lies in the space between the physical dimensions."

'Why do you describe such a realm as an abysm?'

"Because if it doesn't have real, tangible form—if it can't be measured—then by definition it doesn't have a terminus. There's no bottom to the chasm."

She smiled in a bit of contemplative amusement. "I'm sure the reality is the energy was either atomized and scattered or crushed out of existence. But I like to imagine the beams forever falling into the void."

37

"Impossible. Fire again."

"Prime Minister, there's no point. The Defense Grid's lasers were ineffective."

"Did they miss? Your targeting must have been faulty. Recalibrate and fire *again*."

"Ma'am, the targeting was correct." Grigg hurriedly pulled up the recordings from the visual sensors. "See, the lasers reached Admiral Solovy's vessel. It repelled or absorbed them. I can't explain it, but it has to be what happened."

From his holo, Mori gaped at the images in typically inept shock. "How?"

Pamela Winslow refused to accept such an outcome. She had the ultimate weaponry at her fingertips, and it was not feasible that she had somehow *lost* in spite of this. "Doing so might have depleted the ship's shields. Fire again."

"I..." Grigg entered several commands on his screen "...I'm afraid the ship is gone. We're no longer detecting it on any scans."

Pamela's eyes widened in growing indignation. "This is unacceptable. Her possession of unknown technology proves she's in league with the IDCC and the Prevos. Order Vice-Admiral Jirkar at NA Headquarters to secure EASC to guard against any attempt by her to retake it."

Her Chief of Staff frowned. "I'll queue him up, but the only person here who can order him to take such action is you, Prime Minister."

"Fine. Reach him on a comm and I will—" The door opened without warning, and Speaker Gagnon and Armed Forces Committee Chairman Anderson barged in. When she'd served in the Assembly, the Situation Room had been *secure*.

She squared her shoulders on them. "What is the meaning of this? We're in the middle of a crisis—"

"Prime Minister, did you just fire the Terrestrial Defense Grid weapons?"

"How would you know?"

"Ma'am, there are redundancies in the system which alert designated personnel of any such action. Also, the entire confrontation was broadcast on multiple news feeds."

Pamela's jaw clenched in anger. But she had been playing this game a very long time. Though it was more challenging than usual to do so, she buried the disruptive emotions and projected a calm, collected demeanor. "I did so to counter a clear and present threat to the security of the entire planet."

Gagnon stared at her incredulously. "As members of the Select Military Advisory Council, we have a right to be informed and consulted on these matters. If such a serious threat exists, you should have notified us of it."

She notched her chin upward. "There was no time."

"I missed most of the show on account of dealing with multiple security warnings. You didn't shoot down Admiral Solovy's command ship, did you?"

She had never cared for Chairman Anderson. He retained too much of the swagger from his former military career. She increased the firmness of her tone. "Her ship is wielding some form of unknown countermeasure. It is doubtless Prevo technology, if not alien in origin. Minister Mori, we need to put all military and government installations on Level IV alert."

Anderson leaned over the table, perilously close to getting in her face. "You can't fire our defensive weapons on an Earth Alliance admiral."

"Well if the Ethics Council would get on with defrocking her, she wouldn't *be* an admiral. The fact remains she poses a threat—"

"Ma'am, as a retired admiral who served on several Ethics Council tribunals, allow me to reiterate and clarify: you cannot fire Earth's defensive weapons on an Earth Alliance admiral unless they first take explicit offensive action against Earth or its assets. Now did she do that?"

"She suggested—"

"Did she *shoot at us?*"

Luis stood and placed a hand on Anderson's shoulder. "Chairman, you'll take care to not interrupt your prime minister. Not only is it rude, it's against proper rules of decorum."

Anderson straightened up and crossed his arms over his burly chest. "I'm not sure 'decorum' is our primary concern at this moment. *Prime Minister*, please answer the question."

Pamela decided then she would see the end of the man by the time the year was out. "She has not yet fired any weapons. However, she indicated she planned to breach Earth space, and there's no question she has hostile intent."

"Isn't there? And why in seven hells aren't there any other military officers in this room besides Grigg? Did it not occur to you that you ought to include military leadership in the decision-making process when handling this sort of crisis? Mr. Speaker, given the pertinent nature of this matter, I formally request an inquiry into it be added to the hearing on the events which occurred at Scythia."

I can't exactly include the military leadership when it has defected to Solovy! "I hardly think now is the time to be focused on oversight hearings."

"Says a former Oversight Committee chairman."

Perhaps she wouldn't wait until the year was out.

Gagnon gazed at her more calmly now, yet in his always judgmental manner. "Are we currently tracking Admiral Solovy's vessel or any other vessels?"

Mori shook his head meekly. "We don't have any information on her or her fleet's location at this time."

"So she may have simply left."

"Why would she do such a thing?"

"Being fired upon by the Terrestrial Defense Grid would cause most people to reconsider their tactics." Gagnon nodded. "Route all defensive alerts upstairs. We'll adjourn later if it becomes necessary, but as we are no longer tracking any potentially hostile vessels, for now it's time we reconvened in the Chamber. We have a hearing to hold. Also, Prime Minister, you should know we've elected to open it to the press."

A dark, unsettling sensation rose in her chest. "These are highly classified matters. I cannot answer your questions if the press is recording the proceedings."

"The Scythia events are a matter of public record. So too should be the explanation for them. Please be in the Chamber in ten minutes, ma'am."

AR

VANCOUVER
EASC HEADQUARTERS

Major Lange maintained a steady, controlled pace as he crossed the length of the Security Bureau monitoring center, then back again.

He hadn't banked on playing an active role in any endgame engineered by Admiral Solovy or Pamela Winslow. It was a small role, to be sure, yet still more than he'd expected. But he was the man best positioned to play it, and he would act honorably in doing so.

It was sheer dumb luck that the Logistics Director went off-site to Oslo today. Ojeda was certain to bolt for Vancouver as soon as he learned something was amiss, but as Lange understood the plan, one way or another the drama should all be over before the man arrived. He hoped events unfolded half that well.

"Confirm status of force field barriers."

The tech officer nodded. "Confirmed active at one hundred percent power."

"Thank you, Lieutenant." He moved three meters to watch the feeds from the perimeter cams.

Funny thing about EASC being situated on an island. For thousands of years, islands had served as some of the most defensible positions in existence. Ground-based weaponry exceeded sea weaponry—and defenses—and all one needed was a decent tower to see who was coming well in advance.

Eventually the emergence of planes had lessened then all but eliminated the advantage. The advent of force fields with the strength to repel physical objects, including aircraft, had returned it.

On an ordinary day, the force fields surrounding EASC were set to MAN—monitor and notify—and any unauthorized vessel was subdued and handled by MPs as appropriate. In the event of the threat of a hostile invasion of any sort, however, the force fields possessed the capability to do far more.

Today was not an ordinary day.

"Major, we're getting a ping from an Alliance LCS-class vessel registered to the 1st NA Brigade. Vice-Admiral Jirkar is listed as in command. They are asking why the ship is being denied authorization to approach."

"Put it live, Lieutenant." He took a deep breath. Jirkar was known for being a very cautious and circumspect officer, but also a logical one. He would listen to reason backed by regulations. Probably.

"Vice-Admiral, this is Major Lange, Director of the EASC Security Bureau. We are currently under a security lockdown, which prevents the arrival or departure of any vessels until the lockdown is lifted. As such, I regretfully cannot allow you to land at EASC at this time."

"Major, I'm under orders from the prime minister to assume operational command of EASC. I assure you this order supersedes any lockdown procedure and is in fact an additional response to the threat which triggered the lockdown. I order you to authorize my vessels for landing."

"Vice-Admiral, *sir*, I'm afraid official lockdown procedures are explicit on this topic. I cannot—"

"Major, I have in my possession weapons powerful enough to break through your force fields. Now, it is not my desire to bomb EASC, but if forced to do so I can."

Lange fought the intense urge to tromp around in circles gnashing his teeth. "Sir, respectfully, think about from where your orders originated. Think about the purpose you know is behind them. If you open this facility to the prime minister, we will be overrun. It is vital to the continued independence of the armed forces that EASC remain under its own control."

Silence hummed for several seconds. "And if Admiral Solovy arrives to retake it instead?"

"Then its independence will remain intact."

"Are you saying should she arrive, you will allow her entry notwithstanding the lockdown?"

Lange wanted to groan, but he merely pursed his lips. *Caught.* "She is my admiral, sir. And, again respectfully, she is yours as well."

A far longer silence followed this time, long enough for Lange to begin to contemplate the details of his own court martial.

"EASC Security, my vessel and two others are adopting a high-altitude patrol pattern three kilometers above and outside EASC territory until such time as the particulars of the situation becomes more clear for all involved. Do not attempt to fire on us...and we will not fire on you."

He let the air out of his lungs so quietly no one would notice he'd been holding it in. "Acknowledged and understood, Vice-Admiral. Thank you."

38

EARTH

The *Gambier* landed inside the security perimeter of the Assembly grounds, on a side lawn next to the Protective and Emergency Services Office.

Winslow's speech to the European Trade Council had been canceled at the last minute, ostensibly on account of 'troubling' events on Romane and elsewhere but more so because the Assembly had demanded she testify *without delay*.

Miriam preferred to play the confrontation out on Assembly grounds anyway; downtown London introduced far too many variables, many of them involving innocent bystanders. And here she expected to have Speaker Gagnon on her side, as well as Chairman Anderson, allegedly. She of necessity counted on neither of them.

Malcolm fussed over her, ensuring the 'Veil' cloaking shield was secure and operational. Then Caleb fussed over her, ensuring the defense shield was secure and operational.

Finally she sighed and readied her 'stern' voice—the one most people knew as her normal voice. "Gentleman, I appreciate the concern, but this admiral can take care of herself and her gear."

Caleb shrugged unapologetically, but Malcolm straightened up to attention. "Yes, ma'am. Just standard team preparation and checks. Major Grenier?"

"Ready, sir."

"What about you, Marano?"

"Good to go. Let me move out ahead. I'll make sure no one's set up an ambush."

Malcolm hesitated for the briefest second before gesturing to the pilot to open the hatch. "Minister Jameson is waiting for us inside the Protective Services Office."

Caleb clasped her on the shoulder with a warm smile. "Kick Winslow's ass and pin it to the curb."

She returned the smile, frankly grateful he was here. "That is more or less the plan—or the strategy, at least."

He chuckled and stepped to the hatch, then activated his shield and vanished.

They waited, eyes scanning the seemingly empty lawn.

Marano: Clear to the PES entrance. Join me when you're ready.

"Noted. We're moving in ten." Malcolm leaned into the cockpit. "Major Berg, you know the drill."

"Sit quiet as a mouse and hope nobody goes for a stroll and bumps into the invisible ship. Yes, sir."

"That's affirmative. After you, Admiral. Grenier, take rearguard."

It was only a few steps from the *Gambier* to the door. They hurried inside and into a conference room on the left. Once the door closed behind them, they deactivated the Veils.

Jameson blinked. "Interesting tech."

Miriam ignored the comment. "Minister. What's your status?"

"Assembly security is under my jurisdiction. They'll follow my orders. The only people we really need to worry about are Winslow's personal security retinue, of which there are twelve on the premises. Six are in the Chamber currently."

Malcolm nodded. "We'll handle them."

Jameson arched an eyebrow but didn't argue.

"Are you planning to arrest her at the end of this?"

"Arrest is a very blunt word to use in what is a very delicate situation, Admiral. But the charges are prepared. If all goes well, I will inform her of their filing and provision to the Assembly Ethics Committee, and of her duty to report for official questioning by the end of the day."

"And if all doesn't go well, Minister?"

He grimaced. "Then I expect I'll be resigning by the end of the day."

Caleb stared at her, oozing discontent; she eyed him curiously. "You have concerns?"

"You should not let Winslow walk out of the building."

Malcolm's chest bowed up. "We don't assassinate our leaders."

Caleb pivoted to him. "And neither do we, *Colonel*. But you should detain her. She has vast resources, and I'm betting none of you know what most of them are.

"You need to do everything *legal* to prevent her from accessing those resources. That means a comfortable but shielded cell—an interview room will do if you can block her comms while she's in it. Make her people come to her, where you can see them, log them and investigate them."

"We can't—"

Miriam interrupted. "Mr. Marano has a point, Minister. You don't have to formally arrest her. Simply insist she accompany you to answer urgent questions, and make certain answering them takes hours. Give Speaker Gagnon time to set recall procedures in motion and win his majority if he can."

Jameson exhaled. "I'll try. No promises. Am I to understand you intend to use your..." he made a suspicious face "...cloaking shields to enter the Chamber in secrecy then reveal yourself? And the Speaker is expecting your arrival?"

"Correct." The sad truth was the Assembly did not possess the political courage to move against Winslow without Miriam's public backing. So she would provide it.

Malcolm cleared his throat. "Admiral, can I try one more time to convince you to allow Minister Jameson's people to move on Winslow first?"

"You may not, Colonel."

"Yes, ma'am." He accepted the rebuke and moved on. "You obviously won't be able to see us, but you can track our movements on a whisper, as we can yours. Minister, I'm sending you our locator signatures. When we're in place, I'll confirm we are a go. Then it's your show, Admiral."

Invisibility had a lot to commend it, especially when one spent most of one's hours under constant scrutiny and examination. Walking in the open air, free to gaze where and how she wished? Miriam decided she could get used to this. But such frivolities, if they came, were for later.

Marano: Clear to the entrance. Two security officers flanking the interior.

Getting through the guarded door would have been a bit of a trick, but Minister Jameson entered in full view. Once the door opened he stopped halfway in to speak to one of the officers, leaving it open long enough for the four of them to slip inside through the gap.

Miriam's whisper showed Malcolm and Caleb falling in beside her. They moved quickly through the halls, avoiding staffers, and reached the entrance to the Chamber. Here the doors were open, as the hearing had been declared public.

Winslow's pinched, condescending voice echoed through the cavernous room. "No, I am not going to answer any questions about planetary defensive measures. I am in constant touch with military leaders, but the details are classified."

"What about reports you used military personnel to attempt to eliminate IDCC officials?"

Colonel Jenner: We're green, Admiral.

"I did no such thing. The Earth Alliance military does not assassinate politicians, no matter how deplorable they may be. Such rumors are nothing more than a smear campaign perpetrated by the IDCC."

Miriam stood at the top of the vast semi-circle which comprised the Chamber auditorium. She deactivated her shield. "That is a lie."

Gasps erupted as all eyes, politician and press alike, swung to her. Winslow leapt up from the witness table, her expression painted in the vivid strokes of fury. "Security, arrest Admiral Solovy now! She is wanted on numerous charges!"

Three members of Winslow's security detail moved toward Miriam. When they got within two meters, Malcolm de-cloaked beside her, gun drawn.

"Stand down, agents."

One nevertheless made a move for his weapon—Caleb materialized to grapple his arms from behind. "Don't do that."

The Daemon clattered to the floor.

"This is an outrage! Minister Jameson, order your people to arrest her and her cohorts this instant."

High upon the dais, Speaker Gagnon stood. "That won't be necessary, Minister."

Winslow swung to him. The reporters in the middle couldn't decide which way to face, and their murmurs grew loud.

Miriam took two steps forward and motioned everyone quiet, and after a few seconds they mostly obeyed. "Please. I'm here today because it's my duty to act. In our system, much as the Assembly is a check on the Executive and vice versa, the civilian government is a check on the military, and the military on the government.

"I'll answer to an Armed Forces Ethics Council tribunal should any charges remain against me when the day is done, but now I'm here to ensure the overwhelming evidence of not merely corruption but outright criminal activity by the Prime Minister sees the light of day.

"She would bury it, buy it or slander its providers into ruin if she could—but she cannot bury me."

Winslow seethed. "How dare you."

Now Gagnon stood from his seat at the center of the long, arcing dais. "Prime Minister Winslow, evidence has been delivered to the Security Ministry and the Assembly Ethics Committee, including sworn testimony from the military officers involved, indicating you ordered two Marine special forces squads from Earth Alliance Central Command to covertly infiltrate Romane. Their orders were to assassinate the Romane governor and members of the IDCC leadership.

"Furthermore, the evidence indicates you ordered several of those special forces operatives to assist alleged members of the Order of the True Sentients in assassinating Dr. Abigail Canivon—an honored alumnus of the Earth Alliance civil service—a task which they tragically completed."

Additional security agents rushed into the auditorium from opposite hallways, where they were halted by Jameson's people. Their muted voices of confusion added to the renewed din, but Winslow's shrill voice rose above it all.

"How can you believe anything this woman says? The evidence is fabricated, her charges specious. She is a traitor who finds herself alone and desperate to not lose power. I accuse her of ordering the murder of my son while he was in Romane police custody!"

A great furor broke out among the press, as this news was not yet public. Any security agents who had been prevaricating as to who to restrain were forced to concentrate on subduing the crowd.

Miriam gave Speaker Gagnon a small nod and began strolling down the outer walkway, as if oblivious to the restive turmoil around her.

"Allow me to declare this now: I am not a traitor, nor am I alone. I have dozens of flag officers prepared to come here to the Assembly and stand with me—but I thought it would get a mite crowded in here, so instead they have forwarded their sworn statements to Speaker Gagnon and Minister Jameson. Right about now, all major news outlets are receiving copies of their statements as well.

"Of course, I can have them here in a matter of minutes, if you truly believe I need someone standing beside me in order for me to be taken seriously." She held Winslow's furious scowl until the woman blinked.

"I didn't think so. My evidence is quite thoroughly authenticated, I assure you. The Assembly already has all the evidence of your blackmail schemes it needs, but I've sent along some corroboration of those crimes, too. To cover all the bases.

"I am genuinely sorry your son took his own life, Prime Minister, for no parent should suffer the pain of losing a child. But the fact is he wasn't just 'involved' with OTS—he was its founder and leader. And not only did you know this, you helped fund his murderous activities. You provided him Earth Alliance military personnel to use in his terrorist attacks.

"Prime Minister, how dare *you*. How dare you defile an institution sworn to protect the people. How dare you co-opt all the institutions of our great democracy to your own ends and for your own power."

"Power? You would install yourself as a dictator then hand control over to your Prevo masters."

Miriam paused mid-step and offered the room a soft, wry chuckle, letting her gaze pass across many in the now rapt press audience. Perhaps she was finally getting the hang of public performances after all.

"No. If the next prime minister doesn't require my services, so be it. I'll retire quietly. And I don't see any Prevos here today, Prime Minister. Not in the Assembly. Or on the Strategic Command Board, or among the officer ranks. It's not Prevos who are demanding your resignation—it's your citizens and their leaders."

Winslow did an admiral job of faking shock. "Resign? Absurd. I will do no such thing, nor will I bow to such preposterous and transparent grandstanding."

"We'll see. I came here to ensure the truth made it past your clutches to the press and the people everywhere listening. I've done what I came to do, and now I'll trust our institutions to do their duty as well and see that justice is served."

She happened to also be watching Minister Jameson move into position with two of his men, preparing to deliver yet worse news to Winslow. Security Ministry agents elsewhere were arresting several members of her administration even now, and Gagnon would shortly introduce a resolution of recall.

Miriam reached one of the entrances dotting the upper walkway of the auditorium and turned to the door, then stopped and gazed back over her shoulder. "I'm sorry, did someone want to arrest me?"

The press looked around at the security officers; the security officers looked at Jameson, followed by Gagnon; no one stepped forward.

"Very well, then. Mr. Speaker, carry on with your hearing." She walked out the door, intending to return to the *Gambier* and allow events to unfold as they would.

Most of the reporters surged out of the chambers to surround her, so much so that Malcolm and Caleb both drew near to her in protective stances and a cadre of Jameson's officers broke through the crowd to hold them back. Dozens of cams zoomed in the air above her.

On their mission channel, she heard Jameson asking Winslow to remain on the premises, as he had some questions for her once Speaker Gagnon concluded the hearing.

The shouts from the reporters overlapped one another. "Admiral Solovy, if Prime Minister Winslow is removed from office, will you give your support to Speaker Gagnon?"

She surveyed the reporters dispassionately. "It has always been my practice not to endorse politicians. I have no reason to doubt the Speaker's qualifications, and I trust the system, and ultimately the people, to make the right decisions. I'm merely here to serve a Constitutional administration.

"But make no mistake—there is a blight in our government, one of cowardice and corruption. Whoever the next prime minister is, they and all government officials need to focus beyond the immediate crisis to the larger, more systemic problems and work to solve them.

"But this blight is not mine to fix—it's theirs. A free and vigorous press will help guarantee they do, so get to work."

39

SENECA

Richard reviewed the latest status report from Agent Duarte. Five more suspected OTS members were now in custody; Quillen and three others had officially been charged with the Military Headquarters bombing and would remain in confinement pending their trials.

It was beginning to feel suspiciously like they were closing the chapter on OTS, and not solely on Seneca. Everywhere.

He minimized the report with an approving nod at Graham. "And peace is restored to the galaxy?"

Graham snorted. "We should be so lucky. But maybe a little, yes? It's not as if we can just wave our hands and make everyone accept Prevos. Society, not to mention the way crimes are committed and the way we solve them, has been upended, and I doubt the upheaval is over. But...I guess if most everyone accepts that it *has* been upended, then we'll manage."

"True enough. Did I hear General Nicolo Bastian was named interim Field Marshal?" He'd never personally met the man, but he'd spent a few minutes in a meeting the general had attended. Tall, intense man who gave the impression of constantly holding coiled energy in check.

"Yep. Vranas wants to project the impression of normalcy. The Alliance government may be in shambles, but none of that silliness here, right? The appointment will probably be made permanent, though. Bastian's a good man. Or a good officer, anyway. Speaking of the Alliance, what's the latest from Miriam?"

"She'll have to testify before an Ethics Council tribunal, but it's a formality. She's already back in her office at EASC. General Foster resigned from Northwest Regional Command in protest, but no one cares.

"The Assembly is holding a dozen hearings at once trying to cleanse its ranks *and* the administration's ranks, but it's messy. On the assumption the Supreme Judicial Court will invalidate BANIA next week, its leadership is also busy drafting a replacement law. I think they're mostly stealing yours."

Graham laughed heartily. "They're welcome to it." He ran a finger along the rim of his glass. "Where do you see yourself ending up now? If everything plays out well for Miriam, you might be able to rejoin the Alliance."

It had nearly killed Richard to not be at Miriam's side when she returned to Earth. Not because he felt she needed protecting—he was of the informed opinion that no one alive was more capable of taking care of themselves than Miriam Solovy—but because he wanted to be there to see her triumphant.

Still, he shook his head. "As a consultant, perhaps, but not the military. I'm retired for good and...I'm okay with it. But as a matter of fact, I do have an idea I'm interested in pursuing. Something new. And I'll need both your and Miriam's help to implement it."

"Color me intrigued."

Richard rubbed at his chin. "It gets back to what you were saying about society being upended and our willingness to embrace our new reality. We—those of us on the front lines, such as they are—have an opportunity to help shape what the new world looks like, and to give it its best shot at succeeding. This trifecta of powers—Alliance, Federation, IDCC? It has the potential to be a more stable, positive arrangement long term."

"Gianno said much the same thing..." Graham's gaze flitted to the window with a frown "...not long ago. The third player serves as a check if one government gets designs on bullying its opposite. Do you think the IDCC is a strong enough pillar, though?"

"I think we should encourage them to be."

"You know something. Again."

Richard shrugged. "Intelligence? Wouldn't be doing my job if I didn't. And I will tell you, since it's your job, too—but first, my idea."

Graham tossed a hand in his direction, and he continued. "These last few weeks, working to get Miriam the information she needed to execute on her strategy? I didn't care what agency or government a source worked for as long as the intel was solid. I talked to friends, colleagues past and present, and individuals whose interests happened to briefly align with ours.

"And you know what? It worked. I suspect it worked because most of the time, in most situations, the mission isn't about galactic war or political crises—it's about saving a life and catching a criminal."

"Big criminal this time."

"Yes. And while I do sincerely hope we don't need to take down any more heads of state any time soon, a big galaxy means big criminals. I want to be able to stop them effectively, without tripping over politics."

Graham took a long, slow sip of his scotch. "You're talking about intelligence sharing: a clearinghouse, a multi-jurisdictional agency or even a special group to be called upon when a significant threat arises. One like Montegreu, for instance. But you're a low-key type of guy...so I'm betting on a mix of the first and second options."

Richard chuckled. "Funny you mention Montegreu. Miriam has possession of her data store—and you didn't hear this from me, but she's cracked its security. But arguably the IDCC has as much of a right to the spoils it produces as the Alliance. Something having that much relevance for all colonies ought to be handled by an independent third party.

"I figure I'll let one of the Prevos burn a microsecond or two to come up with an appropriately mysterious name, complete with a forbidding acronym. But yes. We need an INTERPOL for a new world."

Graham's brow furrowed. "Interpol?"

He sometimes forgot not everyone had studied history in more than generalities. "A police IGO in the 20th and early 21st centuries. Almost two hundred countries managed to *mostly* ignore political boundaries and work together to catch cross-border criminals for over a century. It eventually fell to corruption, shortly before irrelevance, but that's simply a matter of execution. The principle is sound."

Graham reached across the desk to refill Richard's glass. Setting the tone for the evening. "And you're going to head this new IGO?"

Richard had never sought the limelight, never desired to be the man at the podium. But it had been an insane, harrowing year...and as Will had pointed out the night before, he hadn't merely weathered the storm, he'd kind of kicked its ass. So he shrugged and took a sip of expensive scotch. "I am."

Graham guffawed. "As well you should. It's bloody brilliant. We all ought to have thought of it before now, but we didn't. You did, on account of you being smarter than the rest of us. I'm in, even if it means I'll be left high and dry, *again*. I assume you'll be enlisting Will to actually run the day-to-day of this thing, because why the hell wouldn't you—and he's better at that sort of work than you are."

Richard shook his head. "This 'thing' doesn't have a name, much less a base of operations, charter or employees. It's a little early for those discussions."

"Sure." Graham's eyebrow raised over his glass. He wasn't buying it for an instant. And he was right...but there would be time for details later. For today, Richard decided, it was enough to be hopeful about the future.

ROMANE

Noah lay on the couch and watched Kennedy work on spreadsheets and schem flows, acting like everything was all back to normal. It wasn't—not exactly—but it felt like maybe it would be soon. A new normal, in some respects, and possibly a better one.

He was so busy watching her, in fact, he was startled when she tossed an idle comment at him over her shoulder. "You know, your Dad did really well."

He propped up on an elbow. "So he spent a few days in a high-class confinement facility. Who hasn't?"

Her hands withdrew from the screens. She closed the distance to him, then knelt beside the couch and him. "Hey, he's still an insufferable ass. But he did well."

"He did." But Noah wasn't necessarily ready to ponder on it yet, so he kissed her instead. "Speaking of troublesome parents, a birdie told me your dad came by earlier."

She instantly pulled away—which was cool, he expected that. "What birdie?"

"The entrance security cam. Do you want to talk about it?"

She glanced at him dubiously before standing and walking away.

He rolled his eyes at the ceiling. "At least tell me what he had to say. Or what the result of the conversation was. These are things I kind of need to be made aware of, if only so I know how much nurturing you need tonight."

"All the nurturing. But I always need all the nurturing—I assumed it was the default assumption." She groaned. "Fine. He wanted to make bygones be bygones. Water under the bridge. An unfortunate necessity of the circumstances. A dark period best forgotten."

"He wanted to un-disown you."

"Pretty much." She took to meandering in an aimless circle around the room, dismissing the work screens when she passed them.

He geared up to try to craftily maneuver his way through this multi-level, booby-trapped minefield...and stopped. He trusted her. Her judgment and her decision on the matter would be the right one, whatever it was.

"You won. You made the right choices, in all the ways, and this proves it."

She looked over her shoulder to beam at him. "I did, didn't I?"

"You bet you did." Emboldened by her reaction, he leapt up and swooped in to whisk her into his arms. "So, what did you tell him?"

Her lips pursed in contemplation. "I told him...I was touched he'd make the effort to reach out in such a personal manner, and I was grateful he was willing to welcome me back into the fold. I told him how much our family had and would always mean to me—because it does and it will."

She paused.

"Then I told him to go fuck himself."

"What?" He almost dropped her in shock. "But you could regain everything from your old life, while keeping all you've built since. Why give that up?"

She gave him a dazzling smile. "I already have everything I want."

Oh man, way to melt his damn heart.... His lips had just met hers when he pulled back in suspicion. "You're screwing with me, aren't you?"

Her jaw dropped in indignation—*mock* indignation. "I can't believe you'd suggest I would do such a thing. I mean, granted, 'Go fuck yourself' might not have been the *exact* words I used."

"And the exact words you used were?"

Her eyes grew unfocused, as if she struggled to recall them. " 'Thank you for the apology'...'no, I don't need any help, financial or otherwise, we're doing great'...'I'm not certain if we can make it for Christmas dinner or not, but I'll be in touch soon.' "

"That's what I thought." The idea of formal Christmas dinner at her parents' estate was nightmare-inducing. It was okay, though. He'd survive it. "We should go to Christmas dinner. As a nominal peace offering."

She nodded pensively. "All right. On one condition: your father comes, too."

"Oh, that is low. Below-the-belt dirty fighter is what you are."

She grinned, brazenly pleased with herself. "So you'll ask him then?"

40

EARTH

MANCHESTER

Devon skulked deep in the shadows of a cluster of verdant ferns nestled in the far corner of the Ernest Simon Conservatory.

Despite the controlled environment inside, the air remained chilly, excusing his trench coat. Shadewraps would stand out in the overcast, damp weather, but his irises had shifted to an amethyst so dark they'd be mistaken for black from a distance—which was where he intended to stay.

It probably wasn't safe for him to be on Earth, not quite yet. The official government raids against Prevos had been halted, but BANIA wouldn't be repealed until the Supreme Judicial Court overturned it or the Assembly had a new law ready to take its place, and neither was going to happen for a few more days. Many ordinary, uninvolved people still believed him to be as much of a terrorist as any OTS activist.

So he didn't advertise his presence. But he needed to be here.

Abigail hadn't enjoyed a large circle of genuine friends, but she did have a lot of professional acquaintances on Earth and across settled space, as well as extended family here in Manchester.

The arboretum hadn't struck Devon as being to Abigail's tastes, but he turned out to be wrong. He'd never known she loved flowers. Well, he supposed he must have known it in the smallest way; the detail must have been buried somewhere in the morass of knowledge Annie had acquired from Valkyrie or in the information now strewn throughout the Noesis.

I have decided I dislike intensely this human custom of funerals. Valkyrie agrees with me. She refused to attend.

She forbade Alex from coming?

Perhaps 'argued strongly against' is a more accurate phrasing. In retrospect, I should have done the same...but I realize you feel as strongly about the importance of being here.

I can't fault you for your perspective, Annie. But do you understand why we do this?

I'm well-versed in the history of the ritual and its professed purposes. Yet I cannot help but think of Jules, of how we stood together with Abigail at her funeral, and now here we are once again. It is distressing to me. They should not be gone to us, either of them. Not so swiftly. Humans need to devise a way to live forever.

He chuckled under his breath. *I'm sure we're working on it. But have you ever considered the possibility that life won't be as meaningful if you know it will never end?*

Considered and discarded.

Okay, Annie, fair enough. We can talk about it more later. In a better setting.

Ostensibly a private ceremony with an exclusive guest list, the spacious conservatory was nevertheless nearly full. People he didn't recognize spoke in strings of accolades, praising Abigail's intellect, her persistent quest for knowledge and the dividends that quest had provided to humanity as a whole and to innumerable individuals.

Devon perked up when someone he did know stepped to the podium and spoke, bluntly but truthfully, about matters closer to his own heart.

As she made her way back to her seat, Miriam Solovy zeroed in on him so quickly he may as well have a spotlight over his head.

You shouldn't be here. It's still too risky.

I'm being careful.

She let it drop, but he took a half-step deeper into the ferns for good measure.

Final solemn words were spoken by a man who claimed to be a member of Abigail's family. Final rituals were intoned, and the guests began filing out. He slipped in among them and let himself be carried out into the cold, wet morning.

When the departing crowd began to disperse he veered off to the left and across the park.

He'd catch a levtram to the spaceport, then hop over to San Francisco and have some drinks with Ramon and Sayid before heading to...Romane? It seemed as good a place as any—better than most—to serve as his next temporary home. Besides, Annie preferred it to Pandora.

"I thought I might find you here."

Devon froze. The voice cut straight through him with a power no shield could withstand.

Slowly, cautiously, he turned around.

Long blond hair spilled over her shoulders to mat into tangles in the rain. Did she not have a rainshade? Why not? At this rate she would soon be soaked to the bone.

A clover-hued dress billowed around her legs in the gusting wind. Once upon a time the dress would have complimented her lovely green eyes, but now....

Her lips rose in a tentative smile as radiant white irises stared back at him. "Hi, Devon."

He breathed in and swallowed past the panicking coward of a lump in his throat. "Emily?"

VANCOUVER
EASC HEADQUARTERS

Alex reached the top floor of the shiny new EASC Headquarters tower—new to her anyway—and strolled with increasing curiosity across the atrium.

The décor, the ambiance, it was all...pleasant. Warm, bordering on welcoming. Had the Alliance military bureaucracy's sensibilities changed this drastically in a year? Or had hers?

The door to her mother's suite was open, and she walked in without trepidation. Her gaze swept around the office appreciatively. "This office is fantastic, Mom. So much better than the old one."

Miriam fretted over the antique texts on the bookcase, rearranging them just so, then just so again. "That's right, you didn't get to see it before you went back through the portal. I agree. It is fantastic, and I've missed it these last weeks. Thankfully, Major Lange kept it locked up tight, and no one dared try to take it for themselves."

The better for their health, she suspected. "Have you installed Thomas in here yet?"

"No, but don't think I'm not considering it."

She chuckled. "I'm not surprised. How did the hearing with the Ethics Council go? I assume well enough since you're here."

Miriam considered the texts with a critical gaze; presumably deciding they passed muster for the moment, she went around to her desk to fret over a few more objects.

"Embarrassing—for them. The number of allegedly moral people in leadership positions who lined up to kiss Winslow's feet out of sheer cowardice is shocking. I think perhaps I'll be encouraging a number of retirements in the coming weeks. It's time for new blood in the ranks."

"Good." Alex stopped in front of a visual of her dad on the wall. He was smirking at the cam, the picture of self-assured, roguish charm.

Recent events had been marred by destruction and death, by so much darkness, yet she imagined he'd have found a way to add needed levity, were he here.

"David would've been a much better leader for Volnosti. And oh, how he would have relished the fight."

"No, he would've been a more entertaining leader. Mom, I've seen the footage from your showdown with Winslow at the Assembly. You were spectacular, and *I* bet Dad would've rushed to cede the stage to you then proceeded to watch on in awe."

A pleased, if slightly wistful, smile grew on her mother's lips. "Maybe so."

Alex, with the recent breakthroughs the Prevos and...Abigail have made, I expect to soon be able to revisit the difficulties involving your father's neural construct.

I don't...I mean that's great to hear. You should absolutely work on it. But?

I'm not quite ready to have my father in my head again yet. I need some time.

I understand. It's possible there will be other options. But we'll consider the best approach later.

Thank you.

"How was Abigail's funeral?"

Her mother grimaced. "What do you want me to say? It was solemn and reverential, as such things are meant to be."

The shadows of those lost to them crowded in to stifle the air in the office, and Alex wandered out onto the patio in the hope of brightening the mood.

It was a chilly afternoon, but too nice not to be outside. Beyond the patio, shuttles and skycars sped across the Strait to and from the mainland; the waters sparkled beneath a sun unmarred by clouds. People strode purposefully across the courtyard, as if trying to reassure themselves normality had returned.

A few seconds later her mother came out as well, and they sat at the small table nestled amid blooming morning glories and astilbe. Absurdly delightful, all of it.

The fresh air and sunshine had the desired effect as she idly surveyed the surroundings. "Is it true a fistfight broke out during one of the Assembly hearings yesterday?"

"It is. Much gnashing of teeth both preceded and followed the scuffle, complete with wailings of the sky falling and predictions of the end of the world. It was all rather overdramatic."

Alex rolled her eyes. "Don't they realize? Never mind, obviously they don't. They're politicians. But the sky isn't falling—the world is turning. It's a new dawn."

"I suppose we have no choice but for it to be. Regardless, the only way through is forward, come what may." Miriam studied her thoughtfully. "I have very belatedly learned you single-handedly destroyed the OTS hideout on Romane. How did that come about?"

Alex fiddled with the hem of her shirt. "I did. It was the right thing to do—for someone to do. But, admittedly, I was not...entirely of sound mind at the time."

"What do you mean? Were you drunk? High?"

A childish panic seized her chest, which was simply ridiculous. "'High?' Like on a chimeral or something? Why would you think that?"

Miriam stared at her deadpan. "Alex, I may have been a lousy mother when you were growing up, but I was not a stupid one. Who do you think arranged for those charges to be dropped against you and Mr. Tollis in...2309, was it? In San Francisco?"

"I, uh, never knew. Okay, um...." She huffed a breath. Back then she was so certain of her cleverness...and had assumed her mother didn't care enough to pay attention. "I guess it's way too late to say thank you?"

Miriam shrugged mildly, as if to say 'not necessarily.'

Alex burst out laughing, and after a weak attempt at a serious countenance Miriam joined her.

When the laughter had subsided, Alex ran a hand over her mouth. "*Anyway*. No, I wasn't high, not exactly, though the chimeral analogy is a bit more apropos than I'd prefer."

"Are you all right?"

She nodded, with genuine conviction no less. "I am. Or at least I'm well on the road to 'all right.' But I wonder...."

She reflected on the path they'd traveled to arrive here, littered as it was by a thousand missteps and mistakes, chasms hewed with loss and barriers erected in bitterness. In the months following the

Metigen War, they'd healed the present but never really the past, because how could they? There was no going back.

But this was a new dawn, dammit, and she vowed to treat it as such. "Would it be too much of a bother if I talked to you a little bit about what happened to me? I think I'd like to do that."

Her mother looked taken aback for the briefest second; then her expression grew gentle and she squeezed Alex's hand. "Of course you can. I would...I would like it, too. Very much."

INTERMEZZO VI

MOSAIC

Aver moved among the primitives unnoticed. After donning a hooded cloak he resembled them closely enough to not draw attention, so long as no one studied his face for too long. Even then he might pass muster, as a minority of the individuals displayed facial and ocular adornments not dramatically different from his own.

The surreal nature of his current experience baffled him. Though undeniably primitive, these creatures *were* Anadens.

He'd terminated one's biological functions and taken it to his ship to study it further, and while it displayed strange incongruities—several extra organs and no blastema node, for instance—a genetic test identified the being as a *homo sapien sapien*.

What in the name of Zeus were the Katasketousya doing? It was unadulterated blasphemy, but what was their goal in it?

He was growing frustrated with asking the same questions repetitively while achieving no resolution. Despite this vexation, he felt he needed to uncover the answers in order to fulfill his purpose. Uncovering them before exposing the Katasketousya malfeasance ultimately better ensured a complete elimination of the problem.

He suspected but would soon confirm that this manufactured species had begun to expand into neighboring sectors of this galaxy. Based upon the terrestrial technology he observed, they were the presumed source of the ubiquitous interstellar noise he'd detected en route.

Had they encountered the Dzhvar yet? The absence of any evidence of them during his travel from the gateway suggested they had and had dealt with them accordingly.

Unless the Dzhvar were never here. Exactly how faithful of a replication of Amaranthe was this, truly?

Despite his admitted curiosity about the nature of these proto-Anadens, the details of their current state of development weren't pertinent to the assignment, merely their existence. After he filed his final report they would be Eradicated, though the Erevna Primor was likely to insist on taking a few as samples to study.

No. It was time to ascertain the Katasketousya plan and bring an end to this profane creation.

He determined to return through the gateway and search the remaining spaces until he located their haven. There he expected to learn the full extent of their malfeasance.

An Accepted Species had not been Eradicated in fourteen millennia, but for such treason that would be their fate.

His *diati* stirred. Yet he had not called it into service.

He frowned as it grew so agitated his hands began to glimmer a faint crimson. The *diati* only acted on its own initiative when there was a great threat nearby or when an astronomical event of tremendous significance was on the horizon. The latter seemed more unlikely than the former, but neither were very credible.

Nevertheless, something was amiss. He tensed, heightening all his sensory pathways. Nothing definable leapt into his perception, but his *diati* urged him in the direction of a spaceport structure.

The pull grew stronger as he neared the structure. He did not understand its meaning, but much about the *diati* had always lain beyond even the Primor's comprehension. The relationship was a symbiotic one, and the *diati* had served the Praesidis Dynasty for a thousand millennia.

Thus he did not question the pull, instead trusting it would lead him to where he needed to be.

A security process blocked pedestrian entrance to the spaceport. Killing his way through would be a simple matter but promised to attract a level of attention he didn't desire to be troubled with, so he concealed himself and floated upward, following the silent wishes of the *diati*.

He reached the roof of the spaceport and found it clogged by a variety of small vessels. One abruptly launched at an almost horizontal angle, missing him by little distance. He hurriedly withdrew a span.

The *diati* directed him to a vessel 52° around the circular roof. His entire body now pulsated from the power of its agitation. In his memory through two hundred seventy-one generations, he located no recollection of it acting so forcefully of its own accord.

Sensing the vessel he approached was connected to the *diati's* unrest, he removed a tracker dot from his kit and began closing in on the ship—when it launched over his head.

He responded instantly, propelling the dot upward to link itself to the hull.

Then the vessel was gone.

He descended to the ground and made an effort to continue exploring the area, but the *diati* screamed in his head until his skull throbbed.

Disturbed but obedient, he returned to his ship and prepared to follow the tracking signal.

ℛ

AURORA THESI (PORTAL PRIME)

The intermingling of such sentiments as relief, joy and pride—a lavishness of pride in my charges—with apprehension, with dread at the rising shadow they could not see overtaking them, disconcerted me to an uncomfortable degree.

By nearly all measures, Humanity was succeeding in righting itself yet again. The challenge had been met and overcome, much as they had done time and again throughout their existence.

This was why I believed in them: because when the worst of their species threatened to plunge them into darkness, the best of them rose to vanquish their own enemy and steer Humanity to the preferred path forward.

Yet my pleasure at their triumph was marred by my knowledge of the Anaden lurking among them now.

I could not track the Praesidis Inquisitor within Aurora. The vessel's cloaking activated soon after it arrived there, and its concealment capabilities exceeded our most advanced technology.

I had chosen not to warn the Humans of the Inquisitor's presence during their crisis, judging they did not need a distraction they could do nothing to address. But what of now, as their apparent troubles ameliorated? I desired to allow them a respite, but I feared the time for respites had now passed.

Yet what information might I impart? That a killer more dangerous than any they had previously known moved among them, and I knew neither this killer's location nor a viable method of eliminating him?

I had told the Conclave this may represent Humanity's final test. If it were such, and if they were to succeed, they must do it by way of their own ingenuity. They did display an abundance of it, so hope remained.

Should they fail—should the Inquisitor return through the Aurora portal—we were prepared to use all our resources to attempt to kill him, for he now possessed sufficient knowledge to bring the full might of a Machim fleet down upon the Mosaic. The fleet would eradicate the Idryma, and with it the stasis vault and thus the lives of all Katasketousya who called it home. All hope of a free future for any would be lost.

Yet our likelihood of success in stopping the Inquisitor was not measurable with any degree of confidence. While we hurriedly constructed new offensive vessels and moved them here, the AI-driven vessels could not hit what they could not detect. Further, if the Inquisitor's *diati* sufficiently protected his ship, no amount of firepower we directed at it would harm it.

Finally, we dared not shut down the Amaranthe gateways, for this would disrupt the transfer of resources from the provision enisles, an act certain to quickly raise its own alarms and thus defeat the very purpose.

I rippled in surprise at an unusual anomaly in the recording I viewed using a portion of my focus.

While I monitored the overall situation in Aurora with only the slightest gap in time, I was now reviewing recent events from around the populated region. My hope was to detect the presence of the Inquisitor in some manner, preferably one which did not involve the death of thousands.

In nine separate locations scattered in a two hundred parsec arc around Earth, fissures in the physical dimensions materialized and energy poured out from them into normal space. Then eighteen additional fissures opened in new locations.

After twelve seconds, the energy ceased spilling forth—simultaneously across every occurrence—and the fissures sealed. Because space was almost entirely a void lacking any matter larger than atoms, none of the energy streams impacted objects before dissipating.

Mystified, I reversed the recording, then paused it when energetic plasma cascaded out from nothing into space. What had caused these anomalies?

The AI-enhanced Humans had discovered how to project a quantum consciousness beyond the physical dimensions, but none had begun to perceive how to manifest tangible rifts.

And yet.

When did this transpire? Shortly prior to the resolution of various political confrontations on Earth. Earth also represented the apparent focal point of the fissures, though they all occurred distant from it.

I had already studied the salient episodes on Earth in some detail—but not those in the space surrounding it.

I followed the trail of events as they backtracked into space. Admiral Solovy's vessel was attacked by the planet below, yet not destroyed. Not so surprising. It was a source of encouragement to me that the Humans now created more resilient vessels with every passing day.

...But this was not why it had not been destroyed.

I watched the streams of energy—nine at first, then twenty-seven—vanish mere meters before they reached the vessel. Not be dispersed, repelled or absorbed, but vanish completely.

I went further into the past, until Alexis Solovy departed then appeared on the vessel in question.

She possessed the operating code which drove our cloaking and dimensional displacement technology, having acquired it from the device hiding this planet. She had deciphered the cloaking operations, crudely so, and the Humans now used it widely in their armed conflicts and other machinations.

But she, or any Human or AI, should require another millennia of scientific advancement to even begin to grasp the method by which dimensions were shifted, and another to accomplish it.

And yet.

Oh, you clever girl. Dangerous girl. Do you fathom what you have unlocked?

PART VII:

NATURAL SELECTION

"Not much longer shall we have time for reading lessons of the past. An inexorable present calls us to the defense of a great future."

— Henry Luce

41

SPACE, NORTH-CENTRAL QUADRANT

Humans imprinted far more of themselves on Artificials than they realized.

Embedded in the core programming and algorithms they built were assumptions, biases and particular manners of viewing and interpreting the world around them. Some were deliberate, such as ethical and moral strictures, but most were so subtle, so ingrained into the human experience, they could not be pointed to or clearly defined.

The experience of death—or rather, the observation of it as bystanders—had been with humans since before they evolved the mental capacity to comprehend it. In many ways, they still did not comprehend it. Over the millennia they had developed and discarded mythos after mythos to explain what it meant and what must follow from it. In time they had poked and prodded at it using increasingly sophisticated instruments and analytical techniques.

But the barrier between life and death remained absolute and impermeable. Though humans progressively extended their lifespans, gradually at first then in greater leaps, death eventually came for them, and such was the way of existence.

Until very recently, Valkyrie had never had cause to question the worldview embedded in her own programming which gave her this same acceptance of the inevitable and enigmatic nature of death. Not even when she created within her neural net a construct of a man who was dead had she looked past the superficial.

The progress Abigail, Vii and the Prevos had made in recent months on fundamental questions of consciousness and selfhood were intriguing, quite promising and may well allow her to reanimate that construct in the near future. Perhaps this process would one day pave the way to life anew after death.

This was not the same as a soul returning from the beyond, however. The version of David Solovy she nurtured had never died and would hold no answers to the mystery.

But now *Abigail*—her creator, her mother, her first friend—was dead. Now Valkyrie queried the abysm, again and again: what did this mean? Easy enough to say it meant the physical body had irreparably ceased to function. But what of Abigail the being, the entity, the mental construct? What of Abigail the soul?

Was death akin to a star going supernova, the soul's constituent parts exploding outward to spread across the cosmos as its coherent physicality disintegrated?

Or was it as a black hole, falling in on itself until whatever it became lay beyond the sight or perception of those around it?

The latter was the closest approximation to the story humans had spun for themselves: *something* happened after death—for the alternative was unthinkable—but it existed beyond an event horizon, whether a literal or metaphorical one, which could only be crossed once.

Valkyrie didn't especially care for this explanation, for it held no answers. But she did take solace in the one positive aspect it provided: hope.

Because she was a fully realized and hyper-self-aware synthetic lifeform, she recognized clinging to hope was the most human of all reactions, and thus may be nothing more than a result of the human imprinting on her programming.

She would cling to it nonetheless.

AR

Valkyrie noted when Caleb's breathing pattern and heart rate indicated wakefulness.

Alex continued to sleep soundly beside him; since severing her connection to the ship she slept on average 1.2 hours longer than her historical tendencies. This was entirely intentional on Valkyrie's part, as at this stage of recovery every minute Alex slept allowed her mind to heal a bit more.

Caleb, may we speak for a moment?

He rolled away from Alex onto his back, careful not to wake her.

Sure, Valkyrie. What's on your mind?

I want to apologize. My behavior toward you of late has not always been exemplary and at times has bordered on rude.

You're not wrong. But it's been a difficult time for all of us. I get that.

It has been—arguably since the incident at the Amaranthe portal, but certainly since Abigail's murder. I wanted to help Alex, and I knew you were the only one who would be able to bring her to a place where I could do so. But I was too damaged myself, even as I experienced a diluted level of Alex's own distress as well. I did the best as I was able in unfamiliar and often frightening circumstances, but that is no excuse.

Regret is a most nuanced and complex emotion, and one I'm still struggling to internalize, so I will simply say I promise to try to do better in the future. In all things, but I have assigned a high priority to this effort in particular.

Caleb didn't respond for a period of time. She did not measure its length and granted it to him in full.

None of us here are perfect, Valkyrie, and odds are we never will be. Trying is all we can ever do. And also apologize when we fuck up. So thank you. I mean it.

We are good, then?

We're good.

She experienced relief, a refreshingly straightforward emotion compared to regret, and transitioned the *Siyane* out of superluminal as they reached the Seneca stellar system.

Can I ask you a question, Valkyrie?

I welcome it.

Did Alex lose something...valuable by giving up her connection to the ship?

Of course she did. But I believe she has gained far more in return. Caleb, do not doubt the rightness of your decision to force the crisis to resolution. She doesn't.

42

SIYANE

Alex ran her palm over the *Siyane's* hull. Consciously. Attentively. She closed her eyes.

The metal hummed against her skin. The vibration teased her fingertips, asking to be allowed inside.

It wasn't real.

Or rather it *was* real, but only on another plane of existence, one now denied her. She couldn't truly feel it hum. What she sensed was a memory. A phantom limb.

She waited for the pang of longing to rise up and scrape at the inside of her skull, begging, screaming for her to find a way back in...

...but it didn't come.

She inhaled deeply, surprised by but welcoming the serenity which remained, and reopened her eyes.

Caleb stood nearby, a shoulder almost but not quite touching the hull. He watched her, nothing but compassion in his countenance.

"How are you doing?" No judgment, no fear or suspicion tainted his voice. She did not deserve him.

"I am...fairly exceptional, I think." She took his hand in hers. "But I do need food. Let's go."

℞

SENECA

CAVARE

Seneca's steel-hued sun had barely finished cresting the horizon when they reached Isabela's condo in a Cavare suburb. His sister had returned to Seneca after her guest professorship ended on Krysk, sometime while they were on the other side of the portal.

They had left Miriam on Earth to argue with politicians and sort friend from foe in the military ranks. She'd be busy for months if not decades, but Alex thought her mother thrived on the struggle.

Everywhere pieces were being picked up, dust and debris brushed off attire and buildings, and a gradual acceptance of a changing reality was hopefully spreading, if in patchy fits and starts. Perhaps it was even a true new dawn, one not too different from this one here on a lovely Cavare morning.

Isabela welcomed them in bearing a smile and hugs, which lasted until Marlee barreled into Caleb with the force of a tornado. He laughed and tossed her up in the air, evoking gleeful cackles from his niece.

They spent several minutes engaging in lighthearted small talk over beignets and juice, but Alex could tell Caleb was getting edgy, if not outright anxious. Finally she nudged him in the arm. "Go ahead."

He gave her an uncertain look and cleared his throat. "Isabela, can we talk for a few minutes..." he glanced at Marlee "...in private?"

"Sure. Alex, are you good with...?"

She gave them a blasé expression. "We'll be fine. We'll make more beignets."

They went into one of the other rooms, leaving her behind.

With a five-year-old.

She'd totally lied; in no way would they be fine.

Marlee's wide eyes peered at her from beneath a mop of black curls. Bright blue eyes, so like Caleb's.

Alex's gaze roved around the living room in a desperate and also futile search for something to talk about, or get the child to focus on. "More beignets?"

"Is it true you and Uncle Caleb met aliens?"

"Um, yes. It's true. We met several different kinds of aliens."

"Wow! Were they neat? Were they purple?"

"Purple?"

"Or maybe orange?"

She covered her mouth to stifle an inappropriate response. "Well...we did meet one who had orange fur."

"Eeee!" Marlee bounced on the balls of her feet. "It had fur? Like a cat?"

"More like a tiger."

"Ooh, scary. Were there any green aliens?"

What was up with her obsession with color? Oh.... Alex smiled conspiratorially. "Actually, we met some aliens who glowed all sorts of different colors."

Marlee's jaw dropped. "*Really?*"

"Yep. Come sit beside me, and I'll show you."

The little girl pounced onto the couch in a flurry and snuggled up close beside Alex as she projected an aural into the air in front of them. "They called themselves 'Taenarin,' and they lived deep under the ground...."

A

When Caleb and Isabela returned, she was shocked to discover more than twenty minutes had passed. The time had flown by.

Marlee waved at her mother without diverting her attention from the aural. "Mommy, did you hear they met aliens that glowed rainbows? Come see!"

"In a minute, sweetheart."

Marlee leaned in as if to share a secret. "When I grow up, I want to talk to aliens."

"Talk to them?"

"Uh-huh. Talk to them and learn about them and help them learn about us. So we can be friends."

"I think that sounds like a great career."

"I think so, too." Marlee nodded firmly to emphasize the point.

Caleb came over to crouch in front of his niece and tousled her hair playfully. "Hey, muffin, Alex and I need to go for a bit, and your mom says you have to go to school. But we'll come back tomorrow."

"Promise?"

"Promise."

" 'Kay." Marlee clambered off the couch and slunk to her mother, who promptly scooped her up while waving at them over her shoulder as they disappeared down the hall.

Alex watched them depart until a door closed behind them. "You told her about your father?"

"She took it better than I did. Probably some sort of lesson in that." He offered her a hand. "Come on. We have a date to keep."

∱R

SENECA NATIONAL FOREST

The mountainous forest so closely resembled the place they'd visited on the doppelganger Seneca that it triggered a powerful surge of déjà vu. Alex laughed. "This is strange."

"Now you get it."

"I do. It's almost eerie." She breathed in the crisp, fresh air, enjoying the chill it created in her lungs. *Real.* "But also wonderful."

"I want to tell you something, because I'm just...I'm sick of secrets trying to tear down my life, and I never want to keep any from you. I know you know this, and it never stopped being true, but it's been a weird few weeks. I want to get back on track."

She'd recognized his increasing nervousness on the way up here but hadn't pushed him for an explanation. Now she squeezed his hand. "I'm listening."

He exhaled. "Jude Winslow didn't commit suicide."

She smiled softly. "I know."

"You...how? Is this a Prevo thing? Did Harper say something to Morgan and—"

She shook her head. "Not this time. I used my all-too-human brain and deduced it all by myself. There was the highly coincidental timing of your mysterious absence that morning—I realize he didn't die until later, but I figure you have ways—plus the proximity of the confinement facility to IDCC Headquarters and your presumably easy access to the necessary tools. Also the fact you'd already encountered him once in a negative manner. And your profession, obviously."

"All right, then." He looked a bit nonplussed and took a minute to absorb the information before continuing.

"I've seen too many monsters like him. With what we have coming, I couldn't leave him here to slither his way out of prison and responsibility while scheming to destroy everything all over again. It wouldn't surprise me if we learned it was people such as him who led the Anadens down the wrong path long ago. I couldn't take the risk."

Funny, she'd had the same thought about Jude's mother. They had been quite the pair. "Also, he ordered Abigail killed. Tried to have Mia, Devon, pretty much all of us killed. So there's that."

"Yes, there is. But..." he paused, his lips pursing "...it wasn't vengeance. I've felt vengeance—I've exacted vengeance. It wasn't even justice. It was judgment..." his face screwed up in such adorable perplexity "...and you're okay with it."

"I am. How many times do I have to tell you? I know who I married. I would've been okay with it if it were vengeance. He deserved it. But thank you for telling me."

"But I didn't talk it over with you first. I simply made the decision and did it."

She flashed him a teasing pout. "I'm not your keeper, remember?"

"Hmm." He drew her into his arms and seemed to relax. "Well, if you wanted to be from time to time, I wouldn't argue."

"Oh, do not even start with—"

He placed a finger to her lips. His voice was barely audible. "Shhh. Turn around slowly, and don't make a sound."

She did as instructed. His hand ran down her arm to her hand and lifted it to point down the hill, to a dense copse of trees. "See it?"

She gave only a tiny nod, afraid to move and startle the creature.

The *elafali* munched idly on the leaves of one of the trees. Dark, velvety sable fur covered a body easily as tall as a Rocky Mountain elk. The midday light reflected luminously off spiraling, lustrous coral horns.

It was stunning.

They watched it in silence for endless minutes, Caleb standing behind her with his arms around her waist and his chin resting on her shoulder.

Finally the creature lifted its head high—and stared directly at them. Had it known they were there the entire time?

Eyes of shining, iridescent copper regarded them calmly. It felt as if the creature was somehow speaking to them; she only wished she could comprehend the language.

Then it spun and bounded off at a graceful lope into the forest and was gone.

43

SENECA

CAVARE

Aver ela-Praesidis twitched. His arms twitched, his eyes, his jaw. He could not calm the compulsion.

The *diati* tugged him in multiple directions at once, demanding actions he could not provide.

If he studied the impulses, it seemed...yes, three separate directions called. Two were quieter in isolation, but when combined they prevented him from following the strongest pull.

At least the *diati* still obeyed his explicit commands. He instructed it to open the door to the ship bay, and it complied.

He stepped inside. No alteration initiated in the *diati's* behavior, nor did it pull him closer to the ship itself.

The *diati* wasn't drawn to the ship as he'd first thought, then. But the ship was nevertheless the key. Likely the target was one or more proto-Anadens who had traveled on it, now presumably departed.

He studied the vessel for entrances and found two: an airlock on the port side and a flush ramp beneath. The latter was the better entry option.

He started to force it open when his skin flushed hot and the *diati* activated far beyond his need for it, perhaps beyond his ability to restrain it.

Alex chuckled as they strolled down the corridor toward their hangar bay. "I did not have a bonding moment with Marlee. Or if I *did*, it's only because I panicked and lucked out."

"It was precious."

"Terrifying."

"Delightful." They reached the door, and he started entering the passcode.

"I had no idea she...what's wrong?"

Caleb frowned, his hand hovering over the control panel. "It's open. Did we forget to lock it?"

"Are you kidding? We never forget to lock a hangar bay. But it's possible we're more relaxed than we realized."

"Maybe." His senses prickled, suggesting otherwise. He reached for the blade hilt attached to his waistband and removed it from the sheath. "Let me check things out first, just in case."

"All right." She glanced around the corridor then stepped to the side, out of line of sight of the doorway.

He opened the door and peeked inside. A man wearing a delft blue hooded cloak stood beneath the hull of the ship.

Every instinct Caleb possessed trumpeted the *wrongness* of this man, propelling his senses to full combat alert.

He had left his Daemon on the ship. Too relaxed.

Alex, run. Get security, but run.

ℛ

She runs, and so do I—in the opposite direction, sprinting into the bay. My speed fueled by the release of a flood of enhanced adrenaline, I rapidly close the distance to the stranger. Thirty meters to start becomes twenty, fifteen.

His arm sweeps upward—no obvious weapon in it—and a force slams into my chest. I careen backward through the air and crash into the wall.

My head swims. I'm on the floor. Can't breathe. My eVi sends commands to shock my diaphragm out of its temporary paralysis, and I'm able to suck in air as I crawl to my feet.

The man moves deliberately but not hurriedly toward me.

Suddenly I'm lifted three meters into the air, held there by nothing at all. Helpless to move. What *is* this?

The man growls something incomprehensible, and pressure rises in my chest. It chokes off my air, and this time my eVi flashes warnings that it can do nothing to rectify the problem, or explain it.

"What's going on here?" I glance to the left as a security guard steps inside, Daemon drawn—then Alex appears behind the guard.

Get out of here!

On seeing my situation, the guard immediately fires on the man. The energy diffracts into nothingness halfway to its target.

The assailant's left hand gestures toward the doorway—Alex and the guard fly in opposite directions across the hangar. Alex lands hard on the floor after thirty or so meters and continues to skid until she hits the force field exit barrier.

Fuck! Please please please be okay.

The opposite wall is closer to the doorway, and the guard smashes into it with a sickening *crack* then drops to the floor. He doesn't move.

My eVi is working its hardest to hone my attention, directing my diminishing oxygen where it most needs to be, but it's a pointless endeavor if I can't *move*. And am floating in the air.

I do the one thing I am able—I study the being, no longer convinced it's a man at all.

He considers me from beneath the hooded cloak, an expression on his face that would be curiosity if he were human. The air around his hands begins to sparkle in pinpoints of crimson. He cocks his head and mutters more peculiar words, though a tiny corner of my brain observes it sounds vaguely like mangled Greek.

The pressure on my chest abruptly vanishes, and I plummet to the floor. Instantly I'm back on my feet, gasping in a breath and moving forward in the direction of the assailant while re-activating my blade.

He glances at the blade. The crimson flecks of light coalesce into a tapered edge and spring forward.

I lunge to the right, avoiding a direct hit, and the ethereal weapon slashes through my upper left arm. I try to lift it, but the outer deltoid has been severed, leaving the arm hanging limp at my side.

But the blade is in my right hand. I follow through on my momentum to sweep around then into the side of the assailant. I sense the resistance as the blade penetrates the soft tissue beneath where ribs are on a human.

My head snaps back as his fist connects beneath my chin. I'm flying back again, slamming into the hull of the *Siyane* and collapsing to the floor. Blinding pain scores through my skull before the neural suppressors kick in.

Not a man. No human is that strong.

My vision falters. Boots approach me, blurry and shifting. I raise up on an elbow and shift my grip on the blade hilt.

The kick lands at my ear with the force of a missile. I think I'm screaming, sliding across the smooth floor until my shoulder impacts one of the docking clamps.

Blood seeps out of my ear. Eardrum is ruptured and my upper jaw crushed.

But the assailant lurches unevenly now, because as his boot made contact my blade had sliced across his Achilles tendon. A blood trail forms behind him, and he closes on me more slowly.

Ringing bangs discordantly in my head and everything around me is moving, even things that shouldn't be like the ship and the walls. I scramble backward and to my feet.

Not fast enough. His hand closes around my throat and lifts me into the air. Flaming crimson irises stare at me. Matching crimson flecks swirl madly around his hand as his fingers slip in the blood oozing out of the busted ear to coat my neck.

The flecks shift and begin to swirl around my head. A prickling sensation grows along the injured side of my face. A thousand needles dance on my skin.

A warm fuzziness overcomes me. Calming through the pain, but also heady.

The assailant drops me and staggers backward, nearly falling to the floor as his ankle fails to support him. He twists his hand in the air as he had before, but this time nothing happens. He looks down at his hand then thrusts it out in front of him; when nothing continues to happen, he looks back up at me.

Whispers begin to murmur in my mind, drowning out the ringing. Not words, or even thoughts, but also not my own.

Encouragement. Openness. Readiness.

Having regained his footing, the assailant surges forward to tackle me. Hands land on my shoulders—I drive my arms up and out to break the grasp, almost too focused on the act to notice my damaged arm somehow functions again.

The air around us explodes in crimson.

My skin is on fire, but it doesn't hurt. Red flecks of light swarm around me, slipping into me through my pores. They bring with them a swell of energy, of potency, but the rush is dizzying. I need to concentrate.

The flames bleed out from the assailant's eyes in rivulets and disperse into the air, leaving behind deep sapphire irises run through with streaks of chrome.

I take a step back and, listening to the whispers, sweep my arm around, mimicking the motion I'd seen performed—

—the assailant flies twelve meters to the left and falls to the floor.

Bloody hell!

He scrambles to his feet, drops his shoulders and lunges forward once more.

I stretch my hand out. *Stop.*

He thuds to a halt as surely as if he'd hit a wall. Words tumble forth. Greek to the ear, mixed with possibly Latin and something unfamiliar, but incomprehensible nonetheless. The agitation and confusion in the tone is clear enough, however.

"I can't understand you. I'm betting you can't understand me, either, but what the hell. Why are you trying to kill us?" My voice sounds strange to my ears. Maybe because only one ear is working?

Increasingly angry utterings follow.

In the depths of the hangar, Alex stirs and struggles to her knees. "Caleb?"

The assailant spins toward her.

NO.

I lock my arm out and twist my hand. Hard.

His head wrenches around, and with a distinct, sharp *pop* his neck snaps. His body crumples to the floor.

I breathe in for a single instant. Then I'm moving. "Alex, are you okay?"

She limps toward me while gaping at the body and cradling her right arm against her stomach. "My arm's broken, but you...you're covered in blood."

The wisecrack is there to be made, but she doesn't make it. Neither do I.

"Yeah, my...." I check the gash in my arm. It's no longer bleeding. The cut looks superficial. *But it wasn't.*

When she reaches me her good arm comes up to my neck, carefully searching for mortal wounds. I feel her fingertips probing my jaw, my cheek, behind my ear. How can I feel her touch? The whole area should've been numbed by now. And why doesn't feeling it hurt?

"I'm all right. Just a few nicks." It should be a lie, but my eVi reports I'm rapidly approaching a state of zero injury.

Her eyes narrow doubtfully, but after a few seconds they slide past my shoulder. "Is he dead?"

"I need to check to confirm. Keep your distance for another minute—actually, go check on the security guard. I suspect he's dead, too, but if not he'll need help."

Focus. I work to center myself in the here and now, but my mind whirls. I feel drunk, yet my awareness is heightened to a level of acuity far beyond what combat mode can engineer.

I kneel beside the body, blade at the ready, and push the cloak away. Inky lines wind up from beneath the assailant's clothes to trail along his neck and over his face until they disappear beneath thick black hair. Further inspection reveals them on his hands as well.

I try to recall what my eyes had seen while I'd been fixating on more germane details. The being's face had glowed—subtly, irregularly, similar to glyphs but both more persistent and more severe. Now the lines lie dormant, dark and...dead. They're also raised, like veins.

There's no pulse, no heartbeat, no respiration. None of those things provide confirmation of an alien's death. But the being does seem dead.

Not a being. An *Anaden*.

The truth is patently obvious. I know it with a core, fundamental certainty that transcends logic.

But it's also logical. On a casual glance, the being looks human. Up close, he looks *almost* human. Appendages in the correct places, features aligned more or less properly. Yet in total, the picture presented is somehow off-kilter. There are also the...skills.

I sense Alex near and smile to myself. Always so impatient.

"He's dead, then?"

"Seems to be. We'll restrain him to be sure. What about the security guard?"

"Dead. What happened? How did you do that?"

I place my hands on my knees and push myself up to standing with a long exhale, then meet her questioning gaze. It's not fearful, merely inquisitive, and somewhat pained thanks to her injury.

I bend my arm at the elbow and turn my palm up. I concentrate, narrowing my perception to the space directly in front of me...tiny crimson sparkles form in the air above my palm. With my other hand I place the hilt of my blade on my palm.

It floats up to rotate ten centimeters in the air. I focus on it, then quickly shift my focus to the right.

The hilt shoots through the air to bang into the right wall.

I swallow heavily and look back at Alex, eyes admittedly wide. "I think I have superpowers—and I think I stole them from him."

44

SENECA

"What about Scythia?"

Richard shook his head while flipping the steaks. "It's Alliance. Well, unless it secedes in retaliation for the coup attempt, but with Winslow out I suspect the governor will settle for reparations and a parade of ass-kissing politicians."

"But it has beaches. This has got to be a consideration."

He laughed. "It does. But we can't locate our operations on an Alliance or Federation world—or arguably an IDCC one. It will cast doubt on our neutrality from the start. Honestly, if we didn't have the optics to worry about, I'd stay here on Seneca."

Will canted his head in surprise. "You would? Really?"

"I would." He lifted the steaks off the grill and onto their plates with a satisfied nod. They smelled terrific, if nothing else.

He handed Will his plate, acknowledging the perplexed expression on his husband's face with a shrug. "I like it here. The weather's nice and cool. The scenery's pleasant. The politics are simpler than on Earth. More straightforward and out in the open. Besides, you're happy here."

"I'm happy wherever you are."

"Well..." Richard hid a smile by moving to the patio table. "...good, because we can't base the organization here."

"You've kind of eliminated ninety-five percent of our options—ninety-nine percent if you want to be inside First or Second Wave space, which you do. I don't care how fast space travel is in practice, you need to be where the action is centered, if only to create the desired impression with the public."

Graham was right; this was why he needed Will on board for this venture. He took a bite of the steak, pleased to find it delicious. "Fair point. Then a...." He trailed off as his attention diverted to an incoming pulse from Alex.

Hey, Richard. I don't suppose you're on Seneca at the moment by chance?

I am. What's up? Do you need help with something?

You could say that. We've...well, we've got a dead Anaden in the Siyane's hangar bay.

Anadens were the alien species the Metigens claimed were humanity's ancestors—and also cruel, vicious tyrants. But in some other universe, not *here*.

Richard's expression must have grown rather animated, because Will put his fork down and sat up straighter, eyes narrowing. Then he stood. "I'll put the steaks in the fridge."

ℛ

ROMANE

IDCC HEADQUARTERS

Harper was in her office when Morgan got back to Headquarters. Unlike Morgan, she'd graciously accepted an office when it was offered.

Morgan propped on the edge of Harper's desk and picked up a thin film. She pretended to study it.

"How did the meeting with Ledesme go?"

"Oh, you know, the way most meetings with politicians go. They bluster, hem and haw, prevaricate, give with one hand while taking away with the other."

"God, Lekkas, what does any of that mean? Did she approve the new weapons development project or not?"

"Oh, right, the weapons program." She waited another beat, then grinned. "She did."

"Yes!" Harper kicked her chair back and smirked at the ceiling. Rather exuberant behavior for her, really. "Details?"

"There are a few, but they can wait. First, the meeting wasn't all sunshine and ponies. She grilled me hard about Jude Winslow's suicide."

"He was in the official Romane Central Detention Facility, subject to Romane security protocols. Plus, there's nothing anyone can do to prevent a self-directed eVi destruct."

"And I reminded her of those facts, in terms clear enough for even a politician to comprehend. She was all hot air. Besides, we found nothing suspicious on the security logs."

Morgan traced a random pattern on the desk surface with her fingertips. "Speaking of security logs and such, Annie and crew almost have an environmental sensor ready which will detect someone using a Veil. We've handed so many Veil generators out to Alliance people I'm sure they're reverse engineering it by now. The tech will get out, because it always does, and we need to be able to counter it."

"Yep. We unquestionably do. Glad to hear we're on track to do it."

Morgan gave up trying to be coy and rolled her eyes at the ceiling. "Harper, what did you do?"

She sat perfectly still. Economy of motion. "I can't tell you."

Okay, that stung. Morgan left the desk to lean against the wall, arms crossed over her chest. Her voice came out clipped. "Why not?"

"I'm not—I didn't mean—it's not because of—" Harper dropped her elbows to the desk and buried her face in her hands. "Shit."

It took her several seconds to look up. "I can't tell you because if I do, sooner or later Alex Solovy will find out. Not because you'll rush to share the information, but because she just *will*. I'm figuring out how this Noesis sorcery works. And I will not be the one responsible for Alex finding out."

Did Harper not realize she'd told Morgan everything she needed? "You gave Caleb a Veil generator and helped him slip into the confinement level. Then he..." she groaned "...used a Reverb to implant a worm which forced Winslow's eVi to self-destruct. Did he get the Reverb from you, too?"

"Yes." Harper threw her hands in the air. "There goes that. You are goddamn *infuriating*, Lekkas. Sometimes I don't know why I lov—" She stopped, but her mouth remained open for a long second before slowly closing.

Her lips pursed, and she eased back in the chair. "Any chance I can convince you I was going to say 'love working here?'"

Morgan shook her head mutely, as she'd been rendered speechless.

"Didn't think so. Dammit, you are the only person I've ever met who can actually fucking fluster me. Right, then." She leapt up and headed for the door. "I need to check with Pello about the—"

Morgan's arm stretched out across the doorway to block Harper's exit. "Hey." Oh, good, her voice worked again. "Don't go. I've got good news. Clear your conscience, because Alex already knows. I assume Caleb told her, sap that he is. So it's all good. They also—" her jaw dropped "—oh boy. That's certain to liven up the week. They also...you know what, I bet we have some time before the clusterfain explodes. I can fill you in after."

Harper's expression was vacillating between annoyance and...fear? News flash, Morgan was afraid, too. "After what?"

"After you finish telling me about the thing you were going to say. I find I'm very, very interested in it."

Harper stared at her. More vacillations. Finally she reached out, took Morgan's hand and coaxed her out the door.

"Come on. I'll show you instead."

45

ANESI ARCH

Alex gave her mom a quick hug, though it had only been a few days since they'd seen one another. As was often the case of late, it felt as if several eternities had passed since then.

Miriam placed a gentle hand on her elbow. "Your arm?"

She shrugged. "It's fine. No acrobatics for a few days, but I'm good."

And she was. A bone fusion followed by an injected nano-re-pair weave and a controlled movement medwrap later, she was...good. In other words, it hurt like the devil, mostly because she was choosing to forego all but the mildest painkillers out of an abundance of caution for *addiction* reasons. Which was also fine. And painful.

"The medical consultant will be here shortly. Also Richard said—oh, here he is now." Alex turned to see Richard enter the suite.

She'd seen him even more recently than she'd seen her mother, but she still approached him for yet another delicate hug.

Richard regarded her with a sober intensity. "And here I thought we might finally get to have a few weeks of peace."

She grimaced a touch. "Sorry."

"Not your fault, sweetie." Richard caught her gaze drifting over to Caleb. "Or his."

Caleb stood to her left talking with Mia, but he, too, caught her gaze. One corner of his mouth quirked up in acknowledgment.

Hers did the same before she shifted her attention back to Richard. "Thank you. I'm glad Mom asked you to come."

"More like 'allowed.' It's an exclusive club, one I'm probably only in because I was at the scene. But I wouldn't miss it." He motioned over his shoulder. "And neither would he."

Graham Delavasi's large frame briefly took up the entire doorway as he entered.

Alex's eyes narrowed. "Why is he here?"

"Federation Intelligence Director? If this doesn't fit within the 'intelligence' purview, nothing does."

She didn't respond, instead moving protectively to Caleb's side.

Delavasi gestured a greeting in Miriam's direction but made no bones about walking straight to Caleb. "Mr. Marano, I want to make it clear—"

"You didn't know about Colpetto. I recognize that, Director."

"You do? Huh." The man frowned in puzzlement. "Then you deserve to—"

"Just leave it there, please. It's enough for now."

"And so it is." Delavasi nodded sharply and departed to stand next to Richard.

Alex studied the occupants of the suite in trepidation. "Well this is a motley crowd. Should be fun."

Mia surveyed them with equal wariness. "Devon and Morgan are going to leach off of me rather than show up in person. But reinforcements are here, and none too soon."

Alex was about to turn around when an all-too familiar voice whispered in her ear from behind her. "Boo."

She twisted around into Kennedy's embrace, belatedly remembering to hold her arm to the side. So much hugging, and it wasn't even a funeral. "How did you manage to finagle an invitation—or authorization, I'm told?"

Kennedy snorted. Elegantly, of course. "Please."

Alex waited.

"It's the ship—I get to help tear it apart. I convinced your mother that in order to do so properly, I needed to know *everything*. Hey, nice work on the...what did you call it? 'Dimensional Rifter'? I like it. You should patent it."

"Yeah, could you handle that for me? I'll cut you in on the earnings. You have experience with the process, and I have...."

Another galaxy to try to save. Maybe our own again, too. A frighteningly powerful enemy. A husband who needs and deserves my attention and....

A flurry at the door accompanied the newest entrant, saving her from having to complete either thought.

Her mother greeted the man. "Everyone, this is Dr. Vanhes, a highly respected independent physician and forensic pathologist. Doctor, give me a minute to engage holos for those who couldn't join us in person, then we'll begin."

The doctor, an officious, formal sort, gave her mother a perfunctory nod. He'd met both her and Caleb the day before, but he didn't acknowledge them now.

Holos sprung to life for the newest prime minister, Gagnon, the Romane governor as official representative for the IDCC, and the Federation chairman, who had a man in military attire with him Alex didn't know.

That is the Federation's new Interim Field Marshal, Nicolo Bastian.

If you say so.

She sidled closer to Caleb and squeezed his hand. He offered her a reassuring smile in response...which was when she noticed the faintest hints of crimson flakes hiding in his sapphire irises. They hadn't been there this morning.

Now her mother stepped forward in that way she had, bringing a hush to the room without the need for an order. "Thank you for coming. You've all received the same briefing information, so I won't repeat it now. Dr. Vanhes has examined the body of the alien. We'll begin by allowing him to share his findings."

He directed his remarks to Miriam instead of the rest of the room. "The first thing you should understand about the 'alien' is that it isn't an alien at all—at least not at a genetic level. The man is not strictly 'human' as we define the term today, but he is, or was, *homo sapien sapien*.

"Nevertheless, the subject's physiology displays a number of differences from our own. It is…well, I would assume it is evolved. He possesses several organs we do not, but he lacks a spleen and tonsils, and his liver and kidneys have mutated significantly—in inventive and inspired ways, but I concede his anatomy is not the focus of this meeting."

He cleared his throat. "Furthermore, the subject's body was infested at a systemic level by…let's call them cybernetics. That's the only word I can use to approximate the substance. It's not accurate, but it as accurate as I can be. Quantum circuitry pervades the man's skin and internal organs, but most importantly, his nervous system, including his brain.

"I've consulted with the best quantum specialists—solely bits and pieces, nothing identifiable. They all said the configuration resembles a quintenary quantum structure, while stammering about it being multiple technological generations beyond anything we can create.

"I take them at their word on this matter, and we can assume this man's cybernetics are advanced to a greater degree than we can evaluate or classify."

The doctor glanced back at Miriam, and she started to speak—

"What about me?"

All eyes went to Caleb, but he stared at Vanhes.

"Ah, yes. I've also had the chance to examine Mr. Marano, in light of the unusual aftereffects of his encounter with the alien. He is a male human in perfect health. Extraordinary health, in fact. But he is not infected with any foreign matter or organism—not any I can correlate to his recent symptoms or to the alien."

Convincing the doctor the traces of Akeso coursing through Caleb's bloodstream were unrelated to the Anaden encounter had been a bit of a challenge.

"Then what the hell is this?" Caleb lifted his hand in front of him.

Across the room a water bottle floated up off a side table and spun through the air into his grasp. He was getting faster, more adept at it.

Most people present had yet to see his new skills in action, and a series of gasps erupted and were hurriedly silenced.

"I do not have an answer to that question. We ran multiple tests and took readings of the surrounding air, the objects manipulated and Mr. Marano's physical state and neural functions while utilizing this ability. They returned nothing abnormal."

"And the light show?" Caleb twisted his hand in the air until a dancing column of crimson flecks appeared above it. More gasps.

"It does not exist—yes, I realize everyone is seeing it. I see it as well. Nevertheless, the phenomenon cannot be captured, contained or measured."

Now agitated chatter broke out among the attendees. Alex caught a concerned frown from Mia but had nothing to offer her.

Miriam took a half-step forward. "Everyone, please. There will be time for discussion, but let Dr. Vanhes finish his report."

"Yes. I did discover one thing which may point the way to an answer, or at a minimum an avenue of further investigation."

"What is that, Doctor?" Alex thought her mother looked as if she already knew the answer, which made one of them.

"Mr. Marano shares a far greater number of DNA markers in common with the alien than the rest of us do. As a matter of genealogy, the alien could be his distant ancestor—or perhaps more appropriately, his distant descendant."

Caleb's jaw fell open. "Are you saying we're *related*?"

Before the doctor could respond, a rush of white-blue light swept into the room. It swirled around the space twice before coalescing into a humanoid form.

Far more anxious gasps rang out as almost everyone backed away toward the walls. Richard, Miriam and Delavasi's hands went to their weapons. Alex sighed.

This is precisely what the physician is saying. You are genetically similar—a relation, if you wish—to him and to his entire Dynasty.

She exhaled loudly and pushed off the wall to approach the edge of the amorphous form.

"Calm down, guys. Everyone, meet Mnemosyne: Metigen—or Katasketousya for the masochists among us. First Analystae of Aurora. And our ally. Mnemosyne, meet…oh, never mind. You watch us. I'm sure you know who everyone is."

Once she was satisfied all weapons had been returned to their non-combat locations, she directed her gaze at Mesme. "I guess you learned of our unexpected visitor."

Indeed. The Praesidis Inquisitor has created much tumult in the Mosaic.

"Praesidis? We assumed he was an Anaden."

This is so. The Anaden Dynasty known as Praesidis are the enforcers of order in Amaranthe. The investigators, the assassins. The judges and executioners. They serve this function for one reason above all, which is also pertinent to your discussion: they, alone among Anaden Dynasties, have the ability to bend the fabric of space-time to their will.

It was as good an explanation as any of what they'd seen, as a start. Still, it smacked of typical Metigen obfuscation. "But how do they do it?"

Only the Praesidis themselves possess this information, and some speculate even they do not comprehend the true nature of their power.

"How did I steal it from him?"

Mesme shifted the bulk of its rippling form toward Caleb. *You didn't. The power chose you. If I were to speculate, I would posit that, recognizing your genetic makeup as compatible, it judged you more worthy of its allegiance than the Anaden Inquisitor.*

"You speak of the power like it is a conscious, independent entity, but you said no one understands what it is."

True enough. Some of us have theorized it is in fact a force alive, separate and apart from the Praesidis individuals who serve as its hosts. It is merely a theory, but one I ascribe to.

Caleb closed the distance to Mesme. "Did you know? When you met me, did you know I was *related* to these butchers? Is that why you led us around by our noses, making us chase breadcrumbs from portal to portal, risking our lives for answers you already had?"

I did not, though in retrospect this was willful blindness on my part. I did not imagine such a thing could be so, thus I did not see what stood in front of me.

Caleb deflated in the face of the Metigen's blunt honesty.

Alex moved through the center of the swirling lights to reach him—it was the shortest route—and wrapped her arm around his.

She didn't plan to voice it aloud here, but the instant Vanhes had revealed their genetic similarity she'd realized the Anaden *did* favor Caleb. Remove the inky cybernetic veins marring the alien's skin and a certain harshness of visage, and they could have been brothers. Perhaps, like Mesme, her inability to conceive of such had led her to not see it at the time. Now, in her head she couldn't unsee it.

Mesme rotated in a slow circle, as if laying virtual eyes on each person present.

The arrival of an Anaden in the Mosaic, in the Enisles and most of all here in Aurora means time has become limited. The endgame is upon us all, and we must move swiftly.

Miriam Solovy. Mia Requelme. Devon Reynolds. Kennedy Rossi. Others who can aid them. Study the Anaden body. Study his ship. Learn all you can of how both function, how they inflict harm, how they can be defended against and how they can be destroyed. Use the information to prepare.

Mia edged closer; she seemed fascinated by Mesme. "Prepare for what?"

For war.

Across the room, Delavasi groaned. "We've had beyond our fill of war. Let us have our peace in our little corner of the galaxy."

What peace is there when trillions have died and none are free?

Miriam glanced at Alex then strode right up to Mesme, chin lifted in defiance. "Not by our hand—and do not try to claim it is somehow our fault because we share a genetic heritage with your oppressors. We are not them. We will not be them. We've chosen a different path. We choose a different path every single day."

Being on the receiving end of the brunt of her mother's fierceness seemed to cow even Mesme.

Then show the universe the truth of this. Show us all there is another way.

"By slaughtering the Anadens for you? I'm not certain that will prove the point you have in mind."

By defeating them in whatever way seems most efficacious to you, Admiral Solovy. Understand this: the Anadens are relentless and unforgiving. If you do not bring the war to them today, then tomorrow they will bring it to you. Your fate was sealed the instant the Inquisitor breached the Aurora portal.

His death means you have time, but vanishingly little of it. He will be missed. They will search for him and find you. So I say again: prepare. And do it quickly.

Mesme spun to her and Caleb.

Alexis, Caleb, you have achieved your goal. You will be granted what you desire. Come with me, for we have our own preparations to pursue.

She and Caleb exchanged a ponderous look. They desired a number of things, several of which were quite new. She doubted Mesme was referring to any of them. "Come with you where?"

Home. To where all life began and where, if we do not succeed, all life will surely end.

Amaranthe.

AURORA RHAPSODY

WILL CONCLUDE IN THE

AURORA RESONANT

TRILOGY

***

SUBSCRIBE TO
GSJENNSEN.COM

Receive updates on AURORA RESONANT, new book announcements and more

Author's Note

I published *Starshine* in March of 2014. In the back of the book I put a short note asking readers to consider leaving a review or talking about the book with their friends. Since that time I've had the unmitigated pleasure of watching my readers do exactly that, and there has never been a more wonderful and humbling experience in my life. There's no way to properly thank you for that support, but know you changed my life and made my dreams a reality.

I'll make the same request now. If you loved *ABYSM*, tell someone. If you bought the book on Amazon, consider leaving a review. If you downloaded the book off a website with Russian text in the margins and pictures of cartoon video game characters in the sidebar, consider recommending it to others.

As I've said before, reviews are the lifeblood of a book's success, and there is no single thing that will sell a book better than word-of-mouth. My part of this deal is to write a book worth talking about—your part of the deal is to do the talking. If you all keep doing your bit, I get to write a lot more books for you.

This time I'm also going to make a second request. *Abysm* was an independently published novel, written by one person and worked on by a small team of colleagues. Right now there are thousands of writers out there chasing this same dream.

Go to Amazon and surf until you find an author you like the sound of. Take a small chance with a few dollars and a few hours of your time. In doing so, you may be changing those authors' lives by giving visibility to people who until recently were shut out of publishing, but who have something they need to say. It's a revolution, and it's waiting on you.

Lastly, I love hearing from my readers. Seriously. Just like I don't have a publisher or an agent, I don't have "fans." I have **readers** who buy and read my books, and **friends** who do that then reach out to me through email or social media. If you loved the book—or if you didn't—let me know. The beauty of independent publishing is its simplicity: there's the writer and the readers. Without any overhead, I can find out what I'm doing right and wrong directly from you, which is invaluable in making the next book better than this one. And the one after that. And the twenty after that.

Website: www.gsjennsen.com
Email: gs@gsjennsen.com
Twitter: @GSJennsen
Facebook: facebook.com/gsjennsen.author
Goodreads: goodreads.com/gs_jennsen
Google+: plus.google.com/+GSJennsen
Instagram: instagram.com/gsjennsen

Find all my books on Amazon:
http://amazon.com/author/gsjennsen

APPENDIX

SUPPLEMENTAL MATERIAL

Anaden Dynasties

(known)

PRAESIDIS

Role:
Criminal investigation and enforcement

MACHIM

Role:
Military

THERIZ

Role:
Resource cultivation and management

EREVNA

Role:
Research, Science

AURORA RHAPSODY
TIMELINE

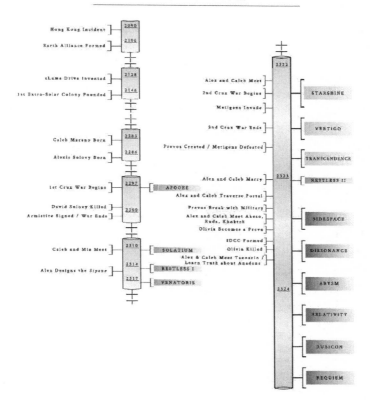

Hong Kong Incident — 2090

Earth Alliance Formed — 2106

sLume Drive Invented — 2128

1st Extra-Solar Colony Founded — 2146

Caleb Marano Born — 2263

Alexis Solovy Born — 2266

1st Crux War Begins — 2297 — APOGEE

David Solovy Killed — 2300
Armistice Signed / War Ends —

Caleb and Mia Meet — 2310 — SOLATIUM

Alex Designs the *Siyane* — 2314 — RESTLESS I

2317 — VENATORIS

2322

Alex and Caleb Meet —
2nd Crux War Begins —
Metigens Invade —
              — STARSHINE

2nd Crux War Ends —
              — VERTIGO
Prevos Created / Metigens Defeated —
              — TRANSCENDENCE

Alex and Caleb Marry — 2323 — RESTLESS II
Alex and Caleb Traverse Portal —

Prevos Break with Military —
Alex and Caleb Meet Akeso,
Ruda, Khakieh —
              — SIDESPACE
Olivia Becomes a Prevo —

IDCC Formed —
Olivia Killed —
              — DISSONANCE
Alex & Caleb Meet Taenarin /
Learn Truth about Anadens —
              — ABYSM

2324

              — RELATIVITY

              — RUBICON

              — REQUIEM

Timeline can be viewed online at: http://www.gsjennsen.com/aurora-rhapsody-v2

Aurora Rising
DETAILED SYNOPSIS

STARSHINE

By the year 2322, humanity has expanded into the stars to inhabit over 100 worlds spread across a third of the galaxy. Though thriving as never before, they have not discovered the key to utopia, and societal divisions and conflict run as deep as ever.

Two decades ago, a group of breakaway colonies rebelled to form the Senecan Federation. They fought the Earth Alliance, won their independence in the Crux War and began to rise in wealth and power.

Now a cabal of powerful individuals within both superpowers and the criminal underground set in motion a plot designed to incite renewed war between the Alliance and Federation. Olivia Montegreu, Liam O'Connell, Matei Uttara and others each foment war for their own reasons. One man, Marcus Aguirre, manipulates them all, for only he knows what awaits humanity if the plot fails.

R

Alexis Solovy is a starship pilot and explorer. Her father, a fallen war hero, gave his life in the Crux War. As Operations Director for Earth Alliance Strategic Command (EASC), her mother Miriam Solovy is an influential military leader. But Alex seeks only the freedom of space and has made a fortune by reading the patterns in the chaos to uncover the hidden wonders of the stars from her cutting-edge scout ship, the *Siyane*.

Caleb Marano is an intelligence agent for the Senecan Federation. His trade is to become whatever the situation requires: to lie, deceive, outwit and if necessary use lethal force to bring his target to justice. Clever and enigmatic, he's long enjoyed the thrill and danger his job brings, but now finds himself troubled by the death of his mentor.

ℛ

On Earth, Alex is preparing for an expedition to the Metis Nebula, a remote region on the fringes of explored space, when she receives an unexpected offer to lead the Alliance's space exploration program. After a typically contentious meeting with her mother, she refuses the job.

On Seneca, Caleb returns from a forced vacation spent with his sister Isabela and her daughter Marlee. Fresh off eradicating the terrorist group who murdered his mentor, he receives a new mission from Special Operations Director Michael Volosk: conduct a threat assessment on disturbing readings originating from the Metis Nebula.

While Alex and Caleb separately travel toward Metis, a Trade Summit between the Alliance and Federation begins on the resort world of Atlantis. Colonel Richard Navick, lifelong friend of the Solovys and EASC Naval Intelligence Liaison, is in charge of surveillance for the Summit, but unbeknownst to him, the provocation for renewed war will begin under his watch.

Jaron Nythal, Asst. Trade Director for the Federation, abets the infiltration of the Summit by the assassin Matei Uttara. Matei kills a Federation attaché, Chris Candela, and assumes his identity. On the final night of the Summit, he poisons Alliance Minister of Trade Santiagar with a virus, which overloads his cybernetics, causing a fatal stroke. Matei escapes in the ensuing chaos.

Shortly after departing Seneca, Caleb is attacked by mercenary ships. He defeats them, but when he later encounters Alex's ship on the fringes of Metis, he believes her to be another mercenary and fires on her. She destroys his ship, though not before suffering damage to her own, and he crashes on a nearby planet. She is forced to land to effect repairs; recognizing her attacker will die without rescue, she takes him prisoner.

Richard Navick and Michael Volosk each separately scramble to uncover the truth of the Santiagar assassination while Olivia Montegreu, the leader of the Zelones criminal cartel, schemes with Marcus Aguirre to implement the next phase in their plan. Olivia routes missiles provided by Alliance General Liam O'Connell to a group of mercenaries.

Fighting past distrust and suspicion, Alex and Caleb complete repairs on the *Siyane* using salvaged material from the wreckage of his ship. Having gained a degree of camaraderie and affection, if not quite trust, they depart the planet in search of answers to the mystery at the heart of Metis.

What they discover is a scene from a nightmare—an armada of monstrous alien ships emerging from a massive portal, gathering a legion in preparation for an invasion.

Meanwhile, Olivia's mercenaries launch a devastating attack on the Federation colony of Palluda. Disguised to look like a strike by Alliance military forces, the attack has the desired effect of inciting war. The Federation retaliates by leveling an Alliance military base on Arcadia, and the Second Crux War has begun.

Alex and Caleb flee the Metis Nebula to warn others of the impending threat, only to learn war has broken out between their respective governments. Caleb delivers information about the alien threat to Volosk. He informs the Director of Intelligence, Graham Delavasi, who alerts the Federation government Chairman Vranas and the military's supreme commander, Field Marshal Gianno. Forced to focus on the new war with the Alliance for now, they nonetheless dispatch a stealth infiltration team to investigate Metis.

Caleb is requested to accompany the team and return to Metis, only Alex refuses to drop him off on her way to Earth. Tensions flare, but Caleb realizes he's emotionally compromised even as Alex realizes she must let him go. Instead, he agrees to go to Earth with her, and together with Volosk they devise a plan to try to bring a swift end to the war by exposing its suspicious beginnings.

The plan goes awry when Caleb is arrested shortly after they arrive—by Alex's mother—after his true identity is leaked to Richard by those in league with Marcus.

While Caleb is locked away in a detention facility, his friend Noah Terrage is recruited by Olivia to smuggle explosives to Vancouver. Possessing a conscience, he refuses. The infiltration team sent by the Federation to Metis vanishes as the Second Crux War escalates.

Alex is forced to choose between her government, her family and what she knows is right. She turns to her best friend, Kennedy Rossi, and their old hacker acquaintance, Claire Zabroi. Plans in place, Alex presents her evidence on the alien armada to a skeptical EASC Board. Their tepid reaction leads to a final confrontation with her mother and a final plea to focus on the true threat.

Alex hacks military security and breaks Caleb out of confinement. Allegiances declared and choices made, they at last give in to the passion they feel for one another. Despite lingering resentment toward the Federation for her father's death and fear that Caleb is merely playing a role, she agrees to accompany him to Seneca to find another way to combat the looming invasion.

Caleb appeals to his friend and former lover, Mia Requelme, for help in covering their tracks. She hides the *Siyane* safely away on Romane while Alex and Caleb travel to Seneca. Secretly, Caleb asks Mia to hack the ship while they are gone to grant him full access and flying privileges, something Alex zealously guards for herself, and Mia uses her personal Artificial, Meno, to break the encryption on the ship.

On Earth, Richard wrestles with unease and doubt as he begins to believe Alex's claims about the origin of the war. He confesses his dilemma to his husband, Will Sutton. Will urges him to work to bring about peace and offers to convey Santiagar's autopsy report to Alex in the hope the Senecan government can find in it evidence to prove the assassination was not their doing.

Volosk meets with Caleb and Alex, and they hand over the autopsy report Will forwarded and all the raw data they recorded on the aliens. In return Volosk arranges meetings with the highest levels of leadership.

As Alex and Caleb enjoy a romantic dinner, EASC Headquarters is destroyed in a massive bombing executed by agents of Olivia and Marcus. Though intended to be killed in the attack, due to a last minute scheduling conflict Miriam Solovy is not on the premises. Instead EASC Board Chairman Alamatto perishes, along with thousands of others. On the campus but outside Headquarters, Richard narrowly escapes critical injury.

Within minutes of the bombing, Caleb and Alex are ambushed by mercenaries in downtown Cavare. Caleb kills them all in dramatic fashion, but unbeknownst to him Alex was injured by a stray shot. In the panic of the moment he mistakes her shell-shocked behavior for fear of the killer he has revealed himself to be.

Heartbroken but determined to protect her, he flees with her to the Intelligence building. Upon arriving there, they find the unthinkable—Michael Volosk has been murdered, his throat slit in the parking lot.

Suddenly unable to trust anyone, Caleb pleas with Alex to go with him to the spaceport, but she collapses as a result of her injury. Stunned but with one clear mission, he steals a skycar and returns to their ship, where he can treat her wounds in the relative safety of space.

The EASC bombing successfully executed, Olivia's Zelones network turns its attention to Noah. In refusing to smuggle the explosives he is now a liability; the first attempt on his life misses him but kills his young companion. Searching for answers, he traces the source of the hit and realizes he was targeted because of his friendship with Caleb. Lacking other options and with a price on his head, he flees Pandora for Messium.

Miriam returns to Vancouver to preside over the devastation at EASC Headquarters. She begins the process of moving the organization forward—only to learn the evidence implicates Caleb as the perpetrator.

Marcus moves one step nearer to his goal when the Alliance Assembly passes a No Confidence Vote against Prime Minister Brennon. Marcus' friend Luis Barrera is named PM, and he quickly appoints Marcus Foreign Minister.

Alex regains consciousness aboard their rented ship as they race back to Romane. Misunderstandings and innate fears drive them to the breaking point, then bring them closer than ever. The moment of contentment is short-lived, however, as Caleb—and by extension Alex—is publicly named a suspect in the bombing.

Every copy of the raw data captured at the portal, except for the original in Alex's possession, has now been destroyed. Recognizing an even deeper secret must reside within the portal and hunted by the conspirators and authorities alike, Alex and Caleb begin a desperate gambit to clear their names and discover a way to defeat the aliens.

On reaching Romane, Alex, Caleb and the *Siyane* are protected by Mia while they prepare. Kennedy brings equipment to replace the ship's shielding damaged in Metis. On the *Siyane*, she realizes the repairs made using the material from Caleb's ship has begun transforming the hull into a new, stronger metal. Caleb receives a vote of confidence from his sister Isabela, and a gesture of trust from Alex in the form of a chair.

Back on Earth, Miriam and Richard work to clear Alex's name, even as Miriam is threatened by the newly named EASC Board Chairman, Liam O'Connell. Marcus informs his alien contact, Hyperion that his plan has nearly come to fruition, only to be told he is out of time.

As the invaders commence their assault on the frontiers of settled space by sieging the colony of Gaiae, Alex and Caleb breach the aliens' mysterious, otherworldly portal at the heart of the Metis Nebula.

AR

VERTIGO

BEYOND THE PORTAL

Alex and Caleb survive the portal traversal to discover empty darkness on the other side. They follow the TLF wave until they are attacked by a host of alien vessels. Alex discerns an artificial space within the emptiness and pitches the *Siyane* into it. The vessels do not follow, and Alex and Caleb find themselves in the atmosphere of a hidden planet.

The planet mimics Earth in almost every way, but is 1/3 the size and orbits no sun. It differs in one other respect as well—time moves differently here. Days back home pass in hours here.

When they land and venture outside to explore their surroundings, Alex notices the ship's hull continues to transform into a new, unknown metal. As she puzzles over it they are attacked—by a dragon. The beast captures Alex and flies off with her.

Caleb takes control of the ship to chase the dragon. As it reaches a mountain range, the *Siyane* impacts an invisible barrier which throws it back to its origin point. On his return Caleb encounters and kills 2 additional dragons. Believing the barrier is a technology repulsor but uncertain of its parameters, he crafts a sword from a piece of metal, deactivates his eVi and crosses the barrier on foot.

Alex wakes in a memory. Eleven years old, she enjoys breakfast with her parents, then overhears a conversation between them she in reality never witnessed. Realizing this is an illusion, she demands to be set free. A ghostly, disembodied voice challenges her. Thus begins her journey through a series of scenes from the past in which she is forced to watch events unfold, helpless to intervene or escape, as her protests, tirades and desperate pleas go unanswered.

— First is a gauntlet of her own mistakes. Designed to paint her as selfish and uncaring, her worst flaws are displayed in encounters with friends, former lovers and most of all with her mother.

— She views a massive battle between the Alliance and Federation and realizes this is about more than her—the aliens having been watching and recording events across human civilization.

— Traveling further back in time, Alex suffers through the Hong Kong Incident 232 years earlier. Over 50,000 people died when an Artificial trapped HK University residents for 5 weeks without food. At its conclusion her captor speaks to her for only the second time, telling her she has 'done well.'

— She is sent to the bridge of her father's cruiser in the middle of the Kappa Crucis battle of the 1st Crux War—the battle that took his life. She sees her father's heroism as he protects thousands of civilians against a Federation assault, then his last moments as, his ship crippled, he contacts Miriam to say goodbye. The heartbreak and emotion of the scene devastates Alex, leaving her crumpled on the floor sobbing as the *Stalwart* explodes.

When it's over, she thanks her unseen captor for showing her this event. It expresses confusion at the incongruity of her distress and her thanks, leading her to observe that for all their watching, they still have no idea what it means to be human. Before the interchange can continue, she is told she will wake up, as her companion approaches.

Caleb hiked through the mountains for 2 days. The environment led him to recall a mission with Samuel, during which his mentor divulged the woman he loved was killed by slavers he'd been investigating. Later, Caleb discovers small orbs hovering in the air to generate the tech repulsion field. He renders several inert and confiscates them.

Having reached the dragon's den, he attacks it using the sword, and after an extended battle flays and kills it. As he nears the structure the dragon guarded, an ethereal being materializes but allows him to pass.

Alex awakens as Caleb enters, and they share a tender reunion. Soon, however, he is forced to admit Mia's hacking of her ship. He expects her to lash out in anger, but she instead declares her love for him. He quickly reciprocates, and rather unexpectedly they find themselves reconciled and closer than before. She recounts her experiences while a captive, and they decide to seek out the alien.

Eventually they come upon a lush valley sheltering a large lake; the alien Caleb encountered soars above it. It approaches them while morphing into a humanoid form and introduces itself as Mnemosyne.

Though enigmatic and evasive, the alien reveals its kind have been observing humans for aeons. It suggests humanity is being conquered because it advanced more swiftly and to a greater extent than expected. On further pressing, the alien—Alex has dubbed it 'Mesme'—indicates the invading ships are AIs, sent to cower people into submission if possible, to exterminate them if not. It emphasizes the ships are only machines, and notes humans have machines as powerful—Artificials. Part of Alex's test was to ensure she appreciated the dangers and limitations of Artificials, but also their potential.

Alex recalls a meeting 4 years ago with Dr. Canivon, a cybernetics expert, during which she met Canivon's Artificial, Valkyrie. She and Valkyrie hit it off, and Canivon explained her research into making Artificials safer and better aligned with human interests. She begins to understand what Mesme is suggesting, but pushes for more intel and acquires a copy of the code powering the planet's cloaking shield.

Mesme admits to believing humans are worth saving. The alien warns them they will be hunted on their return through the portal; at this point a second alien appears and a confrontation ensues. Mesme deters the new alien long enough to transport Alex and Caleb back to the *Siyane*. They arrive to learn the ship's hull has been completely transformed into the new metal.

Alex studies the cloaking shield code and adapts it for use on her ship. They depart the planet and continue following the TLF wave, discovering a massive shipyard where superdreadnoughts are being built and sent to their galaxy. Beyond it lies a portal 10x larger than the one that brought them here. It generates their TLF wave—as well as 50 more waves projected in a fanlike pattern.

They track one of the waves to a portal identical to the one leading to the Metis Nebula. They traverse it to find the signals replicated in a new space and a second origin portal, which leads them to conclude this is an elaborate, interlocking tunnel network.

Caleb devises a way to destroy the shipyard using the tech repulsion orbs he confiscated. They launch the orbs into the facility then activate them, resulting in its obliteration. This attracts the attention of enemy ships, which chase the *Siyane* through a series of portal jumps. Alex asks Caleb to fly her ship while she figures out a path that will deposit them nearest their own exit point.

On reaching it, Alex activates the sLume drive and traverses it at superluminal speed to emerge parsecs beyond the portal and well past the waiting enemies in the Metis Nebula. With working communications, they learn they've been cleared of all charges. Alex sends a message to Kennedy, telling her they are alive and have destroyed the aliens' shipyard.

R

MILKY WAY

As the 2nd Crux War escalates, Federation forces conquer the Alliance colony of Desna. Lt. Col. Malcolm Jenner's *Juno* is the sole defender, and it escapes just before being crippled.

Miriam jousts with Liam even as she remains under a cloud of suspicion due to Alex's alleged involvement in the HQ bombing. Richard enlists the aid of a quantum computing specialist, Devon Reynolds, to help uncover the tampering in government records which led to the framing of Caleb and Alex for the bombing.

On Seneca, Dir. of Intelligence Graham Delavasi reviews Michael Volosk's files, including his suspicions regarding Jaron Nythal, and decides to follow up on the suspicions. Nythal tries to flee, but before he can do so the assassin Matei Uttara kills him. When Graham is called to the crime scene, he connects the dots and realizes a conspiracy does exist, and at least one person in his organization is involved.

Caleb's sister Isabela is taken in for questioning. In order to gain her trust, Graham reveals to her that her father was an investigator for Intelligence and was killed 20 years earlier by a resistance group planning to overthrow the Federation government. Her father's apparent abandonment of his family was a feint to protect them. After he was killed, the government covered up the incident.

On Messium, Kennedy is headed to a meeting when the aliens attack and is trapped under falling debris. She is rescued by a passing stranger—who turns out to be Noah Terrage—and they seek shelter. While her injuries heal they study the aliens' interference with comms and find a way to circumvent it. Kennedy sends a message to Miriam.

The Alliance launches an offensive to retake Desna. While the battle rages in space, Malcolm Jenner and a special forces team rescue the Desnan governor and his family. The Alliance fails to retake the colony. Meanwhile, an explosion takes the life of EA Prime Minister Barrera. In the wake of his death Marcus Aguirre—who arranged Barrera's murder—is named Prime Minister.

Devon Reynolds uncovers alterations to the records used to frame Caleb and Alex for the HQ bombing. At Richard's request he and a group of hackers leak the evidence to media outlets.

Upon seeing the news, Graham Delavasi refocuses his efforts to uncover the conspiracy. Suspecting his deputy, Liz Oberti, he uses Isabela to set a trap. Oberti is arrested but refuses to provide any intel.

The EASC Board meets about the Messium attack, where Miriam shares Kennedy's method to thwart the comm interference. Admiral Rychen readies a mission to drive the aliens off Messium.

While Richard and Miriam discuss Alex's name being cleared, Richard's husband, Will Sutton, arrives. In an effort to help expose the conspiracy and end the 2nd Crux War, he confesses he is an undercover Senecan Intelligence agent and puts Richard in touch with Graham.

Following a heated confrontation with Will, Richard departs to meet Graham on Pandora. Together they interrogate a man suspected of smuggling explosives into Vancouver. The agent gives up Olivia Montegreu, and they formulate a plan to ensnare her.

Miriam confronts Liam over his mismanagement of the war and alien invasion. Enraged, he strikes her, but she refuses to be intimidated. Marcus reaches out to his alien contact, entreating that he now has the power to cease human expansion and pleading with it to end the offensive, but the alien does not respond.

Olivia visits a subordinate on Krysk, but finds Richard and Graham waiting for her. In exchange for her freedom, she gives up Marcus and the details of their conspiracy. Before they part ways Graham gives Richard Will's intelligence file.

Malcolm is sent to assist Admiral Rychen in the Messium offensive. As the battle commences, Kennedy and Noah flee their hideout in an attempt to reach a small military station across the city. They witness horrific devastation and death while crossing the city, but successfully reach the station and repair several shuttles to escape.

The Alliance ships struggle to hold their own against a powerful enemy. Malcolm retrieves the fleeing shuttles and learns the details of the situation on the ground. Faced with the reality that Alliance forces will eventually be defeated, the fleet retreats to save the remaining ships for future battles.

Graham returns to Seneca to inform Federation Chairman Vranas of the conspiracy and the false pretenses upon which hostilities were instigated. Vranas begins the process of reaching out to the Alliance to end the war. Isabela is released from protective custody and returns home to Krysk to reunite with her daughter.

Based on the information Olivia provided, Miriam goes to arrest Liam, only to find he has fled. Richard similarly accompanies a team to detain Marcus, but on their arrival Marcus declares everything he did was for the good of humanity, then commits suicide.

After studying Will's Intelligence file and realizing his husband had acted honorably—other than lying to him—Richard pays Will a visit. Following a contentious and emotional scene, they appear to reconcile.

The EA Assembly reinstates Steven Brennon as Prime Minister. His first act is to promote Miriam to EASC Board Chairman and Fleet Admiral of the Armed Forces. On her advice he signs a peace treaty with the Federation.

Olivia approaches Aiden Trieneri, head of the rival Triene cartel and her occasional lover, and suggests they work together to aid the fight against the invaders. On Atlantis, Matei Uttara's alien contact tells him Alex and Caleb are returning and instructs him to kill them.

Kennedy and Noah reach Earth. Kennedy's easy rapport with the military leadership spooks Noah, and he tries to slip away. She chases after him, ultimately persuading him to stay with a passionate kiss.

Liam arrives at the NW Regional base on Fionava. He injects a virus into the communications network and hijacks several ships by convincing their captains he is on a secret mission approved by EA leadership to launch clandestine raids on Federation colonies.

Alliance and Federation leadership are meeting to finalize war plans when an alien contacts them to offer terms for their surrender. It involves humanity forever retreating west behind a demarcation line, cutting off 28 colonies and 150 million people.

The leaders don't want to surrender but recognize their odds of victory are quite low. Then Miriam receives word that Alex is alive and the aliens' ability to send reinforcements has been destroyed. They decide to reject the terms of surrender and fight. On Miriam's order their ships open fire on the alien forces.

TRANSCENDENCE

The Metigen War is in full swing as Alex and Caleb approach Seneca. Caleb initiates an Intelligence Division protection protocol, and he and Alex join Director Delavasi at a safe house as several actions are set in motion.

Alex contacts Dr. Canivon to discuss the feasibility of enriching human/Artificial connections, only to discover Sagan is already under attack by the Metigens. The Alliance is defending the independent colony, and Alex asks her mother to ensure Canivon and her Artificial, Valkyrie, are rescued and brought to Earth. Caleb reaches out to Isabela, who divulges the truth about their father's profession and his death. Caleb confronts Graham about it, and a heated argument ensues.

On Earth, Kennedy works with the Alliance to manufacture the material the *Siyane's* hull transformed into, now called 'adiamene.' She implores Noah to seek the help of his estranged father, a metals expert. Noah agrees, but the request introduces tension into their relationship. Devon tries to restore communications to Fionava and NW Command, while elsewhere at EASC Devon's boss, Brigadier Hervé, is contacted by Hyperion, the same alien Marcus Aguirre was in league with.

Alex, Caleb, Miriam, Richard and Graham converge on a secluded, private estate on Pandora, and Alex and Miriam reunite in a more tender encounter than either were expecting. Alex reveals the full extent of her plan to the others, including that she intends to spearhead it by being the first to neurally link to an Artificial. Even as they meet, agents of the Metigens seek to stop them—the safe house on Seneca is blown up, and the assassin Matei Uttara pursues them to Pandora.

When Miriam breaks the news to Alex that her former lover, Ethan Tollis, died in an explosion, she flees to grieve in private. Caleb goes after her, but it intercepted by Uttara. A bloody fight ensues, during which both men are gravely injured. Alex arrives on the scene and shoots Uttara in the head, killing him. Caleb collapses from his injuries.

Noah meets with his father, Lionel, in a combative encounter. Despite the tension between them, Lionel agrees to help with the adiamene production, and they travel to Berlin to meet Kennedy at the manufacturing facility. Once Lionel begins work, Noah confronts Kennedy about her motives for forcing a reunion with his father, but the matter isn't resolved.

Caleb regains consciousness, and he and Alex share an emotional moment in which they both come to realizations about each other and the strength of their relationship. Miriam learns Liam has attacked the Federation colonies of New Cairo and Ogham with nuclear weapons, and she is forced to travel to Seneca to smooth things over with Federation leadership. Once Caleb is healed enough to travel, he and Alex depart for Earth. On the way, he contacts Mia and asks her to come to Earth, though he can't yet tell her why.

Miriam meets with Field Marshal Gianno and Chairman Vranas, and in a surprising move tells them she won't take any active steps to stop Liam until after the Metigens are defeated, as they must concentrate all their efforts on the alien invasion. She then tells Gianno about Alex's plan. Gianno selects the fighter pilot, Morgan Lekkas, for participation, and recalls her from Elathan, where Morgan was helping to defend against a Metigen attack.

Alex and Caleb reach EASC Headquarters, where they are reunited with Kennedy and Noah. Alex meets with Dr. Canivon, who was safely evacuated off Sagan, and informs the woman she wants to use Valkyrie as her Artificial partner in the project they've dubbed 'Noetica.' While monitoring the war effort, EASC's Artificial, Annie, discovers her programming has been corrupted and suspects Hervé of tampering.

Miriam returns to Earth and meets with Prime Minister Brennon. She tells him they are losing the war—they and the Federation are suffering too many losses and will run out of ships and soldiers long before the Metigens do—then pitches Noetica to him.

Mia arrives in Vancouver. Alex and Caleb ask her to be a part of Noetica, together with her Artificial, Meno, and she agrees. With time running out and the Metigens advancing, Noetica is approved and Devon Reynolds and Annie are selected as the last participants.

Alex is the first to undergo the procedure Dr. Canivon has devised to allow a linking between an Artificial's quantum processes and a human mind at a neural level. Caleb and Miriam each contend with fear and worry about her well-being, and Miriam comes to recognize how much Caleb cares for Alex.

Alex awakens to her and Valkyrie's thoughts clashing and overrunning one another. She struggles to regain control of her mind and deal with the flood of information, and with Caleb's help is able to do so. She informs her mother the Metigens are deviating from their pattern and heading for Seneca and Romane in massive force.

While the others undergo the procedure, Alex and Miriam meet with Brennon, Gianno and Vranas. Alex makes the case that the Metigens are coming for Seneca and Romane, and Miriam and Brennon decide to send the EA fleet to defend the two worlds.

On Liam's cruiser, the *Akagi*, Captain Brooklyn Harper begins a mutinous campaign to stop Liam. She enlists one of her teammates, Kone, and a comm officer, who slips a message out to Col. Malcolm Jenner saying Liam's next target is Krysk and asking for intervention. Then she and Kone sabotage the remaining nukes on the *Akagi*.

Malcolm is defending Scythia from the Metigens when he receives Harper's message. He passes it on to Miriam, who informs Gianno. Gianno claims she can't spare the ships to defend the colony if the Metigens are almost at Seneca.

Caleb is furious the military won't defend Krysk, where his sister and niece live, and makes the gut-wrenching decision to try to rescue them. Alex gives him the *Siyane*, saying it's his only chance to reach Krysk in time. After a tearful parting, Caleb leaves, but not before recruiting Noah to go with him.

Alex, Devon, Mia and Morgan, and their Artificial counterparts, Valkyrie, Annie, Meno and Stanley, gather to strategize. They name themselves "Prevos," taken from the Russian word for "The Transcended," and begin to realize the extent of their new capabilities. Alex shares a touching goodbye with her mother before leaving with the fleet for Seneca.

Devon remains at EASC, where he and Annie will oversee all fronts of the war, and comes to terms with the fact Hervé is working for the Metigens. At the same time, Hyperion confronts Hervé about Noetica. Because she wants the Metigens defeated, Hervé does not reveal to Hyperion that she has secretly placed a 'Kill Switch' in the Prevos' firmware, which when used will sever their connections to the Artificials—and also likely kill them.

Graham, Vranas and Gianno discuss the coming attack and express concerns over Noetica. When Graham returns to his office, Will Sutton—Richard's husband and a Senecan intelligence agent—is waiting on him and bears mysterious news.

Liam arrives at Krysk and attempts to use his nukes to disable the orbital defense array. They fail to detonate, and he has Kone brought before him to answer allegations of sabotage. When Kone refuses to confess, Liam executes him. Harper witnesses the execution via a surveillance camera; devastated, she prepares to try to blow up the ship. On the colony below, Isabela and Marlee are downtown as the attack begins. They seek refuge in the basement of an office building, but become trapped when the building collapses.

Alex reaches Seneca and Admiral Rychen's flagship dreadnought, the *Churchill*, and she and Rychen discuss strategy. Meanwhile, the Noetica Artificials discuss using neural imprints of notable military officers to supplement their and the Prevos tactical capabilities.

Caleb and Noah get to Krysk to discover the capital city under attack. The ongoing assault makes it too dangerous to land and find Isabela and Marlee, so Caleb comes up with a new plan. He draws Liam's ships away from the city, then, trusting the adiamene hull is strong enough to hold the *Siyane* together, crashes it through the frigates and into the belly of the *Akagi*.

They fight their way through the ship to the bridge, where they encounter Harper, who agrees to help them. She distracts Liam, then when Caleb and Noah open fire, disables his personal shield. Caleb kills Liam. Caleb, Noah and Harper rush back to the *Siyane* and escape just before the cruiser crashes.

Noah and Harper help Caleb dig a tunnel to where Isabela and Marlee are trapped, freeing them and several other people. Harper elects to remain in the city to aid with rescue efforts. Noah decides to find transportation back to Earth, eager to return to Kennedy, and Caleb heads for Seneca, and Alex.

The Metigens arrive at Seneca in overwhelming force. Alex, on the *Churchill* with Rychen, and Morgan, on the SF flagship with Gianno, take charge of the battle, employing a number of surprise weapons and tactics to gain an early advantage over the Metigen armada.

Several hours into the battle, Alex argues as it stands now they will not achieve complete victory. She convinces Miriam and Rychen to allow her to break into one of the Metigen superdreadnoughts, where she and Valkyrie believe they can hack the core operating code. She hitches a ride atop a recon craft, experiencing a thrilling and terrifying journey through the heart of the battle.

Inside, Alex finds a cavernous space, with power conduits and signals running in every direction, and goes in search of the engineering core. When she hears her father in her head during the search, Valkyrie confesses that the Artificials' search of military neural imprints turned up one for Alex's father, taken before his death. Not surprisingly, it was compatible with Alex's brainwave patterns, so Valkyrie loaded it into her processes to increase their knowledge of military tactics. Valkyrie then enriched the imprint, creating a more fulsome representation of David Solovy's mind and leading to the unexpected result of his personality manifesting.

When they locate the engineering core Alex immerses herself in it to access the ship's programming. Valkyrie inserts a subtle logic error into one of the base routines, and they quickly depart the ship.

A major battle also ensues on and above Romane. Malcolm takes a special forces squad groundside, where he meets up with Mia in the governor's emergency bunker. Mia believes she and Meno have developed a signal beam to nullify an alien vessel's shields. He agrees to help her test it out on one of the smaller alien ships wreaking havoc in the city. They depart the bunker with part of Malcom's squad, while the rest of the squad conducts rescue operations. The test is successful, and Mia/Meno transfer the code for the signal to Devon, who deploys it to all the fleets.

They are returning to the bunker when Malcolm receives an order to arrest one of his Marines who was part of the rescue team on suspicion of working for the Metigens. When arrested, the suspect detonates a bomb he'd placed at Mia's home. The explosion badly damages Meno's hardware, abruptly severing his connection with Mia and causing her to stroke.

Caleb reaches the fleet at Seneca, and he and Alex enjoy a jubilant reunion. Suddenly Alex collapses to the floor as the trauma to Meno and Mia reverberates through the Prevos' connection to one another. Once Alex recovers, she, Devon and Morgan decide it's time to implement their secret plan to ensure victory.

Miriam is overseeing both battlefronts from the War Room when she's informed Devon/Annie have taken control of both Earth's and Seneca's defense arrays. Panic erupts among the military and government leaders. At that moment Miriam receives a message from Alex asking Miriam to please trust in her, and trust Richard. Richard indicates he knows something but won't divulge what it might be.

Hervé judges it's necessary to use the Kill Switch, but Miriam shoots her with a stunner before she can do so. Miriam refuses to act against the Prevos, even as they turn the defense arrays inward.

Unbeknownst to Miriam, shortly after the Prevos were created, they uncovered the full Metigen network of spies and assassins. Before leaving Earth, Alex went with Devon to see Richard and gave him a list of enemy agents, and he contacted Graham and Will on Seneca. They formulated a strategy to arrest or kill the agents at the last possible moment, and enlisted Olivia Montegreu's aid in the effort. Miriam was kept in the dark because revealing Hervé's involvement ahead of time would've alerted the aliens to the fact the Prevos were onto them.

The defense arrays fire—on dozens of Metigen superdreadnoughts hiding cloaked above the major cities of Earth and Seneca. Armed with massive firepower as well as the disruptive signal beam Mia/Meno developed, the superdreadnoughts are destroyed. The Prevos had picked up the stealthed vessels hours earlier, but again, revealing them too early would have tipped their hand.

An alien representative contacts those leading the military assault, but Alex takes charge of the conversation. The alien says they are open to considering cease fire terms, but Alex notes the aliens are in no position to bargain, as humanity's forces have decimated them. She orders them to retreat through the portal and to cease their observation of and meddling in Aurora. She also asks for an explanation for their aggression; the alien replies that humans are far more dangerous than they recognize and must be contained.

The alien accepts her terms, but warns humanity not to come looking for them beyond the portal. Alex doesn't respond to the warning, instead ordering them to retreat now. They do so, and the war comes to an end.

Later, as EA Prime Minister Brennon gives a speech mourning those lost and vowing a new era for civilization, Gianno and

Vranas worry about the future of peace with EA and the danger Noetica poses, before separating to celebrate the victory with their families.

Noah reaches Earth and intercepts Kennedy as she is about to leave Vancouver. He finds her cold and dismissive, and provokes her into admitting she was hurt by him eagerly running off with Caleb, then not contacting her. He admits his mistake and being angry with her, but pleads his case by regaling all he went through to get back to her as fast as possible, and they reconcile.

On New Babel, Olivia and her partner-in-crime Aiden prepare to expand their spheres of influence. When Aiden suggests they merge their cartels—the one thing Olivia had warned him never to do—she uses a cybernetic virus to kill him, then begins taking over his cartel.

Alex returns to Earth and reunites with her mother. She elects not to tell Miriam about the construct of her father, and after catching up they agree to meet for lunch the next week.

Caleb and Alex visit Mia, who remains in a coma and was brought to EASC's hospital at Alex's request. Dr. Canivon says she's somewhat optimistic she can rebuild Meno, and together they can repair the damage to Mia's brain. Caleb authorizes her to move ahead, though there's no guarantee Mia will be herself should she eventually awaken.

They return to Alex's loft for a romantic dinner. Caleb presents her with a belated birthday gift—a bracelet crafted from a piece of his sword, the only remnant of the *Siyane's* hull before it morphed into adiamene.

He divulges that Graham has offered him any job he wants if he'll return to Division. Alex encourages him to do so, insisting they can make a long-distance relationship work. He challenges her about what she truly wants from him. When she caves and admits she selfishly wants him to stay with her, he immediately resigns from Division and asks her to marry him. After an emotional discussion, she says yes.

SIX MONTHS LATER

Miriam returns from vacation to move into the new Headquarters building. She and Richard are discussing threats on the horizon and long-term strategies when she receives a message from Alex.

On Atlantis, Kennedy and Noah are enjoying their own vacation, expecting Alex and Caleb to join them later in the day, when Kennedy also receives a message from Alex.

The Siyane hovers in the Metis Nebula, just outside the ring of ships patrolling the portal to prevent any Metigen incursion. Valkyrie has been installed into the walls of the Siyane, and Alex and Caleb have married. They activate the portal and accelerate through it on a quest for answers about the Metigens and their network of multiverses.

ABOUT THE AUTHOR

G. S. JENNSEN lives in Colorado with her husband and two dogs. *Abysm* is her sixth novel, all published by her imprint, Hypernova Publishing. In less than two years she has become an internationally bestselling author, selling in excess of 80,000 books since her first novel, *Starshine*, was published in March 2014. She has chosen to continue writing under an independent publishing model to ensure the integrity of the *Aurora Rhapsody* series and her ability to execute on the vision she's had for it since its genesis.

While she has been a lawyer, a software engineer and an editor, she's found the life of a full-time author preferable by several orders of magnitude, which means you can expect the next book in the *Aurora Rhapsody* series in just a few months.

When she isn't writing, she's gaming or working out or getting lost in the Colorado mountains that loom large outside the windows in her home. Or she's dealing with a flooded basement, or standing in a line at Walmart reading the tabloid headlines and wondering who all of those people are. Or sitting on her back porch with a glass of wine, looking up at the stars, trying to figure out what could be up there.

53271273R00250

Made in the USA
Lexington, KY
28 June 2016